BOOKS BY NEAL ROBERTS

IN THE DEN OF THE ENGLISH LION
A Second Daniel
The Impress of Heaven
A Dragon in the Ashes
All the Men as Mad as He
Shakespeare's Treason

SHAKESPEARE'S TREASON

Book 5 of
In the Den of the English Lion

BY NEAL ROBERTS

O God, I could be bounded in a nutshell and count myself a king of infinite space, were it not that I have bad dreams.

Hamlet, Act II, Scene 2

AUTHOR NOTE

I'd like to take a moment to thank the many thousands of readers who've enjoyed *In the Den of the English Lion* for their encouragement and support. It has always been my intention to take the series from the Lopez case to the end of Queen Elizabeth's reign, as Noah's loyalty to, and affection for, Her Majesty was a driving force behind the whole story.

In the course of the series, I've had occasion to breathe life into so many departed people and to fabricate so many fictional ones that it's indeed painful for me to let them go. Sadly, that's one of the prices of writing fiction.

Whether there will be a new series following Noah into the reign of King James will depend upon your wishes and enthusiasm. If you'd like me to continue the tale of Noah Ames, please drop me an email, whether through my website or my post office box. If there's enough of a groundswell, I'll endeavor to continue Noah's tale into the 1600's, but please bear in mind that it will take a great deal of additional research before I can even begin.

Thanks again, Dear Reader. It's all been for you, and you've made the journey well worth it. God bless you. And God save our gracious Queen.

– Neal

FREE DOWNLOAD

Sign up for Neal's newsletter (bitly.com/FreeHistorical) or visit
www.authornealroberts.com and journey for free to England's
shores in 1558 with young Menachem in the exclusive series prequel
scene, *Escape.*

DEDICATION

To Dear Departed Mom and Dad:
We Love You and Miss You Every Day

ACKNOWLEDGMENTS

First and foremost, to my good friend and correspondent Brenda James, who alone deciphered the code in the dedication to Shakespeare's sonnets and who, together with William Rubinstein, began the long and arduous—but fascinating—task of introducing the true bard to the world.

Next to a good friend, lost much too soon, one of the foremost investigators of the true bard, Dr. John Casson, co-author of the compelling volume *Sir Henry Neville Was Shakespeare: The Evidence* and several other books of great merit and discretion. Dr. Casson is already greatly missed by me and many others, for his insistence on hard evidence and his most valued friendship and guidance.

I'd also like to extend my heartfelt thanks to my treasured wife Myra, to Gigi, to the ever supportive and lovely Jennifer Nagler, Uncle Jack, the Donovans, Good Cousin Barbara (think screenplay), Nadine Rabinowitz (who first brought Mrs. James's work to my attention), John O'Donnell and his friend Alistair Clark, who's a doctoral candidate at Merton College, Oxford (for improving the Queen's Latin in Books 1 and 4), my wife's mother Lily, and all the other relatives and friends who've lent their time, and their moral and literary advice and support to this project. To Dr. Jeffrey Laitman for his advice concerning the progress and treatment of pre-eclampsia in Book 4, and the physical and emotional challenges encountered by those with cleft palates and the progress of Leah's neurological illness in Book 5; any mistakes are solely my own.

To my editor, Martin Jones, I extend my sincerest thanks. To my ever-faithful reader and proofreader Laurel Busch. To my publicist Samantha Williams of Aurora Publicity, for her continuing Herculean efforts in dragging the recalcitrant niche of historical fiction into the 21st century, and to her associate, the world's most patient up-and-coming cover designer, Melody Barber.

Finally, many thanks to my good friend, the talented photographer Jeffrey Loeser, who took the photo appearing on the back cover of this book, and in so doing accomplished the extraordinary task of making me look presentable.

PRINCIPAL PERSONS
OF THE STORY

ELIZABETH, BY THE GRACE OF GOD, QUEEN OF ENGLAND,
FRANCE AND IRELAND

NOAH AMES, barrister, advisor to HM
MARIE AMES, his wife by remarriage
JESSICA, LADY SAINT IVES, his daughter
JONATHAN HAWKING, BARON SAINT IVES, his daughter's husband
ESTHER, his cousin
BETH FERNANDEZ, his cousin
STEPHEN RODRIGUEZ, elder son of Marie Ames
ANDRES SALAZAR, his barrister friend

HENRY NEVILLE, knight, HM's Ambassador to France
LADY ANNE NEVILLE born KILLIGREW, his wife
DAVID "CHEERFUL" KILLIGREW, his wife's nephew
HENRY KILLIGREW, knight, his wife's father

WILLIAM CAMDEN, historian and author

LORD SHEFFIELD, a neighbor
LADY SHEFFIELD, his wife
GARDNER, Senior Yeoman of the Guard
FRANCIS, Yeoman of the Guard
CHESTER, Yeoman of the Guard
AUGUSTINE PHILLIPS, manager, Lord Chamberlain's Men
WILLIAM SHAKESPEARE, owner of a share, Lord Chamberlain's Men
JACOB, former assistant at Drapers' Hall
LEAH, his wife
TIMOTHY, a street urchin
THOMAS LEA, a meddlesome knight
THOMAS DRURY, a meddlesome sailor
MULLIN, an abductor, extortionist, pederast, and murderer, but otherwise
    wholesome gentleman

The Cecil Faction

ROBERT CECIL, LORD KEEPER OF THE PRIVY SEAL, First Secretary of State

FRANCIS BACON, Queen's Counsel

THE LORD CHIEF JUSTICE

THE LORD ADMIRAL

MATTHEW, his footman

JOHN LEVESON, knight, cousin to Sir Henry Neville

WALTER RALEIGH, knight, Captain of the Yeoman Warders

The Essex Faction

ROBERT DEVEREUX, EARL OF ESSEX

LETTICE KNOLLYS, LADY LEICESTER, his mother

LADY ESSEX, his wife

GELLY MEYRICK, his principal attendant

HENRY CUFFE, his secretary

HENRY WRIOTHESLEY, EARL OF SOUTHAMPTON, friend to the Earl of Essex

FERDINANDO GORGES, knight, Captain at Plymouth

CHAPTER 1

THE SUPPRESSION OF Essex's rebellion, far from putting matters to rest, marks the beginning of the most harrowing few months in the life of Noah Ames, when a single slip on his part can result in his dearest friend being torn to shreds and left to rot before completing the greatest testament to humankind ever written.

At mid-afternoon on the thirteenth day of February in the year 1601, Noah is called to the office of Lord Robert Cecil at Whitehall Palace. He quickly takes to his horse, the invaluable Bucklebury, and begins the wintry journey to Westminster from his wife's house in Holborn.

As Noah rides into Whitehall stables, he's surprised to find the diminutive Lord Robert awaiting him in a fretful mood. Mere days earlier, Lord Robert guided the Government through Essex's rebellion—a difficult challenge to Her Majesty's reign—but now his face is pallid and fatigued, as though he's been up for days.

"To what do I owe this courtesy, m'lord?" asks Noah. "I was expecting to meet you at your office."

"Something's come up," replies Lord Robert uncomfortably, "and I need your immediate help."

"Then you shall have it," replies Noah, having no idea what will be asked of him. He dismounts, hands off Bucklebury's reins to a familiar stableman, and brushes the dust of the road off his silk Serjeant's robes.

"Walk with me, Noah," says Lord Robert, leading him into Whitehall Palace.

Noah has always found that walking beside the diminutive Lord Robert presents no problem. *Speaking* with him privately while doing so, however, is always a tribulation, owing to the difference between Noah's height and Lord Robert's. Somehow, Noah always ends up bowing forward to lower his head, and turning his face toward his small companion. In this awkward posture, Noah's always at risk of bumping his head into someone or something, as he cannot see directly ahead. Fortunately, Lord Robert, through long experience, has become the watcher of the way for both himself and his companion.

"Even before my urgent business," says his lordship, "permit me to ask how the ... interment of Master Arden went."

"There is no sadder event, Lord Robert," laments Noah, "than the burial of a young person who's been robbed of such a promising future. Few of his family were able to come to London on such short notice. Some reside as far away as Stratford. Fortunately, Arthur's (and Sir Henry's) cousin Sir John Leveson attended, which was reassuring to all."

Sir John Leveson is one of very few people whose help Noah intends to seek without delay concerning Sir Henry Neville's complicity in the abortive rebellion, as it was Sir John who spoke with Sir Henry before reinforcing and defending the most important military position of the rebellion, namely, Ludgate.

Noah continues. "Arthur's friends attended the interment without exception—even Andres Salazar, who had to ride all the way from Cambridge. All the pallbearers being barristers and long-time friends of Arthur's, each held forth with a mirthful story of their youth together. The merrier each memory, unfortunately, the more it cut like a knife. 'Twas difficult, Lord Robert, quite difficult."

"I can imagine," says Lord Robert. "Arden was an able and welcome presence in Her Majesty's service. Keep his remaining friends together, Noah, and, as my father was wont to say, 'grapple them to your soul with hoops of steel.'"

"I shall," Noah assures him. "And what is your urgent business, m'lord?"

"Two naval officers came to see me a few hours ago," Lord Robert begins. "One was Robert Crofts ... or Cross ... I couldn't make it out clearly. He's a ship's captain. He told me that another officer, one Sir Thomas Lea, had told him last evening that 'it would be a glorious thing for six courageous, brave fellows to go together to the Queen and compel her by force to deliver Essex and Southampton out of custody.' When Lea was unable to enlist any of his preferred six men, he announced he'd do the job himself."

"And where is this Sir Thomas Lea now?" asks Noah.

"That's just it," replies Lord Robert. "No one knows. He could be anywhere, especially as he's likely to be alone. For all we know, he could be in Westminster"—Lord Robert's eyes dart about the hallway—

"why, even here at the Palace of Whitehall." He sighs with fatigue. "It's one of my persistent nightmares that the Queen might be the object of a lone assailant having no care for his own safety. There's no way to be certain of protecting her from that."

"Lord Robert," says Noah, "I know it will be cold comfort to hear, but any notion that Her Majesty is ever completely safe is illusory. We do the best we can by exercising eternal vigilance—which no one does better than your lordship. How may *I* be of service in this?"

Lord Robert snorts and looks up at Noah.

"You can *find* the bastard."

———————⌦———————

BEFORE PROCEEDING FURTHER with the tale, perhaps it would be well to remind the reader of the prevailing political and legal waters in which Noah finds himself.

By said February 13, Lord Essex has been incarcerated in the Tower of London these five days in connection with the late uprising bearing his name. Lord Southampton has been imprisoned there for as long. A few of their subordinate conspirators have also been imprisoned for such time at the Tower, but the more mundane sort has been spread about the local prisons of somewhat lesser security, such as the Fleet in London and the Clink in Southwark.

For Noah's part, a mere three days have passed since Lord Essex secretly imparted to him two explosive facts and assigned him a Herculean task to which he reluctantly agreed. As for the facts imparted by Essex: First, Essex identified their mutual friend Sir Henry Neville as the author of the works publicly attributed to William Shakespeare, confirming Noah's suspicion of many years; second, Essex told Noah that his lordship would soon publicly accuse Sir Henry of complicity in the late uprising.

As yet, however, no accusation has been lodged against Sir Henry by anyone. As Sir Henry departed London on the morning of the uprising to resume his French embassage, hope still lives in Noah's breast that Sir Henry will reach the South Sea and set sail for Paris before Her Majesty's men can overtake him. A foolish hope perhaps, in light of the impediments encountered in moving one's entire household to a foreign land, but one seizes on foolish hopes when reason sees *no* hope for a happy resolution.

The Herculean task that Noah accepted from Lord Essex was to do everything possible to keep Sir Henry Neville and the Earl of Southampton safe from serious harm on grounds of their involvement in the uprising. As no one else is yet aware that Sir Henry will be accused, Noah is severely hampered in his investigation by the need to avoid arousing suspicion, for as soon as Sir Henry falls under a cloud, his escape will be cut off and his capture inevitable.

As for helping Southampton, there seems little Noah can do, as he knows Southampton to have encouraged Essex's insubordination. What's more, Southampton tried to enlist Noah's own cooperation, though in which capacity never became clear, as Noah declined the invitation as soon as he heard it.

"WHERE DO YOU suppose this rebellious Captain Lea is likeliest to be?" asks Lord Robert as he and Noah walk the corridor toward his office.

Noah's mind races to put himself in the shoes of a naval officer preparing to assail the Queen's person, a difficult turnabout for Noah's brain. He stops walking and stands still.

Lord Robert stops beside him. "I'll get you as many men as you need," he assures Noah.

Noah shakes his head. "As for the judicious application of force, m'lord, I'll have to leave that to you. You are far more practiced in it than I, and you haven't time to teach me now. What I *could* use is more information. You said Thomas Lea is a naval officer?"

"Aye."

"What does he look like?"

"Crofts proffered nothing in that regard," says Lord Robert, "and I was so alarmed, I'm ashamed to say ... I didn't think to ask."

"Is this Lea presently assigned to a ship?"

"Aye," says Lord Robert.

"Has he any social contact who might gain him admittance to Her Majesty's court?"

"Perhaps," replies Lord Robert. "The traitorous Sir *Thomas* Lea is a kinsman to the loyal Sir *Henry* Lea, a Knight of the Garter well known to me, and well regarded by all."

Noah cannot conceive of a Knight of the Garter—so few and so loyal—seeking a rebellious cousin's admittance to court.

"Would Sir Henry Lea ever—?" Noah begins.

Lord Robert interrupts, shaking his head vigorously. "Never in a thousand years. More likely he'd slay his traitorous cousin on sight."

Noah's mollified on that score. Lord Robert is as good a judge of character as was his father before him, who was unerring.

An idea occurs to Noah. "Those rooms outside the Queen's Privy Chamber ..."

"With the benches?" asks Lord Robert.

"Yes," says Noah. "I can't quite recall whether any of them has a balcony onto the open air."

Lord Robert searches his memory. "Two of them do," he says. "You don't suppose—Well, shall we go and look?"

Noah gives it some thought, but declines. "I don't think your lordship should be there with me. If we find Thomas Lea, and he's desperate enough, he might try to make a hostage of someone of such high place as your lordship."

Lord Robert regards him skeptically. "What of yourself?"

"The Queen's Jew?" Noah scoffs. "To those unfamiliar with the court, Lord Robert, I expect I'm no more than an oddity, an *amusement* for Her Majesty."

Lord Robert shakes his head emphatically. "You're not going without accompaniment. I'll send two guards there wearing plain doublets. They'll keep away from you unless you beckon them."

⇒∘⊂⟰∘⊂⟰∘⊂══

AFTER MEETING WITH Lord Robert's plainclothes guards, Noah slips out of his chambers and assumes a place on a short queue before the guards stationed at the entrance to Her Majesty's Privy Chamber.

At the head of the queue stand two older women who appear to be of some note, being extraordinarily well-dressed and -mannered, here no doubt to beg the Queen's mercy for husbands caught up in Essex's rebellion. Each carries a small box, surely containing the customary "small gift" for Her Majesty meant to soften her regard toward their erring husbands.

The ladies, who evidently arrived together, ask the guard when Her Majesty might appear, but their inquiry is greeted with little more than a shrug.

A few minutes later, a supercilious clerk appears. Seeing noblewomen present, he emerges to address them. "Her Majesty has not yet supped," says the clerk, bowing formally. "Unfortunately, there can be no assurance that she will emerge this evening. As you can imagine, her time is quite taken up with matters arising out of the late unpleasantness."

While Noah is unable to hear the ladies' reply, the clerk makes no effort to keep his voice down. "If you have letters for Her Majesty," he pronounces, "I can relieve you of them now—with assurances that she will receive them at a time of her convenience."

Once more the ladies murmur, and once more the clerk bows and holds forth. "I am not at liberty to accept *any* parcels intended for Her Majesty. I'm sorry, ladies, but accepting your letters is all I'm authorized to do this e'en."

Another feminine murmur.

"No, madam," replies the clerk to the next unheard question, and for the first time the sheer persistence of these women makes Noah appreciate the clerk's plight and the reason for his haughty manner, "there can be no assurance that others will not read anything you give me before Her Majesty sees it. There are ... *procedures* for such things in the palace of which I have little knowledge, and over which I've no control. Now, I really must be returning to my other duties." At last the ladies relent and hand him their letters.

But before the clerk can recede into the palace, a man strides toward him out of one of the side rooms. "Hoy!" the man shouts, gesticulating with his arms. "A moment, young man!"

The clerk, whose back is already turned, stops, and brings his shoulders up in an evident cringe, as though this same man has already tried his patience more than once this evening.

As the man approaches, Noah gets a good look at him. He's dressed in a doublet of some quality, but other aspects of his appearance distinguish him from those indolent gentlemen who make it their practice to loiter at various points about the palace where they might be seen by Her Majesty.

Although the man's weapons have necessarily been left at the gate, he yet wears the scabbards and other leather items that carried them, and they bear blemishes unmistakably left by exposure to salt water. Leather wears differently at sea than on land, and his leathers all bear the telltale white streaks made by repeated exposure to seawater. His boots, though recently polished, bear similar markings. The skin of his face and hands is weathered and dark, marking him beyond doubt as one who spends most of his time out of doors.

The man's countenance is stern and impatient, as one would expect of someone accustomed to command, but there's also great anxiety on his face. He's pallid and sweaty, as though uncomfortable with the tenuousness of his position.

As he approaches, he speaks as loudly as the clerk did earlier. "Can you tell me, at least, whether Her Majesty is about to go to dinner and, if so, whether she will be accompanied by the Privy Council?"

Before the clerk can reply, Noah steps forward. "Pardon me, sir. I am Serjeant Noah Ames. I couldn't help but overhear your interest in speaking with the Queen and her Privy Council. I personally know several gentlemen who might be of interest to you, but it's unlikely you'll be admitted to see them tonight. However, if you would care to accompany me into one of these anterooms and give me your message, I can assure you I'll relay it no later than tomorrow morning."

At first, the man and the clerk both regard Noah with great surprise, but a look of appreciation gradually dawns on the clerk's face.

The clerk turns to the man and says, "My suggestion would be that you avail yourself of this gentleman's acquaintance, sir. He is no doubt correct that neither Her Majesty nor the Privy Council will admit you tonight."

Though clearly reluctant, the man relents, bowing perfunctorily to the clerk. As he approaches Noah, Noah nods to the clerk, who bows in turn—plainly grateful to be relieved of this persistent fellow—and quickly escapes into the palace before anyone else can call out to him.

―――――――⟶○⟨⟨∞⟩⟩○⟶―――――――

IT TAKES NO MORE than a minute to deduce that this seaman is indeed the sought-for Thomas Lea. He asks Noah to accompany him onto the balcony so he can smoke tobacco, a filthy procedure which Noah has long known signifies exposure either directly to the Americas or to men who've visited there and afflicted themselves with the habit. Noah's assumption that Lea is a smoker is the only intuition he's exercised this evening, and he feels vaguely vindicated when it turns out to be correct. The weatherbeaten fellow, being a gentleman, has no doubt heard that the Queen finds smoking obnoxious and will not suffer to have it about her; hence his choice of a balcony on the open air.

Before the man identifies himself, he casually mentions that he gained entry by invoking the name of a cousin who's a Knight of the Garter. Noah catches the eye of one of the two plainclothes guards and beckons them over.

"Captain Lea?" one asks the seaman.

"I'm Thomas Lea," confirms the man, plainly a bit surprised at being recognized by this stranger.

"Please come with us, Captain," says the guard. "The Privy Council has heard you were here, and has instructed us to bring you forthwith to the First Secretary, Lord Robert Cecil."

"Well," says Lea, turning to Noah with evident satisfaction, "I see you were in earnest when you said you knew men on the council." He reaches out his hand to Noah in friendship. "I'll be sure to mention your name, Serjeant—?"

"Ames," replies Noah, accepting his handshake a bit queasily. Although he bears the man no ill will, he's morally certain the man will not be received by Lord Robert in the tenor he hopes. "Best of good fortune to you, sir."

<hr />

WHEN NOAH STOPS by Lord Robert's office an hour later, Lord Robert is alone and answers his own door.

"Good evening, Noah," he says with some surprise. "I would have thought you'd gone home by now, you did your job with such elegant dispatch."

"So," says Noah, "did you meet with Captain Lea, m'lord, and hear him out?"

Lord Robert goes to his desk and triumphantly holds up a paper with a great red seal at its foot. "I heard him out and have his full confession right here."

"What did he confess to?" asks Noah.

"High treason!" says Lord Robert.

"Did he intend to take Her Majesty captive?"

"Of course."

"He admitted that?" Noah asks with some surprise. "Did he say he'd come alone to Whitehall for that purpose, even without confederates? Seems foolhardy."

"No," says Lord Robert, "Lea said that after his preferred confederates declined to join him, he came here alone to speak with a member of the Privy Council or, barring that, to lock Her Majesty up in her rooms until she were to sign an order releasing Essex and Southampton."

"And," says Noah, "having spoken to a member of the Privy Council, namely, your lordship, he abandoned his plan. So ... is that nonetheless high treason, Lord Robert?"

Lord Robert gapes at Noah in disbelief. "I'm shocked to hear that question coming from the learned Serjeant. As you know, it is high treason merely to mentally *conceive* of using force against the Sovereign. He confessed to much more, namely, attempting to *enlist confederates* in such a cause a few days ago. That was quite sufficient. His coming here alone with the same intention, contingent only upon his success in seeking out a member of the Privy Council, would itself have been quite sufficient. Do you doubt it?"

"No," Noah admits, "but what penalty will the Crown exact?"

At this Lord Robert is quite exasperated. "What's today? Thursday? He'll be questioned again tomorrow, arraigned on Monday on the basis of his confession, and face a traitor's execution at Tyburn on Tuesday."

Noah's perplexed by Lord Robert's certainty and the anticipated pace of the proceedings. "But even Essex and Southampton may not meet such a bitter end, m'lord, and they *led* the uprising. There are many abroad who still speak of it in terms of mere riot."

"Well," says Lord Robert, "I don't know whom you've been speaking with, but I've been speaking with Her Majesty and the Privy Council. The charge is to be open rebellion against the Crown, and the penalties will be ... severe."

Evidently dissatisfied with Noah's dour expression, Lord Robert sighs, shows him to the door, and lets him out. "Noah," he says, "you were right to leave the bloody matters to me. You haven't the stomach for it. You did an excellent job today. Go home and enjoy your growing family. Good e'en."

After Lord Robert closes his door, Noah stands a long time in the hallway wondering what he can do to prevent—or even delay—the like execution of Sir Henry Neville and the Earl of Southampton.

And not a bloody thing is occurring to him.

CHAPTER 2

IN THE NEARLY vacant Throne Room, two pretty young ladies-in-waiting—one brunette, the other blonde—converse in hushed tones as they fuss about the Throne's appearance.

The brunette runs a brush lightly over a swatch on the headrest, evidently ensuring the fabric is free of any stain or catch. She glances about, and pauses when she espies Noah dozing off in a rear pew. Evidently regarding him as someone of no importance, she speaks a bit more loudly. "I know little of these competing claims to the Throne," she tells her pretty blonde companion. "My father says he can't imagine what all the fuss was about, as neither Lord Essex nor Lord Southampton has any claim at all."

The blonde shrugs breezily; evidently, she regards such matters as none of her concern. She removes the silver cover from a tray, revealing an array of ornate baked goods, and begins carefully transferring them onto a fine platter on a table by the Throne.

Noah rubs the sleep from his eyes, praying that these girls complete their duties quickly and begone so he can retrieve a bit of last night's lost sleep. He's come this morning in response to last evening's royal summons, which provided no inkling into the business to be discussed. While ordinarily such an omission would have aroused no anxiety on his part, just now there's one subject—one *big* subject—he hopes to avoid taking up with the Queen, namely, that of Sir Henry Neville, who is no doubt still on his plodding way to Dover *en route* to his embassage in Paris.

Most of last night, Noah tossed and turned, trying with little success to persuade himself that there is no way (at this early date) for Her Majesty to have learned of Sir Henry's participation in the late rebellion. Noah's been assured by Essex that he'll tell no one of such matters prior to his upcoming trial. But that provides little comfort, as Essex is hardly alone in knowing of Sir Henry's foreknowledge of the rebellion and his dashed hope of taking the place of his near relative, Robert Cecil, as First

Secretary of State.

Quite the contrary, it would take the fingers of more than two hands to count how many *more* men know—or who, to save their own lives, might be willing to conjecture aloud—that the stout co-conspirator introduced to them as Sir Helvius Cinna bore a suspicious resemblance to Sir Henry Neville. There are the Earl of Southampton and Sir Henry Cuffe, both of whom undoubtedly know. And there's already talk about Southampton's having begun crafting a confession, one that can save his neck only if it includes mention of every guilty party, including Sir Henry.

The blonde lady-in-waiting, her brow knitted in evident consternation, at last replies to her companion. "And why is everyone so concerned about Richard the Second, anyhow?" she asks. "Whoever is *he*?"

The brunette regards her friend skeptically. "You mean, who *was* he? He was King of England many years ago. In fact, m'lady," she says, "are not you yourself descended from King Edward the Third?"

"So my father tells me."

"Well, then, King Richard was your cousin, for King Edward's eldest son, known as the 'Black Prince,' died before his father, passing the kingdom to *his* eldest son Richard."

A door behind the Throne opens a crack, with such deliberate care that it fails to draw the attention of either lady-in-waiting. Lord Robert unobtrusively inches his way in, a fond expression betraying his eagerness to hear the rest of the girls' conversation. He nods to Noah silently. Noah nods in return.

The blonde purses her mouth, evidently signifying that she is engaged in deepest thought. "But, what I *mean* to say is, why is everyone so interested in Richard *just now*?"

Demonstrating admirable patience for her companion's ignorance, the brunette plops herself onto an upholstered chair. "Because, just before the late uprising, the conspirators paid players' companies all over town to put on Shakespeare's play, *Richard the Second*. You see, Richard was a lawful King of England deposed by his own subjects."

"Why was he deposed?" asks the blonde, without looking up from her biscuits.

"Because, they said, King Richard was too poor an administrator to remain Sovereign."

"But that was so long ago!" says the blonde, shrugging insouciantly. "I mean to ask: In *this* day and age, who is Richard the Second?"

Queen Elizabeth pushes through the door, urging Lord Robert aside. "*I* am Richard the Second," she pronounces, her sonorous voice filling the Throne Room, her eyes flashing with indignation. "Know ye not that, foolish girl?"

At the Queen's appearance, Noah drops from his chair to his knees, yet finds himself unable to avert his gaze as required by protocol.

The ladies-in-waiting gasp and curtsey.

The brunette speaks. "Our deepest apologies, Your Majesty," she says, obviously covering for her dull-witted friend. "We should have completed our task here long ago."

"M'lady," declares the Queen with a curt smile, "my question was addressed rather to your companion." The brunette nods submissively and falls silent.

The weight of expectation has now firmly shifted to the blonde, who shudders abashedly, her eyes downcast. "My apologies, madam. I—I never knew Your Majesty to go by the name of Richard."

The Queen gawps incredulously at the blonde.

Noah rubs his eyes once again, hoping the little dolt will not actually address the Queen as *King Richard.*

"You may both go," says the Queen temperately, and the ladies scamper quietly away.

As they shut the door behind them, Lord Robert adds under his breath, "—to the *library*, 'tis to be hoped."

The Queen sighs despairingly. "As for the flaxen-haired one, Sir Robert, 'twould do her no good. She's illiterate. Most fortunately for her, however, she's as comely as ignorant." The Queen espies Noah. "Why, Serjeant Ames," she says with palpable relief, "I felt *assured* you'd arrive early, and now I see that you have."

Noah rises, adjusts his rumpled robes, and bows with a smile. "Good morning, Your Majesty," he says. "I hope you have been resting well after last week's commotion."

"My repose has much improved, Serjeant Ames, as I hope yours has," she replies, then congenially turns to Cecil. "And yours, Sir Robert?"

Lord Robert bows. "I've slept like a baby, Your Majesty, though the kingdom's cares never truly rest." It occurs to Noah that, although Lord Robert stands as ever at the Queen's side, he's situated himself a few inches *behind* her, something he does only when he wishes to be unseen by her unless she makes the effort to turn in his direction.

"No, the kingdom's cares never rest, as you say," says the Queen, turning back to Noah. "I have a few questions of you, Noah. They'll probably amount to nothing, but they may involve your family or social connections, so I wanted to discuss them with you personally, with no one else present—but for Sir Robert, of course—I trust you have no objection to his remaining?"

Noah smiles at this purely formal courtesy; no one but the Queen decides who stays and who goes. "None in the least, madam. I am yours to command." While Noah tries to appear curious about her questions, dread thoughts of Sir Henry spin in his brain and turn his stomach. "What questions might those be, madam?"

The Queen shifts blithely, as wishing to seem unobtrusive. "Well, to begin with: Have you ever met Master William Shakespeare?"

Despite Noah's steely determination not to betray his innermost thoughts, his smile wavers briefly, and he sees the Queen detect it. She's sharp—for the most part well-meaning—but ever sharp. Lord Robert, in his rearward perch, seems suddenly intent, as though reminding Noah that he's been asked nothing more threatening than a simple question about a man named *William Shakespeare*.

"Yes, madam," replies Noah. "I have met the gentleman."

"How many times have you had occasion to see him?" asks the Queen.

"Oh, let's see," says Noah in his most relaxed manner. "I would have to guess once or twice, yes, *twice* that I can clearly recall—but no more than ... thrice, I expect."

"You've spoken with him at the Globe Theater?" asks the Queen.

Noah finds it unnerving to see Lord Robert so closely tracking his facial expressions. He nods. "I *have* spoken with Master Shakespeare at the Globe, madam." He hopes her inquiry goes no further, as both times Noah met with Shakespeare he was in company with Sir Henry, and the *first* time was not at the Globe, but in Sir Henry's parlor.

"Socially?"

"Well," Noah replies, "I've never been to his home, nor he to mine, madam—if that's of any import." Although a trained questioner would see right through his evasion, Her Majesty is not in that business.

"Have you seen him lately?" she asks, missing his dodge.

Noah shakes his head equivocally. "Oh, I should think not. I would imagine the latest I saw him would have been a couple of years ago, perhaps more than that. If I may, madam: Why is my meeting Master Shakespeare of interest to the Crown?"

The Queen glances toward the stony-faced Lord Robert, and back toward Noah. She shrugs. "No one seems to know where Master Shakespeare *is* at the moment, though Lord Robert has had men seeking him out for days. Lord Robert wishes to speak with him about Essex's hiring of the Lord Chamberlain's Men to play *Richard the Second* on the eve of the late rebellion."

"*Aaaah*," says Noah, as though such a clever thought might never have occurred to him. "Well," he observes, "that's a fairly old play, madam. I know it's reputedly written by Shakespeare, but he's a shareholder in the Chamberlain's Men, after all, so I expect his company has full authority to stage the play without seeking his consent in each instance—so long as permission has been granted by Master of the Revels, of course."

The Queen smirks. "And so long as Master Shakespeare is paid for the performance."

"That, too, of course," replies Noah.

The Queen is momentarily lost in reverie, but then rouses herself. "And what of—?" She turns to Lord Robert. "Oh, who's the *business manager* for the Lord Chamberlain's Men, Sir Robert?"

Lord Robert bows curtly. "Augustine Phillips, madam."

The Queen faces Noah again. "Yes, Augustine Phillips. Has anyone in your family met Master Phillips, Serjeant Ames?"

A strangely crafted question, thinks Noah. *Earlier, she asked whether I personally had met Shakespeare, but now she inquires about the acquaintance of my family members.* Noah realizes he must be very careful here, for, not only did his daughter Jessica meet Augustine Phillips, but she had occasion to speak with the Queen not long after. It's possible that Jessica mentioned her meeting with Phillips to the Queen and, if the Queen already knows about it, Noah had better own up to it without delay.

"Yes, Majesty," he replies. "My daughter Jessica, Lady Saint Ives, mentioned to me that she briefly met Master Phillips in the far west many months ago."

The Queen smiles fondly. "While she was in desperate pursuit of an English military map being smuggled out of the Realm?"

"Quite so, madam," replies Noah, bowing proudly.

"And you, Noah?" asks the Queen. "Have *you* met Master Phillips?"

Noah glances furtively at Lord Robert, whose expression is unchanging.

As though deep in thought, Noah nods, at first uncertainly, and then with greater confidence. "Yes, madam, I met Master Phillips backstage at the Globe, in company with Master Shakespeare." *And also Sir Henry Neville,* he stops himself from adding. "Oh, but I believe I met Master Phillips only the once, and never since. In fact, I confess I might not recognize him if he were to walk through that door right now. Has *Phillips* gone missing as well, may I ask?"

Lord Robert chimes in. "If I may, madam. Master Phillips is here in London, and we have eyes on him."

The Queen turns to Noah. "I was thinking of asking you to assist in Sir Robert's investigation into possibly treasonous performances of *Richard the Second.*"

"Treasonous, Majesty?" asks Noah skeptically.

Lord Robert interrupts. "If I may, madam, at your suggestion I have given some thought to those whose assistance would be most useful to me, and I have *other* men in mind—somewhat less conspicuous—whose, *er*, skills may be better suited to the task, although I look forward to discussing the matter with Serjeant Ames in my chambers after our audience here. Was there something else, Your Majesty?"

"Well," says the Queen hesitantly, "I received a letter from an old friend who I think might be edified by a visit from the good Serjeant."

Noah is pleased that the topic of Shakespeare has been left behind. "Which old friend, Majesty?"

"I take it you are both aware," she says, "that Lady Essex, in addition to suffering through her husband's late sedition, has also suffered the theft of some important jewelry."

Although she awaits confirmation, this is fresh news to Noah. "I was not so aware, madam."

"Oh?" says the Queen. "I would have expected that to be one of the topics between Lord Essex and yourself during your ... lengthy private conferences."

Noah shifts his weight uneasily, a little disturbed to hear that Her Majesty has taken an interest in his conferences with Essex. "Nay, Majesty. His lordship has never broached the theft with me."

She shrugs. "I suppose it's rather small beer in comparison to the penalties presently faced by his lordship."

"Is there something the Crown would like me to do for Lady Essex?" asks Noah.

"Well," says the Queen, "go and see her. I expect her true concern may be a bit different from the problem she stated."

When no more seems forthcoming, Noah bows. "As you wish, Your Majesty."

The Queen perks up out of a brief reverie. "Gentlemen, if you will excuse me, other matters demand my attention just now. Thank you for coming so early, Serjeant, for now I shan't be late for my other appointments." She smiles pleasantly. Noah and Lord Robert bow low. The Queen rises without further ado, departing the way she came.

Lord Robert mutely beckons Noah to accompany him to his chambers.

NEITHER NOAH NOR LORD ROBERT utters a word along the way to Lord Robert's chambers. The guard (whom Noah vaguely recalls as "William") greets them just outside, admits them with a bow, and promptly closes the heavy door from outside.

Lord Robert motions for his guest to take a seat, goes to the window, and stares outward, something Noah has observed him doing whenever wishing to conceal his facial expressions.

The heat emanating from the fireplace is soporific, nearly oppressive. A glowing log cracks loudly, and Noah's chair creaks, both sounds inordinately loud in the suffocating silence of the chamber.

At last, Lord Robert clears his throat to speak, but all that emerges is: "Do you *know*?"

At a loss for a way to respond, Noah says, "M'lord?"

"Do you *know*?" repeats Lord Robert.

"Do I know … *what*, Lord Robert?"

"Don't play games with me, Noah. I ask you again: Do you *know*?"

Noah detects that he's being asked about Sir Henry, but he can't act upon such knowledge until he's sure that Lord Robert already shares it, for if Lord Robert does *not* know that Sir Henry writes plays for the Lord Chamberlain's Men, it would be an unforgivable breach of friendship for Noah to tell him. Likewise, if Lord Robert does not know that Sir Henry was complicit in the rebellion, then Noah's confirmation could result in Sir Henry's arrest and execution. And, if circumstances turn bad enough, Noah could be denied access to Lord Essex, could be forbidden to assist Sir Henry or Southampton, and could even be subject to prosecution himself.

Noah inches toward the less inflammatory of the two Neville topics about which Lord Robert may be inquiring. "I received a note from Sir Henry Neville," he ventures gingerly.

Lord Robert appears to be calculating the implications of Noah's reply. "When did you receive Sir Henry's note?" asks Lord Robert. "Yesterday?"

"No, this past week."

"Why do you mention it now?" asks Lord Robert with an arched eyebrow.

"Oh," says Noah, stretching, "it's just that his notes are always so … well crafted."

"Yes," says Lord Robert, catching on, "he's a remarkable writer, isn't he?"

"*Positively* so," confirms Noah. "One can almost hear his voice while reading."

"Have you ever heard Sir Henry's words spoken aloud … by some-one *other* than Sir Henry?" asks Lord Robert cleverly.

"I believe I have, Lord Robert," says Noah, making a dangerous concession. "Has your lordship?"

Lord Robert nods affirmatively, arching an eyebrow so high that, but for the gravity of the occasion, it would be comical. There's no doubt but that his awkward expression is meant as a mute inquiry whether Noah knows that Sir Henry wrote the plays attributed to Shakespeare.

Noah replies mutely. He nods.

Lord Robert, overcoming a momentary hesitation, says, "So, you *do* know, then?"

Noah refuses to yield his knowledge in the face of anything less than certainty. "Know *what*, Lord Robert?"

Exasperated, Lord Robert overturns the game, whispering, "You know that Shakespeare hasn't written a blessed thing. Correct?"

"So I believe," whispers Noah, then makes a concession of his own. "In fact, his works appear to have been written by our mutual friend."

"Neville?" whispers Lord Robert, studying Noah's face.

"Yes," whispers Noah.

Lord Robert takes a deep breath, obviously relieved to have over-come the impasse. "How did you find out?" he asks eagerly.

Noah has a choice here. He can attribute his knowledge to his dis-covery of the "Shakespeare" manuscript, or he can say he was told by Essex. He considers where the conversation is likely to go if he brings up Essex, and decides to avoid it. "Although I've never told anyone until now, years ago I came upon a manuscript of the third part of *Henry the Sixth* in Sir Henry's study."

"And?" asks Lord Robert.

"It was written in … Sir Henry's hand." Noah waits a moment for the import of that revelation to sink into Lord Robert's mind. "How did *you* learn of Sir Henry's authorship, m'lord?"

Lord Robert sighs. "Oh, I've known of it forever. There's more than wine between Sir Henry's family and mine own, Noah. Sir Henry's mother-in-law (that is, Lady Anne's mother) was my mother's sister, may she rest in peace."

"All in the family, eh?" says Noah.

Lord Robert smirks. "And don't forget that my mother's other sister is mother to Anthony and Francis Bacon."

"Ah, Francis. Our newest prosecutor," observes Noah.

"Indeed," says Lord Robert. "Now that the air is clear, let me warn you that the problem about which Lady Essex seeks the Crown's assistance has *nought* to do with the theft of m'lady's jewels. That matter is already under examination at Star Chamber. I feel certain we'll apprehend the thief, recover the jewelry, and dispense a nice round punishment." He rolls the word "round" in his mouth as though relishing its flavor.

"Then … what is the problem for which Lady Essex requires assistance?"

Lord Robert purses his lips and nods gravely. "Her Majesty wants us … *you*, that is … to provide aid—not to Essex's wife—but to his *mother*."

"Do you mean—?"

Lord Robert brushes a bit of imagined lint from his gown. "I speak of Lady Leicester, whom you may know by the name Lettice Knollys."

Noah nods, amazed.

Lord Robert explains. "When Her Majesty and Lettice were young, they were inseparable, and remained so after Lettice married the Earl of Essex. (Their son now languishes in the Tower of London, as you know.) However, a suspiciously short time after Lettice's first earl died, she married the Queen's favorite, the Earl of Leicester. *That* earned her lifelong banishment from the Queen's court. Then, when Lettice's *second* earl died, she married Sir Christopher Blount (quite a step down, if you ask me), who's now under arrest at the Tower near his stepson, and will likely share his fate. Things are not looking good for Lady Leicester."

Noah is dashed. "But why would Lettice Knollys seek succor from so unlikely a source as Her Majesty?"

Lord Robert shrugs. "She may well be seeking clemency for her son or her present husband … but I doubt it."

Noah is astonished.

Lord Robert smirks. "Does that surprise you?"

"Well," says Noah frankly, "I should think the shared predicament of her son and present husband would rather be foremost on her mind."

"Of course you would, Noah. But then, you're not a woman of name, surrounded by men of renown engaged in the precarious activity of court politics. Noblewomen understand that there's a certain risk inherent in such pursuit, and that their men are ever in great peril, should suspicion arise that their gaze has exceeded their station. Someone in Lettice's position has no choice but to put her matriarchy ahead of any one—or even two—members of her family."

Noah takes Lord Robert's words to heart. "So, she perceives on the horizon some threat to her title and family wealth—even if she were to survive both husband and son. Is that it?"

Lord Robert regards Noah with affection. "Whatever it is, I expect it touches her estate *quite* closely. But enough of this for now. On your way to Lady Essex, I'd like you to pay Her Majesty's warmest regards to Sir John Leveson."

"He of Ludgate fame," observes Noah, feigning indifference while suppressing his excitement at the prospect of speaking with the only man whose assistance might keep Sir Henry from the gallows.

"Even he," replies Lord Robert.

"But Sir John resides in Kent, does he not? And Lady Leicester in … Staffordshire? Sir John's hardly 'on the way,' I should think."

"Don't be absurd," says Lord Robert. "They're both here in London. I've asked Master Treasurer to put Sir John up at your old haunt, Gray's Inn. Lady Leicester has taken up temporary residence with her daughter-in-law Lady Essex at Essex House … at least until conclusion of the trial and its aftermath."

Noah is skeptical. "Wouldn't Sir John feel more exalted by a personal commendation from Her Majesty?"

"No doubt, but I have an ulterior motive in sending you. I want you to congratulate Sir John and privately inform him that his testimony will be required at the upcoming trial of Essex and Southampton. I trust you will find Leveson at Gray's. If he's not there, send word immediately."

"Shouldn't I bring a compulsory writ to serve upon him?"

"He's a *knight*, Noah, and hero of the day. He'll testify without need of compulsion."

"And if he doesn't?"

Lord Robert shrugs. "*Then* you'll serve a writ."

Noah scratches his head. "At that point it might be too late to compel him to testify. After all, a trial takes only a day or two."

"Never you worry. He'll be there, having been reminded by one of Her Majesty's counselors … namely, you."

"How can you be sure? After all, people disappear—as Shakespeare has done. Too bad about Will. He might have been of some help."

Lord Robert smiles knowingly. "Shakespeare hasn't disappeared."

Noah's surprised to see Lord Robert's expression, which mutely says, *Because he's precisely where I put him.*

Noah's dismayed to contemplate that Shakespeare might be in peril, but Lord Robert laughs to see his expression.

"Oh, never worry," says Lord Robert, "he's well enough. Now go, and Godspeed."

CHAPTER 3

SIR JOHN LEVESON swings open the door to his rooms at Gray's Inn, revealing a well-appointed apartment that Noah's never seen before, clearly reserved for special guests. A woman, presumably Sir John's wife, bustles about the kitchen.

"Sir John," says Noah, "perhaps you'll remember me. I am—"

"I know *precisely* who you are, Serjeant Ames," he says with a sincere smile, "and am delighted to see you. Won't you come in?"

Sir John firmly tugs Noah inside by the elbow, then juts his head out of the door, suspiciously glancing both ways before shutting it. His smile resumes unabated. "Sorry for the hugger-mugger, Serjeant. One can't be too careful nowadays. Lord Essex still has quite a few supporters and, by the glowering I get while walking down the street, many of them blame me *personally* for his downfall."

Noah hadn't seriously considered the possibility that Sir John might be in personal jeopardy, should some remnant of the rebellion seek to preclude his giving damning testimony at Essex's trial, or should some ruffian wish merely to vent his spleen at the collapse of Essex's fortunes.

"Just now," continues Sir John, "you seemed uncertain whether I would remember you. Perhaps that's because you have no idea how long ago I *learned* of you. Nor do you have any reason to remember me, I suppose. You were a few years ahead of me at Oxford (though I was at Queen's College, not Merton, like you). Actually, I was introduced to you briefly by my cousin Henry Neville."

Noah is mortified that he has no recollection of the introduction. "Oh, I'm so sorry—"

"Not one bit!" says Sir John. "I was one of several rowdy boys in a group, and there was no reason for you to focus upon me especially."

"But when we met just recently at Whitehall and you asked whether I was the Queen's Jew, I simply assumed we'd never—"

"*Tsk, tsk!*" clucks Sir John's wife, as she emerges from the kitchen.

Sir John obviously realizes at once that he's been wordlessly upbraided for speaking like a vulgar Jew-hater. "You will please forgive me," he says to Noah, "for that absurd, nay, *offensive*, self-introduction on my part, but I'd heard of so many of your exploits at school, and then you seemed to vanish—that was about the time you went on European tour with Sir Henry. The next I heard (which was many years later), someone of your name had bravely defended a Jew at Oyer & Terminer, only then to be exposed as a Jew himself. When I was told of it, I was incredulous that it could be the fellow I'd met back at university. So, when I met you again a few days ago at Whitehall, I meant no insult about your being a Jew—"

Noah smirks. "You were really asking whether I was that same fellow, of course. Well," says Noah, nodding gratefully toward Mistress Leveson, "so I am. And please rest assured that it's a long time since I've taken offense at a friendly inquiry. Your affability more than compensated for the awkwardness of our brief encounter. As I recall, that was the early morning of an unhappy day we had all long dreaded."

Thus reminding himself of the reason for his visit, Noah raises his voice in somber pronouncement with a subtle wink toward the lady. "And now," says Noah, "having been sent to you by Her Majesty, it is my solemn duty ... and honor ... to express the Crown's eternal gratitude for your defense of Ludgate in the face of violent onslaught by Lord Essex and his henchmen. Your efforts had the salutary effect of thwarting his lordship's attempt to take Whitehall Palace, threaten Her Majesty's liberty, and seize her sacred person."

At this, Mistress Leveson chokes up and rushes to her husband's side. She buries her face in his shoulder, which quickly moistens with tears.

"There, there, Christian," says Sir John blithely, caressing her hair and patting her back gently, "Serjeant Ames is just an old college friend come to pay his respects."

This is precisely the way Noah was hoping to be received, yet he cannot allow Sir John to diminish the importance of his accomplishment. "I hope that I *am* such a friend, Sir John," says Noah, "but my visit here is to express the thanks of *all England and Her Majesty personally*."

Noah's stiff insistence on the importance of Sir John's valor has the effect of doubling the lady's tears of pride and, unless Noah's mistaken, there's now a certain mistiness in Sir John's eyes, too. Noah looks away, and awaits subsidence of this storm of patriotic devotion.

The lady wipes her eyes and turns to Noah. "Serjeant Ames ... we have been unable to bring our customary servants to Gray's Inn, but would you care to share our humble fare this fine day? I have a nice bit of beef and … well, no pork."

"That is most kind of you, madam, and I hope that someday not far off I shall be granted an opportunity to share a calm repast at your table. As for today, however, I've been dispatched from the Tower upon two important errands, this being the first and by far the more pleasurable. Alas, the second is equally urgent, and duty beckons." He looks at his feet. "There are one or two things I need to discuss with Sir John privately, however."

"Oh, of course!" says the lady. "I'll leave you two alone."

Noah smiles and bows. "Thank you, madam."

The lady kisses her husband's cheek, curtsies, and returns to the kitchen, discreetly closing the door behind her. Sir John extends his hand toward a chair at the table and takes an adjacent seat.

Noah whispers, "I also wanted to thank you for humanely allowing your men to seek a surgeon's help for my two young—assistants."

Sir John nods glumly. "And now at last *I've* been given the opportunity to express my condolences for the loss of your two young barrister friends. And I have some thanks of my own to share."

Noah raises his eyebrows inquisitively.

"I don't know what you said to Essex before the common fighting began, but it deflated him quite. He was unable to recover his wind, which made things simpler for us defenders."

Noah smiles. "I merely told him that his principal attendant had been arrested." His smile turns to an earnest frown. "If I could have struck him with my open hand, I would have done."

"Well, perhaps it will provide a bit of vicarious relief for you to know that I shot his hat off."

Noah can feel his face redden, and he bursts into laughter. In a moment, he controls himself and whispers to the bemused Sir John. "That was you?"

"Well," says Sir John, "I couldn't trust the others to do it, as it required great accuracy and their weapons were old and long disused. My pistol, however, had just been cleaned and resighted and I wanted to send his lordship a message he could not mistake. And I knew that, in the general melee, no one would be able to tell where it came from." He leans forward and whispers. "Incidentally, I expect you'll keep that between us."

"For all time," Noah assures him quietly, "and I shall treasure your confidence for just as long, Sir John. Incidentally," he says, "I have two things to tell you, one of which must remain confidential, and you shall soon see why. But first to Queen's business. You know that your testimony will be essential at the fast-approaching trial of Essex and Southampton?"

Sir John nods as though he was expecting this. "I'll be there. Just say when and where."

"I'll send you a note to that effect. Lord Robert was confident we could count on you, and I see he was correct in his judgment of your character. It's an unerring gift he inherited from his father, Lord Burghley."

"But that's not the *secret* matter, is it?"

"No," says Noah, becoming quite earnest. He looks deeply into Sir John's eyes. With little more to rely on than Lord Robert's character assessment, Noah is about to take his own life in his hands. "I must ask you a few questions, and I ask you not to repeat them to *anyone*, so long as you can do so within the law. And I shall protect your answers to the same extent."

"Sounds reasonable," Sir John replies.

"They relate to your dear cousin and my selfsame fondest friend."

Sir John caresses his beard with the back of his right hand, and he nods gravely. Something in his expression betrays that, like Noah, he's been dreading to be questioned about Sir Henry.

Noah whispers. "You know that Sir Henry is on his way to Dover for the crossing to Calais, yes?"

Without looking at Noah, Sir John nods slowly.

Noah continues. "On the day of the rebellion, did you have occasion to speak with Sir Henry, or to receive a writing from him?"

Sir John looks down at the floor. "Pardon my answering a question with a question, Noah, but why do you ask?"

"Well," Noah whispers, "I was … nearly certain that I saw him at Whitehall that morning, shortly after you and I parted ways—although I couldn't swear to it in a court of law."

Sir John shifts his gaze to Noah's, as though struggling to see into his soul. "Well," says Sir John, "suppose it *were* Sir Henry you saw, although I can't be certain what, or whom, you saw. What difference would it make?"

Noah takes a deep breath. "I suppose it's possible that Sir Henry guessed—and I'm not saying that he did—that Essex's rebellion would take place that day and that Essex would move through Ludgate in the general direction of the Tower, and would later try to pass through the gate in the opposite direction in an attempt to take Whitehall."

"And?" says Sir John.

"And … Sir Henry *may* have wished to ensure that Essex's way back through Ludgate would be barred by an armed contingent. And he might have enlisted a trusted relation to command the gate. Someone … such as yourself."

Sir John takes a deep breath, and Noah has no doubt he's put his finger on the truth. Sir John remains silent a moment. "But it would make no difference, would it? I mean, no accusation has been lodged against Sir Henry, has it?"

"Not to my knowledge," replies Noah. "I believe none has … as yet."

"Then, what harm if Sir Henry attempted to frustrate Essex's foul intentions?" Sir John studies Noah's grave face. "Oh, God," says Sir John without awaiting an answer, "I can see by your face that *someone* is going to inform on him. Am I right?"

"I am duty-bound to refrain from telling you why I believe so, but yes. I ask you to believe only that it shan't be *I* who does so, and that I shall do everything in my power to keep Sir Henry from the gallows. That's why I asked to speak with you privately."

Sir John now works his beard with both hands. "You know, I have quite a good reputation in Kent, and a promising career. If it were true that Sir Henry had enlisted me, would I be required to give public testimony to that effect? I should care to avoid that."

"The question *might* arise in a public forum," says Noah, "as no one has any clue how you turned up in precisely the right place at exactly the right time. But if it *can* be kept private, say, as in a clemency hearing attended only by you and Her Majesty (and one or two of her most trusted counselors), then I promise to strive against the forces of the Devil himself to make it—and keep it—*private*."

Sir John lets out a long sigh. "Then I shall be doubly in your debt, Noah, for saving both Sir Henry *and* my reputation." He extends his right hand.

Noah shakes the proffered hand, nods, and rests his left hand on their conjoined hands as a further sign of assurance. He leans into Sir John and whispers. "I shall be in attendance at Essex's upcoming trial at Westminster. After you give testimony there, please tarry in the hall until the close of proceedings that day, which will almost certainly mark the end of the trial. I shall meet with you there and we can discuss how you may assist in garnering clemency for Sir Henry."

"Why must the trial be complete?"

"Because it's only after completion that we'll know for certain that Sir Henry's name has not yet come up. On the other hand, if Sir Henry's name *has* come up at the trial, we may need to proceed immediately … and a different way."

Sir John nods gravely.

⟶∘◦⟵⟶∘◦⟵

OUTSIDE GRAY'S INN, Noah is about to remount Bucklebury when he notices that he's being observed from some distance by a mounted, black-clad figure partially concealed behind a snow-covered tree trunk.

Careful not to allow his gaze to linger on a possible tracker, he considers whether it would be better to stop at his nearby home in Holborn or to proceed directly to Essex House to confer with Lady Essex and her mother-in-law Lettice Knollys. After a moment's thought, he concludes that in returning home he would almost certainly lose his tracker, something he'd prefer to avoid. (The irony does not entirely escape him that he's come to regard a hostile tracker less as a threat than as a potential source of important information.)

Noah decides to take neither such course of action. Instead, steeling himself for some unwelcome memories, he proceeds to the nearby Saracen's Head, ostensibly for a small ale. When his tracker does not follow him in, Noah summons over the tapster's blond boy and seats him across the table, where they can converse under the tapster's watchful eye.

"Do you know who I am, boy?" Noah asks quietly.

The boy, who can't be a day older than eleven years, seems a bit in awe of Noah. "You're the barrister what killed that bad man here at the inn," he replies.

There are so many misconceptions in the boy's understanding (which he no doubt shares with the tapster and everyone who frequents the tavern), Noah decides not to correct him, but rather says, "Sometimes we have no choice but to defend ourselves."

Though the boy seems dubious, he's evidently curious.

"What's your name?" asks Noah. This young man is so reminiscent of David Killigrew at the same age, Noah would be unsurprised to learn he likewise comes from Cornwall.

"I'm Timothy, suh," says the boy with a smile.

"How would you like to earn yourself tuppence, Tim?" asks Noah.

"Tuppence?" asks the boy, glancing over his shoulder at the tapster, who nods in encouragement.

"Yes," says Noah, "all you have to do is take a slip of paper to my home, which is quite near here on High Holborn, and hand it to someone."

"To *anyone*?" asks the boy.

Noah shakes his head. "To someone *in particular*. To Lord Saint Ives, in fact."

The boy seems excited to meet the famous hero of Saint Ives. As the boy consults with the tapster, Noah writes a brief note, blots it, and awaits the boy's prompt return.

"The master says I can do it, suh, but I've got to be paid before I take the note."

Noah smiles at the tapster, who salutes humorously, and returns his attention to the estimable Timothy. "You drive a hard bargain, young man, but ... very well. You must not, however, deliver the note to anyone but Lord Saint Ives. If he's not there, bring the note back here and"—he points to the blaze in the fireplace—"toss it into the hottest part of that fire."

"Do I get to keep the tuppence, suh?"

"Will you make sure it's consumed by the flame?"

"I'll watch it burn, suh."

Noah rises from his chair, hands the boy tuppence, tousles his hair, and whispers, "Then you may keep the tuppence, and I'll give you an *additional* penny."

"Oh, but how will you know, suh?"

Noah's taken aback. "Are you a man of honor, sir?"

"I am," the boy shoots back.

"Then I shall rely on your word."

Wide-eyed with astonishment, the boy stuffs the note and the coin into his pocket. A thought occurs to Noah, and he bends down to speak with the boy eye-to-eye. "And if Lord Saint Ives reports to me that you brought that note to him, Timothy, I shall see that you get *tuppence* more, instead of just an extra penny."

The boy is downright excited by the prospect of getting a fair start on a shilling for having simply delivered a note to a residence mere paces away. "But how will I know he's told you, suh?"

"Because, much like you, *I* am a man of honor."

The boy smiles, and dashes for the rear door.

Noah nods to the tapster, walks out of the front door and remounts Bucklebury, relieved to see from the corner of his eye that his tracker has not given up on his quarry. And, if fortune favors the good, the tracker will soon have a tracker of his very own.

CHAPTER 4

A FEW MINUTES LATER on the same bleak and wintry day, Noah sits uneasy atop Bucklebury, mournfully clopping along the Strand on a roundabout approach to Essex House. Through its windows, formerly lined with books to guard against the stray shot from outside, Noah can see that Essex House has been returned to a peacetime footing. Not a single window is broken or damaged. All the books have been reshelved.

Out of doors, the house retains no sign of its month-long occupation by Essex's men-at-arms, nor of the abortive rebellion that whimpered to its close here. Indeed, the only remaining sign of the recent commotion is the heavily trampled snow on the lawn, where a chaos of muddy bootprints has been sharpened, hardened, and brought to a high polish by a fine icy powder drifting in off the Thames.

Noah approaches the house, where the new stableman admits horse and rider through the gate. A few drops of blood on the frozen snow remind Noah of the fierce firefight that flashed out through these very windows that night, yielding four gory bodies that were carried over it, their lifeblood draining onto the winter landscape.

He wonders with disgust whether the blood had been mopped up before Lettice Knollys accepted her daughter-in-law's invitation to take up residence here, where she could more readily seek the Queen's aid in preserving what is evidently of utmost importance to her: wealth and position.

Knocking on the front door, Noah half expects it to be answered by the wicked Caim. But, of course, Caim's dead, courtesy of Cuthbert Bennett. The new footman emerges and politely admits Noah inside by the very door through which he was manhandled mere days ago. They pass quietly down the same hall where Noah feared he was seeing young David for the last time.

It takes Noah every bit of determination to suppress his bitterness at these aristocrats, to whom the lives of family members count for but little, and those of plain folk nothing.

"Serjeant Ames?" says a young woman in the library.

Noah turns toward the voice. In the dull grey light stands an elegantly dressed young woman of pleasant appearance, with obvious intelligence behind the eyes, as befits a daughter of First Secretary Walsingham and former wife of Sir Philip Sidney. She can only be Lady Essex. He bows low. "That I am, m'lady, though I'm surprised to be recognized, as I have no recollection of being introduced to your ladyship, and that's something I'd surely recall with great fondness."

"I was told you would be coming," she says, and points up toward the higher storeys. "Also, I caught a glimpse of you the other day, during the … the …"

Her evident sadness has her stuck for the word.

"Commotion?" Noah offers sympathetically.

"Commotion. Just so." She smiles wanly. "Who would have thought that the best English word would come so easily to one born in a foreign land?" She offers him a chair, which he assumes only after she's taken an adjacent seat.

He's pleased to have distracted her from her main troubles, and so continues to chat. "Actually, my family is English—or as English as Hebrews can be—and we spoke English in our home even in our 'foreign land.'"

"My husband, Lord Essex, told me of your command of the language. More precisely, he *warned* me."

"I assure you, madam, that you have nought to fear from my skill in English (paltry though it may be)—or in any other language. And I hope his lordship informed you that I have never employed such skills against his interests."

"So he has assured me," she says wistfully, "and yet, there he lies in that fetid place."

"I wish I could mitigate his lordship's discomfort, madam. But, as I cannot, I am here by Her Majesty's leave to provide what assistance I may to *your ladyship*."

Lady Essex seems unsure how to proceed. "I have a confession to make," she says at last.

He chuckles quietly. "I fear you've come to the wrong *church* to make confession, m'lady," he says, and is delighted by her titter of appreciation.

"A palpable hit," she replies. "But, what I meant was: 'Tis not truly I who seek your aid."

Noah does his best to look mildly surprised. "'Tis *not*?" he asks, and cringes at the half-heartedness of his own dissimulation. He was once so much better at feigning enthusiasm about this sort of polite fakery. "Then … for whom might you be seeking aid, may I ask?"

"Lady Leicester," she admits in a whisper.

He nods as though in need of a pause. "M'lord's dear mother," he says sagely.

"Yes. She is concerned about a possible adverse claim to her title and property." She observes Noah's face for any sign of protest, and then simply assumes it's coming. "Now before you storm out of here—"

"Never fear that, m'lady," he says gently. "I hope I'm not reputed to be as petulant as all that."

"Have you no fear of angering Her Majesty?" asks Lady Essex. "After all, Lady Leicester has been banished from court for life."

"Does Lady Leicester's predicament pose a problem also for your ladyship?"

"Oh, certainly, Serjeant. Very much so."

"Her Majesty has instructed me to help you." He shrugs. "And so I shall, insofar as it is in me to do it."

Lady Essex breathes a sigh of relief. "I am pleasantly surprised to hear it." She rises. "Permit me to fetch Lady Leicester."

Noah rises and bows.

WARY IS THE MOST apposite term Noah can conjure in his head to describe Lady Leicester as she enters the library and approaches him in company with Lady Essex.

Lady Leicester is a good deal older than her son's wife, as one would expect, though she was surely quite fair of face in her heyday, and has maintained a pleasant figure. Yet her looks are marred by worry and … suspicion.

As her sole preoccupation ought to be her son's likely execution, that she's preoccupied by a threat to position and property makes Noah queasy. He puts aside his feelings, and bows.

"Lady Leicester, it is a privilege to make your acquaintance." He bows to kiss her extended hand.

"Lady Essex informs me," she begins cautiously, "that you have been sent by Her Majesty. Is this so?"

"'Tis, m'lady."

"And you are a Jew, is *this* not so?"

Noah sighs briefly. "'Tis, madam."

"Well," she says with a shrug, "if Her Majesty's father could appoint a butcher's boy Lord Chancellor, I suppose she can have a Jew advisor."

More slap than caress, thinks Noah. He remains silent, more from weariness than resentment. She'll need to ask him for help, which ought to put things on a more even footing.

"My daughter-in-law informs me that the Queen has sent you to assist me," says Lady Leicester.

"Her Majesty has sent me rather to assist the *younger* Lady Essex, madam. As your daughter-in-law has assured me that your problem is likewise a problem for her, however, I see no reason to consult Her Majesty concerning your ladyship's interest in the matter."

Lady Leicester, evidently both impressed and displeased by his response, chooses to upbraid him. "So, you take it upon yourself to decide the issue on Her Majesty's behalf?"

Tough old bird, thinks Noah. "Not in the least, madam, as my assisting your ladyship was in no way precluded by my instructions, whether explicitly or implicitly." He waits a beat to see if she backs down. When she doesn't, he rises, as with reluctance. "Of course, if your ladyship deems it inappropriate for me to proceed without clarification—"

"That shan't be necessary," she says. "I shan't even ask that these affairs be kept secret from Her Majesty, as I expect any such request would be ignored." Her comment trails off into a barely perceptible interrogatory note.

She won't even deign to put the matter to me as a question! She's been vying all the while for control of the conversation—for control of me—and I refuse to yield.

As she's asked no question, she's entitled to no answer. Noah stands mute, and they look unblinkingly into each other's eyes for an interval that young Lady Essex, at least, evidently finds uncomfortable.

"Mother," says Lady Essex, "I doubt that Her Majesty's interests will be involved in a solution to your … problem. That being the case, I can't imagine why Her Majesty would pry."

The old woman says merely: "Serjeant Ames?" Again, she declines to pose a question to him.

"Madam?" he replies, as though failing to understand.

She regards him warily, obviously suspicious of anyone who plays the game so well. "What have you to say to that?"

To avoid any imputation of insubordination, he says, "As to whether Her Majesty's interests might be threatened in resolving your ladyship's current posture, I cannot judge, as I know not the nature of m'lady's predicament. However," he turns reassuringly toward the younger lady, "so long as Her Majesty's interests are in no way imperiled, I should feel no compulsion to inform Her Majesty of any confidential communications between you ladies and your humble servant."

Lady Leicester snorts, and mumbles, "Humble, indeed."

Noah smiles and bows to Lady Leicester. "Humble or no, m'lady, I am at your service and shall help you in any lawful way I can." He points to a chair adjacent to the one he formerly occupied. "Would your ladyship have time to discuss the matter with me now?"

Head held high, Lady Leicester deigns to accept the proffered chair, and Noah takes a seat. To Noah's surprise, Lady Essex excuses herself, leaving him alone with the older woman.

"It might move matters along," says Lady Leicester, "if you were to tell me what you know about my situation."

Noah finds this a bit unnerving. The lady is famous, so to be ignorant of something important about her life might make him appear unschooled, even disrespectful.

"Very well," he says. "I shall tell what little I've learned of m'lady's position, but please bear in mind that much of my knowledge is based upon mere rumor." He sighs, and begins. "M'lady is a grandniece of Queen Elizabeth's mother Queen Anne Boleyn, and was Her Majesty's closest friend from the earliest days, even before Her Majesty was crowned. M'lady was married to Walter Devereux, First Earl of Essex, and was for a time known as 'Lady Essex,' which is, I expect, a title still appurtenant to m'lady, although I'm no expert in such matters."

"Correct so far," she says, looking well pleased.

"M'lady then befriended Robert Dudley, Earl of Leicester, Her Majesty's long-time favorite. M'lady's then-husband, Walter, Lord Essex, traveled on Her Majesty's service to Ireland, where he passed of an illness."

"Dysentery," she specifies, though it has long been rumored that Essex died rather of poisoning at the hands of Robert Dudley aforementioned.

"Robert Dudley, Earl of Leicester," he continues, "then married with m'lady some time after Essex's passing."

"*More than two years* after," she adds, "and don't forget it."

Noah bows his head compliantly. "At that time, m'lady adopted the primary style of 'Lady Leicester.' It was also at that time that your ladyship fell from Her Majesty's grace—"

"To put it mildly," she interjects with a sniff. "Satan was thrust out of heaven with less dispatch."

"—and your ladyship was banished from court thereafter," says Noah. "To universal dismay, Lord Leicester died shortly after the defeat of the Spanish Armada. Your ladyship married Sir Christopher Blount (currently committed to the Tower) shortly thereafter—"

"Shortly thereafter!" exclaims Lady Leicester. "*Shortly?*"

"I beg your pardon, m'lady. As I mentioned, I have very imperfect knowledge of such matters."

"Is *six months* 'shortly,' Serjeant?" she demands.

Noah blushes and scans the floor. "I meant nothing by that word, m'lady. A lady—or *any* woman, for that matter—may remarry at any time she chooses after her husband's death. *Any* interval is therefore 'decent' for such purposes, I would argue."

She's mollified by his emendation. "And you would argue rightly. Continue."

Noah's a bit rattled. "I know not *where* to continue, madam."

The lady rolls her eyes heavenward. "Children, Serjeant," she says in a most patronizing manner. "*Children!*"

"Very well," he replies, "but I remind your ladyship that these matters were rather overheard than told to me in reliable manner."

The lady nods.

"Your ladyship had borne Lord Essex several children, eldest of whom was the Second (and present) Earl of Essex, now most unfortunately committed to the Tower."

With no sign of grief, she nods for him to continue.

"During your ladyship's marriage to Lord Leicester, you bore him a male child, Lord Denbigh, who most unfortunately departed this veil of tears long before reaching his majority. I regret to raise this painful matter, m'lady, but, as I expect you are aware, it could be of some present significance."

She nods with visible anguish. "Is that all the children of whom you are aware, Serjeant?"

As Noah approaches a point of great sensitivity, he speaks hesitatingly. "No. I ... understand ... that his lordship of Leicester brought with him to the marriage ... a male child."

"A *foundling*, Serjeant?" she demands drily. "Was this child discovered in a basket on the Nile?"

Well, he wouldn't have been the first, Noah thinks, but has the good sense not to utter it aloud. "As I have no knowledge of the origins of such child, madam, I would much appreciate *your* continuing this … exegesis." He berates himself for his choice of words, which she pounces on.

"*Exegesis*, Serjeant? Are we expounding upon the Book of Exodus?"

"I chose my word poorly, madam. What sprang first to my mind was 'tale,' but that would have been an even worse choice, as it would have implied that your ladyship and I are jointly composing a work of fiction."

"Very well," she says. "I shall continue. Leicester had begotten this male child of Lady Douglas Sheffield, of the renowned Howard family, who had theretofore been widowed by Lord Sheffield. The child had been born out of wedlock, and so had no right to inherit from his father; however, the child's father made him his namesake, having him christened 'Robert Dudley.'"

Noah nods. "Aha."

"What does *aha* mean in this context, Serjeant?" she demands.

"Well, of course I must hear the remainder of the narrative, m'lady, but there's an old saying: 'Bastardy is the barrister's best friend.' That is to say, illegitimacy raises so many justiciable questions that the barrister who handles them shall never want for paying work. Tell me, m'lady, was the young Robert Dudley adequately provided for in his father's will?"

Lady Leicester glowers. "Although in his will the earl repeatedly referred to his namesake as 'my *base* son' (thus acknowledging the bastardy), the boy was *magnificently* provided for in his father's will. He received a large fortune in lands lying far and wide. I have had a copy made of Leicester's will and, before you go today, I shall lend it you for perusal at length."

"You have me on the hip, m'lady," says Noah, throwing up his hands. "As young Robert was so well provided for, *where comes the dispute?*"

In rough reply, Lady Leicester tosses onto the table a worn note that's been folded over several times. Noah takes pains to open and flatten without tearing it.

On one side is written in remarkably clear handwriting: *Lettice Knollys, Lady Essex,* an impudent form of address depriving her of her later-acquired title, *Lady Leicester.* On the reverse, a date occurring about a month ago has been written, and the following words appear in court script: *No valid title belonging to your ladyship having been omitted, as shall soon be seen by* all. *All* is underscored. The note is unsigned and lacks a return address.

"How did this note arrive?" asks Noah.

"It was slipped under the door at my country residence."

"Is the handwriting familiar to your ladyship?" asks Noah.

The lady shakes her head. "Not in the least."

"Are you familiar with the handwriting of young Robert Dudley?"

"Most certainly."

"And this is not his," he posits.

"Most certainly not, nor has he ever complained to me about the inadequacy of the provision made for him under his father's will."

Noah sits back pensively. "What do *you* make of this note, your ladyship?"

"How do you mean?"

Noah is baffled. "Well, the only possible purpose of sending a note such as this would be to unnerve you, which is not something you—or the younger Lady Essex—should be made to suffer, especially at this difficult juncture in your lives. I expect the note is prefatory to some further contact, perhaps a demand for money. I also expect that there is some meddler involved, of whom it is to be hoped young Robert has no knowledge. Has anyone contacted you about this note or its subject matter, or sought any payment from you?"

"No."

"Well, I shall be pleased to accept into my care the copy of Lord Leicester's will, and shall study it with great interest. Until you receive further contact from whoever wrote this note, however, I doubt there's much we can do, other than to ready ourselves. We shall at least do that."

A FEW MINUTES LATER Noah is fully cloaked for his departure, and the front door stands open before him.

Young Lady Essex approaches him from behind. On her approach, the doorman dutifully withdraws.

"Serjeant Ames," she says, "Please understand that Lady Leicester is far more grateful to you than she lets on."

Though Noah doubts it, he nods graciously.

She asks, "Do you suppose you'll be able to help her?"

Noah weighs his answer carefully. "I'm unsure whether the note was sent by authority of the young Robert Dudley, but let's hope it wasn't, for the only way the matter can get out of hand is if he intends to prove that his parents were married to each other at the time of his conception."

"And what would be the practical effect of such proof?" she asks.

"One result could be a judicial holding that the Earl of Leicester's marriage to Lady Leicester was bigamous, and therefore a nullity."

Lady Essex's eyes open wide and she gasps. "Oh, my word! The shame! The *shame* she would suffer!"

Noah turns to her. "While I doubt that Lady Leicester is unaware of anything I'm now saying, I did not wish to upset her by mentioning it, and I beg you to refrain from repeating to her what I'm about to tell you."

She chafes her hands together.

Although Noah didn't wish to leave Lady Essex in a quandary over such contingencies while her husband will soon be on trial for his life, she's left him no choice. "If Lady Leicester's marriage were to be nullified from its inception, it would mean that young Robert Dudley has been the rightful Earl of Leicester since his father's death. And, worst of all (in my humble estimation), property believed to have descended to Lady Leicester by virtue of her marriage to Lord Leicester would revert instead … to young Robert."

"My word!" she whispers excitedly. "How can the law allow him to challenge their marriage after he's been so handsomely provided for, and has accepted the benefit of his father's will?"

"I suppose it's possible," says Noah, straining for happier alternatives, "that her ladyship's solicitor required young Robert *to release* any such claim before delivering property to him under the will, although I have no grounds to believe that such a release was in fact signed. I even have some question whether such a release would have the force of law, in light of England's rather strict laws of descent." He shrugs. "A release is merely one of several possibilities requiring investigation. But if no such release was signed, then young Robert's claim cannot be barred by his acceptance of such of his father's wealth as he has already received."

And now the lady frets openly.

He berates himself. *Why did I allow myself to be engaged in such questions prematurely?* "Madam," he says, "for Lady Leicester's sake, I must beg you to becalm yourself. Such questions may never in fact arise. The note may have been entirely unauthorized by young Robert, in which case it's probable that nothing will ever come of it. Why, even if young Robert did authorize the note, or if he were to awaken one fine day and decide to challenge the marriage, he might simply fail in his proof. It happens all the time. So, you see, it is entirely premature to lose hope."

She looks up at him imploringly. "May I ask you for another bit of assurance, Serjeant?"

He's been dreading this moment and hoped to avoid it entirely, but he can see it's about to arrive nonetheless.

She asks with great trepidation, "Serjeant, in your experience ... do you think there's a chance my husband will not be put to death for what he did?"

He steels himself to deliver the news. "I regret to say that things are likely to go badly for him, madam."

She weeps, nearly choking into her kerchief.

"Madam," he says, "although Lord Essex has set a difficult course for himself, there is always hope that Her Majesty may stay her hand. In any event, I have spoken with Lord Essex at length, and he is determined to make his peace with his Maker regardless of the outcome of his trial."

His words appear to restore to her some level of equanimity, and he's amazed to see it, as he finds no comfort in them himself.

As he's about to bid farewell, a lone horseman passes by on the Strand moving in the direction of London, his features set in stark relief against the steely sky. Although his black hair has been tied back, it's unmistakably Andres Salazar, who must have remained in London after the obsequies for Arthur Arden.

All at once, Noah realizes that his note did in fact reach Jonathan, and that *Andres* volunteered to follow Noah's tracker, who has just now moved off toward London with Andres hard behind.

"I must take my leave of you now, m'lady," says Noah anxiously. "Would it be possible for me to reach the stables through a rear door?"

"Yes," she replies, "but why?"

"I'd rather not be seen leaving Essex House at this time."

CHAPTER 5

HAVING FOLLOWED THE horseman on a ragged northeasterly path through the City of London, Andres earnestly hopes his quarry will come to rest within the walled city, for if he's forced to follow him through Bishopsgate, his knowledge of streets and neighborhoods may fail him and there's a possibility he'll be unable to provide Serjeant Ames with a precise description of the rider's destination. (And, which seems even worse, he could miss tonight's supper with his beloved Barbara Bell.)

Andres begins to lose hope as the rider passes through Bishopsgate and disappears north of the city wall. As it would be a pity to lose him after tracking him this far, he hastens to catch up. Passing through the gate himself, he spots the rider slowly studying the front of each small cottage he passes, as though unsure which is his. The rider slows at last before a cottage he finds familiar.

Although Andres briefly considers riding nonchalantly past his quarry to get a closer look, he thinks better of it; perhaps someone's been watching for the rider's return and will spy Andres riding past.

Instead, Andres stops a few cottages behind the rider, steers his mount behind a mighty oak, and dismounts. He peeks around the tree's massive trunk and watches the rider tie off his horse and step inside the cottage, shutting the door behind him.

Although Andres could, with the little he's already seen, specify the cottage's location to Serjeant Ames (he need only count each cottage between the rider's and Bishopsgate), he'll deem performance of his task deficient if he fails to learn the man's name—or some other tidbit to aid in his identification.

Andres is surprised to see a squat, middle-aged man waddle down snow-covered Bishopsgate Street straight up to the front door of the rider's cottage, and knock. Andres wipes his brow in the realization that, if he'd approached the cottage heedlessly, this fellow, who for all he knows may be in cahoots with the rider, might have trapped him in a tight spot indeed.

As the visitor waits at the rider's door, Andres studies his appearance. He has that self-satisfied look of one who feels he's achieved much in life by pecuniary standards (and what other standard would such a fellow apply?): a bit corpulent, his clothing worn but dear. He's what one might call a *burgher*.

"Who is it?" demands the occupant through the closed door, with the world-weariness of a person of high estate who really ought not be bothered with the mundane cares of the commercial classes.

"I'm pleased to catch you at home, suh," says the burgher, affecting surprise at his good fortune, when all the while he was likely watching across the way for his quarry's return. "'Tis I. Groatsworth."

After a brief delay, the door opens just enough to permit a voice to emerge.

"What can I do for you, Master Groatsworth?" asks the rider in a clear baritone voice.

"If I might come in, suh?" There's a thoughtful silence on the other side of the door, which Groatsworth evidently finds a bit perturbatious. "That is, *if* you have but a moment, suh."

The door creaks open reluctantly, just enough to admit the rotund little fellow, but no wider to be sure. Unfortunately, because of Andres's vantage point beside the cottage, the fellow disappears from view as he enters.

Andres ties off his horse and slinks through the small snowy wood to the near side of the cottage, which fortunately has no windows. Confident that Groatsworth will not be invited in past the vestibule, he steps mincingly toward the front of the cottage and ducks below a barely open casement to hear what's going on inside. He fiddles with his boots, should anyone find his conduct suspect. In a moment, he picks up the thread of the conversation inside.

"Well, you see, Master Drury," wheedles the burgher, "the small advance you ... kindly handed to me upon your assuming occupancy at this ... *sumptuous abode*"—Andres can almost *hear* the burgher's arms spreading wide in an exaggerated flourish—"ran out some days ago. In fact, it was my understanding that you would be staying only a few days—"

"I *told* you," says the impatient lodger. "I had no idea how long I would need to stay. As it turns out, I have only now begun to achieve some slight success in my endeavors in London. *Here*," he says, clinking a few coins into the burgher's hand, "how much more time will this cover?"

"I'm delighted that you have begun to succeed in your endeavors here," says the burgher affably, as though the news of his tenant's success has completely distracted him from his purpose in coming.

Bloody likely, thinks Andres.

There's a moment of silence as the landlord counts the money. "Oh, but suh," he says apologetically, "this amount covers your occupancy only up to a week ago. You still owe rent for this past week—and I hope you are prepared to give an advance for a few weeks more."

Andres hears something heavy being pulled down from inside the very wall he's leaning against.

"What are you *doing*, suh?" asks the burgher in horror.

The occupant replies nonchalantly. "Pray, continue, Master Groatsworth. As I'm unwilling to pay to occupy this … *tumbledown shack* … any longer, I thought it best to allow my *friend* here to do my talking for me."

Friend? At first Andres derides himself for making the dangerous mistake of undercounting the cottage's occupants. But then the unmistakable sound of a firearm being prepared for service reveals that the occupant's *friend* is in fact a musket.

"But, suh!" says the burgher anxiously. "There is *no need*—"

Andres sprints back toward his hiding place behind the great oak as quietly as the icy footing allows, nearly sliding into his horse. He peeks around the oak once again and spies the cottage's front door swing wildly open and the burgher frantically waddle out, striving in vain to accelerate. The burgher lumbers halfway across Bishopsgate Street, slipping on the uneven ice every few steps, but thus far remaining vertical.

Behind Groatsworth, a barefoot Master Drury emerges with a loaded musket and stands just outside the door, obviously harboring no intention of either following the burgher or shooting him. Glancing about to ensure there are no witnesses, he fires his musket into the sky with a loud report.

The burgher leaps into the air higher than Andres would have imagined possible and lands on his ample bottom in the middle of Bishopsgate Street, flailing for purchase in the snow like an overturned beetle (all to Drury's unguarded amusement).

Regaining his footing at last, the burgher rubs his bottom and waddles indignantly to a cottage across the way. Before opening the door, he shoots a sharp glance back at Drury, imparting unmistakably that he'll get *even* for this indignity. He enters the cottage and slams the door behind him, apparently unhurt except for his wounded pride—and possibly a bruised bottom.

Drury snickers. As though the burgher were still there to hear, he says: "Do come again."

And with that, the little crisis seems to have passed.

Drury smirks and shoulders his smoking musket but, as he turns to reenter the cottage, he spies snowy footsteps leading off the porch into the woods. Alarmed, Andres holds his breath.

Drury's eyes follow the footsteps to Andres's hiding place and flicker with the realization that he's being spied upon. Though Drury quickly adopts an air of nonchalance, Andres knows full well that he's been spotted by his quarry and is quite certain he'll be pursued.

Andres unties his horse and leaps into the saddle, grateful for two things. First, Drury's musket can't be fired again without being reloaded. Second, Drury's icy feet must be soaking wet (their heedless owner having stepped barefoot out into the snow) and will need to be toweled off before boots can be slipped on. The combination of these two advantages should—other things being equal—give Andres time to escape on horseback.

Andres shakes the reins, and his mount bolts forward, back through the gate and south into London.

Normally, someone fleeing on a thoroughfare as straight as Bishopsgate Street would be expected to escape his pursuer's line of sight by making a sharp right turn onto Wormwood to hug London Wall until he's achieved a safe distance. Andres, however (believing himself to have a one-minute head start on his pursuer), chooses instead to remain on Bishopsgate for an additional quarter-mile, then turn right onto Threadneedle Street.

Even a pursuer who saw Andres turn onto Threadneedle would expect him to ride hard until he'd put a mile or so between them, so Andres quickly decides to frustrate his pursuer's expectations by dodging into the small remaining segment of Saint Christopher's Alley north of Cornhill.

Having reached a place of relative safety, Andres ties off his horse in a doorway and watches for his pursuer to pass him by in the busy traffic on Threadneedle Street.

"Hiding from someone?" asks a male voice behind him that nearly strikes him dead with fright. Although the voice does not belong to Drury and is strangely familiar, Andres is still unnerved to realize that *anyone* would know where he is, having taken such pains to avoid detection.

He turns suddenly to find himself face-to-face with David Killigrew, with his renowned blond mane flowing smugly in the breeze.

"Cheerful!" says Andres. "What the devil are you doing here?"

David puts his hands on his hips and says in good humor, "I might ask you the same, Master Salazar!"

From another doorway in the alley emerges a young blond boy with a smudged face, wearing a feathered cap that Andres recognizes as having belonged to David in younger days.

"Shall I wait on the corner now, suh?" the boy asks David in a manner that strikes Andres as entirely too familiar.

Indignant that this little fellow has been allowed to tag along on serious business, Andres says to him, "And what are *you* doing here?"

The boy puts his hands on his hips in imitation of David, and replies, "I might ask you the same, Master Salazar!"

It's all Andres can manage not to burst into laughter.

"David," Andres says drily, "at last you've found an acolyte. He even resembles you." Regaining his sense of mission, he adds, "For your information, Master Killigrew, the man who followed Serjeant Ames, whose name happens to be 'Drury,' is now in pursuit of your humble servant."

"*Excellent* strategy, Andres," says David, barely suppressing a laugh. "Is it your master plan to draw him to Serjeant Ames? Because—perhaps you'll recall—those were *not* your instructions."

Andres points his chin at the boy. "Who's this young fellow?"

"Timothy," replies David. "He brought the note to Lord Saint Ives asking one of us to follow Serjeant Ames's pursuer."

"Pardon me, Master Salazar," says the boy. "The man chasin' ye. What's he look like?"

Andres looks to David to see whether he should answer. When David nods approval, Andres replies: "Brown hair, tall and lean, well-dressed in black clothing of different shades, wearing a gold cross on a gold chain. His horse is a roan."

The boy nods. "That's what I thought," he says pensively.

"Do you *know* him?" asks Andres in wonderment.

"No, suh," says the boy, "but he just rode by while you gentlemen were talkin'."

Andres's eyes go wide. "Did he look this way?"

"I doubt it, suh. He was movin' fast, like he was runnin' from a ghost."

David turns to the boy. "Timothy, go stand on the corner, somewhere no one will notice you. If he turns back this way, come and tell us first thing."

The boy looks inquiringly at David. "Same wage, Master David?"

David smirks. "Tuppence *'tis*, but don't grow accustomed to these outrageous wages, young man. There's more to life than money."

"Sure," says Timothy. "There's all the things money can buy, like *food*." He smiles broadly and gives David a military salute. Quick as thought, he darts from the alleyway and out of sight.

Andres turns to David. "You and I can't be seen together. If Drury recalls only me, he'll think he was followed by a Spaniard. But if he sees us together, eventually he'll draw a connection to Serjeant Ames. And—not to change the subject—when this is over with, you'll have to tell me how you knew to find me in this miserable alley. I decided only at the last second to take cover here!"

"*Esther* told me where you'd be," says David, withdrawing into a doorway to wait with the horses.

Andres hides his face in his cowl.

Two minutes pass. Five.

Just as Andres decides he's evaded his pursuer and it's time to call off the vigil, he hears a horse gingerly approach the mouth of the alley. The hoofs draw to a stop, and a man furtively dismounts.

Andres withdraws further into the shadows, placing his hand on his dagger. Eerily, the sounds of traffic seem to have faded entirely. His heartbeat drums in his ears.

A man in black appears at the alley's mouth. It's Drury, and he appears not to have spotted his quarry yet. As he takes a slow, hesitant step into the alley, a shiny metal object tinkles onto the pavement before his feet. As he crouches to identify it, a larger metallic item falls to the ground before him with a thunk.

It's his golden cross, still attached to its golden chain!

As Drury stoops to pick it up, he's bludgeoned across the back of the neck, and falls to the pavement in a heap.

The small figure that shadowed him into the alley doffs his cowl and smiles broadly.

"Tuppence, please!"

———————⇒∘⫸∘⇐———————

A SHORT WHILE LATER in Westminster, Noah approaches William, the guard outside Lord Robert's chambers. William regards him doubtfully. "I know Lord Robert wishes to speak with you, Serjeant Ames, but right now there's a distinguished visitor in there, come down to attend the trial of Essex and Southampton, and I'm not sure Lord Robert would wish to be interrupted."

Noah nods indulgently. "I quite understand, William, and defer to your superior knowledge of Lord Robert's custom. I'll return in an hour or so."

As Noah turns about to walk away, William says after him, "Please to remain a moment, suh. For all I know, Lord Robert wishes to introduce you to this fellow."

Noah turns, pleasantly surprised. "Who's with Lord Robert, William?"

But William is already knocking at the door. Hearing a muffled voice from inside, he walks in and closes the door behind him. In a moment, he comes back out with a smile. "I was right, suh. Please go inside."

Noah takes a hesitant step into the familiar chamber, where Lord Robert stands at the window next to a fellow with a long bulbous nose, about Noah's age, but bent forward as one who's spent most of his life in intense study.

"Ah, Noah!" says Lord Robert, "it's most opportune that you've come." He turns toward the scholarly gentleman. "Master William Camden, permit me to introduce to you Serjeant Ames, a valued advisor to Her Majesty."

Delighted to see Camden's face light up in recognition of his name, Noah says, "It is indeed a privilege to meet you, Master Camden. I have much admired your work in the *Britannia*, since reading one of the earliest editions at the library of my good friend Sir Henry Neville."

Not only is *Britannia* the best history of Britain ever attempted, but it's equally a marvel of cartography and British lore.

Camden smiles gently. "A *capital* gentleman is Sir Henry," he says. "I have met him and would very much like to see him while I'm in London for tomorrow's trial. I should value his legal knowledge. Will Sir Henry be attending?"

Lord Robert interjects an answer. "I'm afraid that would be quite impossible, Master Camden, as Sir Henry is well on the way back to his embassage in France."

Camden's disappointment is evident, but then he brightens up. "Tales of Sir Henry's friend, Noah Ames, have been circulating since I attended Oxford. Would *you* be that same Noah Ames, Serjeant?"

Noah bows ceremoniously. "At your service."

"Your legal exploits are renowned, Serjeant," says Camden. "Lord Robert, would you be willing to have Serjeant Ames sit by me at the trial, so that he might fully apprise me of the significance of events? That is, of course, if he's not needed as counsel there."

"As Queen's advisor *not* assigned to the case," says Lord Robert, "Serjeant Ames will be seated somewhere behind counsel's table." He turns to Noah with one eyebrow raised. "Noah, would you be willing?"

"*Thrilled!*" exclaims Noah, barely believing his good fortune. At the same time, he can't help but wonder whether the same honor would have been bestowed upon any barrister who happened to walk into Lord Robert's chambers at that instant. "In fact, I came here just now to ask Lord Robert's permission to be accompanied at the trial by Jonathan, Lord Saint Ives."

Lord Robert seems taken aback at Noah's question. "*Baron* Saint Ives is welcome to participate on the *jury*, of course, in which case he would be seated with his peers."

Noah shakes his head dourly. "I have spoken with him, Lord Robert, and he feels entirely too ... conflicted ... to sit in judgment of Lord Essex."

"*Conflicted?*" says Lord Robert. "Why, if every peer having private griefs against Essex or Southampton were thereby disqualified, there would be no one left to judge them. You might assure Saint Ives that among those sitting in judgment will be Lord Grey, whose enmity for Southampton is well known to have descended into personal violence from time to time. Lord *Cobham* will be sitting, as well, whose death was one of Essex's chief objects. If we proceed along that line, Lord Chief Justice Popham will not only be sitting in judgment but testifying for the Crown—as *he* was forcibly detained by Essex throughout the rebellion."

Camden seems confused. "Are such grudges not grounds for disqualification?"

Lord Robert looks to Noah to reply.

Noah shakes his head mournfully. "Peers of the Crown cannot be disqualified on such grounds."

"That seems absurd," observes Camden. "Why, the verdict must often be a foregone conclusion."

Lord Robert interjects. "'Tis one of the 'privileges' of nobility, I'm afraid. In trials of commoners, other commoners *can* be disqualified on such grounds. But peers can be judged by any other peers." He turns to

Noah. "Serjeant, you certainly *may* bring Lord Saint Ives as your guest. He'll feel more at ease behind counsel table no doubt, having spent some years there before being made baron."

"It's settled, then," says Camden. "We three shall be seated together. Is that to your liking, Serjeant?" he asks with a devilish flair that strikes Noah as humorous in one so scholarly. Noah bows with pleasure, and Camden changes the subject. "Do you know that Lord Robert has been trying to distract me from revising the *Britannia*?"

Lord Robert looks away.

"I had no idea," says Noah in good humor. "Why *ever* would he do that?"

"He prefers that I write the annals of Her Majesty's reign. *That* is why!"

Noah takes Camden's hand reassuringly. "Sir, there could be no one better suited to do so, and no Sovereign more worthy of your renowned efforts. I personally would subscribe prior to publication."

Camden shrugs. "Well, I suppose it would be a relief to undertake a project where I won't be hounded for inclusion by every notable family in Britain, as I *have* been while writing the *Britannia*. One would have thought I was revising the Domesday Book, so that anyone omitted would be left without land or title."

"Look on the bright side," says Lord Robert. "At least you're acquainted with everyone of importance in the Realm."

Noah smiles sympathetically. "I doubt that writing the annals of Queen Elizabeth's reign would provide any relief on that score, Master Camden. Everyone would wish to be mentioned there, too."

Camden sighs. "I suppose that knowing everyone of importance has its advantages, after all."

There's a light knock on the door, and William enters.

"Lord Robert, there is a young gentleman here to see Serjeant Ames." Immediately behind William, uninvited, stands a smiling young blond boy in a feathered cap. Noah recognizes him as the messenger he dispatched from the Saracen's Head.

Two strong arms reach into the room, seize the boy by the elbows and draw him out.

Fortunately, Lord Robert and Camden react to the boy's unexpected appearance (and disappearance) with heartfelt laughter.

Red-faced, William resumes as though the boy hadn't barged in. "Lord Robert, there's a Master Salazar here who wishes to see Serjeant Ames."

Lord Robert nods. "Well, gentlemen, that was a welcome relief in light of the solemnities we shall face tomorrow. Serjeant Ames, why don't you see what's going on?"

Camden bows. "I shall see you and Lord Saint Ives bright and early at Westminster Hall, Serjeant."

Noah leaves with a bow.

———————⊸∘⊂✦⊃∘⊂———————

ONCE OUTSIDE LORD ROBERT'S CHAMBERS, Noah sees with mild annoyance that he's been fetched by a triumvirate consisting of Andres, David, and of course young Timothy, who has already made a premature appearance.

"I'm sorry to have embarrassed you, William," says Noah. "Rest assured it shan't happen again."

"Oh, it's all right, Serjeant Ames," says William. "I've got a few little imps of me own, and so does Lord Robert."

"Nonetheless," says Noah, scowling at the boy.

"Serjeant Ames," says Andres urgently, "we have discovered the surname of the man who followed you to Essex House."

Noah draws his visitors out of William's hearing, and regards Andres with mild curiosity, which Andres rightly takes as his cue to speak.

"His name is 'Drury.'"

"Thank you, Andres. Is that all you can tell me of the fellow?"

"No, sir, there's much more."

To Noah's great surprise, at the opposite end of the long hallway appears Lord Chief Justice Popham, walking swiftly towards him and waving a paper in his hand. "Serjeant!" he shouts. "A word, I pray."

Noah turns to his companions and speaks low. "That's the Lord Chief Justice. The first of you to make so much as a peep, I shall personally *hang*." He glowers at the wide-eyed Timothy who, for the first time, seems to recognize the gravity of events taking place here at Westminster.

Noah takes a few steps forward and awaits the approaching judge.

"Noah," says the Lord Chief Justice, "a request for service of a criminal summons has come in. The offense involves the discharge of a deadly weapon." He glances at the paper he's been waving. "A musket, evidently. The summons is sought by the landlord of some cottages just north of Bishopsgate. Hah!" he says, reading further. "Has the ironic name of 'Groatsworth.'"

Andres and David exchange a knowing glance.

"When must the summons be served?" asks Noah.

"The request seeks service as soon as possible. I want a calm head in charge when the summons is served, but every Crown barrister in Westminster is tied up in tomorrow's trial. Would you be able to handle the summons?"

Noah lets out a breath. "I've just told Lord Robert I would be at Westminster Hall before the trial begins and would remain there with a special guest of the Crown."

The Lord Chief Justice raises an eyebrow. "Special guest?"

"Camden."

The Chief Justice is clearly impressed. "The historian?" he asks. Noah nods. "Well, we'll all have to be on best behavior, won't we? That's quite a feather in your cap, Noah."

"I'm looking forward to it, m'lord," says Noah with a hint of self-satisfaction. "But, if the summons can wait, I shall take a few armed men with me at the conclusion of tomorrow's proceedings straightaway. If it's already dark, I'll go first thing the following morning."

"Well," says the Lord Chief Justice, "if it were to await anyone of equal seniority, it would take *days* longer, so by all means, go. And thank you." He hands the paper to Noah and quickly disappears down another hallway.

"I can't believe it!" exclaims Andres as he approaches with the other two.

"*What* can't you believe?" asks Noah, dismissively patting the paper he's just been handed. "It's just a workaday summons—"

"See who's being served," says Andres excitedly.

Noah studies the paper. There's the name right at the top. "One … 'Thomas *Drury.*'" The name rings familiar. "Is that the man who followed me?"

Andres smiles. "Delivered right into your hands!"

Noah feels as though he's stepped into a whirlwind. "I have to catch my breath, and I have some papers to file. All three of you, meet me at my home without delay."

Timothy nearly jumps for joy at being invited along.

Andres protests apologetically. "But I've supper this evening with Barbara … and her parents."

"When?" asks Noah.

"Two hours from now."

"Plenty of time," Noah assures him. "I'll meet you at my home. Meanwhile, keep an eye on *him!*" he says, scowling at the boy.

CHAPTER 6

THERE'S A KNOCK on the door at the Ames residence, and Serjeant Ames's cousin Esther opens it. It's her betrothed, the dashing David Killigrew, who she's delighted to see is openly smitten to see her.

"Master Killigrew," she says in good humor, "might I ask whom you wish to see—other than your humble servant?"

Remembering himself, David says, "Yes, Esther. Serjeant Ames told the three of us to meet him here." He tilts his head to indicate two young fellows loitering a respectful distance away.

"Ah, visitors," she says. "As Mistress Ames is away in town, I'll need to fetch Lady Jessica."

Before David can say another word, she disappears. In a moment, a weary-looking Lady Jessica appears with Esther behind her. As David bows, he remarks to himself (not for the first time) how much alike they look.

"Good e'en, David," says Lady Jessica. "Esther tells me that Serjeant Ames told you to meet him here, and that you've brought two additional visitors." She leans out through the doorway to see who they are. One is Andres Salazar, a well-regarded and frequent guest.

The other is a little blond boy wearing a feathered cap. Although his face and bearing are pleasant enough, his face is smeared with dirt and his whole appearance rather disheveled.

Lady Jessica turns to David. "Did you wish to await the Serjeant out of doors?"

"Actually, it's a bit nippy out here, m'lady," David replies. "I was hoping we could await him in his study."

"Did he say when he would be here?" she asks.

"Well, he was at Westminster and had a few remaining errands to complete. In an hour or so, I should expect."

Lady Jessica shakes her head. "Where did you find that boy?" she asks.

"*Find* him?" David says. "I suppose it was Serjeant Ames who *found* him—at the Saracen's Head."

"Where does the boy reside?"

David seems confused by the question. "Well, I'm sure I don't know—"

"Has he any family?" she asks.

David shrugs. "I'm afraid I don't know much about him, madam."

Lady Jessica shakes her head impatiently. "So typical of Father." She whispers something to Esther, who disappears into the house.

Lady Jessica takes a step out of the door and points to an outbuilding on the plot across High Holborn where her new house is under construction.

To David's surprise, a welcoming stream of grey smoke rises from the outbuilding's chimney.

Jessica detects his surprise and reassures him. "My lord has recently let that cottage to Master Jacob and his wife Leah," she says. "They'll be assisting us in preparing the house for occupancy. There's a tub in the cottage. Please take the boy there and have him thoroughly scrubbed."

"*Scrubbed*, madam?" asks David with astonishment. "On a February day?"

Lady Jessica nods emphatically. "Hair and all. He's absolutely *filthy*, David. Can't you *see* that? This house is clean and we've a newborn living here, so we have a choice, you see. Either this lad enters the house in his filthy condition bringing with him whatever infests street urchins nowadays (thereby rendering the whole house filthy) or—?" She raises her eyebrows and waits for him to speak.

"Or we clean him up first," says David.

Lady Jessica nods as to an apt pupil.

Just then, Esther reappears carrying some clothing and undergarments suitable for a boy Timothy's size.

"These clothes," says Lady Jessica, "were among Yetta's effects when she died. They've been thoroughly cleaned. They'd been worn by any charge in need of them, and your young friend there fits the bill. Take the lad—and these clothes—to Jacob and bring the lad back in them once he's clean. Burn his old clothes. Keep his wet hair covered while he's outside, or he'll catch his death of cold. Meanwhile, Esther will stoke the fire in Father's study to help the boy dry off upon your return."

As David meekly accepts the clothing and swaggers toward his friends, Jessica watches with bemusement as Esther's gaze lovingly follows David's progress.

"You should take heed, Esther," Lady Jessica admonishes. "As you can see, men are all alike in some infuriating respects. For one thing, they seem to lack any innate appreciation of the difference between outdoors and indoors. And they all need to be reminded of the susceptibilities of the very young and the very old."

Esther offers a wistful defense. "But when they're properly guided," she says, "they can be such a blessing."

Lady Jessica smiles and arches an eyebrow. "And there's our downfall," she says, closing the door on the wintry day.

⁂

NOAH'S SEATED ALONE in his study with (for some unknown reason) an unusually hot fire, when his son-in-law walks in.

"Lord Jonathan," says Noah, rising, "Good news. Lord Robert has approved your accompanying me in counsel's corner at the trial tomorrow. Better still, we'll be seated with William Camden."

Jonathan looks momentarily perplexed. "The author of *Britannia*?"

Noah smiles. "The very same."

Jonathan seems unenthusiastic.

"Are you not pleased?" asks Noah. "If not, Lord Robert has reminded me that you are welcome to sit with your peers—"

Jonathan shakes his head. "I'm not sitting in judgment of Essex and Southampton. Too much past business. I'm delighted to meet Camden, of course. What civilized man wouldn't be? But I'd just as soon be left to my own thoughts. I expect Essex will be convicted and sentenced to death."

Noah admires Jonathan's maturity. "Years ago," he says, "such a prospect would have pleased you roundly. No longer, I take it."

Jonathan shrugs. "I have every reason to cheer Essex's destruction," he says. "I still blame him indirectly for the loss of Graves. And now I must add poor Arthur Arden and both Bennetts to the butcher's bill. Still—"

There's a knock at the front door. Ignoring it, Noah nods. "It's hard to see a man condemned to death—or even a long term of imprisonment—no matter his grievous sins. Still," he sighs, "that's the business we're in: Bringing men to justice, if for no reason other than to serve as an example for the like-minded."

The swarthy Andres enters the study and bows to both Jonathan and Noah. "M'lord. Serjeant Ames. As instructed, I've brought David

Killigrew and Timothy. May I bring them in?"

Noah nods. As Andres goes to fetch the other two, Jonathan assumes his place in a chair beside Noah.

Andres enters with David. Last to enter is a remarkably clean Timothy, with his hair in a well-worn towel. Behind him stands a solemn-looking Jacob, who removes the towel from Timothy's head and combs the damp blond hair dangling to his shoulders. Jacob places a chair with its back to the fire, and seats Timothy there.

Noah addresses the lad tongue in cheek. "I hope your accommodations have been satisfactory, Goodman Timothy."

Timothy bows hesitantly. "I'm sorry, suh. I know not what that means."

Noah nods indulgently and restates the proposition more simply. "I hope that you've been treated well since arriving here."

The boy's face turns red and his eyes well up. "Oh, I *have* been, suh. I've been treated wonderfully well. I was given a hot meal with … *meat* and *gravy* in it." Timothy seems overwhelmed with gratitude. To everyone's astonishment, he covers his face with his hands, and softly weeps.

Lord Jonathan says incredulously, "Certainly, Timothy, it wasn't the first hot meal you've ever eaten?"

The boy wipes his eyes on the damp towel and replies, "Not the first ever, suh, but the first in … a *very* long time." He looks to Jonathan. "I'm sorry, young suh … I only saw you once. That was today, and I'm not sure how I should call you."

Noah replies. "You may call this gentleman 'Lord Saint Ives' or 'm'lord.'"

Timothy's eyes go wide. "Why, you'll be the first nobleman who's ever spoken to me … m'lord," he says, and drops to his knees.

Lord Jonathan gestures for Timothy to rise and resume his seat. "Thank you for your courtesy, Timothy," he says kindly. "From now on, a single bow upon entering the room will serve just fine."

"Aye, suh … m'lord."

"Where do you live, lad?" asks Noah.

"Oh, here and there, suh," Timothy replies, shifting uneasily.

"Have you a mother and dad?"

"I did, suh, but they were taken by plague."

"Oh," says Noah with dismay. "How unfortunate! How long ago were they taken?"

"About three years, suh."

Jacob speaks up. "If I may, Serjeant. I've known the boy since right after his parents died. He's been very helpful at the Draper's. He more than earns his keep." Jacob looks down sadly. "I do not know him to have a steady home."

Noah leans forward sympathetically. "But where do you rest your head at night, Timothy?"

The boy seems a bit dismayed at this intrusion into his privacy, but answers dutifully. "Master Tapster allows me to sleep behind the fireplace most nights, suh, in that big room at the Saracen's Head that they use for special occasions." Noah realizes with a start that the boy is referring to the room where he was nearly poisoned to death by Nerezza. "If the room's in use, I have to look somewhere else. But I never beg, suh. *I'm no beggar!*"

"No, we can all see that," says Noah. "You have practical skills, and you're prepared to work hard for your keep."

Jacob clears his throat, steps up to Noah and Jonathan, and addresses them in a hush. "The boy has *some* skills you may frown upon, gentlemen, as you shall see. If you permit, I'll stay for the remainder of your meeting."

Noah and Jonathan exchange a curious glance. "Very well," says Noah, and Jacob returns to his former place. "Let's get down to business, as Master Salazar has an engagement for which he's nearly due. Andres, tell us what you've learned about the man who followed me on horseback."

Andres perks up at the prospect of leaving presently. "We've learned that his name's Thomas Drury, and that he hails from Hawstead, Suffolk. I followed him to a rented cottage just outside Bishopsgate, where I saw him chase his landlord out into the snow with a musket, then discharge it harmlessly into the air—to make a *point*, I suppose. Drury caught sight of me and gave chase. Although I thought I'd escaped him by riding hard into London and dodging into an alleyway, he must have realized how I'd given him the slip, as he doubled back and entered the alley where I'd hidden."

"Did he confront you there?" asks Noah.

Andres shakes his head. "He was bludgeoned unconscious before catching sight of me."

"Bludgeoned? By whom?"

Timothy's youthful voice chimes in. "By *me*, suh," he says sheepishly.

Surprised, Noah turns back to Andres. "Did you leave Master Drury out of doors in an unconscious condition in this icy weather?"

Andres nods. "We did, Serjeant. But we tied off his horse and leaned him up against a building out of the wind. He was coming to as we left."

"Did you search his person?"

"We did," replies Andres. "He was carrying a couple of letters, neither of which made mention of you, Serjeant Ames."

"What did the letters say?"

"They seemed to be 'letters home' about a sea voyage he'd been on. One mentioned his having made the acquaintance of someone of ostensible importance."

"Whose acquaintance had he made?" asks Noah.

"In all the excitement," says Andres abashedly, "I forgot the name."

Noah then looks to David, who's quite defensive. "Please don't look to *me*, Serjeant," says David, as he glowers at Andres. "I didn't read the letters. I thought it sufficient for *one* of us to do so."

"No matter, suh," says Timothy, reaching into his pocket and placing two letters on Noah's desk. "Here they are."

Noah's astonishment quickly turns to mirth, which leads to a general laughter that seems to confuse Timothy.

"Did I do right, suh?" asks the boy.

"Well," says Noah once the laughter dies down, "I can't condone a general practice of bludgeoning people and filching their private papers, but in this instance I can see how it made sense to you."

Noah glances through the letters while the others wait silently. The handwriting is crisp and legible, and vaguely familiar. It leans left, as though written with the left hand. He's inwardly startled when his eye catches the name *Robert Dudley*, but he pretends not to have noticed anything and returns the letters to the table. "Thank you, gentlemen. I shall hold onto these and peruse them after dinner. Master Salazar, you may go, with my thanks. And please pass my blessings along to the family Bell. As for the rest of you, including you, Jacob and your wife Leah, I invite you to sup here with us. As for you, Goodman Timothy, who've just eaten dinner, you shall have a place at supper, regardless."

Jacob interrupts again. "Pardon, Serjeant. Before we all go: Timothy, please show these gentlemen the other items you took from Master Drury's person."

Timothy braces himself, removes an item from his pocket and places it carefully on the table. It's a small badge bearing an insignia that no one seems to recognize. From his other pocket Timothy removes a heavy gold cross on a golden chain. Although he tries to lower it gingerly onto the desk, it's so heavy that he can't prevent its making a profound thud. Andres and David cannot hide their shock.

Noah sighs. "Is that *all* of it?" he asks with exasperation.

Timothy nods emphatically.

Noah points to the items on the desktop. "These will ... all ... have to be returned surreptitiously to Master Drury tomorrow. For now, however, I shall hold them here for safekeeping." He leans sternly toward Timothy. "Have I your word, sir, that you will filch nothing from our families, servants, or houses?"

Timothy chokes up, but rather than make a prolonged defense, he says, "I swear, suh. I'm no thief. I took those things because I thought you'd wish to see them."

Noah nods. "And so I did," he says, rising with a smile.

Jacob says, "With your permission, Lord Saint Ives, and yours as well, Serjeant, I'd like the boy to stay with me and the missus at the cottage for a time."

Noah and Lord Jonathan nod their assent, and the meeting is adjourned.

But in truth Noah's unsure what to make of this light-fingered urchin.

—————————⟫∘❦∘⟪—————————

AFTER DINNER, Noah and Lord Jonathan return to speak privately and have a sherris.

"Well," says Lord Jonathan, "the boy was well-enough behaved at supper."

"He was," Noah agrees. "After the trial tomorrow, we'll serve that warrant. I'll have Drury brought to the landlord's cottage without giving him time to don his coat." He removes Drury's personal items from a desk drawer and hands them to Jonathan. "At that point, please hand these to Timothy, tell him to enter Drury's cottage and leave them in separate pockets of his coat. Tell him he must get out straightaway, or he'll be caught." He ponders for a moment, and adds, "Tell him not to take anything else while he's there."

"Won't Drury see these items when he returns home?" asks Jonathan.

"Eventually, and that's the point. He'll wonder whether he simply misplaced them. After all," says Noah with a devious smile, "who ever heard of a cutpurse returning the booty?"

Jonathan smiles. "It seems you have matters well in hand, Noah," he says, slouching into his chair, "so why do you seem so on edge?"

Noah looks into Jonathan's face, wondering if he should share his fears. "This is the last evening when I can be sure Essex will not make a full confession."

Jonathan regards him skeptically. "Why should you care *when* Essex makes peace with his Maker?"

Noah sips his sherris. "If Essex were a Hebrew, he'd pray privately and be done with it." He sighs. "But that's not the way of the Church of England. I'm not worried about Essex's *Maker*, who's historically been the Paragon of discretion. It's Essex's *confessor* that has me worried. Lord Robert quickly learns everything the divines find out."

"What could Essex say that Lord Robert doesn't already know?"

Noah shrugs, allowing himself to be led toward disclosing some matters to Jonathan, which would be a great relief. "I suppose he *could* incriminate someone."

"But you yourself have told me that Lord Robert already knows everyone who was involved in the rebellion, as well as his degree of involvement."

"Yes, that's true," says Noah. "At least, I *think* he does."

Lord Jonathan sips his sherris and is silent for a time. Suddenly, to Noah's surprise, he rises and quietly closes both doors to the study. Jonathan resumes his seat, takes a deep draught, and looks Noah in the eye. "It's Sir Henry, isn't it?"

Noah is mortified. The heat of embarrassment flashes over his face. "Why would you say that?"

"Because I'm not stupid, Noah. You said that Essex might tell his confessor of someone's involvement, but that Lord Robert probably knows everyone involved. So, it's the *confessor's* knowledge, not Lord Robert's, that worries you. That can only mean that Lord Robert is now forbearing to act against a co-conspirator (someone he obviously cares for) but will feel *impelled* to act against when the secret is discovered by someone *else*. Lord Robert is obviously not worried about *your* finding out—for numerous reasons, chief among which is that you already *know* of this person's involvement in the rebellion; otherwise, you would not be fretting about it now." Jonathan takes another sip. "So the co-conspirator is someone both you and Lord Robert care for. And why would you be concerned about the *timing* of the confessor's discovery? Why, because the co-conspirator is already on his way out of England, and Lord Robert hopes he'll be gone before he's named. Who fits that scenario better than Sir Henry Neville? Indeed, who else fits it at all?"

Noah wipes his eyes and sinks down into his chair. "I haven't been sleeping, Jonathan. Every bloody night when I close my eyes, all I can see before me is my old friend Henry on a cart at Tyburn, with some faceless barbarian slicing his ample belly open and burning his entrails in front of his face." He feels his gorge rise. "I couldn't bear to see it," he says quietly. "I should surely go mad."

"What are you doing to avoid it?" asks Jonathan sympathetically. "Perhaps I can help."

"Other than to keep the secret, there's not much you can do for now. Actually, there is one thing you *can* do, although I cannot tell you how it's related. At tomorrow's trial, Sir John Leveson will testify about his defense of Ludgate against Essex's men. I need him to await me outside the courtroom, so that I may speak with him after the trial is completed. Don't approach him. Just keep an eye on him, and come and rouse me if he appears to be … leaving early."

"Simple enough," says Jonathan.

Noah rises to retire, evidently having forgotten the additional topic of Thomas Drury.

"And what of Drury?" says Jonathan. "Have you figured out why he followed you?"

Noah sits back down. "Not really, but one of his letters indicates that he recently met one Robert Dudley."

"The Earl of Leicester's son?"

Noah nods.

"Of what significance is that?"

"Young Robert," says Noah, "is reputed to have been born out of wedlock."

"What of that?"

"This is also secret," Noah admonishes. "Robert Dudley may be preparing to claim that his parents were in fact married, which would make him rightful heir to his father's estate, including his title. If borne out at trial, that would leave Lady Leicester with very little property, and *no* title except *Lady Essex*, which was her station before marrying Leicester."

"But what has any of this to do with Drury?"

"Perhaps nothing, but I expect Drury was following me because Her Majesty (in roundabout manner) had just charged me with assisting Lady Leicester. After I left the palace," he says, omitting his visit to Leveson, "I naturally went to visit Lady Leicester to discuss the matter. She produced an unsigned note threatening to expose the flaw in her title. It just seems more than coincidence that Drury, who'd just met Robert Dudley, was following me to Lady Leicester's lodgings at Essex House."

"But how could he have learned you were appointed to assist Lady Leicester?" asks Jonathan.

"The only way Drury would know is if someone in the palace told him immediately after I was appointed."

Jonathan rubs his beard. "The plot thickens."

Noah shakes his head. "Just what I need while I'm trying to save Sir Henry's hide: a subplot."

CHAPTER 7

ON THE CHILLY MORNING of the great trial, Noah arrives early with William Camden to secure their favored seats at stately Westminster Hall. The rafters echo with the tapping and shouting of workmen putting the finishing touches to a large makeshift courtroom built for the occasion.

Camden gazes up at the ceiling in awe. "I've come here many times, of course, but each time, I marvel at this hall as though I've never seen it before—especially the roof."

"Quite the wonder, isn't it?" says Noah, though in truth he barely notices the roof after all these years practicing law in its shelter. "It allows for an unobstructed view anywhere in the hall."

"Yes," says Camden, "that was made possible by the advent of the hammer beam, of course."

Noah looks to him questioningly.

Camden points at an edge of the ceiling. "See those short horizontal beams protruding from the walls, supported by struts?"

"Yes, I see them," says Noah.

Camden nods. "They're most of what's holding the roof up over our heads. The Egyptians didn't invent the hammer beam. The Greeks never came up with it; to the contrary, the interior of the Parthenon is cluttered with colonnades whose sole purpose is to hold up the roof. The Romans came no closer. And yet," he says with wonderment and pride, "less than a generation after England is conquered, the Conqueror's son hires a few English masons—and they design and implement a way of holding up the largest roof in Europe without columnar support, making what is effectively the largest unobstructed room … in the known world." He smiles. "That's one way to create a sense of community and grandeur in a newly conquered people, I suppose."

Noah smiles appreciatively to have such a wonderful storyteller bringing life to surroundings so familiar that he's rarely paused to contemplate them.

The din of effort in the makeshift court dwindles to a few masons checking for any unsoundness in their completed work.

Camden points to the newly finished court. "Tell me, Serjeant Ames, what is the *name* of this court?"

"It's the Queen's court, of course," Noah replies.

"Is not *every* court the Queen's court?" asks Camden.

"Well," says Noah, "this temporary one's built on the site of the Court of Queen's Bench—'King's Bench,' when we're ruled by a king—but today's court is not constituted as Queen's Bench, although the two courts do have certain officers in common. For example, the presiding judge of either such court is the Lord Chief Justice of Queen's Bench."

"Has Queen's Bench always been held here?" asks Camden.

Noah shakes his head. "Not always, no. Originally, it was called *Curia Regis*, and it was itinerant; that is, it traveled wherever the Sovereign traveled." He shrugs. "'Wherever the king holds court is the king's court,' as they say." He suddenly realizes what Camden's getting at. "The growing notion that a court can exist as an institution apart from the Sovereign is of fairly new vintage, at least by English standards, and it's strongly denied by the Sovereign. In fact, as you will see today, especially in trials of public note, the Sovereign is sure to send a conspicuous emissary to assure the world that all cases are being adjudicated under Her Majesty's authority, according to Her Majesty's laws, and in Her Majesty's royal name."

"Ah," says Camden, as though Noah's cast a new light on things. "So, *that's* what accounts for the double meaning of the word 'court,' as denoting either a place where a subject may seek the Sovereign's intervention *or* a place where justice is meted out under law."

Quite enjoying himself, Noah points toward the front and center of the room, where an elevated canopy of state sits above an imposing-looking chair and an equally distinguished footstool intended for its occupant. "There shall sit the Lord High Steward, signifying Her Majesty's Presence. At his feet, if you will—lower down, in any event—will sit the judges presiding over today's proceedings." He points to either side. "The numerous seats to the side of the well (steeply inclined, like those in an amphitheater) will be occupied by Peers of the Crown, with the uppermost rows occupied by those of highest position. Just now, those would be earls, as the Kingdom is currently dukeless (as you well know). Seated in front the earls (but below them) will be barons, and so on down the hierarchy."

Camden points to a series of tables in front of him. "And who shall occupy those?" he asks.

"Those are for the prosecutors, some of the best lawyers in all England," replies Noah. "I know many of them quite well."

"And this oddly shaped double table immediately before us?" asks Camden.

A feeling of dismay turns Noah's stomach, and he takes a few breaths before answering. He turns gravely toward Camden, who appears shaken to see the change in his aspect. "Those, Master Camden, are for the guests of honor."

Camden takes but a moment to realize what that means. "The accusèd earls?" Noah nods. "So we shall be watching the proceedings from nearly their viewpoint?"

Noah nods curtly and changes the subject. "Master Camden, once court is convened, which you will recognize by the familiar 'oyez, oyez,' all in attendance will be admonished not to speak during the trial. The judges are quite earnest about that. Any conferences among those in attendance must be moved outside before they so much as begin. I would recommend, therefore—unless you wish to exit and re-enter the courtroom (which would be much frowned-upon and likely prohibited)—that you now bring out whatever scraps of paper you may have in your bag and place them on the table here. That way, if you wish to converse, you can write me a short note, to which I shall respond in kind."

"Capital idea!" says Camden, who fishes in his bag and removes some scraps together with some ink and a couple of ink-stained quills.

Noah looks about them and realizes that the last workmen have left, and a few somber-robed officials wander about. "I wonder where Jonathan is," he muses.

At that precise moment, a rear door swings open and Jonathan comes racing breathlessly to his chair. Noah cannot help but smile, as Jonathan looks much the same as he did years ago—if one were to ignore the distinguished coat of arms on his sumptuous black robes, of course.

Jonathan nods respectfully to Camden and turns to Noah. "I was arranging assistance for the service of summons on Master Drury later today. I made it here just in time. The judges and other dignitaries are lining up outside." He glances about. "Indeed, a few seem to be here already."

"Any sign of Essex or Southampton?" asks Noah.

Jonathan's expression suddenly turns grave. "I just saw the carriage being dispatched to the Tower to fetch them." He glances about and his eyes light despondently on the table immediately before them. "From the looks of things," he says dourly, "we'll be seeing quite a bit of them—and quite soon."

Noah is concerned for his young friend's frame of mind. "Jonathan," he intimates, "you must steel yourself for the inevitable. 'Tis upon us."

Camden, surprised by Noah's fatalism, evidently feels impelled to interject. "Surely, Serjeant, things cannot be so bleak as *that*."

"Master Camden," Noah says indulgently, "half the men judging the accused will be witnesses to their wrongful acts. The other half will be their *victims*." He shakes his head dourly, to Camden's further dismay. Jonathan merely folds his hands impassively.

A few spectators scurry in and take seats elsewhere in the rear. No sooner has the last been seated than three deep booms fill the room, emanating from a baton rapped thrice against the other side of the door at the front of the courtroom.

A court officer opens it and enters.

"Oyez, oyez!" he bellows.

All rise, and the pieces begin to move.

In front of Noah's rearmost table, the seven prosecutors file in, altogether denominated "Queen's Counsel," consisting of Queen's Serjeant Yelverton, Attorney General Edward Coke (with whom Noah has tangled more than once), Master Francis Bacon (the only prosecutor to pause to bow to Jonathan and acknowledge Noah and Camden), and others whom Noah recognizes, but with whom he's had little business.

Seven judges assume the central seats that Noah pointed out to Camden. Of these, Noah is best acquainted with Lord Chief Justice Popham of Queen's Bench, who casts a polite nod in Noah's direction (which, on second thought, Noah feels fairly certain was directed at Camden).

Before this impressive judicial panel appears a prefatory display of such pomp as even Noah has never seen in one of Her Majesty's courtrooms.

The Lord High Steward enters the hall followed by seven Sergeants at Arms who lay down their ceremonial maces before him. The King at Arms and a gentleman usher carrying a long white rod, flank the Lord High Steward.

Sir Walter Raleigh, Captain of the Tower Guard, appears at the door, taking in the scene before he enters. His nimble eye quickly finds Noah and, in a show of breathtaking panache, winks at him.

Sir Walter is followed by forty of his men, foremost among whom Noah is most pleased to see Senior Yeoman Gardner, moving as a man of a certain age, assisted by the younger Francis, who himself seems less than fully recovered from a shoulder injury suffered in Her Majesty's service some months ago. Assisting the two of them is Chester, a recent addition to the Tower Guard recently brought to London by David Killigrew.

As the assembled remain on their feet, Camden leans over to scratch a note onto a scrap of paper and slides it to Noah: *Always such pageantry?*

Noah writes immediately below it. *Only for trials of Peers. Quite rare.*

One of the Sergeants at Arms rises, and raises his voice well above the pitch of the earlier proclamations. "The Lieutenant of the Tower of London shall return his precept and bring forth the prisoners, Robert Earl of Essex, and Henry Earl of Southampton."

Until now, the courtroom has been quiet, but for a few necessary footsteps and the accompanying rustle of papers and robes. But now, even that small bit of noise has ceased, as though everyone has stopped breathing at once. Noah closes his eyes for a moment, and the absence of sound is so profound that he momentarily imagines the courtroom vacant. Opening his eyes again, however, he sees everyone still there and all eyes fixed on the door.

The first thing to enter is the shiny blade of a headsman's axe, which the Gentleman Porter carries aloft before him, purposefully aiming the edge *away* from the prisoners. Although Noah's seen such imagery countless times, it never fully loses its effect, and he feels empathy for those who gasp at the sight. Naturally, everyone's mind races ahead to the posture of the axe should the prisoners be convicted and sentenced to death; the condemned prisoners would be escorted out of the door, but with the edge purposefully aimed *towards* them.

The Gentleman Porter hands the clerk the precept that instructed him to fetch the prisoners. Essex and Southampton are escorted into the courtroom separately. Meeting before the judges, they kiss each other's hands and embrace.

Noah finds the difference between their countenances quite remarkable. Southampton, barely twenty-eight years of age, trembles visibly, his posture slumped, face ashen. For a brief moment during their embrace, the desperate Southampton seems literally to collapse into Essex's arms, which hold him up unflinchingly. Though Essex is barely eight years older, he seems preternaturally serene, a man who's survived all the terrors of the world and is prepared to face their end.

Noah glances toward Jonathan, who looks back at him worriedly, evidently occupied by the same thought: Essex's complacency in the face of near-certain death bodes poorly for the fate of Sir Henry Neville. After all, a man who fears nothing but divine punishment will zealously unburden his soul—with little regard for the worldly burdens he thus imposes upon those yet living.

The prisoners are marched to their table. Southampton seems oblivious to his surroundings, but Essex nods to Noah.

The name of each Peer is called and answered as present. With a few of them, Noah is personally acquainted; the first such to be mentioned is Lord Thomas Howard.

When the name of Lord Grey is called, Essex laughs aloud and tugs at Southampton's elbow. Southampton seems quite jarred by the interruption.

"M'Lord Chief Justice," says Essex—his confident voice ringing out through the courtroom—"shall we prisoners be granted the same privilege as conferred upon any other private person—that being to challenge the participation of any person with whom we have just cause? I ask not for mine own sake, as it matters little to me, but rather for the sake of the fine earl who stands beside me."

Lord Chief Justice Popham confers briefly with his brethren, clears his throat, and pronounces: "Verily, the law does not allow a challenge to any of the Peers, for such is the credit and estimation of the Peers of England that they are neither compelled to an oath on arraignments, nor subject to any exception."

Attorney General Coke rises from his chair just in front of Essex and holds forth with precedent. "Should it please the court, the rule was established in the case of Thomas, Lord Dacre during the time of King Henry the Eighth, and has remained so ever since."

Essex whispers briefly to Southampton, who shrugs wanly. Essex turns back to the Lord Chief Justice. "We prisoners are satisfied with this answer, m'lord," he pronounces.

Uncharacteristically, Coke turns his head toward Essex and nods politely at Essex's acquiescence.

Though Coke's recital of precedent is quite correct, Noah shakes his head silently. It will be frustrating to listen to Coke pontificate as though his were the only possible view of the law. But Essex lacks any right to have a lawyer stand beside him to provide counsel and speak on his behalf.

And, in any event, Noah is not his lawyer.

CHAPTER 8

NOT A SINGLE WITNESS has yet been heard, but Attorney General Coke has filled the courtroom with his stentorian tones all the while. To persuade the Court that, in finding high treason, it may infer without proof that it was the prisoners' specific intention to kill the Queen, Coke presents prior cases in which lowly subjects have been found guilty of high treason though the Sovereign's death was clearly outside the scope of their intentions.

Coke stops his speech short and slowly scans the courtroom to be sure every eye is upon him—a ploy that even Noah must admit Coke has oft used with great effect. He begins again in a lowered voice: "If, as in these past cases, millers and masons, poor mechanical persons, intending to overthrow enclosures, shall be said to be guilty of treason in devising the death and destruction of the King"—now his pitch rises—"what shall we say when so many *earls, barons, and knights,* having assembled on a sudden three or four hundred persons, and expecting a multitude of followers, intend to take—*not* a slender fort—but *the Tower of London*; to invest—*not* a mean village—but *this great city*; to surprise—*not* the mansion of the Lord Mayor—but *the sacred palace of the Queen*? This must needs *imply* that they intend the death and destruction of the Queen, and is higher than the highest treason!"

Now Coke condemns Essex for confining in his library those sent by the Queen to persuade him to relinquish his plans. "To the Earl of Essex, Her Majesty very graciously sent the Lord Keeper, the Earl of Worcester"—he waves his arm in genteel manner toward the Judges' Bench—"the Lord Chief Justice, and the Comptroller; two of them of the earl's own blood, the others never bearing him any malice, as I think m'Lord of Essex himself will confess; these charged him upon his allegiance to the Crown to lay down his arms and dissolve his troops. Now mark the fury of this rebellious company! They immediately cried out to Essex: 'Kill them! Kill them! We shall have the fewer to deal with. They do but abuse you and plan to betray you!' And yet, when the earl left the house,

Lord Essex abandoned these Councillors to this very same vulpine rabble! Thank God for preserving their lives! And the earl, before leaving the house to go into the city, gave the order that if he and his accomplices should miscarry in London—as they did—these esteemed Councillors should be *slain*!" Coke casts a contemptuous glance at Essex. "Why should I stand upon further proofs?" he asks aloud. "Why, the treason is so evident that the earl himself will not deny it!"

Essex rises in a huff. "Will your lordships give us our turns to speak? For Master Attorney General plays the orator, and abuses your lordships' ears with groundless slanders against us. He speaks like some corrupt country's favored orator, famous for arguing other men out of their lives."

The Lord High Steward bestirs himself in his lofty chair. "It is fitting, m'lord, that the evidence should first be delivered, and *then* your lordships should be at liberty to speak as you wish."

Essex shakes his head. "We urge your lordships to allow us first to answer generally to the charges against us, and afterward to each item of evidence *as it is delivered*. Otherwise, our memories will be overcome with detail and we'll cede the advantage to our enemies by failing to answer each particular point."

Noah cannot help but smile. He couldn't have said it better himself, and is delighted to see that the judges deem Essex's request reasonable.

"Granted," says the Lord High Steward with little hesitation.

Essex is obviously surprised by the success of his objection. "At this point," he says, "we beg the Court not to consider what may be said by these gentlemen"—he points to the prosecutors before him—"but only what shall be directly and plainly *proved*."

The written testimony of several witnesses is then read before the jury. Essex casts aspersion on their testimony on grounds that they have been conveniently placed outside the reach of the Court and are unavailable to be cross-examined. Noah knows this to be a common, though devious, practice of prosecutors in London.

Essex denies to the Court that the prisoners in his library (to whom he refers as "guests") were subjected to the whims of an undisciplined rabble. "I never heard such words as 'Kill them! Kill them!'" he protests.

Coke leaps upon Essex's denial, addressing the Bench. "Might m'Lord Chief Justice declare whether your lordship heard those words, 'Kill them! Kill them!'?"

The Lord Chief Justice, plainly reluctant to offer his testimony in a case in which he serves on the Bench, replies in calm and measured tones, "I did hear those words spoken behind my back, but I cannot say directly whether m'Lord of Essex heard them or not."

Thereafter, the Lord Chief Justice and many other witnesses testify to a progression of events, and their testimonies coincide with one another down to the last detail, leaving Essex to fall back upon the unpersuasive words he repeatedly uttered that day upon leaving Essex House for London, namely, that his enemies had plotted against him and sought his life. By the demeanor of the jury, no one takes those assertions seriously.

Essex bestirs Southampton to declare, as he did on the day of the rebellion, that Lord Grey had recently fallen upon him and his servant as revenge for grudges dating back many years to their service in Ireland together.

Lord Grey rises and speaks. "I protest I owe m'Lord of Southampton no malice. God knows that I do not wish to press someone in such abject fortune as he, but what I did to him in the street was not in respect of our old quarrel, but rather for new injuries."

Southampton musters his strength. "Your lordship did mistake me," he says. "I never intended you any injury at that time."

To avoid diversion of the trial into collateral matters, the Lord Steward calls an end to this colloquy between Southampton and Grey.

Essex says, "But there is also Sir Walter Raleigh, who sent to Sir Ferdinando Gorges at Essex House, attempting to turn him against me and threatening dire consequences should he instead remain loyal to me. Against my objections, Sir Ferdinando met with Sir Walter on the River Thames, within sight of Essex House. There Sir Walter once again threatened harm to those loyal to myself. Upon Sir Ferdinando's return to Essex House, he spoke some encouraging words concerning the likely success of our endeavor, though his courage failed him at the last.

"And later I heard that Bales, the scrivener at the Old Bailey, confessed that he'd been forced to counterfeit my signature on at least a dozen letters. Was it unreasonable for me to detect in that a Government conspiracy against me?"

Coke feigns exasperation. "By my troth, this is true. But Master Bales has offered information that he was procured to do so by one John Daniel—*one of your own men*—and that it was for the sole purpose of enabling you to deny that you had signed such letters in the event they came to light."

Essex pounds his hand on the desk. "You say it, Master Attorney General, but you're not under oath, nor *would* you say it under oath, for you surely know that John Daniel is an arrant thief who stole a casket of my wife's jewels. How likely is it that I would have trusted a man after he'd done that to me? My family's estate is under siege in more than one way, if you don't know it already, and I can only thank God that my judges today are not so uncharitable as you are!"

Coke smiles at Essex derisively. "My lord, we shall soon prove what you are, and what your pride of heart and aspiring mind have brought you to."

But the sanctimony is too much for Essex. "Ah, Master Attorney," he retorts, "lay your hand on your heart and pray to God to forgive us *both*."

Coke ignores the remark. "The Crown calls Sir Walter Raleigh."

Essex waves his hand dismissively and mutters in a stage whisper, "What's the point in swearing a fox?"

Sir Walter takes the oath and offers his testimony. "As I knew that my friend and kinsman Sir Ferdinando Gorges had, without leave, left his post at Plymouth," he says, "I sent for him to come to me. Although at first he declined, eventually he agreed to meet with me in separate wherries on the Thames by Essex House, at which time I warned him to leave Essex's band, for otherwise he'd be spending a great deal of time in the Fleet Prison. He dismissed my warning and warned me in turn that Essex had a greater force than I knew and that, if I were to try to unseat him, I would have a bloody day of it. He shoved off and, as he did so, I saw several men with firearms descend the river steps from Essex House and take a few long shots at my departing wherry. Sir Ferdinando assures me that, upon his return to Essex House, he strove mightily to persuade m'Lord of Essex to abandon his designs on the Queen."

Essex protests. "That differs entirely from Sir Ferdinando's report as delivered to me at Essex House. I demand to hear his statement."

Sir Walter steps down.

Camden shoots Noah a glance, and scribbles to him: *What is the point of disagreement?*

Noah shrugs and writes, *Unclear as yet. Wait.*

Sir Ferdinando's first written statement is read aloud, which appears not to touch upon whatever point of disagreement Essex has in mind. But Sir Ferdinando's second written statement, given only yesterday, describes a disputed meeting at Essex House on the eve of the rebellion.

The question among Lord Essex's supporters, says Sir Ferdinando's second written statement, *was whether to attempt first the court at Whitehall or the Tower, or to stir his friends in London first and storm both the court and Tower at the same moment. The majority resolved that both should be stormed at once. I disliked that counsel, and told them that their numbers were likely insufficient to carry it off, and advised them to think of something else, for I doubted they could plan arrangements for such a foray. They immediately set about expounding some division of labor among them in the taking of the court, at the successful conclusion of which ploy m'Lord of Essex would have presented himself to Her Majesty.*

Essex rises. "I desire to have Sir Ferdinando Gorges face to face," he says.

Sir Ferdinando is sent for and appears, looking soldierly but ill at ease. Handed a copy of his two statements, he reads them aloud in strong voice. When he finishes, he adds orally to the written statement, "I advised the earl, when he returned from the City to his house, to go forthwith and submit himself to Her Majesty."

Essex stares at Sir Ferdinando silently quite a long time, until at last the witness squirms under the scrutiny. There is not a sound in the courtroom, as everyone is eager to learn whether Sir Ferdinando freed Essex's prisoners for no reason other than to escape the hangman's noose that surely awaited him if he'd done otherwise.

At last, in a sardonic voice dripping with skepticism, Essex says, "Good Sir Ferdinando, I pray you speak openly whatever you remember. With all my heart I desire you to speak freely. I see you wish to live, and if it please Her Majesty to be merciful to you, I shall be glad and will pray for it; yet I pray you"—he hesitates a moment and continues with a note of disgust—"speak like a *man*."

Sir Ferdinando bristles under Essex's contempt and brings his spine erect. "All that I can remember I wrote in my earlier statement. Further I cannot say."

Essex purses his lips and shakes his head. "Sir Ferdinando," he says, "I wish you might speak anything that might do yourself good; but remember your reputation, and that you are a gentleman. I pray you answer me, *did you advise me to leave my enterprise?*"

Noah turns to Camden to indicate that Essex has at last reached the point of his disagreement with the witness. Camden nods in understanding.

Sir Ferdinando seems wilted as he answers. "My Lord, I think I *did*."

"Nay," says Essex firmly, "it is no time to answer now upon *thinking*. These are not things to be forgotten. *Did you indeed so counsel me?*"

Sir Ferdinando looks away from his questioner to some indefinite spot in the courtroom. "I did," he mutters wistfully, but by this point not a soul in the courtroom believes him.

"Why, my lords," says Essex, "look upon Sir Ferdinando, and see if he looks like himself. All the world shall see—*by my death and his life*—whose testimony is truest."

Camden quickly writes, *Was the point important enough to present Essex with a major success?*

Noah nods his head and writes, *The jury now doubts Sir F's testimony. All of it!* He underscores his exclamation.

Evidently emboldened, Southampton speaks up for the first time in a long time, and Noah notices what no doubt many have seen before: that Southampton is a very pleasant-looking man with a sonorous and thoughtful voice. His words emerge as seemly and sincere. "Good Sir Ferdinando, satisfy the Court what was intended amongst all our conferences and consultations."

The witness seems relieved that Southampton's question is free of Essex's dripping sarcasm. "Some delivered their minds one way, some another. But by the oath I have taken, I never knew nor heard any thought or purpose of hurt or disloyalty intended to Her Majesty's person."

The court dismisses Sir Ferdinando, who leaves the courtroom without hesitation.

Southampton turns to the judges. Although he speaks out of turn, he holds forth with great pride and is allowed to speak for his life without interruption. "I protest I bear all loyalty in my heart towards her Majesty. Inasmuch as I have offended her, I am heartily sorry for it, and do in all humbleness crave her pardon. But as touching the consultation at Drury House, though many things indeed were propounded, nothing was performed nor even resolved upon, all being left in the end to the Earl of Essex himself. Some advised it would be best to surprise the court only; others to take the court and Tower at once. Yet *neither* of these was done. How can this be construed as treason? It is true we consulted at Drury House about the securing of my Lord of Essex's free access to Her Majesty, but for no purpose other than to prostrate ourselves at Her Majesty's feet, humbly submitting ourselves to her mercy, and laying forth to her our grievances, whereof we thought she'd been misinformed by others. This was the whole scope and drift of all our meetings, and that this was without any treasonable thought, for my own part, I take God to witness. My Lords, I desire the opinions of the Judges, whether a thing consulted upon can be treason though it is never executed, nor spoken of—nor so much as known to be treason. True, we talked of going to the court; the Tower was also discussed, but both were *rejected;*

and we went forth into London, a matter we never spoke of at all. And *this* Master Attorney General wishes to call treason? For my own part, I knew nothing of my lord's intent to go into London in the morning when I came to Essex House. I had no arms, but my sword which I usually wear; and I was accompanied by only ten of my servants, and they were footmen and lackeys. When I was in London, I heard nothing of the proclamation declaring us traitors, for I was distant by the length of a street. Let m'Lord Burghley tell if *he* saw me in London. I never drew my sword once all day."

Here is perhaps someone worthy of the aid that Essex seeks for him, thinks Noah.

The Lord Steward, who had until now sat back impassively, leans his head sympathetically toward Southampton, a very telling shift. The shift in the jury's sympathy is likewise palpable.

But its effect on Coke is perverse. Noah recalls that Coke has ever been unable to overcome a witness's ability to garner sympathy, and he's always countered it ineffectually by pounding the witness with precedent and abstract rules finding no home in the merciful human breast. As the Judges declare at Coke's request, Southampton's legal point is incorrect. Neither a specific intent to harm the Sovereign nor knowledge of illegality is necessary to a charge of high treason.

But nobody (save perhaps Coke) wants to inflict a traitor's death upon a handsome, well-spoken, sympathetic young earl. Though these peers will have no real choice but to convict Southampton along with Essex, as Southampton has already hinted, his real audience is Her Majesty the Queen, and there can be no doubt that his contrition will be reported to her at length by the Lord Steward.

And, failing that, by Serjeant Ames.

———————————— ᐅ◦ᑕ◖◗◦ᑯ ————————————

THE TRIAL CONTINUES APACE. Francis Bacon, who has spent much of his adult life beholden to Essex, nevertheless performs his prosecutorial duty admirably.

Lord Robert Cecil, for his part, seizes upon the opportunity to defend himself under oath against Essex's incessant and groundless accusations of fealty to the Infanta of Spain. After hearing Lord Robert out, Essex sincerely begs his pardon and is graciously forgiven his trespass.

"The Crown calls Sir John Leveson to come forth and be sworn," says Coke.

Noah and Jonathan sit up smartly, for Sir John is the man who may hold the key to Her Majesty's clemency for Sir Henry Neville—if only Noah can get Leveson to persuade Her Majesty that Sir Henry renounced his participation in the rebellion by arranging armed opposition to it.

Coke steps forward and, with obvious respect for the witness, asks him what he did on the day of the rebellion.

Sir John replies. "I came from the city with a company of pikemen and musketeers for the Queen. Some of my men were too inexperienced and others too old for serious action, but they did their level best that day. When the Earl of Essex and his men passed through Ludgate on their way into London, I commanded a chain be drawn across the gate against their return. When he returned that way with a much smaller contingent, my men refused the earl passage. After awaiting the outcome of individual combat between men bearing terrible grudges against one another, Lord Essex drew his sword and ordered Sir Christopher Blount to fight his way through. Blount obeyed with great resolution, falling briskly upon one man, Waite, whom he killed. Blount was wounded and taken prisoner. One Tracy and several other citizens were killed. My men, having turned away Lord Essex's, did not pursue, as Essex's men scattered and retreated toward the river."

There being no further questions for Sir John, he steps down but does not immediately depart. Seeming distracted and somehow reluctant to leave, he loiters briefly (making no apparent effort to spy out Noah), then leaves the way he entered.

Noah worries that Sir John may have forgotten his promise to remain in the courthouse until the trial's conclusion, so that they might discuss which course might best aid Sir Henry.

But decorum forbids Noah to send after Sir John while the trial continues.

AT THE CONCLUSION of all the evidence, the Lord High Steward stands. "The Lieutenant of the Tower shall escort the prisoners from the bar." Essex and Southampton, heads bowed, follow their custodian out of the courtroom.

The Lord High Steward turns toward the jury. "The Peers shall now retire to consider their verdict," he pronounces, whereupon the Peers are escorted away from the makeshift courtroom into an area ordinarily occupied by the Court of Chancery.

The noise level of those remaining in the courtroom rises immediately. Noah glances up at the windows. The fading grey light of the winter afternoon will soon disappear. He wonders whether he'll have enough daylight left to serve the warrant upon Drury while allowing young Timothy to return all the stolen effects surreptitiously. But foremost on Noah's mind is Sir John Leveson's befuddled exit.

Noah turns to Jonathan. "M'lord," he says rather pointedly while Camden looks on, "would you be so kind as to locate Sir John?"

Jonathan regards him dubiously at first. As Court technically remains in session, a barrister ordinarily needs leave of Court to go. But for *Lord Saint Ives* things are less tightly controlled. "Certainly, Serjeant," Jonathan replies and leans into his father-in-law with a cautionary word. "But if I leave now, I may not be readmitted. So if the verdict returns before I do, I pray you mark it, as I shall surely wish to know the outcome." The request is facetious, of course, as word of the verdict is sure to spread through London like wildfire. Noah nods and watches Jonathan part through the door Leveson used a short time earlier.

After Noah and Camden have conversed freely a few minutes, the Lord Chief Justice catches Noah's attention and beckons him to the Bench with a crooked finger. Noah sits up vigilantly, wondering if he's about to be called to task for allowing Jonathan's premature exit.

"Pardon me a moment, Master Camden," says Noah.

As Noah approaches the Bench, he bows low, his heart pounding. "M'Lord Chief Justice?"

Though Popham is by now speaking with one of his brethren, he allows himself to be interrupted and turns to Noah. "Serjeant, does it appear you'll have enough daylight to serve the warrant?" asks the Lord Chief Justice.

Noah's heart returns to its normal rhythm, relieved that he is not being admonished. "M'lord, I know no rule of law prohibiting the service of an arrest warrant after sundown."

Popham smiles wryly. "No, indeed. I suppose anyone who commits a crime assumes the risk of being arrested by moonlight."

"Just so, m'lord," replies Noah.

Just then, Lord Thomas Howard, foreman of the jury, strides into the courtroom, heading straight for Popham. But on the way, he catches sight of Noah and, to Noah's dismay, addresses him before acknowledging the Lord Chief Justice.

"Good e'en, Serjeant Ames," he says, as jovially as the somber occasion will allow. "It's been too long since our meeting with the Lord

Admiral at Mountjoy's residence up in the country."

The Lord Chief Justice's eyes open wide, and he regards Noah with something like amazement.

Lord Thomas turns to the Lord Chief Justice. "M'Lord Chief Justice, I've been dispatched to you by a few of the jurors who require additional explication on two points."

"Which points?" asks Popham, but before Lord Thomas can answer he holds up his hand. "Pardon me, Lord Thomas, but there's no need for you to state these points more than once." Popham beckons over the Lord Chief Justice of Chancery and the Lord Chief Baron. "M'lords, Lord Thomas has asked us to address the jury on a couple of points." Turning to Lord Thomas, he says, "Go ahead, m'lord, if you please."

"Both points go to the question whether something's high treason," says Lord Thomas. "First, as I understand it, the Peers wish to know if it's high treason for a subject to attempt to garner such strength to himself that he can compel the King to govern otherwise than in accordance with his own royal authority and direction."

Popham silently polls his two brethren, who nod their heads in turn. Much to Noah's amazement, Popham then looks to *him*. Non-plussed, Noah is about to remind Popham that he's not entered any appearance in the matter before the Court, but then realizes that as a Serjeant he's a part of the jurisprudential establishment of the state, and can be called upon to offer his opinion regardless of the occasion. Once again he's about to answer when something else comes to mind, namely, how the expression of his opinion might adversely affect the fortunes of Sir Henry and Southampton. Then he realizes it's unlikely to affect those matters one way or the other. Add to the mix that the answer to the jury's question is obvious.

Solemnly, Noah nods his concurrence, embarrassed by his own hesitation.

"And what's the second question, m'lord?" asks Popham, evidently amused by Noah's qualms.

"The other question is a bit more theoretical," says Lord Thomas, "and I don't know why it needs to be answered at all. It pertains to the reason underlying the—*legal presumption,* I suppose one might call it— that every rebel understands his rebellion to encompass the King's murder. The question is this: Is the basis for such presumption that no rebel would willingly suffer a King to survive because he might eventually punish or take revenge against the rebels? I think that's what the Peers wish to know." Lord Thomas shrugs. "At least—that's the best

I can restate the question."

"And well done," says Popham with a respectful nod. "If it please you, Lord Thomas, would you be so kind as to tell the jury that we will be with them anon?" He continues apologetically. "The brethren would care to discuss this question briefly amongst ourselves before coming to speak with the jury, you see."

"Oh, certainly," says Lord Howard, bowing. "M'lords." He turns to Noah and nods respectfully. "Noah," he says in parting.

"Serjeant Ames," says Popham as soon as Lord Howard is outside his hearing, "is it simply my imagination or do you hold some ... *influence* over Lord Howard?"

Although Popham's question comes near the mark, in truth it's a miss. The truth is that Noah's influence is not over Lord Howard (though Howard knows of it) but rather over Mountjoy, who is Essex's replacement in Ireland, and it arises out of Noah's detection and suppression of Mountjoy's unauthorized correspondence with King James of Scotland.

"None in the least, Lord Chief Justice," Noah replies. "Lord Thomas is too much the force of nature to fear disclosure of private matters." He bows and returns to his chair beside an apprehensive-looking Camden.

"Have we heard from Lord Saint Ives, Master Camden?" Noah asks. Camden shakes his head worriedly. "Is something wrong?"

"I haven't the foggiest," replies Camden, "although I fear his lordship has been absent longer than expected, has he not?"

Noah plops down into his chair. "He has," he confirms anxiously.

⇒∘⊂⊅∘⇐

ABOUT TWENTY MINUTES LATER, Popham and the other judges return from their conference with the jury.

A half-hour after that, the Sergeant at Arms formally hands a written note to the Lord Steward. The Lord Chief Justice immediately calls the Court to order, and the Peers file back into the room, taking their former seats.

The Lord Steward addresses Lord Howard loudly and formally. "My Lord Thomas Howard. Have the Peers decided whether or no Robert Earl of Essex is guilty of this treason whereupon he has been indicted, upon your honor?"

In accordance with the custom upon such unhappy occasions, Lord Howard prepares to make answer by bending his body and laying his left hand upon his right side. "Guilty, my lord," he pronounces somberly.

"Guilty of high treason. Upon mine honor." The Court then poses the same question to each of the remaining Peers, from the lowest to the highest, and the answer each time is the same.

Against all judgment and all odds, Noah has thus far harbored hope that things might go differently for Southampton, but his hopes are soon dashed.

"My Lord Thomas Howard," says the Lord Steward. "Have the Peers decided whether or no *Henry Earl of Southampton* is guilty of this treason whereupon he has been indicted, upon your honor?"

Once again, Lord Howard bends his body and lays his left hand upon his right side. "Guilty of high treason, my lord," he says. "Upon mine honor."

The Sergeant at Arms says, "Lieutenant of the Tower, you are commanded to bring your prisoners to the bar again."

After a brief delay, the Lieutenant of the Tower leads Essex and Southampton before the bar. Once again, Essex is sober but calm; by contrast Southampton's eyes are swollen and his complexion splotched with red.

The Clerk of the Crown, speaking first to Essex, says, "Robert Earl of Essex, you have been indicted by two several indictments of high treason. You have pleaded not guilty, and for your trial you have put yourself upon God and your Peers. The Peers here (who have heard the evidence, and your answers in your defense) have found you guilty. Now what can you say for yourself, why you should not have judgment of death?"

Noah is amazed at Essex's self-possession.

"I say only this," says Essex, "that since I have committed that which has brought me within the compass of the law, I am willing to die. My own life I do not value, but I entreat your lordships to interpose with Her Majesty to grant my Lord of Southampton her gracious pardon. He may yet do Her Majesty good service. I do not speak to save my own life"— he takes a crestfallen moment to look about at all present, many of whom he long counted as friends—"for *that* I see were now but in vain. I owe God a death, which shall be welcome whenever it pleases Her Majesty. But to satisfy the opinion of your lordships and the world, I declare that, however I may have been in this action misled to transgress the law, I never had any treacherous or disloyal intentions towards her Majesty."

Then the Clerk of the Crown demands of Southampton in turn why judgment of death should not be pronounced against him.

"My lords," says Southampton, "I must say for my part, as I have said before, that my ignorance of the law has made me incur this danger, and that I humbly submit myself to Her Majesty's mercy. And therefore, my Lord High Steward, and my Lord Admiral, seeing that I am condemned by the letter of the law, I pray you truly to inform the Queen of my penitence, and be a means for me to Her Majesty to grant me her gracious pardon. I know I have offended her; yet if it please her to be merciful to me, I may, by my future service, deserve my life. But since I am found guilty by the law," he sighs despondently, "I do submit myself to death, yet not despairing of Her Majesty's mercy."

The Lord High Steward listens patiently and pronounces with evident world-weariness: "The Court awards judgment as follows: that you both shall be led from this place to the place from whence you came, there to remain during Her Majesty's pleasure; from thence to be drawn upon a hurdle through the midst of the city to a place of execution, there to be hanged by the neck and taken down alive, your bodies to be opened, and your bowels taken out and burned before your face; your bodies to be quartered, your heads and quarters to be disposed of at Her Majesty's pleasure. And may God have mercy on your souls."

At this point, the Lieutenant of the Tower holds the axe aloft and pointedly turns the glinting blade toward the prisoners, who precede him out of the Courtroom.

The Peers are dismissed and file out, and Court is adjourned.

Camden begins collecting his papers, including the torn notes he's exchanged with Noah. "Serjeant," he says, "I thank you most heartily for your guidance. I see now why you felt so certain of the outcome—"

He's interrupted by Jonathan who races into the Courtroom, disheveled and ashen. He stands before Noah, breathing heavily.

"Jonathan!" exclaims Noah, "I'm relieved to see you. What took you so long to return? I'd begun to wonder whether you'd been abducted!"

Jonathan just stands there breathlessly, filled with evident dismay.

When no answer comes, Noah says, "You *weren't* abducted, were you?"

"No, Serjeant," says Jonathan. "But Sir John Leveson *has* been."

CHAPTER 9

AS THE COURTROOM is rapidly clearing out, Noah laments how little he can accomplish for Sir Henry and Southampton without Leveson's cooperation. And now there's real urgency about it. *Why, Essex might implicate Sir Henry as early as tonight!* And there's simply no case for clemency without Leveson.

He strains for answers. Could Leveson have been abducted by some-one *wishing* death to Sir Henry or Southampton? But such a person would have needed to know how important Leveson would be in saving them. And no one does know. *Or do they?* A jolt of fear rides up his spine. As he often does, Noah suppresses his own excitement by assuaging those around him.

"Calm down, Jonathan," says Noah as serenely as possible, "and tell me everything that happened after you left the courtroom."

"I caught a private word with the Lieutenant of the Tower," says Jonathan, "while he awaited the carriage returning Essex and Southampton to their quarters." Jonathan scowls. "He confirmed to me that both earls had been convicted of high treason. But—tell me, Noah—was the sentence death in *both* cases?"

Noah glances momentarily at Camden, who follows the discussion with evident interest.

"Yes, Jonathan," replies Noah glumly, "a traitor's death for both."

Jonathan's wind rushes out of him in a single breath, and he collaps-es in the nearest chair, overtaken by pervasive sadness. "It's to be *Tyburn*, is it?" he asks. The question is rhetorical only, as he knows full well that Tyburn is where a traitor's death is meted out.

Noah takes an adjacent chair and draws it up to Jonathan. Camden remains standing, rapt withal.

"Jonathan," says Noah in his most fatherly manner. "For us to do anything to help those, *er,* two gentlemen, I must know what happened to you during your absence."

Jonathan nods, and furrows his brow distractedly. "I was—I was searching," says Jonathan. "I began by asking those in authority where Sir John had gone, and no one—not *one*—could tell me. I—I began swinging open the doors of every carriage remaining in the courtyard. Needless to say, the occupants were furious to be disturbed." He points to his coat of arms. "Without this, Lord help me, I'd have been arrested for a criminal, or taken to Bedlam as a madman."

As Jonathan becomes lost in thought needlessly contemplating the outcome of an arrest that never happened, Noah tires of his reticence and brings him up short. "And *then*, Lord Jonathan?" he demands.

"And then," Jonathan proceeds as in a trance, "I quickly moved toward the gate that leaves Whitehall, asking all and sundry if they'd seen Sir John. They seemed to have no idea whom I was asking about, and stared back at me like so many sheep. I even went out through the gate—"

"On foot?" asks Noah.

"Yes. So taken aback was I by Sir John's utter disappearance that I never thought to retrieve my horse. Besides, which way would I have ridden? I had no idea which direction *he* took."

Camden interjects, "Pardon me, m'lord, but what makes you think he was abducted and didn't simply leave of his own free will?"

Jonathan nods. "When I gave up, on my way back here some lowly fellow—who'd heard I was inquiring—told me that he saw two rough-looking men escort Sir John into a waiting carriage that sped off."

"Did he describe the men?" asks Noah.

"I paused momentarily to think," replies Jonathan abashedly, "and by the time I turned to him, he was gone."

"Gentlemen," says Camden, "why is Sir John needed in aid of the Earl of Southampton?"

Noah and Jonathan lock eyes. Noah turns to Camden. "We're not at liberty to discuss such matters, Master Camden, and I would request your word as a gentleman that you will repeat nothing of what you've heard pass between Lord Saint Ives and myself this afternoon."

"I give you my word without hesitation," says Camden. "It's just so exciting. You know," he sighs, "*I* considered going into the law—"

"Well, if it's *excitement* you're after," says Noah, causing Camden's eyes to sparkle with interest, "you'd be welcome to accompany Lord Saint Ives and myself in serving an arrest warrant."

"Now? In the dark?" asks Camden.

Noah nods.

Camden is full of suppressed excitement.

"Why, I would *love* to ride along!"

———————⟶◦⬳◦⟵———————

FORTUNATELY, THE THREE-QUARTER MOON has risen early this evening and the clouds have blown away. The carriage arranged by Jonathan draws up to the door at Westminster Hall, and he steps in after Noah and Camden.

"My word," says Camden as the carriage moves off, "riding from a full-blown trial to serve an arrest warrant! Is this a normal day for you gentlemen?"

"A bit unusual," replies Noah, "a bit long." But neither he nor Jonathan is in a mood to engage in casual banter.

After a quiet moment during which only the clop of hooves is heard, Camden asks, "So, who is this summons about?"

"The name is Drury," replies Jonathan distantly.

Camden nods with satisfaction. "Fine family. Whose arrest are they seeking?"

Noah and Jonathan laugh for the first time since learning of the earls' sentences.

Jonathan replies. "No Drury is having anyone arrested, Master Camden. Rather, a Drury is *being* arrested."

Camden's expression turns sour. "If this is the family Drury with whom I'm familiar, they *do* have black sheep—but few."

"Oh?" says Noah. "Who's the worst of the lot?"

Camden gazes at the ceiling of the carriage as though searching his memory. "That would be Thomas, I expect."

"Ah," says Noah, "you've hit the mark on your first try. He's our man. What do you know of him?"

"More than I care to," sniffs Camden. "In fact, he is known to spend time in company of that very John Daniel excoriated by Lord Essex during the trial."

Until now, Noah had thought himself quite attentive at the trial, yet the name is at first unfamiliar. Then it occurs to him. "*Daniel?* You mean the man that Essex testified stole his wife's jewelry?"

"The same," sniffs Camden. "Drury is sure to recognize me, as his was one of those families insisting to be included in the *Brittania*. And they sent *him*, of all people, to persuade me."

Jonathan's interest has been piqued. "What did you tell him—I mean, about including his family?"

"I told him what I'd told all the others," replies Camden, "that not every family could be mentioned, but that I would try to give them their due. He tried to bribe me," he says, "with stolen money, no doubt."

The carriage passes out of the city through Bishopsgate just as the remaining sun dies, and quickly comes to a halt before the complainant's cottage.

A portly little fellow peeks out of the front door and steps outside to greet them. Noah, Camden, and Jonathan step down from the carriage, while the constables remain on the driver's bench.

Noah draws Jonathan aside for a private word before acknowledging the complainant. "What of the *boy*?" he asks quietly, avoiding any mention of Timothy's name.

Jonathan nods reassuringly and whispers, "I expect he's waiting behind Drury's cottage, as arranged."

Noah turns to the complainant. "Master"—he glances at the complaint—"Groatsworth, I presume?"

"I am Groatsworth, m'lords." With much bowing and scraping, he invites them into his home. Though humble in size, the cottage is nicely appointed; inside, a pleasant fire blazes and a lady (every bit as portly as Groatsworth himself) fusses about the kitchen.

"Madam," says Noah, bowing, "I am Serjeant Ames. This is Lord Saint Ives"—she lets out a short gasp at the name of the heroic lord, and draws her left hand up to her heart—"and *this* gentleman, who is here merely to observe, is Master Camden, of whom you may have heard." To Camden's evident disappointment, his name is unfamiliar to both the burgher and his lady.

The woman curtsies broadly. "Welcome, welcome, gentlemen. It's valiant of you to come out on this bitter evening. May we offer you a warm beverage?"

Noah declines on behalf of them all. "Nay, madam; we're here on Crown business and shan't be long. However, would you be so kind as to permit us to entertain Master"—he feigns seeking out the name in the complaint—"*Drury* in your parlor here, to see if this matter requires an arrest—or whether some accommodation can be reached?"

The woman looks to her husband, who nods. "Why certainly, Sheriff—"

"Ames," says Noah. "*Serjeant* Ames."

"Why, of course, sheriff," she replies, curtseying again. Though there seems no malice in her mistaking his name, it irks Noah just the same. "Won't you gentlemen take seats here," she says, "and we can send for Master Drury?"

"That won't be necessary, Goodwife Groatsworth. Lord Saint Ives has already dispatched the constables to fetch Master Drury."

The woman's eyes open wide. "Oh, no, Sheriff Eams. You have mistaken me for my dear departed mother. I am Master Groatsworth's *daughter* Maude."

Sheriff Eams? She's not only demoted me to a non-judicial officer; she's changed my surname.

The three visitors have barely taken seats when there's an official-sounding knock at the door. Maude opens it. The constables enter, hauling a manacled and coatless Thomas Drury inside by the elbows.

Noah points to a chair opposite his in the little parlor, and the constables drop Drury into it. He signals for the constables to wait outside. They bow, and close the door behind them.

Jonathan's grave countenance betrays some slight concern about Drury's coatlessness. "Please pardon me, gentlemen," says Jonathan. "I've … something to attend to outside. I shall return anon." He steps out.

Noah takes a moment to size up Drury. The firelight plays on Drury's eyes as they dart from face to face. To Noah, he seems more annoyed than afraid.

"Master Thomas Drury?" asks Noah.

"Who are *you*?" Drury retorts.

I'm the barrister you followed to Essex House the other day, Noah would like to say. But if Drury chooses to pretend he's never set eyes on his inquisitor, Noah is prepared to play along.

Maude berates Drury. "You caitiff!" she scolds. "This is *Sheriff Beans*! And these other two gent—"

Sheriff Beans, is it? I'll show her.

Noah interrupts. "Thank you, *Maeve*. I'll do the introductions." He turns to Drury. "I am Serjeant Noah Ames, sir, here on Queen's business. Now I shall ask you one more time. *Are you Thomas Drury?*" Drury says nothing. "I assure you, sir, if I need to ask you that question again, it will come with a blow."

To Noah's dismay, Camden interjects. "He's Thomas Drury, all right. I could never forget that insolence."

Drury squints at Camden. "Master Camden. Is that you, sir?"

Noah throws up his hands in exasperation and gestures for Camden to answer.

Camden replies. "'Tis I."

"What are *you* doing here?" asks Drury. "Have you come to identify me?"

"*Tut, tut!*" says Noah. "Down to business. But first, a point of personal comfort. Master Drury: Did the constables decline to allow you to don your coat before coming here?"

"No, sir," says Drury, a little abashed. "I couldn't *find* it."

"You couldn't find your coat, sir?" asks Noah incredulously.

"No," says Drury. "My personal items have been disappearing lately." He looks suspiciously at Groatsworth, who gapes back at him with horror at the silent accusation.

Although Noah knows little about Timothy, he knows enough to associate him with missing personal items. But, what is *this*? Timothy's supposed to be *returning* items, not stealing additional ones.

"Well, that's neither here nor there," continues Noah. "When we've done here, if you find out who took your personal items, I strongly advise you to file a complaint with the civil courts, and not to take matters into your own hands—which seems to be difficult for you."

Drury takes the point, and arches his back proudly. "Serjeant, would you be so kind as to inform me why I've been dragged through the snow—with or without a coat—to Master Groatsworth's parlor?"

"Before we get to that," says Noah, "Master Drury, may I assume that your present cottage is not your permanent residence?"

Drury sniffs at the impertinence of this most mundane of questions. "I hardly see what difference that makes."

Noah peers at him suspiciously. "Of course not, Master Drury, as you have no expectation of why you were summoned here."

"'Dragged' is more like it," pouts Drury. "Perhaps you might inform me why it's important."

Noah shakes his head impatiently. "Whatever may be my purpose in summoning you, Master Drury, I assure you it wasn't to explain to you legal notions of relevance. When a man refuses to divulge something as plain as the location of his residence, I often find he's hiding a good deal more. Now, where *is* your permanent residence, sir?"

Drury seems disappointed to learn he won't get far through outright resistance. "My family resides at Lincolnshire. You might have asked Master Camden. He's visited there."

Much to Noah's annoyance, Camden chimes in. "You own some of the family's estate there, do you not?"

Drury nods.

Noah shakes his head. "Do you presently reside there with your family?"

"Not at present," says Drury.

Something occurs to Noah. "Do you also own a portion of Drury House here in London, on Drury Lane?"

Drury's scowl shows this to be something of a sore point. "If you must know, my father left that entire place to his eldest son, my brother William. And before you ask, Serjeant, no, I have not come to see William. I doubt he's even there. And even if he were, he's let it be known that I'm unwelcome."

"I see," says Noah.

For the first time, Drury volunteers a bit of information about himself. "I'm a seafaring man, presently seeking a situation on a vessel."

"Is that what brings you to London?"

"Look here—" begins Drury angrily, but Noah cuts him off.

"Keep a civil tongue in your head, sir, or you might just lose the latter. Now, is your search for a seafaring position what brings to you to London just now?"

Drury obviously weighs which answer might be more advantageous to him. "Yes, it is," he replies. "Is there some law forbidding such a search?"

"Hardly, sir," says Noah. "Have you had much success in such endeavors of late?"

"No."

"But Master Groatsworth avers in his statement," says Noah, "that you mentioned you were finally beginning to make some headway in your endeavors here."

Drury nods reluctantly. "That's true, but I wanted to put him at ease. I thought that, if he were to perceive me as having some success, he would feel mollified about his prospects for receiving my rent."

Groatsworth snorts with derision and turns away.

"I see," says Noah. "So, I take it you have in fact had little success here. Is that correct?"

"Correct," admits Drury.

"Wouldn't you be more likely of success seeking a ship in, say, Plymouth or Dover?" Noah shrugs. "Falmouth?"

Drury obviously hadn't anticipated the question. "I suppose I might," he replies sullenly.

Noah leans into Drury. "Then, would you care to come clean and tell me your present business in London?"

Drury gets his back up. "*Seafaring* is my present business. Just because I'm having no success at the moment doesn't mean I've misrepresented my business."

As Noah can see he's getting nowhere with this line of questioning, he draws a paper from his pocket. "I have here a warrant for your arrest under this gentleman's oath."

"*Arrest?*" protests Drury. "Upon what grounds?"

Groatsworth is incensed and blurts out, "Upon those grounds across the way that you occupy without payin' for!"

Now Drury is outraged. "Serjeant Ames, now I ask *you*, is it a crime to fall a week's arrears in rent?"

"Well, it oughta be!" says Groatsworth.

Noah sighs with exasperation and shakes his head. "That's *enough*," he shouts. "No one will speak unless *I* ask him a question!" Now that he has their attention, he says in as conciliatory a manner as he can muster, "To answer your question, Master Drury. *No*, being a week's arrears in rent is not in itself a crime, but rather a matter for the civil courts. What *is* a crime, however, is firing a weapon at one's landlord."

"I—" begins Drury.

"Do not speak!" Noah says threateningly, and Drury backs down. "Now, for what it's worth, that is the charge upon which I have come, and upon which you will be arrested if you two gentlemen are unable to arrive at terms. But first I wish to see if there is, perhaps, more to the story than is contained in this complaint. Master Groatsworth, would you tell Master Drury what you swore to in the complaint?"

Groatsworth bows. "I visited Master Drury at his sumptuous abode— what *I* own—to collect the rent. Instead of payin' me like he ought, he took down his musket and chased me from my own cottage." His face reddens with embarrassment, but he plods on. "And then—having once got rid of me—he fired the musket, causing me to fall on my arse in the middle of Bishopsgate Street."

Noah suppresses a smile. "Were you struck by the shot, Master Groatsworth?"

"No, suh," replies Groatsworth sheepishly.

Maude can no longer contain herself. "Sheriff Green, I can testify that me dad's rear was quite bruised, and he was in a lotta pain."

'Sheriff Green' am I now?

Noah holds up his hand. "Please, *Mary*," he says, retaliating with a name-change of his own, "the same rules apply to you as to everyone else." He turns to Groatsworth. "Does Master Drury still owe past rent?"

"He *does*, suh," says Groatsworth. "Hasn't paid me a farthing since the … incident."

Noah looks to Drury. "Master Drury, have you the wherewithal to bring yourself current in rent?"

Drury, though obviously appreciative of the opportunity to stay out of jail, replies, "I doubt I do, sir. I seem to have ... lost ... several items of value, one of which I could have posted as security, as its value greatly exceeds the amount of any *possible* arrears."

"Can you describe it?" asks Noah.

Although a bit confused as to the point of Noah's question about property he no longer has, Drury cooperates. "It *was* a signet badge, sir, made of gold."

Yes, thinks Noah, *I've held it in my hand.*

Drury continues. "Though the badge has some sentimental value to our family, if this gentleman would have accepted it to secure my indebtedness to him, I would have posted it as security. That is, *if* he were to kindly drop these charges. As for my *weapon*"—he waves a hand dismissively—"when I fired, I stood only a few feet from him and could easily have struck him, had that been my intention. But I never fired *at* him, rather in the air, just to emphasize my point. I see now it was highly inappropriate for me to do so." He sighs. "Unfortunately, I seem to have lost the badge a few days ago, so I'm unable to offer it."

"Where were you when you lost it?" asks Noah, eager to see what lengths Drury will go to in order to avoid reference to his being knocked unconscious while seeking out his pursuer.

"I don't know for certain, sir," Drury says evasively.

"Do you suppose it might still be in your cottage?"

Drury shakes his head with resignation. "I've searched everywhere, sir."

"I'm going to ask you to try again," says Noah, knowing full well that—assuming all's gone to plan—it's been secretly left in the cottage by Timothy. "I've often found misplaced items in mine own closet, having failed in my search several times."

Drury shrugs dubiously, but appears resigned to repeating his search.

Noah calls in the drivers. "Constables, please escort Master Drury back to his cottage and give him an opportunity to search for something he may have misplaced—a small item of jewelry. And, while there, give him a moment to put on a coat."

———— ⇒∘《∅∘⊂ ————

JONATHAN STRIDES ALONE to the rear of Drury's cottage. There's nothing much here besides woods and a small jakes.

The recent snow has been disturbed, as though there's been a struggle. *If there was a fight here, whose fight was it? Who won and who lost?* Though Jonathan would like to get a better look at the whole area, he can't light a torch because he can't risk being seen back here. At any moment, Noah will be sending Drury back to this cottage to find the valuables filched from him the other day.

Something lying on the ground glints in the moonlight. He takes a step closer, and spies a smattering of coins recently fallen onto the snow; a shilling and a few pence, apparently dropped during the fracas. As Jonathan knows that Timothy's penury would never have allowed him to pass up free booty, he begins to worry about the boy. *Did he contest with someone ... and lose? Or was he simply too rushed to scoop up the coins? What's become of him?*

Soon, Jonathan's eyes adjust to the darkness well enough to detect the light of a small taper burning inside the cottage. He takes a step closer and realizes that he's peering through a little window into a sleeping room, perhaps the only one. Moving closer until his nose nearly touches the glass, he spies furtive movement by the closet. As its hinged door is wide open, he can see the closet consists of an open cavity with a single shelf above.

Apparently, Drury's coat has been returned to him, as it's hanging from a peg on a wall near the closet.

Jonathan is greatly relieved to catch sight of Timothy's long blond mane bobbing about as he performs the task he should have completed a quarter-hour ago, carefully placing personal items into the pockets of Drury's coat. Although the taper's light is weak, it's sufficient to reflect off Drury's golden cross as Timothy deposits it into one of the coat pockets.

Suddenly, across the street a front door slams, startling Jonathan. Peeking around the corner, he's alarmed to see the two constables escorting Drury straight toward the cottage from which the oblivious Timothy has not so much as begun his escape. In Jonathan's estimation, the speed of Drury's approach would prohibit Timothy's safe exit from the cottage even if he were to leave immediately—unless there's another exit as yet unseen.

Jonathan's seen one side of the cottage and the rear, and there was no door on either of them. He earnestly wishes to check the remaining side for a door, but time simply will not permit it. He has no alternative but to warn Timothy to conceal himself.

Jonathan knocks quietly on the glass, and Timothy twirls around, his eyes agog, his right hand plunging into his pocket for his dagger. Fortunately, he quickly realizes it's Jonathan.

Jonathan brings his hand up toward his face so it can be seen through the little window, and points toward Groatsworth's cottage, excitedly mouthing the words: *They're coming!* To avoid being seen, Jonathan backs away from the cottage, quickly trots out in a wide circle in the dark, and comes up behind the constables.

Startled, the elder constable twists about to see if he's being ambushed. "Oh, m'lord," he says as he recognizes Jonathan, "ye scared the life outta me." He bends over to catch his breath and clutches his chest.

The younger constable puts his arm around the shoulders of his winded colleague. "Come on, Sam. You've got a few more scares left in ye. Don't give up on me now."

The elder looks up at his young friend and smiles. "Don't you worry, lad. I'll be buryin' *you* years from now!"

Lord Jonathan is relieved to find that he's caused no harm to the constables, and glad that he's given young Timothy an extra moment to conceal himself, although he can't imagine *where*, as no obvious hiding-hole had presented itself when he peered inside through the tiny window.

Lord Jonathan trots a few steps ahead and draws abreast of Drury, who seems surprised that he's being approached in such a friendly manner.

Drury nods respectfully. "Welcome, m'lord, although I'm embarrassed to tell you that I've nothing to offer you in this worthless cottage that's caused me so much trouble. Not so much as a goblet."

Lord Jonathan nods indulgently. "In that regard, Master Drury, I'm sorrier for you than for myself. I've come along to ensure that we search *everywhere* your property could possibly be hiding." Just using the word *hiding* gives him a chill up the spine, as it comes perilously close to suggesting that something (or someone) is hiding in the cottage. He must now enter the cottage with the wildly inconsistent dual purpose of ensuring that Drury finds his property but does *not* find Timothy.

They reach the porch.

The elder constable, still a few yards behind them, shouts, "M'lord! Please don't go indoors just yet!" As he steps onto the porch, he smiles at Jonathan, removes from his pocket a taper jabbed into a humble pewter candlestick, and lights it with his companion's torch. He takes the lit taper inside and emerges in a moment with Drury's musket. "Is this all, suh?" he asks Drury. "No other firearms?"

Drury shakes his head. "None."

"No pistols?" asks the constable skeptically.

"None. That is to say, none *here*."

"All right," replies the constable. "*Here* is all we're concerned about just now. I'll hold this musket while you go inside with m'lord." He hands the burning candle to Jonathan and stands aside.

"Thank you, constable," says Jonathan, thinking how much more likely he is to succeed in both purposes now, as the constables evidently feel no further need to enter.

Stepping inside with Drury, Jonathan lights an additional taper. Drury accepts it and immediately begins searching a desk by the entrance, providing Jonathan with an opportunity to step into the back bedroom where he saw Timothy stuffing the items into Drury's coat.

The coat still hangs on the same peg. There's no sign of Timothy, but the closet door's been closed, so it's a fair bet Timothy's in there.

"*Hoy*, Master Drury!" shouts Jonathan. As Drury stamps back toward the bedroom, Jonathan adds, "I thought you said your coat was missing."

No one could dissemble the surprise on Drury's face in seeing his coat. "Good God!" he shouts. "Where did this come from?"

"Is it yours?" asks Jonathan innocently.

Drury reaches his hand into a pocket and draws out the very signet badge he's promised to pledge as security for his rent. "Looks like it," he says, reaching into the other pocket. To his amazement and obvious relief, he draws out his weighty golden cross. Quickly reaching into an interior pocket he draws out his missing correspondence.

Jonathan nearly laughs aloud when Drury speaks to him, amazed. "Well, I—I—I have no idea how these got here. By my troth, m'lord, they were not here when the constables arrived. I could not find even the coat, let alone these valuable items." Suspicion breaks out over his face, together with a righteous anger. "Why, the bastard who returned these things must have been the same one who stole them. He might be here still!"

Before Jonathan can stop him, Drury grabs his flickering taper, swings open the door to the closet, and plunges into its recesses.

Jonathan's heart hammers in his chest with the certainty that Drury will find the boy. But after a breathtaking moment, he can see that the reckless search has come up empty.

Jonathan discreetly glances up at the interior shelf and sees Timothy's wide eyes peering down at him from the rear. Jonathan's breath (and, he can swear, his heartbeat) stops for a moment, as though the fabric of time itself has been stretched across tenterhooks.

Jonathan grabs Drury by the collar, and in a single motion draws him out and slams the closet door behind him, leaving Timothy once more safe in the dark. He assumes command of the situation by sheer vocal force, as he's seen Noah do on numerous occasions.

"Master Drury," Jonathan declares loudly, both to intimidate Drury and to ensure that he's heard by the constables, "have you located the item that Serjeant Ames sent you here to fetch?"

Drury stops, amazed by Jonathan's suddenly commanding tone. "Why, yes, m'lord, but—"

"No 'buts' about it, Master Drury," shouts Jonathan. As he hoped, the constables have taken his severe tone as their cue to enter the room. "You may don your coat, if you wish. Then, take with you the formerly lost items, and return to Serjeant Ames in the company of the constables."

"But, m'lord," says Drury as he's being dragged away, "the one who stole them may still be upon the premises!"

Jonathan raises his hand and assumes an air of judicious equanimity. "A moment, constables!" The constables stop as they're just about to drag Drury out through the front door. "Master Drury, are you suggesting—if those items were *ever* stolen—that the thief has lately *returned* them to you?"

"Why, I suspect that very *thing*, m'lord!" says Drury.

Jonathan looks at him as though he's daft. "Then … what would have been the point in stealing them in the first instance?"

"Why," says Drury, his eyes darting about for an explanation, "I'm sure I don't know."

Jonathan looks to the constables, who burst into laughter. "Well," he says, smiling despite himself, "I'm sure *I* don't know either!" He turns to the officers. "Constables, kindly bring Master Drury to Serjeant Ames. I shall be there anon."

"Sorry, m'lord," says the elder. "The rules require one constable to remain here until Serjeant Ames has departed the scene."

Jonathan hesitates, searching his mind for a way to extricate the poor, trapped Timothy. "Very well," he says. "Give me a moment alone to see if I can find any evidence in the bedroom supporting Master Drury's outlandish suspicion that some varlet has had the temerity to return his 'stolen' property."

"Aye, m'lord," says the elder constable, still grinning. "We'll await you on the porch."

Jonathan returns to the bedroom, closes the door, and cracks open the closet door. "Timothy?" he whispers.

"M'lord?" comes the whispered reply.

"I'm afraid you're stuck here for the duration. This may take a while, and it's going to get precarious. Stay down where no one can see you and wait for Master Drury to step out to relieve himself. Then, meet me at the stables in Old Jewry."

"But, how soon do you suppose Drury will go to relieve himself, m'lord?"

Jonathan can hear the boy lowering his young bones as far as possible on the shelf. "Oh," says Jonathan with a snicker, "quite soon. I'm sure of it."

Having done what he can for the boy, Jonathan follows Drury and the elder constable back to Groatsworth's cottage.

ENCUMBERED BY THE NEED to make polite conversation for the sole purpose of passing the time, Noah's relieved when Drury returns to Groatsworth's cottage wearing his coat and carrying a few small items.

Before the constable and Jonathan can even follow Drury inside, Noah says, "Besides your coat Master Drury, what did you find?"

"Well," says Drury, "all the items I lost have been returned to me."

"How fortunate!" says Noah. "Have you found the signet badge you'd post as security for your indebtedness to Master Groatsworth here?"

"I have,' says Drury, "but I believe my cottage has been broken into."

Lord Jonathan and the constables enter and join Noah in listening with great interest.

"You mean," says Noah, "that your items were stolen from your cottage?"

"N—no, sir," says Drury, "not exactly. I believe they were stolen elsewhere and that someone broke into my cottage and left them there."

Noah exchanges a glance with Jonathan, as though to say, *This man is mad.*

Jonathan says, "Master Drury expressed the same conjecture to me when he found the items in his cottage just now."

"At least he's consistent," remarks Noah skeptically. "Master Drury, why would someone do that? I mean, steal your personal belongings only to … break into your residence and return them to you?"

"I've no idea," replies Drury.

"Well, ordinarily I *would* suggest you bring your case to the courts, but … whom would you accuse?"

"No idea, sir."

Noah nods. "Precisely. Why, even if you were to identify the thief and sue him in a civil court for replevin, he would simply defend on grounds that he'd returned the items to you. So, even if you were to discover who took them, you would still have no legal claim, except perhaps for a technical 'trespass to land,' which would yield only nominal damages, even if proven."

Drury is confounded. "What if I'd needed the items when they were unavailable to me because the thief had taken them?"

Noah weighs that hypothetical case. "I suppose the thief could be liable for any special damage you suffered during that time. Did you … suffer any special damage?"

Drury admits glumly, "None, sir."

"Well, then, it seems you must be satisfied with the return of your items, does it not?"

"I suppose so," says Drury.

"Very well, then," says Noah, "as none of that has any bearing on Master Groatsworth's complaint against you, would you care to show us the badge of which you spoke earlier?"

Drury removes it from his pocket and hands it to Noah.

Noah takes it and stoops to examine it in the firelight. "This is solid gold, Master Drury?"

"Aye, sir," comes the reply.

Noah beckons Groatsworth and hands him the badge. "Are you satisfied with this security, master?"

Groatsworth studies the item with great interest. He seems to be confident in his ability to tell real gold from fake. "I'm satisfied, Serjeant Ames, and I'll withdraw the complaint, so long as I retain this as security for Master Drury's rent."

"Master Drury?" inquires Noah.

"That is satisfactory, Serjeant," says Drury, "and I apologize to Master Groatsworth for the incident with my … musket."

"Master Groatsworth?" inquires Noah.

"Apology accepted," says Groatsworth.

"Lord Saint Ives," says Noah, "have we need of any documentation for this transaction?"

"I believe these two gentlemen heartily need to share a round of small beer," says Jonathan, "after which each will need to sign an informal security agreement."

Noah turns to the lady. "*Mathilda*," he says, knowing full well that's not her name, "would you please bring Lord Saint Ives a cup of small beer for each of these two gentlemen?"

"Certainly, Constable Avery," says the lady as she scurries off.

Demoted again, he notes, *and victim of another name-change.*

Jonathan writes out a short security agreement on paper he brought for that purpose and presents it to Groatsworth for signature. Groatsworth signs gladly and hands it to Drury, who seems a bit fatigued.

"Right here, Master Drury," says Jonathan, pointing to a blank section of the paper, "please write the following words: 'Nothing requested by me having been omitted herefrom, title to said badge has not hereby been conveyed, except upon proven default.'" Drury takes the quill in his left hand, writes the words, and signs his name.

Jonathan asks Groatsworth to initial the addendum, and packs the papers away in Noah's portfolio.

"The scribe will provide a copy to each of you upon payment for his services," says Noah, "which in this case will be limited to a shilling apiece. Is that satisfactory?"

The erstwhile disputants nod their agreement.

Jonathan accepts from the lady the two small beers intended to signify the disputants' newfound amity, and furtively drops a small tablet into Drury's. "Now, does each of you promise," Jonathan asks, "to bring any further disputes between you to the proper authorities, and not to take matters into your own hands?"

"I do," each replies.

Jonathan hands them each a cup.

CAMDEN IS FIRST to step up into the carriage. While he waits inside, Jonathan draws Noah aside.

"Father, I hope that all will soon come clear," whispers Jonathan, "but I must remain in this area for another hour or so. Would you please instruct the constables to bring my horse to the stables at Old Jewry, that is, after they've dropped off Camden at the inn and taken you home to Holborn? Timothy and I will ride together and meet you in your study as soon as we can."

"You must remain here for an *hour*?" asks Noah.

"Perhaps a bit less," replies Jonathan. "I added to Master Drury's beer a nostrum I learned from the late Doctor Lopez. One is never quite certain when it will kick in."

Noah rolls his eyes. "You're incorrigible. Just be careful!"

THE ELDER CONSTABLE returns Drury's musket to the gunrack in his cottage, steps out onto the porch, and pats his young assistant on the shoulder. The two converse jovially on their approach to Noah's carriage, pausing a moment to bow respectfully to Jonathan, then stepping up to their accustomed perches on the driver's bench.

As the carriage rolls away, Camden nods to Jonathan through the retreating window.

Jonathan waves to him with a tentative smile and watches the carriage disappear through Bishopsgate, standing pat until the clopping of hooves can no longer be heard.

Alone at last, Jonathan ambles over to Bishopsgate, concealing himself in a deeply shaded location on the city side of the wall that provides him a clear view of both Groatsworth's and Drury's moonlit cottages.

In a few minutes, Drury steps out of Groatsworth's cottage and closes the door behind him. By the relaxed posture, it appears Groatsworth contributed another ale or two to the original peace offering arranged by Jonathan.

Drury pauses a moment to gaze up at the twinkling stars, then saunters off toward his own cottage. After only a few steps, however, he stops to rub his belly with both hands, as though soothing a sudden cramp. Resuming his progress at a livelier clip, he first moves deliberately, then quickly accelerates to a trot.

Jonathan smiles to see that his wish is about to be fulfilled; the urgent call of nature (albeit aided by physic) should render it impossible for Drury to search his room before running for the pit.

Reaching the porch, Drury opens the door and—to Jonathan's dismay—goes straight to the gunrack, where he pulls down his musket. No sooner does he grasp it, however, than he's impelled by nature to turn and run out of the front door, leaving it open behind him in a frantic race for the jakes behind the other side of the cottage.

Timothy must already have leapt down from his shelf (quite prematurely, if you were to ask Jonathan), for he soon tears down the little hallway and bolts out the open door at breakneck speed, sprinting for

Bishopsgate faster than Jonathan has ever seen anyone move.

Drury must have heard Timothy's footsteps, as he promptly emerges from the jakes with his musket at the ready. But, with his breeches down about his knees, he's too awkward to cut off Timothy's determined escape.

"Come back here, thief!" he shouts as he swings his musket 'round to fire in the direction of the fast-escaping Timothy, but the barrel catches on a post supporting the porch roof and, with too hasty a trigger finger— *boom!*—he inadvertently squeezes off a heavy charge of scattershot that blows the post in two and smashes through the cottage window, making an awful crash.

Unable to withstand the kick of the musket with his knees bound together, Drury totters a moment, then tumbles backward in a helpless heap.

Although Jonathan knows he should run away, he finds himself unable to take his eyes off the unfolding disaster.

After a long moment of quiet, the porch roof cracks loudly and noisily collapses onto a small patch of snowy lawn.

Once the noise subsides, the silence of the night falls over the damaged cottage, interrupted only briefly by one long fart and an anguished cry of dismay.

CHAPTER 10

NOAH IS PLEASED to have finished up at Groatsworth's cottage leaving a general glow of satisfaction among all concerned. Groatsworth has obtained adequate security for the rent, Drury has recovered his lost valuables, and no obvious source of renewed dissension looms on the horizon. Indeed, what untoward event is likely to occur in such a peaceful precinct?

As his carriage clops away, his mind has temporarily escaped the dark cloud of the trial that took place only a few hours ago, and been brightened by the more recent glow of a job well done. On second thought, he shakes his head at the absurd emotional equivalence he's assigned to events of such widely divergent importance. One is undeniably deadly and will soon result in bloody executions, the other trivial enough to be forgotten in a few days' time.

Even Camden, who's made no bones about his distaste for Thomas Drury, is most congratulatory toward Noah, bubbling with good cheer over his own imaginary contribution toward resolving a potentially deadly dispute between neighbors.

Once Camden is dropped off at his lodgings, Noah arrives at home and passes the constables a few shillings to lead Jonathan's horse to the stables at Old Jewry, as Jonathan requested.

Entering the house, Noah is greeted by Cook with a full plate of supper, which he declines for the moment. Abashedly (given the lateness of the hour), he asks her to prepare two additional plates, one for Lord Jonathan and the other for Timothy, who will soon be arriving.

Entering his study, he finds Esther there, reading a book.

"Serjeant Ames," she says apologetically, "we'd no idea when to expect you." She places a scrap of paper in the book to mark her place, and returns it to the shelf.

"I'm delighted that you find respite here in the study, Esther, as I generally do." He kisses her forehead. "Feel free to come whenever you wish."

Esther curtseys, but a concerned look comes over her face before she departs. "The boy is coming," she declares. "Is that not so?"

Noah looks at her askance, as his confirmation seems wholly unnecessary. She's quite *sure* he's coming.

"Who? *Timothy?*" he asks for the sake of normal conversation.

"Yes, the blond boy."

Noah nods. "He's on his way here. Do you know whose company he's in?"

She gazes into the distance. "His lordship's?"

Noah nods hesitantly. "Why do you ask about the boy?" he asks.

"I feel as though he is"—she seems a bit embarrassed—"like me, a little bit."

Noah shrugs. "I've seen no evidence of the second sight in him. At least, not yet. Dear Esther, I need to be alone for a few minutes just now. I hope I shall see you again before you retire for the evening."

She smiles, and goes at once.

Noah looks in his desk drawer for the note threatening to expose Lord Leicester's alleged bigamy, and pockets it.

Cook appears at the door and curtseys. "Serjeant Ames, his lordship and the boy have arrived. The boy was so dusty, I sent him outside to wash his face and hands."

<hr />

JONATHAN AND TIMOTHY stand by the table engrossed in discussion. Spying Noah's approach, they smile and wait for him to take his seat at the head of the table. He invites them to sit on his immediate left and right.

Cook enters carrying three plates heaping with food, and sets one before each of them. Timothy's eyes sparkle with delight, as though he's about to enjoy Christmas dinner.

"Cook," says Noah, "please see we're not disturbed."

She curtseys silently and returns to the kitchen.

At Noah's suggestion, Jonathan says Grace, as prescribed by the Church of England. Noah folds his hands respectfully, while Timothy squirms and joins vocally in prayer.

"Pardon me, Serjeant," says Timothy once the prayer is complete, "I heard you were a Hebrew. Do you say Grace, same as us?"

"Same as 'we,' Timothy," says Noah. "No, ordinarily, I begin supper with a different prayer, but I want you to feel comfortable."

"Please don't change your ways for me, sir," says Timothy ingenuously. "I feel blessed just bein' asked to stay for the meal."

Noah smiles. Necessity is a great teacher of religious tolerance; so he's learned his whole life. As they begin eating, he breaks the silence. "So, gentlemen," he says, "perhaps you would bring me current concerning your activities this e'en."

Jonathan redirects the inquiry to Timothy. "Yes, Timothy. Please tell us how it came about that Master Drury was without a coat when the constables came to fetch him."

Timothy finishes a bite. "Well, when I got there," he says, "Drury was out, and the place was being fleeced."

Noah is astonished. "But how did you know that, Timothy?"

"Well, I got there a bit early and the front door was wide open. So I waited and watched a bit." Timothy echoes himself. "Waited and watched." He cuts some more food and continues. "I knew what Drury looked like, as I'd seen 'im up close, so I knew I'd soon learn if he was inside."

"And what happened while you watched?" Noah asks.

"A beggar man came out through the door," says Timothy, "carryin' a few things. I think he wasn't very good at fleecin' a cottage. Didn't seem to know what he was doin'. The sun wasn't down yet, so I could see 'im pretty clear. He looked to be holdin' just a few things. Some coins in his hand. And he was carryin' somethin' bulky. It was the coat Drury'd been wearin' when I first saw 'im."

"What happened then?" asks Noah.

"He turned to carry his booty toward the woods at the back o' the cottage. Well, I couldn't very well let 'im get away, now could I? For there's the very coat walkin' away as I was supposed to put Drury's things in!" He takes a bite and smiles at Noah, clearly relishing the attention of these fine gentlemen. "So ... I stopped 'im."

"Stopped him?" says Noah. "How?"

"I followed him to the rear of the cottage and struck 'im hard in the lower back when he wasn't lookin'. He fell forward into the snow tryin' to catch his breath, and dropped everything."

"Really?" says Noah.

"Oh, yes, sir," replies the boy. "That's a hard smack to get over. When he turned and saw it was somebody as young as me who struck 'im, he started comin' at me, like I was gonna be an easy mark. But I showed *'im* somethin'."

"Showed him something?" echoes Noah.

"Showed him this!" says Timothy. Barely pausing between bites, he draws a surprisingly well-made dagger-and-sheath from his pocket and lays it on the table. "When he sees that, he decides it's most important to get away with all his fingers and toes. Suddenly, the coat and coins don't look so important to 'im. Then he just blows out of there like a pile o' soot." A look of sadness suddenly surfaces on his face.

Surprised at the turn of emotions, Noah asks, "Have you regrets about the beggar man, Timothy?"

For the first time since sitting down, Timothy stops eating. His face flushes and he speaks slowly, from the heart. "Well, sir, he had no coat himself. Here he'd thought he'd got one to last him a few winters, and I come along and take it back." He stares down into his forgotten plate. "God knows *I've* little more than he has even now, and I'm young and able to earn my keep. I suppose I ask myself if he's just *me* in another thirty years. Perhaps *I'll* have no coat. Who's to say I shoulda won this bout? Oh, I had quickness and a dagger," he says with remarkable self-contempt for one so young, "so what I say *goes*. But what's to become of me when quickness is fled?" He slowly shakes his head from side to side, and looks up at Noah, who's on the verge of tears, so touched is he by this young fellow.

Noah places his hand on the boy's shoulder and says contemplatively, "Well, what do you *know*? There's hope for you yet, lad."

Jonathan drinks down his feelings with some wine and winks at Noah.

Timothy smiles at Noah. "Thank you, sir. Anyway, I grab the coat and shut the front door of the cottage, as Drury'll be suspicious if he sees it open. By now, it's gettin' dark. I step off quick into the woods and take cover with the coat. And it's a good *thing* I was steppin' quick or he'd 'ave spotted me."

"Drury returned so soon?" asks Noah.

"*Soon?*" Timothy laughs quietly. "You'd have been able to count no more'n forty, sir. So, Drury goes inside—he's wearin' a jacket, but it's not one that'd get you through a London winter—and he's there for maybe another count of forty, and then this big coach comes through Bishopsgate, and that was *you* all. Well, at this point I know the plan will need to change."

"What happened then?" asks Noah.

"When the constables came over and took Drury away, I snuck into the cottage, hung the coat up on a peg in the bedroom and started stuffin' in Drury's—*effects*, I think you called 'em—and then there's a knock on a little rear window, and it's m'lord here, signalin' to me that the constables and Drury are on their way back. Well, it was too late for me to get outta there. (I'd looked all over for more doors before I even went inside, but there was none to be found.) So, I climbed up on a shelf in the bedroom closet to hide, and figured I'd see what comes, and make my escape when I could. Then Lord Saint Ives and Drury come back and discover Drury's coat all stuffed with his valuables. M'lord spots me on the shelf. Thank God it was m'lord, 'cause if it'd been Drury, my goose was cooked. M'lord tells me to sit tight and make my escape when Drury runs for the jakes, which he did, and *I* did—and here I am."

"Yes," says Noah jovially, "here you are."

A strange, hunted look comes over Timothy's face. His eyes dart about as though he's searching inside himself. "Sir, I don't mean nothin' by it, but—is there a *witch* in this house?"

For a long moment, no one makes a sound.

At last, Jonathan clucks. "*Tsk, tsk!* No witches here. Where did you hear that there was?"

"*Hear*, m'lord? Nowhere. *I feel it in my bones.*"

That's something Noah's never heard from one so young. Young people generally give not the least thought to their bones. "What do you mean, in your bones?" he asks.

Suddenly, Timothy's eyes freeze on a single point far away. "There she is," he says as though to himself. He smiles. "I can see her now."

"What does she look like?" asks Noah.

Timothy smiles more broadly. "She's ... very ... *very* beautiful, and young. She has reddish brown hair and her eyes are ... green? Wait! I've *seen* her ... *here*! She's the one who opened the door when Master Killigrew first brought me here."

Noah sighs. "That would be Esther. My niece. Perhaps she's listening in. I've told her many times not to do that. Lord Jonathan, would you kindly see about her?"

"There'll be no need for that," says Esther's husky voice as she enters the room. "I assure you I was not 'listening in,' Serjeant, at least ... not in the way that you mean."

Timothy rises like a shot and can't take his eyes off her. "Miss," he ventures tentatively, "you oughtn't do that. People are entitled to some privacy in their thoughts."

Esther shakes her head and regards Timothy with amazement. "Most people don't *care* when I'm 'listening in,' if you so call it. In fact, they don't even *know* it. What's remarkable is that you not only felt it, *you looked back at me*! I never met anyone who could do that."

Noah regards Esther with visible annoyance. "Esther, please go to your room. We'll discuss this later."

Esther curtseys and climbs the stairs.

Noah sits down, followed by the others. He rubs his hand over his eyes and mutters, "I cannot believe how long this day has been." Turning to Timothy, he says, "Will you be staying with Jacob and Leah tonight?"

Timothy smiles. "I will, sir. Jacob's wife, Mother Leah, is often in need of good eyes and quick hands, and I'm only too happy to lend her mine."

"Good," says Noah. "Only, Timothy, please say nothing to anyone about Esther's second sight. It is *not* witchcraft, I assure you, but rather something she was born with. She's no devil-worshiper."

"Oh, sir, I'm sorry I used that word," says Timothy abashedly. "It's not what I meant, but I don't know as many words as you, so I pick from what I've got."

Noah smiles. "Please stay and finish your meal, then let yourself out. Lord Saint Ives and I need to retire to the study."

Timothy resumes eating as though not much has happened.

IN NOAH'S STUDY, Jonathan searches through Noah's portfolio and pulls out the security agreement that Groatsworth and Drury signed earlier. He flattens it on Noah's desk and runs his finger down to the inscription made by Drury under his direction: *Nothing requested by me having been omitted herefrom, title to said badge has not hereby been conveyed, except upon proven default.*

Noah takes another writing and flattens it next to the security agreement. "And here is the note received by Lady Leicester, saying *No valid title belonging to your ladyship having been omitted, as shall soon be seen by all.* The words in common are *title* and *omitted*," says Noah.

Jonathan concurs. "Also, the first three letters of *Not*, which begins with a capital letter in both documents. And, also, there's the word *to*."

"How similarly are they written?" asks Noah.

"Well," says Jonathan, "unlike Drury's letters home, he evidently wrote both of these with his left hand. See how the letters all lean left?"

Noah compares the common words carefully. "They're certainly the same handwriting," he says. "So, it was *Drury* who wrote the threatening note to Lady Leicester."

Jonathan scratches his head. "Why does he write with his left hand only *sometimes*?"

Noah shrugs. "My guess is that it affords him the possibility of denying his signature on documents he signs with his left."

"Such as the security agreement," says Jonathan.

"Or a threatening note," adds Noah, yawning. "I don't know about you, Jon, but I'm exhausted. We're doing a good job for Lady Leicester, but she's not the one whose jeopardy is keeping me awake nights. What we must do tomorrow is one thing—and one thing only."

Jonathan completes his thought. "Find Leveson."

Noah nods slowly. "Without him, Sir Henry's doomed." He rises to go to his room, but Jonathan seems reluctant to end their meeting.

Jonathan braces himself and says, *"Er,* there's one more thing I think you ought to know about Timothy's adventure at Drury's cottage."

Noah looks at him apprehensively.

"Timothy got away only in the nick of time, you see. Drury had barely grabbed his musket and run off to the jakes when Timothy—with his hair bound up so he couldn't be easily recognized—ran out of the cottage and off toward London. Drury heard the commotion and ran back from the jakes with his breeches about his knees. He got off a late shot at Timothy, who was quite distant by then."

"So, no harm done?" asks Noah apprehensively.

Jonathan shuffles his feet. "Drury's shot went wild. It shattered every window in the front of the cottage, and ... severed a support beam holding up the porch roof."

Noah's too dismayed to speak.

Jonathan forces himself to add, "And the porch roof collapsed onto the lawn."

While Jonathan waits anxiously, Noah rubs his eyes and takes a moment to compose himself, at last asking, "Drury has no means to trace this to us?"

"None, Father."

"Good. Go to bed."

Jonathan leaves the room, his step a bit lighter, unburdened by the bad news he had to pass along to Noah.

Noah shakes his head, feeling foolish about his earlier sense of a job well done.

CHAPTER 11

NOAH AWAKENS EARLY with Sir Henry on his mind. The sun has barely come up, but his heart is too troubled to allow him to sleep any longer, despite the cares of yesterday. Although Noah and Jonathan were preoccupied after the trial with service of the summons upon Drury, in his mind's eye, Noah imagines what happened at the Tower after Essex and Southampton returned there following their sentencing for high treason.

Essex would have been escorted back to his cell accompanied by the divine of his choice. The divine would have persuaded him to obtain absolution from heaven not only by confessing his own guilt, but by incriminating all others involved in the rebellion, especially those not yet apprehended. And Essex, who by his last words at the trial, swore to make a full confession, would need no persuasion to fulfill his obligation to heaven. At that point (roughly nine o'clock, Noah guesses), Essex would have summoned Lord Robert and a few other ministers, and provided them with a list of everyone having knowledge of affairs at Essex House and Drury House, including Sir Henry Neville.

Heaven only knows what else Essex would have told them, but one thing is certain, Lord Robert would then bring Southampton the list of those incriminated by Essex (probably about ten o'clock), and would have persuaded Southampton that he could expect no mercy from Her Majesty if he were to fail to ratify Essex's list and incriminate each listed man.

Southampton would have cursorily reviewed the list, pen in hand, and pricked down the name of every guilty party with little scruple for the degree of guilt. This entire process would be rife with hypocrisy, of course, for Southampton would be specifying the acts taken by each man to further the object of a conspiracy that he'd just testified was *devoid* of any object.

About midnight, Lord Robert would have prepared his own list of those assigned to arrest each accused man, and would then have assigned a messenger to notify each man responsible for making an arrest.

In the case of Sir Henry Neville, Lord Robert would have assigned a messenger to summon Sir Henry's close friend Serjeant Ames to the Tower at dawn today. The messenger would have been dispatched from the Tower an hour before dawn, and would knock on Noah's door at any moment.

Right on cue, there's an official-sounding knock at the front door, causing Noah to question whether he's been in this business too long. He rises and begins to don his silk robes as quietly as possible so as not to wake Marie.

Cook answers the door and, to Noah's surprise, engages in a bit of friendly banter with the visitor. Though the words are indistinct, the man's voice sounds like that of Francis of the Tower Guard; it would make sense for Cook to be on friendly terms with him, as he recently spent time guarding this house during the rebellion.

Noah grabs his boots, and shuts the bedroom door quietly. Peering down the stairs, he sees Jonathan in earnest conversation with Francis.

"M'lord," says Francis. "I cannot tell *anyone* what business I've come on—not even Serjeant Ames—for I do not *know*."

But Jonathan knows, thinks Noah.

"Well," says Jonathan, "did Her Majesty specify that Serjeant Ames may *not* be accompanied by me?"

Reaching the foot of the stairs, Noah reluctantly says to Jonathan, "M'lord, I expect you will wish to carry out your very important plans for today."

Jonathan seems irritated by the suggestion. "I expect Masters Salazar and Killigrew can handle those," he replies.

"Are they both *still* in London?" asks Noah incredulously.

"They are, Father," replies Jonathan.

Noah shakes his head disapprovingly. "Pretty much as I recall university days. One of them's supposed to be at Cambridge, the other at Oxford, yet both are in *London*." He turns to Jonathan. "If m'lord cares to do so, then round them up in preparation, but I urge m'lord not to accompany me to the Tower at present. As even Francis knows nought of this business, I expect it's secret in character, in which case it may be best for you to have no involvement; best for you, best for Lady Jessica, and best for young Arthur."

Jonathan can see that he's been politely given his instructions. Though he doesn't like them, Noah's point is inarguable. If this is about Sir Henry (and of course it is), *all* of Sir Henry's friends may come under suspicion, including Noah. Best for Jonathan to distance himself, at least until Noah's obtained Crown leave to bring him into the matter.

"Very well, Father," says Jonathan. "Good day, Francis. Perhaps we'll meet again later today."

Francis smiles and bows. "That would be my privilege, m'lord, and I look forward to it."

Jonathan looks at them both uncomfortably and turns away.

Francis leans into Noah. "Lord Robert advises you to ride your favored mount, Bucklebury."

Noah expects he's about to be sent to fetch Sir Henry from whatever point he's reached in his interminable journey to Dover. Bucklebury is strong and well-suited for riding a long distance. Why else would Lord Robert specify Bucklebury as his mount?

⇒∘⟪⟫∘⇐

THERE'S QUITE A BUSTLE about the Tower this early morning. As Francis and Noah enter through the gate, a small company of mounted men with solemn faces passes the other way.

Francis sees Noah watching the procession. "Been goin' on since first light, suh," he says.

Noah nods absently, thinking back to his previous interview with Lord Robert. Lord Robert made sure to find out whether Noah knew that Sir Henry wrote the history plays, but neither had touched upon the possibility that Sir Henry had been involved in Essex's rebellion.

Francis escorts Noah all the way to Lord Robert's chambers until William solemnly allows Noah in without a word, shutting the door behind him.

Lord Robert is seated at his desk, evidently overcome by worry and fatigue. His right eye is ringed in black, and his clothing out of sorts.

"Did you enjoy your sleep, Noah?"

"What little I had of it, m'lord."

"Well, whatever you've had is that much more than *I've* had."

Noah's riding a thin line. Although Lord Robert will have no patience for banter, he's likely to perceive an insult if shown no sympathy for his plight.

Noah decides on the obvious. "So, you've not slept at all, then?" he asks with concern.

"Not a wink. And do you know why?" Lord Robert knows Noah too well to believe he hasn't assembled a fair expectation of what's happened.

Noah shifts uncomfortably. "I'd imagine Lord Essex did as he promised at trial, which was to make a full confession. I expect in doing so, he blamed everyone he possibly could for his own foolhardiness."

"Including his own sister," adds Lord Robert with disgust as he gazes out the window, shaking his head. He turns to Noah with a look of impatience bordering on fury. "Do you know whom *else* he implicated?"

Noah can feel his face fall and his shoulders droop. He stares at the floor. "I ... I fear to conjecture, m'lord."

Lord Robert regards him skeptically. "Have you spoken with Essex since the rebellion?"

Noah nods slowly. "The day after his arrest."

"And did he implicate anyone who'd not been arrested?"

"M'lord, he consulted me by Her Majesty's leave—"

"I don't care if *Christ the Savior or his Heavenly Father* gave him leave—" begins Lord Robert angrily.

"It was not only Essex who received Her Majesty's leave, m'lord. 'Twas I, too, given leave to engage in a legal consultation. For such purposes, Essex was my client, and I am forbidden to report—"

"May I remind you that you work for the Crown, *Serjeant?*" demands Lord Robert, whose enunciation of *Serjeant* drips with sarcasm. "You work for me!" he shouts, rising from his chair. Although under different circumstances, there might have been something humorous about a dwarf menacing a full-size man, there's nothing remotely humorous about this. "Are you holier than those weasels who call themselves 'divines,' who take down every word Essex utters in penitence and repeats it to *me*?"

Noah learned long ago that the way to respond to an angry person is with no trace of anger. "The Crown, in the person of Her Majesty, waived its right to expect my loyalties for purposes of that interview, m'lord. Essex asked Her Majesty for the right to consult with me, and she consented. I'm neither a weasel nor a divine." He straightens his spine. "I'm a *barrister*."

"Yes, all very honorable," Lord Robert says sardonically. "If he'd told you that there was yet another plot afoot against Her Majesty, would you have told me *that*?"

"In a *heartbeat,* m'lord," replies Noah calmly. "There's no right of confidence protecting a client's intention to commit a crime."

Lord Robert is only slightly mollified. "May I ask, Serjeant, if there are any others at this moment in connection with whom you have such divided loyalties?"

Noah's loyalties are not really divided, but he isn't stupid enough to quibble when Lord Robert is so distraught and his meaning so clear. He nods. "As you know, Her Majesty has asked me to provide legal assistance to Lady Essex, which representation has now been extended to assisting her mother-in-law, as you expected."

"Anyone else?" asks Lord Robert.

Noah nods. "At the request of both Lord Essex and Her Majesty," says Noah, "there is another, namely, Lord Southampton."

"Anyone *else*?" asks Lord Robert, as though the list is apparently endless.

"Not—No one, m'lord."

"You were about say 'not yet,' weren't you?"

Noah can feel his face flush. "Possibly, m'lord."

"You *knew* he was involved, didn't you?" shouts Lord Robert, not an inch from Noah's face. Noah's tempted to wipe Lord Robert's spittle from his face, but dismisses the urge.

"*He*, m'lord?" asks Noah, expecting an onslaught.

Instead, Lord Robert steps back, as though he cannot abide Noah's equanimity. "Oh, I'm not going to play this game with you again, Noah. You know *bloody well* whom I mean."

"I surmise m'lord speaks of the same knight about whom we spoke a few days ago," says Noah.

"Say his name, damn you. *Say his name!*"

"Sir Henry Neville?"

Noah's grudging cooperation, however slight, appears to have mollified Lord Robert more than expected.

"You *knew*, didn't you?" asks Lord Robert.

Noah shakes his head sternly. "I knew nothing of Sir Henry's involvement until it was all over. Else, I can assure you I would have taken measures to stop it."

"Have you communicated with Southampton since his arrest?"

"No."

"Have you communicated with Neville since the rebellion was put down?"

"No."

"Well, then," says Lord Robert, "you can only have learned about Neville's involvement from Essex."

Noah merely shrugs. Lord Robert's conclusion is unwarranted, and would be disregarded as mere surmise in a court of law, but this is hardly the time to mention it.

"Do you know why I've had Francis bring you here this morning?" asks Lord Robert.

"I do not, m'lord. Francis could tell me nothing, although he did pass along your recommendation that I ride my horse Bucklebury to the Tower, from which I surmise that you intend to send me with a party to *apprehend*"—he takes a sudden breath, as it makes him physically ill to use that word in respect of his best friend, and his voice breaks—"Sir Henry Neville."

"Yes," says Lord Robert cynically, "but why do you suppose I wanted you mounted on *that* horse? Of what significance is he to Sir Henry?"

Of course. Noah thinks back to that late summer's day at Billingbear. Though he thinks Lord Robert terribly cruel, he replies, "Sir Henry *gave* me Bucklebury as a gift."

"And the horse has stood you in good stead, hasn't he?" asks Lord Robert.

"He has, m'lord. Many times."

"Well," says Lord Robert, "when you overtake Sir Henry, I want him to understand Bucklebury's appearance as signifying that the Crown yet rests safely upon the Queen's head, and that you, Serjeant, are united with the Crown in requiring Sir Henry's return to the halls of justice— even if it means putting your most valuable gift to the Crown's service. Do you suppose the appearance of the horse will have that effect?"

Noah feels defeated, and can make only one answer. "I've no doubt, Lord Robert, that it will have just such effect."

"Very well," says Lord Robert. "I am informed by a reliable source that, as of three days ago, Sir Henry and his family were lodged at the inn at Maidstone."

Noah's confused. "But that's only *halfway* to Dover."

"That's correct, which means that you, traveling light, should over-take him in no more than two days, weather permitting."

"Am I to travel alone, m'lord?" asks Noah.

"You may bring Saint Ives with you, if you wish, so long as you tell him nothing."

"Thank you, m'lord," says Noah.

"Be careful what you say to Sir Henry about his case. Don't be seen as helping him to assemble his story, for he *will* be inclined to lie about at least one thing."

"Which thing?" asks Noah.

"He will certainly say untruthfully that he has not seen Southampton since he was a boy."

"But that's patent rubbish!" says Noah. "Why would he lie about it?"

"Have you read the two long poems Shakespeare published when the theaters were shuttered?"

"Yes," says Noah, "*Venus and Adonis* and ..."

Lord Robert finishes his thought. "*The Rape of Lucrece.*"

Of course! Noah could slap his head for forgetting the dedications until now. "Both poems were both publicly dedicated to Southampton."

"Correct!" says Lord Robert. "So that, if Sir Henry's authorship is discovered, *any* demonstrable connection between Sir Henry and Southampton will naturally show Sir Henry to be lying, and will reinforce the suspicion that he participated in the rebellion. Oh, and one more thing, Noah."

Rarely has Noah been so pleased to hear Lord Robert use his given name instead of his title. "Yes, Lord Robert?"

Lord Robert speaks low and regretfully. "Essex and Southampton are no longer to be called Essex or Southampton, nor are they to be afforded any title of nobility at all. They are simply Master Robert Devereux and Master Henry Wriothesley, until further notice."

"Just so, m'lord?" asks Noah skeptically.

Lord Robert nods emphatically. "On orders of the Queen, personally."

Noah rises and bows. Will Sir Henry receive the same treatment? he wonders.

Lord Robert regards Noah sympathetically. "I'm sorry to have questioned you so closely, Noah. I had to be sure."

Noah bows. "Lord Burghley would be proud."

Lord Robert sighs. "Do you really think so?"

Noah nods. "Of that I've no doubt, m'lord."

"Send for Lord Saint Ives, Noah. If he decides to ride along with you, the Tower stables is ready to outfit you both for the journey. I shall see you in a few days. Oh, and please be sure not to arrive too late to prevent Sir Henry's departure from Dover. There would be hell to pay for that. For *both* of us."

"No doubt, m'lord. Thank you for your confidence."

ESTHER HEARS THE front door close, which means that Lord Saint Ives has left for the Tower. She goes to Noah's study and finds her beloved "Cheerful" David Killigrew in a contemplative mood.

"What troubles you, dear David?" she asks.

Realizing that she's entered, David rises. "I'm waiting for someone. On more Queen's business, I'm afraid. And, no, it has nothing to do with the spicemaid Constance or her mistress … or master."

"I wouldn't assume that it does. And I know that you would come and speak to me if any such eventuality were to arise. For whom are you waiting?"

"You already know, *don't* you?" he asks lightheartedly. "Then why do you ask?"

"I'm only making conversation," she says. "I expect you're awaiting Master Salazar. Is that right?"

"You *know* it is," says David. "I hear Serjeant Ames was a bit dismayed at your parlor trick last evening."

"No parlor trick," she says. "I assure you that I was as surprised as anyone."

"And I'm thinking of bringing someone additional into the meeting," says David.

She nods. "Timothy is about to leave Jacob's cottage to come over here."

David looks at her skeptically. "And how do you know Timothy's coming over here?"

"How do I *know*?" she asks, a bit surprised.

"Yes," says David.

She rolls her eyes. "David, it's dinnertime. He never misses a meal."

Before David can ask Esther why she brought Timothy into the conversation at all, Andres enters and removes his gloves. "Good afternoon, all. I understand Serjeant Ames has an assignment for us."

"Happily, you've arrived just in time for dinner," says Esther.

"Have I?" asks Andres, wide-eyed with feigned surprise.

Now it's David's turn to roll his eyes. He applauds. "Excellent performance, Master Glutton. If ever prizes are awarded for an acting performance, you're sure to take first prize."

Andres scoffs. "Who would ever award a prize for acting?"

"I shall await you gentlemen in the dining room," says Esther as she goes.

Andres sits in a chair before the desk occupied by David. "So, where are the good Serjeant and Lord Saint Ives?"

"Serjeant Ames had gone to the Tower long before I arrived," says David. "Lord Jonathan explained to me that he and Serjeant Ames will be unavoidably 'out of town' for a few days. He could say no more."

Andres nods. "And what has the good Serjeant in mind for us?"

"He wants us to find someone," replies David.

"I hope it doesn't require us to leave London. I'm supposed to return to Cambridge with my betrothèd Barbara and her parents in another day or two. Whom does Serjeant Ames wish us to find?"

"I'll tell you, but you cannot repeat the name."

"Too difficult to pronounce?" asks Andres with a wry smile.

"How clever!" says David. "No, I mean you *may* not repeat it. This is Crown business, Andres, so please be earnest."

"All right," says Andres. "Sorry. Whom are we seeking?"

David leans forward and whispers. "Sir John Leveson."

Andres's eyes shoot up. "The hero of Ludgate?"

"The very same."

"He testified at Essex's trial yesterday, didn't he?"

David nods.

"Did Lord Jonathan say why Leveson is needed, or how he disappeared?"

"Not really," says David. "He told me that Leveson was spirited away immediately after testifying."

"You mean he was abducted from Westminster Hall?"

"From right outside."

Andres is astonished. "One would need to be cheeky indeed to abduct a witness from a courthouse"—upon a moment's reflection, he adds—"*or* well connected."

David nods. "Or both."

"Well," says Andres, "as he was abducted *after* he testified, it obviously wasn't to keep him from testifying."

"True," says David.

"Perhaps he was abducted to punish him for his testimony."

David frowns. "Hardly seems likely, as Leveson testified to things that occurred in public with dozens of other witnesses present."

"Has anyone checked at his home to see if he's turned up there?"

David nods. "Lord Jonathan went this morning to the rooms that Leveson and his wife have taken at Gray's Inn. He said there was no sign of the man, and his wife is positively terrified for him, which is understandable. Serjeant Ames suspects Leveson's being detained somewhere locally for some reason he hasn't yet figured out. In any event, he doesn't wish us to go far afield to investigate. He said he'd pursue the matter further upon his return, if need be."

Andres scratches his head. "That's precious little information to work with. I wouldn't know where to begin looking."

"Nor would I," says David, folding his hands on the desk like an old barrister making a proposition. "I suggest we ask Timothy."

"*Timothy?*" says Andres, at an initial loss. "Oh, *little* Timothy?"

David nods.

Andres laughs despite himself. "We're going to enlist an *eleven-year-old* in finding an abductee?"

"You have a better idea? He's more familiar with the seamy side of London than either of us."

There's a knock at the front door. Instead of waiting for Esther to answer it, Andres opens the door and escorts Timothy into the study.

"Good e'en," says Timothy. When David and Andres hesitate to speak, Timothy breaks the ice. "Is there something I can do for you gentlemen?"

David proceeds slowly. "Timothy, you've been all about town, have you not?"

Timothy regards him askance. "I suppose one might say that, suh."

Andres speaks up. "Have you ever heard of a place where people who are … unlawfully taken … are kept until their families pay ransom?"

Timothy regards them both a bit suspiciously. "I've *heard* of such places," he says tentatively. "Never laid eyes on one, though."

"There's more than one?" asks Andres ingenuously.

"I've *heard*," says Timothy, "that they move such places among houses that lack a tenant for the time being. At any time, there may be as many as three or four in London."

Andres and David exchange an astonished smile. "'Out of the mouths of babes,'" says David, quoting Scripture. "Timothy, do you suppose you could locate them without placing yourself in danger?"

"I could *inquire*, suh," says Timothy, "but it'd take some money. I don't know where they are myself. And informers don't put their lives at risk for nothin', suh."

Andres says, "If we gave you coins amounting to, say, three pounds, how soon do you suppose you might have some useful information for us?"

"Would I be startin' the search right after dinner, suh?"

David laughs up his sleeve at this young mercenary. "Andres, he's of your school, isn't he? Hot meals first!"

Andres ignores him. "Yes, Timothy. Suppose you were to begin searching after dinner?"

"Don't rightly know when I'd have something useful for you, gentlemen," says Timothy, sizing up his prospects. "I suppose I might have something for you by supper. More likely by breakfast tomorrow."

Andres laughs aloud. "Everything runs according to mealtime. I'll warn Mistress Ames to stock up her larder."

CHAPTER 12

AS NOAH AND JONATHAN ride silently abreast in the late afternoon, Kent is a snowy blanket of white where God has wiped away the ugliness of the world, reducing all of Creation to a collection of oversized children's toys where no paint can chip, nor roof leak—where every shape is simple, every edge beveled and soft.

The cold breeze rattles the ice-capped oaks, reminding Noah that this is no hibernal dream. He has no idea what passes through others' minds upon viewing such a scene, but he's noticed over the years that, in the whirring of the wind, he seems always to overhear the sonorous voice of God admonishing the long-suffering Job that His ways are inexplicable to the human mind:

> *Where were you when I laid the foundation of the earth? Tell me, if you have understanding. Who laid its cornerstone, when the morning stars sang together and all the sons of God shouted for joy?*

While the passage has been described by biblical scholars as the humiliation of Job—a reminder that God is God, and man is *not*—the feeling it instills in Noah is rather different. True, it trivializes the importance of Noah Ames, but in so doing it has the salutary effect of trivializing his *cares*.

He imagines himself asking the Almighty, "Why must *I* be the one to arrest my dearest friend?"

The answer would come from on high. "Where were you when I laid the foundation of the earth? Tell me, if you have understanding."

"I don't," Noah would confess. "So, this must all be *Your* fault!"

The shadows grow ever longer. Soon at least one window in every cottage is aglow with the flickering red light of a hearth. *It may be cold out there,* say the tongues of flame, *but it's snug enough in here.*

As darkness falls, Noah and Lord Jonathan cross the River Medway by the old stone bridge and reach the inn at Maidstone, halfway to the silver sea. Though Noah is ever mindful of Lord Robert's admonition not to allow Sir Henry to board at Dover, 'twould be foolhardy to ride on through the coming night. For one thing, by the calendar it will be nearly moonless; for another, the footing is becoming precarious. A horse's broken leg (or even a thrown shoe) would slow them down far more than a night's rest. They dismount outside the inn's stables and hand off the horses to the stableman.

Noah and Jonathan sit in a private room off the inn's dining room.

The innkeeper brings some wine and rough bread before the meal. "The roads to the local farms have been blocked by snow," he says apologetically, "so our baker's been hard put to get his hands on the more refined flour. I hope you gentlemen will find this adequate."

"I'm sure it will be fine, sir," says Noah, wishing he would leave them to their private conversation. He soon obliges.

After a silence, Jonathan clears his throat. "Have you considered how Sir Henry will react when he sees us approaching on horseback?"

Noah shakes his head in dismay. "I've thought of little else since we left London. I expect he's already discussed with Lady Anne that he might be called back to answer questions in the Essex affair."

"D'you think she's aware that Sir Henry may be directly implicated?" asks Jonathan.

"I expect Lady Anne's in the dark about it. Sir Henry would think there's no need to alarm her. He's surely hoping to be carried through to safety by the Queen's good will."

Jonathan says, "You know Her Majesty well. Will he be?"

Again Noah shakes his head. "It will not help him to avoid trial," says Noah. "He'll be interrogated and charged. Whether he'll suffer a traitor's death is another question. I'll do everything I can to avoid *that* horrid outcome." His eyes mist over and his voice cracks. "Good Lord, I hope the boys can find Leveson. I pray he's still alive!"

Jonathan's eyes open wide. "Can you imagine if he's dead?" Realizing that his remark has compounded Noah's anxiety, he quickly changes the subject. "Is there anything you can suggest to Sir Henry that may get him back into Her Majesty's good graces?"

"I'll say all right things," says Noah, "but he won't do as I ask."

"How shall you advise him?"

"Why, of course I'll advise him to tell the truth," says Noah, looking skeptically at Jonathan. "How *else* could I lawfully advise him?"

"Will it help his cause to tell the truth?" asks Jonathan, ignoring the question.

Noah shrugs forlornly.

"Will you ask him about the Drury matter?" asks Jonathan.

"I will, but I must be careful not to vex him. Lady Leicester will be far, far from his mind. He may regard my questions as impertinent, even intrusive."

"Perhaps," says Jonathan, "but suppose you suggest to Sir Henry that Lady Leicester's case is related to his in some way."

Jonathan's suggestion starts Noah's thoughts down a path he's ignored until this moment. *Could* the cases be related in some way? Noah turns to his son-in-law. "Someone apparently wants Sir Henry out of the way for good and all," he says. "Do you suppose it could be *Drury*?"

A DRIZZLE DRIFTS in at dawn the next morning and begins to melt the snow, raising a patchy fog along their path. By eight o'clock, they've been making good time for nearly three hours and so must be nearing the port at Dover, yet there's been no sign of Sir Henry and his family.

Just as Noah begins to fear that Sir Henry's already reached the ship and boarded for Calais, he and Jonathan crest a steep rise looking down into a valley where, through a billowing fog, they spy a train of carts and carriages headed east.

"Come on," says Noah, preparing to shake the reins. "If it's Sir Henry, there's not a moment to lose. We can't be more than ten miles from the port."

"Shall we announce ourselves by firing off a pistol?" asks Jonathan.

Noah's horrified by the idea. "No!" he says. "Let's get ourselves 'round the carts to the head of the train. Stay beside me, remain mounted, don't smile … and *don't say a word*. Sir Henry will know all too well why we've come."

It's begun to rain harder now, which Noah attributes to the nearness of the sea. For the first time this morning, Bucklebury trots through the mud. Passing carts covered in oil cloth, they soon arrive at the front of the train, where several burly men are attempting unsuccessfully to tow the lead carriage out of a rut by means of a rope attached to the axle of another carriage.

Sir Henry stands beside the stranded carriage with his arm around Lady Anne's shoulders watching the work proceed. Anxiety is etched upon both their faces, and their heads drip with rain. As Lady Anne's hearing has begun to fail, only Sir Henry can hear the two horsemen approaching and halting in tandem a few yards away. Sir Henry turns toward them, and his face falls.

For just a moment, Noah sees himself and Jonathan through Sir Henry's eyes, two somber silhouettes against the stormy sky, mounted on black horses, surrounded by patchy fog, rain dripping off.

But even more painful is Sir Henry's obvious conviction that these riders, who've been friends, have now turned agents of death. Without a word, Sir Henry tenderly kisses Lady Anne, who watches as he mounts his oversize horse and trots back toward London, passing Noah and Jonathan with neither word nor glance.

The two horsemen, before turning to follow, bow in their saddles to Lady Anne. But she sees them not at all. Instead, her eyes follow Sir Henry into the receding fog, followed by two faceless horsemen in black.

UPSTAIRS IN LADY JESSICA'S CHAMBER, she lifts Baby Arthur from the floor where he fell asleep, sets him down in his cradle, and kisses his forehead.

As seems to happen whenever a newborn falls asleep during the daytime, a ruckus erupts elsewhere in the house. By the sound of it, something quite heavy is being carried into the kitchen. Jessica *feels* a thud in her ears as the object is evidently placed onto the floor.

"No!" says Cook with some stridency, her stern voice rising up the staircase and trailing off.

The baby shifts uneasily for a moment, then settles back into a slumber.

Although Jessica leaves the room quietly, she plans to unload her concerns on the ears of the offender. "Probably a man," she says to herself as she descends the stairs. "It's about time the ladies were shown some respect in this house."

She marches off to the kitchen where she finds Cook instructing David Killigrew and Andres Salazar on the proper placement of a giant wood-and-metal contraption they've carried into the kitchen over her protest. Each of the men has a hand on it, firmly holding it upright.

Cook has one hand on her hip; the other wags a finger in the men's faces. "This has no place here, gentlemen," she says. Suddenly aware of her ladyship's arrival, Cook turns toward her and curtseys deeply.

The men, evidently unable to bow without allowing the contraption to collapse, nod respectfully to Lady Jessica and pin their eyes to the floor, preparing to be admonished. "G'morning, m'lady," they intone like a couple of schoolboys caught stealing an extra slice of bread.

If Jessica weren't so angry about the possibility of their waking the baby, she would laugh aloud. Instead, her face reddens. "I thought I'd given you an understanding of the difference between outdoors and indoors, and the importance of keeping filth *outdoors*," she says. "Do you remember that?"

In tandem, the men intone, "Yes, m'lady."

"Gentlemen," she says with quiet exasperation, "what is that … *thing*?"

David and Andres look to each other, apparently unsure which of them should try to explain it to her. Either that or, by their extended silence, they're admitting that they don't actually *know* what it is.

"No matter," she says. "I was just making conversation. What I really want to know is: *Where did you get it?*"

Andres clears his throat. "From your family's stables, m'lady."

"Would it then be fair to say," she asks, "that this … device … is used in the care and feeding of horses?"

They nod. "Yes, madam," says Andres, "that is correct."

Lady Jessica makes a show of looking about the kitchen. "Do you see any … *horses* in this kitchen?"

Cook blushes, and titters into her apron.

"No, madam," say Andres and David in listless unison.

Lady Jessica nods. "As I thought. Then I suggest you return … *that* … to the stables or some other place suited for the care and feeding of horses."

Seeming only too happy to oblige, David and Andres begin to lift the device in preparation for moving it.

"Stop," says Lady Jessica impatiently. "Put it down till I'm through." She smooths her skirts. "I came down here only because I had just got Baby Arthur to sleep when this ruckus began. To avoid waking him again, I wish to put an end to what seems a curious endeavor on your part. I suspect I'm going to regret asking this, but why were you bringing this thing into the kitchen?"

"To make room in the stables, m'lady," says Andres.

"Why is more room needed in the stables?"

"We're not at liberty to discuss that, m'lady," says Andres. "Perhaps Lord Saint Ives might satisfy m'lady's curiosity."

The devil he will, thinks Jessica. *He's even more close-mouthed than these two when it comes to Queen's business.*

Evidently finding his own reply inadequate, Arthur volunteers, "We soon expect to need a place offering some privacy about this house, m'lady."

"Why not use the cellar?" she suggests. "That way, you needn't move such contraptions about."

"*Is* there a cellar, m'lady?" asks Andres.

She nods vigorously, a bit surprised that neither Andres nor David knows of the cellar. "It's about the size of this kitchen."

"If I may, madam," says Andres, "where is the *entrance* to the cellar?"

"Well," she says, "there's one in the floor at the rear of the stables."

Andres and David, abashed not to have known it, are delighted to hear it. Apparently unsure whether the cellar would be suitable for their unknown purpose, Andres asks, "Is there much clutter down there, madam, if I may ask?"

"Well, there's a large spice rack and a few casks of old whiskey, but precious little else," she assures him.

"Thank you so much for this information, m—"

"Before you take that contraption out of here," she says, "let me instruct you further. You are to make no further ruckus—and move no other … contraptions—in or around this house without written leave in Her Majesty's own hand, or permission *beforehand* from either Mistress Ames or me; Esther will do in a pinch, as she appears to have retained the good sense God gave her. Are we clear on this?"

"Yes, mum," say Andres and David, as they pick up the machine, silently remove it from the kitchen, and begin moving it back toward the stables. Cook quietly shuts the door behind them.

A baby's cry comes from upstairs. Lady Jessica rolls her eyes and turns about. "*Another* baby heard from," she mutters.

Cook titters again.

———————⟶∘⧼⧽∘⟵———————

AFTER TWO DAYS on the road back to London, the weather has cleared.

Sir Henry has stayed several lengths ahead of Noah and Jonathan through the journey thus far. As they near Maidstone, Sir Henry gallops so far ahead he very nearly escapes their sight.

"If he escapes, it won't bode well for us," says Jonathan with concern.

Noah scoffs. "Sir Henry escape? All twenty stone of him? He's about as well-suited to life on the run as Cheerful to a life of celibacy."

Jonathan's eyebrows rise suddenly. "I was under the impression that David's fondness for the fair sex had ... escaped your attention."

Noah regards him skeptically. "Please, Jonathan. I may be busy, but I'm not blind." He sighs and shakes his head. "Sir Henry won't run for several reasons. First, he's too ungainly and too well-known to escape. Second, he simply has too much to lose. If he were even to *try* to escape, he'd lose any hope of regaining his old life. If he were to fly to France, he'd lose everything he has in England. Finally, if he were to succeed in escaping, he'd put both you and me behind bars for quite a long time. He's just riding ahead to avoid discussion."

"And his aversion to speaking with us makes one wonder whether he would be much troubled by exposing us to punishment," says Jonathan.

Noah shakes his head. "He's preserving our ability to testify truthfully that we never discussed the case with him on this journey."

They pull up to the inn and hand off their horses, but there's still no sign of Sir Henry.

Upon entering the inn, Noah's handed a folded note: *I've taken a private room. My suggestion is that we leave at dawn. We should reach London by sundown. —HN*

CHAPTER 13

SHADOWS CAST BY London's tall buildings stretch eastward over Stew Lane by Queenhythe. On a clear winter's day like this, night will come quickly.

In an alleyway littered with old wherries and discarded equipment, two men and a young boy lounge about in a weathered two-horse cart.

"I feel ridiculous," mutters Cheerful as he lies back on the cart as though it were a bed, his breath visible in the damp cold. "These disguises are absurd."

Cheerful's hair is tied back in a white rag. Black ash has been strategically smeared on his face, especially about the eyes. The others have been similarly defaced, leaving all of them difficult to recognize even in the remaining sunlight. In the dark, their own mothers would draw up their collars and pass them by.

"Well, Master Killigrew," says Andres, looking very much the experienced Spanish seaman in his salt-stained clothing, "it's the best we could do in a pinch. Besides, if you'd just close your eyes and act as though you're enjoying your cup of ale, you'd appear no different from the locals."

"Ah, *vagrancy*," says Cheerful, "or the appearance of it, anyway—just what I've always aspired to." He shakes his head in disgust. "If I'd wanted to fit in with other vagrants, I could have stayed at Falmouth. Plenty of vagabonds at *that* port." He takes Andres's advice, however, and closes his eyes. Before he dozes off, he opens one. "Timothy," he says quietly, "just how certain was your friend that Leveson's about to be moved into that abandoned shack across the way?" Actually, he's being unfair in summarizing the house; though it appears to be unoccupied, it's hardly been neglected. "'Twould be a shame to have wasted all this time and effort, especially with Serjeant Ames due back at any moment."

Timothy finishes watering the horses, and strokes each of them gently before putting down his bucket and approaching Cheerful. "Best to keep our voices down, suh," he advises quietly. "My friend said he was sure, and he's got every reason to speak the truth, since he's got only one shillin', and won't get the other three if nobody shows up in the next half-hour."

Andres laughs up his sleeve. "I swear on a book, Cheerful; Timothy is just a smaller version of you. Timothy, look at that rag you've got your hair tied off in. It's the same as his."

Timothy beams with pride as though nothing could be more desirable than being thought of as a little Cheerful.

The real Cheerful pats his short sword and dozes off.

<hr />

THE NEXT THING Cheerful knows, Timothy's shaking him awake and it's full dark. "Master David," says the boy, reaching back from the driver's bench, "it's time to look sharp. I can hear 'em comin', and we've gotta grab Leveson before they take 'im inside."

Cheerful sits up briskly. Shaking off the vestiges of sleep, he glances about. Timothy holds the reins. Andres is seated next to him at the ready, his sword and dagger strapped to his side, his pistol in his hand.

A heavy torch-lit cart heading west on Thames Street turns noisily onto Stew Lane and rapidly approaches the house across the way. As the cart begins to slow, its three occupants come into view. The one in the rear is manacled, wearing a bag of coarse cloth over his head tied loosely about his neck. The other two men, seated on the driver's bench, are wearing swords. The cart comes to a halt.

As the element of surprise is essential to the plan, Cheerful makes no remark when one of the faces across the way seems vaguely familiar; besides, it's hard to be sure at this distance in the flickering torchlight.

Cheerful and Andres exchange an earnest nod, and Timothy picks up the reins.

"Ready?" asks Andres, cocking his pistol.

David grabs his short sword. "Ready," he intones.

"Ready," says Timothy, his high-pitched voice more suited to a church choir than a rescue party.

"Go," whispers Andres, and the cart bucks forward.

Timothy artfully positions their cart immediately ahead of the prisoner's but aimed the opposite way, out toward Thames Street, thus effectively trapping the other cart while facilitating their own escape.

In the abductors' cart, the two on the driver's bench sit wide-eyed, as though unable to believe their eyes.

Andres sits up and aims his pistol at the driver's head.

"Hands up, gentlemen!"

Cheerful races to the prisoner, who's sightless and disabled with his eyes covered and hands bound. Cheerful helps him down and leads him to their own cart, laying him down flat, so as to render him invisible to the idly curious. As Cheerful hops up and takes his place beside the prisoner, the night remains completely still. No one has moved but he and the prisoner, and fortunately no meddler has happened by.

Timothy glances back at Cheerful, who nods curtly.

This is the dangerous part, thinks Cheerful, as Timothy shakes the reins, and the cart starts abruptly, racing toward Thames Street.

Cheerful glances back and sees one of the abductors from behind reach for a pistol strapped to his side. As agreed beforehand in such eventuality, Cheerful fires his own pistol into the air, making a loud report that disturbs the otherwise quiet night. The abductor abandons all thought of drawing his weapon and cringes instead, throwing his hands up into the air in a sign of total submission.

The prisoner, startled by the gunshot, emits a muffled sound. Evidently, the poor bastard's not only been bound, but gagged, as well. Cheerful is eager to remove such foul restraints and restore the prisoner to his liberty.

Serjeant Ames will be so pleased.

Once safely away on Thames Street, Cheerful lights two torches and hands one off to Andres to help light their way.

NIGHT FALLS ON the Lord Admiral's house in Chelsea. Sir Henry Neville sits alone on his mount, gazing pensively out over the black waters of the Thames, waiting for Noah and Jonathan to catch up—a bit of a surprise to them, as he's kept his distance the whole way and spoken nary a word, other than to ask Noah his destination.

A short way behind, Noah strokes Bucklebury's withers, and turns wistfully to Jonathan. "Sir Henry looks a condemned man awaiting the hangman," he says.

Jonathan is about to reply when he stops suddenly and looks back over his shoulder into the distance. "Did you hear that?" he asks dubiously.

"Hear what?" says Noah.

"It sounded like a pistol shot," says Jonathan, "far away down the river."

"Well, if it was too far away for me to hear it, I imagine it's no concern of ours."

Jonathan shrugs. "I suppose." He looks ahead to the mournful figure of Sir Henry. "I can only imagine what *he's* thinking."

They reach Sir Henry and silently join him in his watch over the river.

Sir Henry begins speaking in a soft monotone, as though to himself, but just loudly enough for them to overhear. "The Lord Admiral's house behind us, to which I'll soon be confined, has served as residence to many notables." He clears his throat. "Katherine Parr lived there. Under the title of Princess Elizabeth, Her Majesty once lived there in the household of Lord Admiral Seymour—long before *she* was crowned and *he* executed for treason. … Lady Anne of Cleves …" His voice trails off, but neither Noah nor Jonathan speaks, as Sir Henry seems to be moving toward a point. "More recently, Lady Jane Grey." He turns to his silent companions. "She went straight from this house to the Tower of London." He releases a long sigh, having no need to say what everyone knows: that she never left the Tower alive. "And I expect your humble servant shall follow suit."

Sir Henry turns to Noah and addresses him on a personal level for the first time since leaving Dover. "Lady Jane's nine-day reign as Queen ended shortly before you arrived in England, Noah. When *did* you arrive, exactly?"

Noah can barely speak, so anxious has he been that his friend of so many years might have decided to dispense with his friendship forever. "I arrived just after Queen Mary passed."

Sir Henry slaps his forehead. "Of course. You delivered groceries to the Tower when Princess Elizabeth was in residence awaiting coronation. My father was there, as you know. My father—" he says, shaking his head dolefully. "It all seems so long ago … as in another life."

"Henry," pleads Noah, "give me a chance to help you, and there shall be much more for you in *this* life." He's never strained to sound sure of something he was so unsure of.

Sir Henry's expression is baleful, yet Noah detects a spark of hope in it. "I daren't hope," Sir Henry says with a wan smile, "but if anyone can do it, I suppose it's you, my friend."

A footman emerges unbidden from the Lord Admiral's house and begins toward them down the walk.

"'Tis not just I, Sir Henry," says Noah. "'Tis Robert Cecil, too."

With the mention of Robert Cecil, Sir Henry's face brightens as though he's received news of a possible royal reprieve.

Noah mutters in order not to be heard by the approaching footman. "And, of course, there's Lord Jonathan here. Keep heart, Henry, and tell the truth."

The footman reaches them and bows to Jonathan. "M'lord. Gentlemen," he says, "though the Lord Admiral is away, yet he has invited you all to dine here this evening."

Sir Henry and Jonathan look to Noah, who replies. "Please thank the Lord Admiral for his gracious invitation. Alas, only Sir Henry will be able to dine here this e'en, as Lord Saint Ives and I have pressing Crown matters requiring immediate attention elsewhere. Please do convey to the Lord Admiral that we very much hope to be invited on an occasion when the Lord Admiral is able to attend."

The footman is obviously surprised that *anyone* would decline dinner at the Lord Admiral's table under any circumstances. "As you wish," he says. "I shall send the stableman 'round for Sir Henry's steed presently. Of course, the Lord Admiral has made sure to obtain suitable, *er,* Crown accompaniment for Sir Henry during his stay here." He bows courteously and returns to the house.

The footman's last message was so blithely delivered that it takes Noah a moment to realize what he meant. *Sir Henry's under house arrest and his guard will be staying in the house as long he does.*

Noah leans into Henry, so no one but Jonathan can overhear. "I must know one thing before going: Did you persuade Leveson to guard Ludgate against Essex's advance on Whitehall?"

Sir Henry's spirit rises at first, but then his face falls. "Oh, but I promised him I would not mention his name if there were an inquiry."

"I've spoken with him," says Noah hurriedly, "and he has very kindly changed his mind, but there's still one problem in enlisting his assistance."

"What's that?" asks Sir Henry.

"He's been abducted, and no one seems to know where he is. His wife is beside herself with worry. Henry, I think someone quite highly placed wishes to put *you* out of the way ... permanently. Making Leveson disappear must seem the readiest way to accomplish that result, as his testimony may be your only hope of securing Her Majesty's clemency. If you can think of *anyone* who hates or fears you that much, write me immediately any time of day or night, and I'll investigate. Meanwhile, rest assured I'll visit you whenever and *wherever* I may.

And one last thing: *Don't lie*, especially about your association with the Earl of Southampton. Good e'en, Sir Henry, and God bless."

Noah and Jonathan start off slowly for Holborn on the final leg of their mournful journey. Though they have each other's company, somehow without Sir Henry, they feel … alone. For some unknown reason, Noah's overcome with the feeling that they'd better hurry. He prods Bucklebury into a trot.

————————⟶∘⟜⟝∘⟜————————

"MIND YOUR TORCHES, GENTLEMEN!" says Timothy. He turns off High Holborn, slows the cart down, and lets the horses guide them through the open doors into the sheltering darkness of the Ames's stables. With cart and horses still attached, it will be a tight fit, but it was all measured out yesterday after they gave the stableman the night off.

Once the stable doors are closed behind them and they're safe from prying eyes, Timothy hops down and waters the horses. Meanwhile, Andres steps off the cart and opens the cellar door.

Cheerful assists their liberated prisoner down the steps, jams his torch into the cellar sconce, and seats the prisoner on a bench. He turns to Andres.

"Are you ready for the unveiling?" he asks.

Just then comes a determined banging at the stable door, followed by a man's muffled shout.

————————⟶∘⟜⟝∘⟜————————

NOAH IS DISGRUNTLED to find his own stables door closed to him. What's more puzzling is it seems dark inside, or nearly so. He and Jonathan dismount and tie off their horses on a post outside.

Noah pounds on the stable door with the meat of his hand and speaks aloud to whoever may be inside. "This is a most disagreeable greeting upon our safe return!" No reply. He turns to Jonathan. "Where the devil is that ingrate Tom, who was *so* pleased when I brought him over from Gray's? I haven't given him the night off."

Jonathan shrugs. "Perhaps Mistress Ames did so."

Noah shakes his head. "If anyone were to presume to do *that*, m'lord, it would more likely be *your* lady. I've noticed Jessica can be a bit proprietary about this place."

"Well," offers Jonathan, "her attitude should change this summer with the completion of a habitable section of her own house across the way."

Sounds of scrambling and secretive conversation make their way through the stable door.

"What the devil is going on in there?" Noah mutters.

The bar inside is lifted and the door opens a crack, letting out a beam of torchlight. Young Timothy slips out to speak with them, shutting the door hard behind him. "Welcome, home, m'lord," he says, bowing. "Serjeant," he adds with a smile.

"Timothy," says Noah with concern, "is everything all right?"

"Marvelous, suh," Timothy assures him proudly, while pretending not to notice the noise coming from the stables.

"*Marvelous*, eh?" says Noah skeptically. "I can only wonder who told you to say that. Stand aside, Timothy."

Timothy begins to speak, but quickly darts aside to avoid being walked over. Noah and Jonathan march into the stables. Timothy follows and shuts the door behind them.

Standing before Noah is Andres Salazar, wearing some kind of face paint and an old sailor's costume.

"Is this some new form of masquerade?" Noah demands, beginning to seethe.

"I can explain, sir," says Andres.

"I should hope so! Lord Jonathan and I return from four days' hard ride and find our entry to the stables barred by a carriage with the horses still tied to it? What are we supposed to do with *our* horses?" His eyes burn into Andres. "What *madness* is this?"

Cheerful tramps up the cellar stairs. The torchlight that escapes as he opens the cellar door is cut off when he closes it behind him.

"We've got him, sir," says Cheerful proudly.

"*Got* him?" asks Noah. "Got *whom*?"

"Why, the very man you've been looking for," says Cheerful.

"Leveson?" asks Noah skeptically. "What do you mean you've *got* him? You've got him in my *whiskey cellar*?"

Cheerful nods emphatically. "Come and see."

A momentary hope rises in Noah's chest, but then reality sets in. Things *never* turn out so perfectly. Something must be wrong.

"Wait!" says Noah. "Let's first establish that I did *not* instruct you to take Sir John by force."

Cheerful's face falls. "We used no force against the gentleman, Serjeant Ames. The only pretense of force was against his captors. Come and see!"

Noah squeezes his eyes shut and cringes. "First tell me what I'm going to see when I go down there."

"We've only just arrived," says Cheerful. "You surprised us. Sir John is still wearing the coarse bag they tied over his head—"

"*They?*" says Noah.

Andres steps forward. "'They,' meaning Sir John's captors, sir," says Andres.

"Who were his captors?" asks Noah warily. "Was there a fight?"

"No fight. We're not quite sure who they were, sir, but little Timothy searched London for nearly two days before learning that Sir John was to be moved at sundown tonight to an old house at the north end of Stew Street."

Noah frowns. "In Queenhythe?"

Andres nods. "Yes, sir. He was being held by two men. We surprised them, and they put up no resistance. As we left, one put his hand on a pistol, so Cheerful fired a blank just to immobilize him till we could get away."

Noah turns to Jonathan. "There's your gunshot on the Thames," he says.

"So it appears," replies Jonathan, turning to Andres. "So, you haven't yet seen Sir John's face?"

"Not I, m'lord," says Andres, looking over his shoulder at Cheerful.

Cheerful shakes his head. "Nor I."

"Nor heard his voice?" asks Jonathan.

"No, m'lord," says Cheerful, "he's been gagged."

"Has the prisoner seen *you*?" asks Jonathan. "Does he know your names?"

Andres and Cheerful exchange a glance and shrug uncertainly.

Noah throws his hands up, goes to the cellar door, and waits for Cheerful to open it. He steps down the stairs and spies a lone figure sitting on a bench, much as Cheerful described. He can't imagine what must be going through the mind of a man in such an apparently perilous situation. The others follow him down, but Noah sends Timothy up out of the cellar. No need to multiply the witnesses.

Noah says to Cheerful, "Remove this gentleman's restraints, take off that wretched bag, and ungag him."

"He'll *see* us," mutters Jonathan in Noah's ear.

Noah scoffs. "Bit late to worry about that, isn't it?"

In a moment, Cheerful removes from the prisoner all the paraphernalia of abduction.

Noah takes the torch from the sconce and brings it close enough to see the man's face. He looks into the black-ringed, bloodshot eyes of a man who is certainly *not* Sir John Leveson.

"Master William Shakespeare," says Noah conversationally, taking a seat on the bench beside him.

Andres and Cheerful swoon at the news that they've freed the wrong man. Neither has even heard that Shakespeare had been abducted.

"Serjeant Ames," says Shakespeare wearily with a respectful nod.

"How are you this evening?" says Noah, as to an old friend sharing a bench in a public park.

Shakespeare rubs his hands together. "Well, Serjeant, to speak the truth, I've had better evenings."

"We'll soon put things right," Noah assures him. "You two!" says Noah, indicating Andres and Cheerful. "Go up into the stables. No one is to enter or leave without my permission." The two dart up the stairs and close the cellar door, leaving Noah alone with the prisoner.

"Master Shakespeare," says Noah gently, "those two young gentlemen were quite concerned when they heard you'd disappeared."

Shakespeare does his best to be cordial. "Theatergoers, are they?"

"Oh, most certainly," says Noah. "They spent several days locating you, and then found just the right moment to pounce on your abductors."

"My ... *abductors*?" says Shakespeare.

"Well, that's who my young friends thought they were," says Noah apologetically. "But you were *not* abducted, were you?"

Shakespeare shakes his head.

Noah asks, "You were in protective custody of sorts, weren't you?"

"After a fashion, I suppose," says Shakespeare. "Oh, but see, I'm not at liberty to disclose—"

"No need," says Noah, waving his hand dismissively. "Robert Lord Cecil is a good friend, and I know his mind as it pertains to you."

"Oh, then you know?" asks Shakespeare.

"I know he wanted you to be free of any baseless inquisition."

"How do you mean, 'baseless'?" asks the reputed playwright.

"I mean, I *know*," says Noah.

"Know *what*?" asks Shakespeare.

"I know that the authorities have no business suspecting you of treason in the playing of *Richard the Second* on the eve of the rebellion."

"Most certainly," Shakespeare assures him. "I had no hand whatsoever in mounting that production."

Noah regards him gravely. "But I know *more* than that," he says.

"What more is there to *know*?" asks Shakespeare cautiously.

"I *know*," says Noah, "that you had nothing to do with writing *Richard the Second*."

Fear of discovery passes over Shakespeare's face, and his eyes seek out Jonathan in the dark cellar.

Noah can see what he's thinking. "Lord Saint Ives knows, too," says Noah. "We have only just escorted Sir Henry Neville back to London, you see."

"Did *he* tell you?" asks Shakespeare.

Noah shakes his head. "No. Very few know, still. Tell me, Master Shakespeare, do you wish to avail yourself of your newfound freedom? If so, you're welcome to have a good supper here at my home, spend the night, and go in the morning at leisure, if you wish."

"I'm afraid that your solution, though kindly offered," says Shakespeare gratefully, "would secure me only one freedom, one which I do not care to exercise, namely, the freedom to be arrested and questioned by the Crown."

Noah nods indulgently. "Ah, I see what you mean. Well, then I assume you prefer to be returned to your protective custody, is that right?"

Shakespeare nods earnestly.

"So it shall be. Just give me a short while to arrange matters." Noah rises, brings the torch over to a cask of whiskey, fills two wooden cups, and hands them to Jonathan. "M'lord, won't you please share this offering with our esteemed guest?"

Jonathan accepts the cups, hands one to Shakespeare, and sits next to him, laughing quietly at Noah's *sang froid* in calling a man forcibly dragged into his cellar an *esteemed guest*.

Noah climbs the stairs and sternly summons Andres, Cheerful, and Timothy. "You three have managed to carry off an amazingly dim-witted feat this evening. You've managed to free the only prisoner in London who doesn't *wish* to be freed. Did any of you think to take a good look at the men who had custody of Master Shakespeare?"

Andres and Timothy shake their heads without hesitation.

But Cheerful looks at Noah guiltily and swallows hard. "I got a look at one of them."

"Did he look familiar?"

"Only vaguely … in the torchlight," says Cheerful.

Noah arches an eyebrow and waits for Cheerful to continue.

"He looked like … like … Chester of the Tower Guard," admits

Cheerful reluctantly.

"How interesting!" says Noah sardonically. "And who would know Chester's appearance better than *you two*, who brought him to London from Cambridge?" He can feel his face flush, and reminds himself to control his temper. "Did it occur to you, Master Killigrew, that it might be"—he shrugs—"*poor practice* to wrest a prisoner away from Her Majesty's Guard?"

"I th-thought," stammers Cheerful, "that Chester might have turned coat against the Crown."

"*Thought?* On the basis of which evidence?" demands Noah.

"Well, I thought the prisoner was Sir John Leveson," says Cheerful, "and could not imagine a lawful reason for him to be in custody."

Noah nods skeptically. "And that brings me to you, Master Timothy. On what basis did you advise these simpletons that the prisoner was Sir John?"

"I was told," says Timothy timidly, "by a fellow about my age who's always been right about such things ... until now. I s'pose he just knew I was lookin' for somebody famous, and Master Shakespeare is famous, so—"

"Enough, Timothy!" says Noah. "And *you*, sir," he says turning to Andres with a moue of distaste, "you were the *adult* in this affair. 'Tis you who are most culpable in relying upon the word of an *eleven-year-old* in seizing a prisoner from Crown custody."

Noah takes a step back and stares them down one at a time in the torchlight. "And that's to say nothing of the likelihood that one or more of you might have been wounded or even killed if you'd been resisted. In all likelihood, the only reason you went unharmed is that Chester recognized *you* and had the good sense to forbear! David, do you suppose Sir Henry Killigrew or his daughter Lady Anne—or Sir Henry Neville, for that matter—would have forgiven me for your death? And make no mistake, they would have pinned responsibility on me! As for you, Andres, how do you suppose Barbara Bell would take the news of your untimely passing? There'd be the end of *her* future."

Lastly, Noah looks down at the blond orphan. "As for you, Timothy, did you give one moment's thought to the pain your death would have inflicted upon Jacob and Leah—who've come to depend on you so heavily?"

This has precisely the effect Noah wished. Timothy's first reaction is to realize with a sense of gratitude that there's *someone* in this lonely world who'd miss him if he were gone. Noah's remonstrance isn't entirely lost on the boy, but the reminder that good people need him has both driven home Noah's point and taken much of the sting out of it.

Jonathan trudges up the cellar stairs, relaxed by the whiskey and conversation he's shared with Will Shakespeare.

"Let's get our story straight," says Noah. "Although I don't expect this matter to become public, if it were to do so, you three were trying to rescue your favorite playwright from unlawful abduction. You'd never *heard* of Leveson, except by rumor that he's the man who saved the day during Essex's rebellion." He turns to Jonathan. "M'lord," says Noah, "do you suppose you might summon Chester here on 'urgent business'?"

There's a polite knock on the stable door. As the others rush to answer it, Noah shouts, "Stop!" The others back away. "I'll answer this myself, if you please."

He opens the door partway and says with copious relief, "Thank the Lord! Just the man I wanted to see." He pulls Chester inside by the elbow.

Chester enters and glances at the others with chagrin. He plainly draws the correct impression that all but Lord Jonathan have been roundly upbraided by the good Serjeant. "Is the ... *prisoner* here, Serjeant Ames?" he asks nervously.

Noah nods. "First, let me apologize on behalf of these young men." He bows, as one in the wrong. "Yes, Chester, Master Shakespeare is here and in good condition. Well, he's got some whiskey in him, but otherwise he's in the same condition as you last saw him." As though an unrelated thought has occurred to him, Noah asks, "Chester, has Lord Robert been informed of this ... shipwreck of a rescue?"

Chester shakes his head. "Not unless *you* told him, suh. I'd just as soon not be the one to tell him we lost the gentleman he entrusted to us."

"Oh, thank God again," says Noah. "I haven't had a chance to contact him. Lord Jonathan and I just returned home and walked into .... this. And please, Chester, instruct your colleague never to tell of it."

Chester smiles. "Can I trust that none of these gentlemen will let on that Master Shakespeare's in custody? From what I'm told—"

Noah interrupts him gently. "Her Majesty knows nothing of it. Well," he says, turning to the others, "none of these four gentlemen will say a thing about it. Kindly swear, gentlemen."

"I swear," says each of them.

Lord Jonathan goes down to the cellar and brings up Master Shakespeare, who looks disoriented and quite weary.

In one of Jonathan's hands are both the bag and the gag formerly worn by the prisoner. Jonathan leads Shakespeare to Chester and hands him the items.

"One thing, Chester," says Jonathan. "If this is all just a disguise and Master Shakespeare is willing to go, then what need of the gag?"

Chester considers, and nods. "Right, m'lord! No need for it," he says, placing the bag over Shakespeare's head and leading him gently out of the stables.

In a moment, the sound of two horses clopping slowly away penetrates the stable door, reminding Jonathan how difficult it can be for a rider to lead a second horse over distance.

"Where's Tom the stableman?" demands Noah.

"We gave him the night off," says Cheerful.

Noah shakes his head wearily. "I might have known. Well, all right. For your disgraceful and hazardous performance—and for giving the stableman the night off without permission—you three will quietly detach the cart from these horses, and then tend to *all* the horses, including m'lord's and Bucklebury. I want them fed, watered, groomed, and put away before you retire. Any objection?" He arches an eyebrow.

It's clear none of the three is prepared to hint at the least objection. To the contrary, Andres steps forward with hat in hand. "I just wanted to apologize, Serj—"

Noah holds up his hand. "I don't mean to be rude, gentlemen," he says, "but it's been a long day, during which m'lord and I arrested a lifelong friend on charges of high treason against the Crown. With the sentencing of Essex and Southampton so fresh in your memory, you need no reminder from me of the possible sentence such charges may bring. I feel the weight of the world on my shoulders just now so, unless you're about to say something extremely urgent, it can wait a day or two. Rest assured: Though you may sometimes act the imbeciles"—he looks fondly into their dimly lit eyes—"I still love you all. Now good night!"

Andres nods respectfully and the other two stand silent as Noah and Jonathan turn and leave the stables. Once they're out of hearing, Timothy says wistfully, "I want to be just like him someday."

"So do we all," says Andres, tousling Timothy's hair. When Timothy reaches up to retaliate, he's tousled from behind by Cheerful.

"Come on, Tim," says Cheerful. "We've got a lot of stable work to do."

⸺◦○◦⸺

AS NOAH OPENS the front door, Jonathan excuses himself wearily and goes up to Jessica's room.

Noah picks up the letters on the floor by the door. Two of them are bills; one for feed, the other for spices evidently ordered by Cook.

The last is a brief note from the Lord Chief Justice, enclosing a letter from Groatsworth detailing the considerable damage inflicted by Drury's musket on his precious cottage. Groatsworth asks that Serjeant Ames be instructed to give Drury a good talking-to and ensure that the costs of repair will be recompensed.

The Lord Chief Justice's covering note is terse: *I thought you had this matter in hand.* Noah's pride tempts him to dwell on the Lord Chief Justice's inapt criticism; perhaps he wonders why a mere Jew should be so highly regarded by the nobility.

But instead, Noah focuses on the rare opportunity presented by the enclosed letter. Groatsworth wants Drury to be given a sound grilling, and Noah's mood is just foul enough to carry it off. Besides, it will present the perfect occasion to question Drury about any grudge he or his ilk may harbor against Sir Henry Neville.

In the matter of Leveson's disappearance, subtlety has done me no good so far, he thinks, *so to hell with it.*

CHAPTER 14

THE TOWER OF LONDON holds prisoners of every station in life, but most are either noblemen or those deemed a direct threat to the Crown. The noblemen are generally treated as such, or at least as noblemen who've deviated from the straight and narrow path to salvation. Their food is better and can be supplied from outside the Tower through one of the approved grocers—at the prisoner's expense, of course. Although imprisoned noblemen are not given the run of the place, Tower personnel (given a large enough vail) can bring them various luxuries, such as paper, pen, and ink, and can allow them to consult records maintained at the Tower.

Those prisoners lacking any claim of nobility, if they're not soon tossed into one of the seedy houses of detention located elsewhere in London, are treated somewhat less well. Their cells are a means of punishment, and are as severe as those of monks, though lacking their cleanliness.

Sir Gelly Meyrick languishes on a cot in one of the latter cells. He's received few visitors, so he's surprised when one morning he receives an unexpected one.

"Visitor for you, Sir Gelly," says the jailer outside his cell.

"One of those 'divines'?" Sir Gelly grunts, rubbing his eyes. "Tell 'im to go to hell."

The jailer snickers and shakes his head. "Not a divine, Sir Gelly, though I've often wished to tell one just as you say. No, this a nobleman: Lord Saint Ives."

Sir Gelly sits up, confused. "Lord Saint Ives? Come to see *me*?"

"Shall I admit him?" asks the jailer, as though it's nothing to him either way.

Sir Gelly ponders the question. "He's alone?" asks Sir Gelly.

"Alone he is, suh."

"All right. Let 'im in," says Sir Gelly, rising and dusting the detritus of a recent meal from his doublet. He takes a seat at a little table, and nudges the other chair away from the table for his visitor.

A metal key is slipped into the lock and turns with a clack. The door is shoved open.

The jailer enters and says. "My lord, here's Sir Gelly."

Lord Jonathan, Baron Saint Ives, enters and slips the jailer a few coins. The jailer bows gratefully and goes.

Sir Gelly rises and bows. "M'lord," he says, "to what do I owe this visit?"

"Rise, Sir Gelly," says Lord Jonathan, "and resume your seat. I shan't stay long, but there's something I've long felt the need to say to you."

Sir Gelly looks at the chair and would like to flop into it, but can't bring himself to do it. "I'm sorry, m'lord, but I can't sit while you're standin'." He smirks half-heartedly. "'Tisn't the way I was reared, I s'pose."

"Very well," says Lord Jonathan, "then I shall join you." He takes a seat at the table. "Sir Gelly, I've come to seek your forgiveness—"

"My forgiveness, m'lord?" says Gelly. "But I never knew you to do me wrong."

"Well," says Lord Jonathan, "there was the incident at the Boar's Head."

"The Boar's Head?" Sir Gelly's eyebrows rise. "Oh, you mean, my flight through the window?" He emits a full-throated laugh. "I've 'ad worse 'appen on a Chelsea mornin'!" He realizes that his sense of resignation has left him focused solely on his own feelings, and that laughter at this moment must appear unfeeling to this young man who's come to make amends. "Is *that* what you want forgiveness for, m'lord? 'Tweren't nothin'. Besides, I was drinkin' pretty heavy, and I get awful mouthy when that 'appens. It's me what should be seekin' *your* forgiveness."

Lord Jonathan remains serious. "Well, no, it isn't specifically for that occasion, nor the time I would have killed you up on the Thame if my pistol had been loaded."

Sir Gelly gives that some thought, as it never occurred to him that Jonathan's pistol might not have been loaded.

Lord Jonathan resumes. "No, it's that I wrongly convicted you in my heart many years ago of injuring my mother by knocking her over with your horse."

"Your *mother*, m'lord?" asks Sir Gelly in wonderment. "I mean no disrespect, suh, but I don't recall ever layin' eyes on m'lady your mother."

Lord Jonathan laughs softly. "She was not a 'lady' in that sense, Sir Gelly. I'm the first of my line to receive noble preferment. No, she was my *adoptive* mother, and I loved her dearly. She lived with my adoptive father in Old Jewry. And they were quite poor. Occasionally, she would set up a cart with some of her handiwork for sale to passersby. One day I heard a horse whinny, followed by a terrible clatter in the street. I emerged from the house and saw my mum lying there. She was badly hurt. Later that day, I heard you having your wounds bound up by one of the seamstresses in the neighborhood. You were … as you say, drunk. At that time, being but a small child, I convicted you in my heart of the offense."

Sir Gelly's mouth hangs open as he strains to recall the details of that day. "Oh," says Sir Gelly, "I remember that day. 'Tweren't me, but rather a drunkard on a horse what knocked everyone over. A sailor, as I recall; in fact, an *officer*. I took me life in me 'ands, but I thrashed 'im good. The way he run down all those poor people! It got me *Welsh* goin'. The men in Old Jewry had to stop me from beatin' 'im to death. They carried 'im off and put him back on his horse in some other part o' town." He smiles fondly. "I thought that was a nice touch." Returning to present day, he says, "So … m'lord's mum was one of those what got knocked over?"

"Yes," says Lord Jonathan, "and I carried that grudge against you until I learned the truth only a few weeks ago."

"How'd ye mum fare, m'lord? Did she come back from it?"

Lord Jonathan nods sadly. "She did, Sir Gelly, but only to die of the plague shortly thereafter."

"Death comes like a thief in the night," mutters Sir Gelly, and his words remind him that his own execution is imminent. "That's a shame, m'lord. My heart goes out to ye. Who told ye the truth about that day, if I may ask?"

"I doubt you'd know him," says Jonathan. "His name is Jacob, and he's getting on in years."

"Jacob?" says Sir Gelly. The name is ringing a bell. "From the Drapers'? *That* Jacob?"

This brings a wan smile from Lord Jonathan. "The same, Sir Gelly."

"Well, if that don't beat all!" says Sir Gelly. "M'lord, you have my forgiveness. With all my heart. Ye never did me no harm, leastways no more'n I 'ad comin'."

"Thank you, Sir Gelly," says Lord Jonathan with a break in his voice.

"That's a load off my conscience. Does that cover Serjeant Ames, as well?"

"*Pshaw!* Only thing *he* ever done to me was save me neck out in Cornwall. Covers *him*, too. Sure."

Jonathan smiles. "Now, I've come also to offer my assistance in your"—his eyes glance about the cell—"current predicament. If you wish, I could offer my testimony in your behalf, and tell the jury of that occasion when I saw you courageously defend the defenseless. Or, if you prefer, I could offer my testimony in an application to the Queen seeking clemency in your case."

While it sounds like an easy offer to make, Sir Gelly knows that for this young man to proffer testimony in his case would cast a pall on his future. He'd be putting his entire life and fortune at risk from the moment he was seen to oppose the implementation of the Crown's righteous vengeance against any who dare threaten it.

Sir Gelly begins to speak, but is at first overcome with the simple decency of this young man. "I—" he croaks, then begins again. "I appreciate the offer, m'lord—I *truly* do—but I do not think your testimony would make any difference in my case. They've already gutted the big fish." He shakes his head. "Small fry like me are just a matter o' cleanin' up, if you take my meanin'."

Lord Jonathan nods solemnly, but comes to terms with Sir Gelly's answer. "Well ... there are *other* ways I could help. I understand you're allowed to bring in food from outside. I could—"

Sir Gelly shakes his head. "M'lord, I'm a veteran o' wars. In war, when the hunger come—I mean *real* hunger—I've 'et things I didn't recognize. Things that don't have names, as far as I know. What I eat in this place is no matter to me." He looks up at Jonathan plaintively. "But there's one thing you *could* do for me, m'lord."

"What's that?" asks Lord Jonathan.

Sir Gelly rises and kneels before Jonathan. "You can forgive *me*, m'lord, for my trespasses against you and your family. 'Tis *I* who'll be in need of forgiveness—and ... sooner than your lordship."

Lord Jonathan's eyes tear up. He places his hand gently on Sir Gelly's head, and croaks out the words.

"Sir Gelly Meyrick, without reservation I forgive you your trespasses against me and my family with all my heart and soul, and shall pray for your salvation. So help me God."

IT'S LATE MORNING by the time Noah leaves Bucklebury at the Tower stables and walks to Sir Walter's chambers. He knocks on the door, which is already open.

Sir Walter rises at his desk with an energetic smile. "Why, Serjeant Ames, please come in."

"Good morning, Sir Walter," says Noah. "After spending all those days on the road, it's good to see you again. Have you sent your men for Master Drury?"

Sir Walter nods emphatically. "Some time ago. They should be here with him at any moment." He glances about. "You may meet with him in this chamber, if you like."

Noah nods. "A most gracious offer, Sir Walter, but your men are known to barge in here unannounced. I'd better take a different chamber to avoid interruption."

Sir Walter swings open the door to an adjacent chamber, where two barrels block the way to the desk. Sir Walter beckons two burly Yeomen Warders to roll the barrels away and wipe a film of dust from the desk and chairs. One brings a burning faggot of wood from Sir Walter's fireplace, places it carefully down in Noah's, and tosses on a few pieces of aged wood. Immediately, the cold room takes on a bit of warmth and a welcome scent of the forest.

"Good as new," says Sir Walter. "Please wait inside. I'll have Drury brought to you." He winks. "More official-looking."

In a few minutes, it's become so warm that Noah opens a window. Just then, flanked by two Yeoman Warders, Drury appears. Though he wears no restraints, his expression is surly. *At least he's wearing his coat this time,* thinks Noah.

Noah beckons them all in. "Thank you, Yeoman Warders," he says. "I shall call upon you later." The Warders bow and move off.

Noah takes his seat behind the desk and motions Drury to the opposite chair. "Thank you for coming of your own free will, Master Drury," he says. "Master Groatsworth asked me to have you arrested, but I thought that excessive."

"You think you're fooling everyone, don't you?" snarls Drury.

Noah sits up. "I beg your pardon?"

"You think you're fooling everyone … acting all proper and law-abiding."

"See here, Master Drury," Noah says with all the world-weariness he can muster, "this interview cannot go well for you, if you're to begin it by making false accusations of illegal conduct."

"You think you're impervious, don't you?" Drury continues. "As though you have no vulnerability whatsoever. Well, I happen to know where you live, and that you have a newborn grandson still mewling and puking in his mother's arms."

Noah is sorely tempted to slap him across the face but decides there's more to be gained by listening. "Thank you, Master Drury, for threatening the family of one of Her Majesty's advisors on Crown business. You've thereby provided me with probable cause for your immediate arrest."

"I didn't threaten anybody," says Drury, sulking now.

"Well, I suppose we can leave that question to Queen's Bench," says Noah. "They'll decide between *my* honesty and *your* wantonness." He stares into Drury's eyes.

Drury turns away and shifts uneasily, nervously watching the door from the corner of his eye, as though expecting the Yeoman Warders to return at any moment. "Well?" he says nervously. "Are you going to have me arrested?"

"I'm considering it," says Noah. "I suppose it depends upon the way this interview goes. Why were you following me?"

Drury's caught at unawares. *"W-when?"* he says, looking frightened, while failing miserably to look indignant.

Noah smiles smugly. Getting that reaction feels even better than slapping him in the face would have. "That's a *stupid* reply, isn't it?" he says. "It implies you've followed me on several occasions. All right, allow me to rephrase it. At *any time* you were following me, why were you doing so?"

"I don't know what you mean," says Drury in a sullen pout.

"Don't you, though? Incidentally, lying to me is not a prudent choice on your part."

"When d'you think I was following you?" demands Drury.

Noah smiles smugly enough to infuriate his subject. "That's not how this works, Master Drury. *I* ask the questions. *Understand?*"

Drury nods, a bit defeated.

"Good, now answer my question."

"I'd heard you were going to visit the one who styles herself 'Lady Leicester,'" says Drury with disgust.

"Heard?" says Noah, "You must have learned where I was going at the same moment I did."

"Perhaps a few minutes later," says Drury.

"From whom did you learn where I was going?" asks Noah.

Drury shrinks in his chair. "I'd rather not say," he says.

"Someone at Whitehall Palace?"

Drury looks at the floor and nods.

Noah decides to let the next question pass for the moment.

"Why would Lady Leicester be of interest to one of your station and occupation?" asks Noah.

Drury sits up impatiently. "What has any of this to do with Master Groatsworth's ruined porch?"

Noah rises from behind the desk. He can feel Drury's frightened eyes follow him as he steps behind Drury, picks up a fire iron, and disturbs the angry embers at the base of the fire. "Have you ever been here at the Tower of London, Master Drury?"

"Not until now," Drury admits.

"Ah," says Noah, "then perhaps there's something you can learn. It was easy for you to get into the Tower, you see, but it can be *quite* difficult to get ... *out*. Now, you can continue to try to redirect my questions and stay here for ... oh, quite a while ... or you can *answer* my questions fully and truthfully and leave this afternoon, none the worse for wear."

"What was your question?"

"Ah, now we're getting somewhere," says Noah, returning to his chair. "Why would Lady Leicester be of interest to one of your station and occupation?"

"Well, I have—quite by chance—met Lady Leicester's stepson, Robert Dudley."

Noah waits for the next sentence, but it seems not to be forthcoming. "And he asked you to look in on his stepmother?" suggests Noah.

"No, of course not," scoffs Drury. "I asked him why he was not styled 'Lord Leicester' after his father, and he replied that he'd been misbegotten of Lord Leicester."

"How ... *misbegotten*?" asks Noah.

"Born out of wedlock," says Drury, "or at least he'd been told as much by his stepmother many times throughout his life. Evidently, his father was spineless on the question."

"'Spineless' seems an ungenerous appellation for Lord Leicester, may he rest in peace," says Noah. "He was known for his courage. Was Master Dudley not well provided-for in his father's will?" he asks, as though lacking any knowledge of the matter.

"Young Robert was reasonably well provided-for in his father's will," says Drury. "But in that selfsame will, his stepmother made his father insert the false word 'base' in every reference to young Master Dudley." Drury smiles cynically. "I hate injustice in all its forms, you see."

Noah nods skeptically. "When you're neither the *beneficiary* nor the *cause* of it, I'll warrant—and yet you have pointed out no real injustice in any of this." Noah begins framing his questions to force Drury out into the open. "If young Master Dudley was base born, he is barred from inheriting his father's title, is he not?"

Drury regards Noah with disgust. "And if young Robert was *not* 'base born,' as you call it—if his mother and father were well and truly betrothed, publicly wed, and held themselves out as husband and wife for several years during which the wife bore live issue of the marriage, namely young Robert, he would rather be *legitimate*, would you not say, Serjeant?"

Drury is a tough nut to crack. "That seems to follow," acknowledges Noah. "But why state a hypothetical case when we know it's *not* the case before us?"

"Oh, is it *not*?"

Noah sits up and feigns impartiality. "Is it? Was Master Robert *not* born out of wedlock?"

Just as Noah had hoped, Drury has his back up now and he seems prepared to shed his former reticence. "Robert was *not* base born. He is legitimate, and as such he is the rightful Earl of Leicester."

Noah shrugs. "But you still have not told me the basis of *your* interest in this. What has any of it to do with *you*, sir? Are you in Master Robert's service?"

"No ... at least not yet."

"What proof is there that this ... marriage took place?" Noah asks.

"Some of those who participated in the ceremony live still," protests Drury. "Though the gentleman who gave Robert's mother away to Lord Leicester has sadly passed, there remain alive many who witnessed it, including the servants. Evidence abounds. And there are believed to be extant writings in the hand of the deceased Lord Leicester acknowledging his marriage; personal letters and such."

"To whom would the earl have written such things?"

"It's commonly believed," says Drury, "that the earl corresponded on the subject with his deputy, Sir Henry Neville."

Just as Noah is about to point out the great difference in age between the late earl and Sir Henry (which would render the possibility of such correspondence quite remote), it dawns on him that Drury is not referring to the 'Sir Henry' he just brought back to face justice, but rather to Sir Henry's eponymous *father*.

The memory of a summer's day at Billingbear rushes back so strongly upon Noah that it's as though it were today, and he's in the library with young Sir Henry. *There is a banned publication somewhere in this library*, Henry had said, *entitled Leycester's Commonwealth, published in Antwerp in 1584*. In later years, Noah would read the book and find in it a reference to old Sir Henry's expectations of great advancement ... should the Earl of Leicester become King someday.

Noah returns to the present. "Have you any grudge against Sir Henry Neville?" he asks. "I mean the one who lives today."

"Grudge?" Drury asks with apparent innocence. "None in the least, although I've heard he's been brought back for questioning in Essex's failed rebellion. I'm glad to have steered clear of that disaster."

"If the deceased Sir Henry kept the earl's letters discussing the question of an earlier marriage," muses Noah, "they would likely have been left in the care of *young* Sir Henry, would they not?"

"Stands to reason," says Drury, evidently unsure what Noah's getting at.

"Why," says Noah, "then Lady Leicester and young Robert Dudley would *both* have incentive to see that the earl's letters to Sir Henry never see the light of day—depending upon what they say about the possibility of the earl's prior marriage."

At first Drury reacts with an expression of utter confusion. But—however subject to criticism he may be on moral grounds—he's never been regarded as dim-witted. To the contrary, his reputation is one of cunning. He sits back with an expression of the cat who ate the cream.

"What better way," says Drury, emitting a chesty laugh, "to ensure they never see the light of day than to put an end to their custodian, namely, the younger Sir Henry?" He leans forward and conjectures with uncanny accuracy. "I can see from your expression that *someone's* trying to scuttle Sir Henry. And you think 'tis *I*." He smiles deviously and shakes his head. "But as I just told you, it's my firm belief that, if any such letters are extant, they would prove young Robert's birth to have been legitimate, so *I* have no incentive to seek Sir Henry's destruction."

Noah realizes at that moment that Lady Leicester has *just* such an incentive. *Was it she who had Leveson abducted—in order to preclude any hope of clemency for Sir Henry?* All this time, he's been straining to identify the holder of some unknown, ancient grudge against the Nevilles, while the answer's been in front of his nose the whole time.

Despite his inner turmoil, Noah forces himself to maintain an accusatory expression. "But since you can't be sure what any such letters contain," he says, "you *have* such an incentive yourself, have you not?"

Drury shakes his head smugly and dismisses Noah's accusation with a silent wave of his hand.

"The jig is up, Master Drury," says Noah. "I have come by a note implicitly threatening to slander Lady Leicester's title. As you will recall, you recently wrote upon a document using your left hand. The handwritings are the same."

Drury sulks. "I know nought of what you speak."

Now it's Noah's turn to smirk. "Yes, you do. I doubt I'll do anything with that note for now, Master Drury, but if you persist in menacing Lady Leicester, I expect she'll find a use for it—and much to your misfortune. Lady Leicester has many friends in high places—higher than I once thought possible. If you care for young Master Dudley, you'll not encourage him to pursue the matter. The Crown will stand united against him, and his effort will avail him nothing but fines to pay. I strongly advise you to turn away from this threat to Lady Leicester. 'Tis *family* business of no concern to you and, should you continue in this endeavor, you shall place both yourself and young Robert Dudley at risk of prosecution. Remember, 'he that troubleth his own house shall inherit the wind.'"

"Ah, *Proverbs*!" says Drury.

Noah rises and paces. To turn from the issue at hand, he blurts out, "Why did you shoot down the porch of Master Groatsworth's cottage?"

Drury is plainly surprised by the sudden change of topic. "It was … an accident," he replies.

"Master Groatsworth's carpenter has provided him an estimate of three pounds."

Drury shakes his head sadly. "Highway robbery," he says dismally.

"Have you three pounds to give him, Master Drury?"

Drury sighs. "I have not that amount with me. I wasn't planning on remaining in London long enough to need more money."

Noah steps away from the window toward the opposite end of the room and cocks his head sympathetically. "Just to satisfy my own curiosity, Master Drury, do you mind explaining how destroying someone's porch with a musket can happen … by *accident*?"

Drury looks at the floor. "To tell the truth, Serjeant, I seem to have my own personal demon. A little blond boy. If I ever get my hands on him, I'll know who's behind this spate of awful luck."

Fortunately, Drury is looking at Noah and not toward the window, for, as if on cue, Timothy's blond mane bobs into view outside, then quickly drops out of sight below the sill.

"Please remain seated, Master Drury," says Noah, betraying more alarm than he wishes. "I must attend to something outside for just a moment." He takes his copy of Groatsworth's letter and shoves it into Drury's hands. "You really ought to read this. Here, let me turn your back to the window so the light is better."

Noah marches outside and finds Timothy sitting on the ground beneath the open window. He shoves the boy under his robes and marches him to Sir Walter's vacant office next door. He brings the boy inside, and stoops to look him in the eye.

"Do you know who that is in the other chamber, young man?"

Timothy shakes his head. "No, sir. I couldn't see from outside."

"It's Thomas Drury, with whom you had a run-in the other night." Suspiciously, he asks, "What did you overhear just now?"

"Not much, suh," says Timothy. "I heard 'im say he knows where you live and that you got a grandson." Anger crosses his face for a moment, but disappears just as quickly.

Noah shakes his head. "Well, did you hear him refer to his personal demon—who happens to be a blond boy?"

Timothy smiles benignly. "I been called worse," he says dismissively.

Noah wags his finger in the boy's face. "He must not see you, so stay right where you are and keep your head down. Are we clear?"

Timothy plops on the floor with his legs folded. "Clear, suh," he says.

Noah steps outside and re-enters the examination room.

"This is mostly a pack of lies, Serjeant," says Drury, indicating Groatsworth's letter.

"We don't take such accusations at face value, Master Thomas," says Noah reassuringly. "We always assume there's another side of the story, which is why we interview the accused. Still," he says, wandering over to the desk, "there's the matter of the three pounds. If I were to tender that amount to Master Groatsworth on your behalf, would you repay me when you return to your home from London?"

Drury looks as though he's been reprieved from an interminable sentence. His eyebrows rise. "I *would*, sir, and count myself fortunate to have met you."

"Very well," says Noah. "Only I ask that you send it to my home."

He winks, something he rarely does, as he regards it as out of character. "That should avoid inquiry about whether I've misappropriated monies given me for the payment of Crown informants." In fact, it's Noah's personal money, so there's no chance of that.

Drury smiles with relief. "I shall surely do so, sir."

"And there's one more favor you can do for me, Master Drury," says Noah cautiously.

Drury shakes his head in dismay. "I might have known. What's that?"

"I ask your word as a gentleman that you shall let the matter concerning Lady Leicester rest for the time being—for two years from now—and that, during such time, you shall do nought to prod Master Dudley to action."

To Noah's surprise, Drury's apparently giving the proposal some thought; he'd thought Drury would simply give his word and then break it.

"Two years is quite a long time to ask in exchange for three pounds," Drury says skeptically.

Noah laughs. "I'm not *giving* you three pounds, Master Drury. 'Tis a loan—and yet I'm asking neither security nor usury. Consider what I'm asking you to be ... a return favor."

"And if I refuse?" asks Drury.

"I'll still lend you the money, but then I'll know what kind of man I'm dealing with."

Drury sighs and casts a look of grudging admiration at Noah, as though he'd bested him at cards.

Finally, Drury nods. "You have my word."

Noah nods and summons the Yeoman Warders. "Please return Master Drury to his home. There will be no charges." He hands three one-pound coins to the elder Warder. "Please hand these to Master Groatsworth, the complaining witness, and explain they're for the carpenter's repairs. And don't forget to bring me a signed receipt."

"Aye, sir," says the elder Warder. "Right away, sir."

Noah watches the Warders escort Drury across the courtyard and leave the Tower. He forces himself to count to sixty, and returns to Sir Walter's office where Timothy dutifully awaits, still seated on the floor.

"Now, Timothy, what is it that couldn't await my return home?"

"It's Sir Henry Neville, suh. His wife and children are back in London from Dover, but her father won't let them back in the house at Lothbury."

Noah regards the boy with concern. "Did he say why not?"

The boy nods, chagrined to repeat such cross words. "He said, 'No traitor to the Crown shall enter my house, except on *orders* of the Crown.'"

Just then Sir Walter Raleigh returns to his office and finds Noah and Timothy engaged in serious conversation.

"Can I offer my assistance?" asks Sir Walter.

Noah turns to him. "We'll be out of your hair presently, Sir Walter. Do you know whether Lord Robert is here at the Tower?"

"You may be in luck," says Sir Walter. "He'll soon be bound for a meeting of the Privy Council at Whitehall, but if you rush, you might catch him still in chambers."

Noah and Timothy bow silently and race to the stairs to Lord Robert's chambers.

CHAPTER 15

LATER THAT DAY, Noah and Cheerful take a carriage to the Lord Admiral's house in Chelsea, where they're greeted by the footman.

"Is Sir Henry in residence?" asks Noah.

"Who shall I say is calling?" asks the footman, pointing his chin at Cheerful.

"Serjeant Noah Ames of the Tower, with Master David Killigrew of … Oxford, if he can ever drag himself up there. No. Say he's of Cornwall."

"Won't you please come in and wait in the vestibule," says the footman, "if you would?"

As soon as the footman is out of hearing, Cheerful says, "What was that comment about Oxford for? I'm in good standing there. In my fact, my grades are quite good."

"I'm sorry, David," says Noah. "I meant no reflection upon you. I was regretting, rather, the excessive number of times I've prodded you to assist me here in London in the past few weeks."

The footman reappears. "Sir Henry has asked me to escort you two gentlemen to the upstairs salon. Please follow me."

They follow him up the stairs past glowering portraits of numerous notables, all no doubt related to the Lord Admiral. Sir Henry awaits them in the library. The footman bows and leaves the three of them alone.

Before beginning, Noah glances about the library. "Where is your guard?" he asks.

"What matter?" asks Sir Henry indifferently as he carefully pours three cups from a casket of light red wine. "We must assume they're everywhere—and they may well be." He glances at the walls replete with paintings and priceless furnishings, any one of which might conceal someone listening in. He finishes the pour, takes his own glass, and motions for Noah and David to partake. "You two seem in earnest. Why have you come?"

Cheerful replies. "We've just left Lord Robert at Whitehall."

"Quite a coincidence," says Sir Henry, collapsing into a comfortable chair by the fire. "I was there only this morning—before the Privy Council." In a brief moment, he seems on the verge of sleep.

Noah and Cheerful take their glasses and assume nearby chairs.

Noah shakes his head. "I must say, Sir Henry, I'm surprised how calm you've managed to remain in the face of present difficulties."

Sir Henry rubs his eyes, and the worry suddenly becomes apparent. He seems on the verge of tears. "I've … *er* … been busy at the Lord Admiral's claret since returning from the council this morning. I'm afraid he's a better host than I a guest." He takes a sip. "What news?"

"Uncle Henry," says Cheerful, "Lord Robert has prevailed upon the Privy Council to issue an order to my grandfather requiring him to allow Auntie Anne and your children—and me—back into the house at Lothbury."

Sir Henry knits his brow. "*Allow?* Has Lady Anne reached London so quickly?"

Noah's confused. "She has, Sir Henry. Are you unaware?"

Sir Henry shrugs listlessly. "I was, until you just told me." He regards them both skeptically. "Did m'lady's father refuse them admittance?"

Cheerful nods glumly. "He did. He said he would not admit a traitor to his house unless ordered to do so by the Privy Council."

Noah reaches into his pocket. "We applied to Lord Robert for such an order immediately. I caught him before he left the Tower for Westminster this afternoon. We stopped at Lothbury, where we found David lingering outside like a lost sheep. David and I accompanied Lord Robert to Whitehall, where he argued valiantly for this order." He withdraws a sealed paper from his pocket and waves it in the air.

Sir Henry, lost in a cloud of spirits, seems vaguely bewildered, and his listlessness is wearing Noah's patience thin.

Sir Henry asks, "Where is Lady Anne now?"

"Where is—*Where is Lady Anne?*" Noah echoes incredulously. "That's what we've come here to find out. We haven't had occasion to consult with Lord Jonathan. In fact, we're not quite sure where *he* is, either. Evidently, 'twas he who dispatched young Timothy to fetch me at the Tower. I haven't been at home since." He shrugs. "Perhaps he's there."

Sir Henry takes another sip. "I would conjecture that Lady Anne is at your home, as well. Where else could she bring the children near the City of London? A public house?" His lip quivers, which downright infuriates

Noah.

"David," Noah says in a commanding voice, "await me downstairs and have the footman bring the horses 'round. We're leaving for Lothbury to serve this blasted writ on your grandfather, then we're going straight away to Holborn to escort Lady Anne and your cousins back to their Lothbury home. I need a private word or two with Sir Henry."

David rises, knocks back his claret in one gulp (in sound Oxford fashion), and leaves the way he came, closing the library door behind him.

Noah stands, approaches Sir Henry so his lips are only inches away from his friend's ear, and whispers, "*Damn* you, Henry! Don't you dare give up. You have too many people depending upon you to enfold yourself in your personal tragedy. And I'll be damned *myself* if I'll pursue your interests while you medicate yourself into oblivion." He knocks over Henry's empty glass, and immediately regrets doing so. Becalming himself, he says, "Count your blessings, foremost among which is that you have well-placed friends."

Noah looks again into Sir Henry's eyes. At last he sees an incipient struggle for purpose, foggy though the brain may yet be.

Sir Henry reaches into his pocket and pulls out a scrivener's document. "I—" he begins, and swallows with dread, "I gave an oral statement to the Privy Council this morning. It was transcribed, and I got two copies. One's for you," he says, handing the paper to Noah. "I warn you, you're not going to like it, but I promise I shall hear your advice before giving further evidence."

Noah kisses Sir Henry on the forehead, and pockets the paper. He's reached the door by the time his friend begins to croak out a few more words. He turns to hear.

"Thank you," says Sir Henry at last, in a strangled voice.

"God bless you, Sir Henry," replies Noah. "Prepare for a fight."

Sir Henry nods slowly. "*Life* is a fight," he intones, as though reaffirming something he's always known.

Noah descends the stairs to the vestibule, where David patiently waits with the Lord Admiral's footman.

"Well, David," says Noah, "we've a call to make in Lothbury."

The footman coughs politely.

Noah has no idea what he's forgotten. "Have I ... misspoken?" he asks.

David smiles. "It appears we'll be back here this evening."

"If I may, Master Killigrew," says the footman in a decidedly erudite, upper-class accent. "Serjeant, the Lord Admiral was most perturbed to hear that you'd declined his recent invitation to dine—"

Noah's eyebrows shoot up. "Wh—But the Lord Admiral was not even going to be present for the meal! I trust you passed along our compliments and informed the Lord Admiral that Lord Saint Ives and I were needed on other Crown business that very evening."

The footman smiles as though *every* invited guest misunderstands the same thing. "Serjeant," says the footman, "I assure you that I informed the Lord Admiral of *precisely* what you said—and of your most courteous reply. But, you see, the Lord Admiral is accustomed to having his invitations regarded as, rather ... *commands*. You will be pleased to know that the Lord Admiral *will* be in attendance at the ... meal, as you call it, and that you, Lord Saint Ives, and Master Killigrew here are ... *invited"*—he winks conspiratorially—"this evening together with your three ladies. I know that you, Serjeant, are happily married, and that the courageous Lord Saint Ives is happily married to your daughter, Lady Jessica, whose reputation, may I say, for beauty, grace, and patriotic courage positively *fascinates* the Lord Admiral. He has expressed a strong desire to meet her."

"You know—" begins Noah, but he's evidently failed to realize the footman is not quite finished.

"The Lord Admiral is well aware that Lady Jessica has recently brought forth a new member of the family, a young gentleman by the venerable English name of 'Arthur,' I believe. If her ladyship cannot find someone to remain with the child, the Lord Admiral has offered to send Lydia—she's nursemaid for half the earls visiting London—to m'lady's home or, if her ladyship prefers, the Lord Admiral will send an escort for your whole company, and her ladyship is welcome to bring young Arthur with her. We are well equipped to attend to children here, and shall have Lydia tend to the child without fail. Of course, that's assuming mother and child are both well, and fit to travel all the way from ... Holborn, I believe?"

The footman's pronunciation of the name *Lydia* is so very upper-class that it sounds as if the name consists of only two syllables: "lid" and "ja."

So unprepared is Noah for this compulsory invitation that he cannot think of a reply.

The footman smiles to see his bewilderment. "Although Master Killigrew here is unwed, I expect he'll have no problem finding an appropriate companion. So, Serjeant, unless the Lord Admiral's royal cousin has commanded you *not* to attend"—he laughs lightly at the absurdity—"we look forward to seeing you all at eight."

Noah smiles at the footman's barrage of well-chosen words. "Well, even I can see how the land lies in this instance," says Noah. "What did you say your name was?"

"I didn't say, sir, but it's Matthew."

"Very well, Matthew. I yield to your superior knowledge of the Lord Admiral's expectations and gladly accept his gracious invitation, but please bear in mind that I'm not sure everyone can be notified in time. In fact, if you would be so kind as to send a note to my home at once informing one and all of the invitation, it would be most appreciated. They will be furious with me if they're given insufficient time to prepare. At this very moment, you see, Master Killigrew and I cannot go there; instead, we must make immediate arrangements for Sir Henry's wife and children to stay in London—which presents me with a bit of a dilemma, I'm afraid. I expect Lady Anne is presently at my home and, if she hears of the invitation, she will be more than dismayed not to be invited."

Matthew equivocates, thinking aloud. "Well, Her Majesty's instructions are that Sir Henry shall receive no visitors."

"Will my family not be visitors?" asks Noah.

"Well, you'll be guests of the Lord Admiral."

"Perhaps the Lord Admiral would care to invite Lady Anne as *another* of his guests?"

Matthew smiles cagily. "I'm certain he'll wish to do so."

Noah's surprised. "Can you extend such an invitation without first raising it with him?"

"He trusts me with such things, I assure you. I shall add her invitation to my note to be sent to your home. Incidentally, which lady shall I have it handed to?"

Noah laughs. "Doesn't matter. Any grown woman there will do. Tell one, tell all, y'know?"

<hr />

FOR WHAT SEEMS AN HOUR, Noah awaits Sir Henry Killigrew in the vestibule at the base of the central stairs at Lothbury. At last, the aged Sir Henry appears at the top of the stairs supported by a manservant, and the two descend deliberately.

"Serjeant Ames," says the dour Sir Henry in his husky voice when they're nearly halfway down, "I've been advised that you wish to speak with me."

Noah smiles. "*Well*-advised, as it turns out, Sir Henry, for to speak with you is precisely my reason for coming."

Sir Henry's eyes dart about. "Where is David? I was told he was here with you."

"He's right outside the front door here, sir. Out of respect for you, he's declined to enter until he's invited in."

"You mean 'unless' he's invited in," sniffs Old Killigrew. At last, he reaches the base of the stairs and dismisses his manservant with a wave of his hand.

"I have here," says Noah, "the order you requested from the Privy Council, so I expect young David shall be invited in presently."

"See here, young man," says Sir Henry, upbraiding Noah for his impertinence, "just because the Privy Council may have given me *leave* to admit my daughter's family—"

"Oh, it's not *leave*, sir," says Noah. "It's a *command*, just as you requested." Noah hands Sir Henry the writ.

Though Sir Henry accepts the writ, he looks away from Noah in light of his insolence. "I take it you have read it?" he asks.

"I have, sir," Noah assures him. "It's quite clear in its tenor. Lord Robert was quite impressed by your refusal to admit Sir Henry Neville and his family, but even *more* impressed by your insistence upon uniting the whole family in this house."

"Hmph," grunts Sir Henry. "I'd no idea that's what I was doing, but very well," he says. "Summon David and he'll be admitted."

"Oh, Sir Henry," says Noah. "I'm so pleased to have brought many more than merely David. Your daughter and her family are even now coming up your drive with all their things." He bows to the old man, who seems rather bewildered by this sudden turn of events, and goes out of the door having no wish to witness the cold greeting Old Killigrew is sure to receive from his ruffled daughter.

Remounting Bucklebury, Noah reminds David of their mutual invitation and rides off to Holborn wondering what kind of greeting he'll receive, having given the ladies so little advance notice of the evening's entertainment.

CHAPTER 16

BY THE TIME Noah leaves Bucklebury in his stables, it's nearly dark. Tom the stableman has rolled out the carriage and busies himself wiping it down, inside and out, in preparation for this evening's short journey to Chelsea.

As Noah can readily imagine the pandemonium taking place in the house, before going inside he steals a contemplative moment to gaze westward toward the sun that's just slipped under a horizon streaked in pink and red. To the south, for the moment the sky has retained its daytime azure, yet a star twinkles brightly there as it never would in full daylight.

Then he ponders the new astronomical theory he learned about from Sir Henry Neville, that the earth revolves about the sun, just as the other planets do. And the possibility occurs to him that the bright body is not a star at all, but rather one of earth's sister planets. He shakes his head. Astronomy is not his field, but it bewilders him that so much he learned at university has lately been discredited—at least by those subscribing to the new theory. He wonders if such a revolution will ever take place in the stodgy field of the law, which is inherently backward-looking.

He takes a breath and opens the door to his house. Before he can even step into the vestibule, a female figure with a towel on her head rushes past, nearly knocking into him. The sound of the house is madness itself, as though every drawer were being drawn open or shoved shut. Same with the closets. Trunks are being dragged about, but as yet he's seen no faces.

At last, Marie gazes down at him from upstairs.

"Well, if it isn't Serjeant Ames!" she says, half in jest. "Perhaps you're here to tell us we've got the time wrong and must be in Chelsea an hour earlier than we were told!"

"No, Marie. You've got the time right, I'm sure. Where's Lord Jonathan?"

"He's asleep in a servant's room," she says and disappears into the upstairs bedroom.

Noah walks to the back of the house and tries the doors to several rooms before he finds Jonathan asleep in one. He takes a seat at the foot of the bed. "I am amazed," he says quietly, "that you are able to sleep through this din."

Jonathan opens one groggy eye. "Oh, 'tis you, Noah," he says. "Sleeping is a method of escape I've had from youth. When women start primping, I start dozing." Instead of opening his other eye, he closes the open one. "Esther's been looking for you. She seemed upset, but she calmed down a good deal before I came in here to dodge the madness." He suddenly opens his eyes and sits up abruptly. "Do you know Esther told me the strangest things?"

"Such as?" asks Noah, dreading a report of yet another macabre vision.

"The little blond boy?" says Jonathan. "Timothy? She says he loves Arthur like a brother."

Noah scowls. "How could he love Arthur? Has he even *seen* the child?"

"Oh, he's seen the baby a few times, and seems fascinated by him, but that's common enough. If you can believe it, she says, 'If you take Timothy in and educate him, he'll be Arthur's lifelong friend, like a caring older brother.' She says Timothy would lay down his life for Arthur's sake. And then she says, as though under a spell, 'During Arthur's eighteenth year, Timothy will save his life, though he may thereby lose his own.' How the devil could she know these things?"

Noah can only shrug. "I've no idea. What did she wish to speak with *me* about?"

Jonathan shrugs. "You're on your own there," he says as he lies back and seems to fall asleep at once.

If he's faking, he's doing a good job of it, thinks Noah. He rises and leaves the room.

Almost immediately, he's spotted by Esther, who looks nearly ready for their excursion. "You look lovely, Esther," he says, "as you always do."

Esther places her hands on her hips. "Serjeant Ames, where have you been?"

"Where have I been?" he echoes without replying, and throws his hands up. He marches off to his study and sits behind the desk. Not until he turns about does he realize Esther's followed him in. Against his better judgment, he tries to explain. "Dear Esther," he says, "I have been racing about London ensuring that Lady Anne and her children will have a roof over their heads tonight. Do you suppose that cause is worthy enough to justify my absence?"

Esther begins brushing her hair absent-mindedly. "Lady Anne and her brood left here only an hour ago. Can you *believe* that her father wouldn't let her return to Lothbury until he'd got permission from the *Queen*?"

She clearly hasn't heard a word he's said. A thousand possible retorts volley about Noah's head, but the best he can do is a privately sardonic, "You don't say?"

She stops brushing her hair, and shakes the brush at him. "They *beat* him," she says earnestly.

The lack of any antecedent to her pronouncement leaves him wondering how she could possibly hope to be understood by anyone unfamiliar with the inner workings of her mind. *What's this? They beat Old Killigrew?*

"Who beat whom?" he asks wearily.

"Near the gate," she adds.

Noah rolls his eyes. "Not Ludgate again."

She shakes her head, as though his conjecture is absurdly foolish and he's simply refusing to take her seriously. "No, the other one. Bishopsgate." She turns and walks out of his study.

Bishopsgate? he marvels, and follows her out, catching up to her in the kitchen. Perhaps dividing his question into smaller parts will yield him an answer. "*Who's* been beaten?"

She points the brush at him again, and shakes it in time to her words. "You know him." She raises her eyebrows as though guessing. "*Dooley?*"

He knows no one by that name. "*Dooley?*" he echoes and shrugs.

"*Tsk, tsk!*" Esther clucks and regards him skeptically, as though he's being deliberately dense. "*Droopy,* perhaps?"

"Oh, yes, Esther!" he says sardonically. "My old mate Droopy of Bishopsgate. Wait!" he says, "Do you mean *Drury*?"

"Yes, that's it, like the name of the local street," she says. She rolls her eyes heavenward. "Sorry," she says as though she's not sorry in the least.

Just then Marie enters the kitchen. "Esther, have you seen my pearl hairclip?" she asks, momentarily ignoring her husband until she turns to him and says, "I want you to know, Serjeant Ames, that Lady Jessica would not have taken her newborn out in this frigid winter for anyone in the world. Not even for the Lord Admiral! It's a good thing her Aunt Beth was available to watch over Arthur, or Lady Jessica would have refused to go, and the Lord Admiral's men would have had to come by and toss her into prison—and me *with* her."

Noah frowns. "Oh, dear," he says to Marie, "there's no call to be so dramatic." He turns back to Esther. "*Who* was beating Drury?"

Marie throws her hands up and marches off.

"No, madam," says Esther to Marie's retreating figure. "I have *not* seen your hairclip." Then her face lights up, and she runs after Marie, who's already climbing the stairs. "It's in your second drawer from the bottom, Mother. I saw it there not long ago."

Esther turns about and is patently surprised to see that Noah's followed her from the kitchen. "Serjeant Ames, did you ask me something?"

Before he can reply, Marie's voice rings out upstairs. "Found it, thank you!" she intones.

Noah gently takes Esther by both wrists to command her attention. "Esther, *who* was beating Drury at Bishopsgate?"

"There were many. Each had a stick and was beating him about the chest and back." She seems to be searching her memory. "No one struck his face."

"But *who* were the people who were beating him?" demands Noah.

Her face softens. "Children. Many children. Oh, they struck him quite hard. But he's alive. Just bruised."

"*Children* were beating Drury?" he asks, and then is himself struck by a possibility. "Could it have been *Timothy* doing the beating?"

She regards him as though he's daft. "Timothy's been at Jacob's the whole time," she says, "tending to the invalid Leah, and doing a wonderful job of it. Leah's losing control over her limbs. Very sad," she says wistfully, "very sad."

"It was *not* Timothy, though," he confirms with a sense of relief.

"Doing the beating? Oh, no, not Timothy, the dear lad."

"Well, thank heaven for that much," says Noah.

Esther adds, "But he *is* the one who sent them."

JONATHAN ACCOMPANIES NOAH to the small outbuilding occupied by Jacob and Leah, and (for the time being) Timothy.

Trudging through the cold past the unfinished brick structure that will serve as the main part of Jonathan and Jessica's new home, Jonathan remarks, "The workmen will be starting again in two more weeks."

"Will they be finished with the main portion of the house by summertime?" asks Noah.

"Who knows?" says Jonathan. "To return to more pressing matters, we'll be leaving for the Lord Admiral's within the half hour. Did you intend to change your robes?"

Noah shakes his head. "No. Silks are fit for every occasion. I doubt the Lord Admiral will be scandalized by the sameness of my appearance. I'm more concerned about Timothy's propensity to take matters into his own hands."

Jonathan nods. "You're rightly concerned," he says. "Timothy is far too young to make such decisions."

As they reach the door, Jonathan knocks lightly.

Jacob opens it, looking quite melancholy. He bows to Jonathan and admits the two newcomers promptly, before much heat can escape.

Jonathan's glad to see that the quarters are quite warm despite the weather. For these three unassuming people, there's ample space, consisting of a principal room with a large fireplace (now housing a goodly fire) and a sleeping room off to one side.

Before the fire sits a table with three chairs; two are occupied by Jacob's elderly wife Leah and young Timothy, who's helping her to eat. Jonathan draws the inference that the third chair was occupied by Jacob until he knocked.

"Please, Jacob, sit," says Jonathan. "We meant no interruption."

"No, m'lord. I'd rather stand if it's all the same to you."

With an expression of incredulity, Leah watches helplessly as her hands twist themselves into a most awkward, painful-looking position, until they appear poised to claw at someone, as might a witch in a folk tale, except that her claws are turned inward on herself.

Before her on the table sits a bowl of porridge and a soiled spoon.

"Come, Mother Leah," says Timothy in kindly manner, "we'll fix that up right away." He picks up a clean, moist rag, deftly wipes away a spoonful of porridge that's splashed across Leah's right hand, wipes the spoon as well, and puts it down neatly beside the bowl. He gives her his sweetest smile. "That's why we let the porridge cool first, isn't that right?"

Leah, near tears, struggles for words, but gives up after a few tries. She seems strangely unyielding as Timothy takes her gnarled right hand and begins to knead it gently, which he does for only a few seconds before the hand begins to relax.

"Give me the other hand now, Mother Leah," he says, and she does so as she stares mournfully at nothing in particular.

Jacob removes a handkerchief and weeps briefly. With reddened eyes, he looks up at Noah and Jonathan and whispers, "She won't let me tend to her so ... intimate-like. He's a godsend, this boy. Made o' the milk o' human kindness. When Cuthbert was ... killed, I thought that she was a goner for sure, but then the good Lord sends us this one, and ... it only goes to show we must never give up hope."

Jonathan places his hand on the old man's shoulder. "She'll want for nought as long as she lives, Jacob, nor will her loving husband. You two will stay with us"—Jonathan pauses to admire what he formerly deemed humble surroundings—"until neither of you has any use for this place."

Jacob takes Jonathan's hand and kisses it. "Thank you, m'lord," says Jacob. "I never in a million years would have guessed that proud little boy in Old Jewry would become our prop in old age. You're a godsend, too. I don't know what Leah or I ever did to deserve such kindness, but it's"—he chokes up and waits for it to pass—"it's more appreciated than you'll ever know."

Leah's hands seem to have fully relaxed now, and Timothy hands her back the spoon. She calmly takes a few spoonfuls, though with little determination. Still, she's getting the job done.

Jonathan turns to Jacob. "Actually, Jacob, we have very little time right now. Serjeant Ames and I came to have a word with Timothy, if you can spare him for a moment."

"O' course, sir," says Jacob. "Tim," he says, "these gentlemen came to have a word with you." He takes the vacant chair and sits at the table. "I'll tend to Leah for a moment. You'll trust me to do that, won't ye?"

Timothy smiles. "Of course," he says. Although he seems about to pardon himself to Leah, he thinks better of it as it's obvious she's oblivious to her surroundings. He gets up, bows to Jonathan and beckons them both into the sleeping room for some privacy. Jonathan and Noah follow him in, and he closes the door behind them.

"What can I do for you, gentlemen?" asks Timothy.

Jonathan motions for Noah to do the talking.

"Timothy," he says, beginning hesitantly, "did you ask your ... young friends to give a thrashing to Master Drury?"

"How do you know he had a thrashing?" he says without surprise. "Miss Esther told you, didn't she?"

"Answer the question, Timothy," says Jonathan. "If you're going to be a gentleman, you must learn to act like one, and that includes learning a sense of honor and responsibility to others."

"A *gentleman*, suh?" asks Timothy. "How could I ever—"

"As long as you behave yourself in a manner becoming my house," says Jonathan, "I shall have you educated, and you shall serve this house at least until you have graduated university, and after, for as long as you wish. But in exchange for this, I will need your word not only to behave yourself with reserve and honor that will bring respect and accolades upon my family, but always to be truthful to the whole family. Especially to me."

Timothy's mouth hangs open, as he begins to see the scope of what's being offered. "M'lord, I shall do so until then, and always ... so long as you allow me to protect Master Arthur."

Noah interjects. "You must learn to protect Master Arthur as a *gentleman* protects those he loves. And that precludes sending your friends to beat a man you hardly know."

Timothy recovers from learning of his good fortune. "Serjeant Ames, I heard Drury say that he knows where you live and that you have a grandson, and that you should feel—" He's at a loss for the word.

"Vulnerable," says Noah, supplying the word against his better judgment.

Timothy nods. "Where I come from, sir, one needs friends and protection from a man like that."

Noah nods. "I understand what you mean, Timothy, but you are young, and not yet fit to know how to take measures proportional to the threat. You must learn restraint."

Timothy looks Noah square in the eye. "I shall do as you say, suh, but I did use restraint."

Noah regards him awry. "You used restraint?" he asks incredulously.

"Aye, sir," replies the boy. "Drury's not dead, and that's no accident, suh."

Noah turns to Jonathan. "M'lord, would you leave me alone with Master Timothy for a moment?"

Jonathan nods and leaves the room.

Noah turns to Timothy and tousles his blond hair. "Young man, you have no idea how fortunate you are. If you manage yourself as m'lord has said, you'll have an interesting and fruitful future."

Timothy is overwhelmed by this favorable change in the winds of fortune. "I know, suh; I'm not stupid. Oh, but it's hard for me to tell a gentleman like you how I feel right now."

Noah smiles wryly. "Oh, I know it well."

Timothy cannot conceal his surprise. "But how could you know how it feels, sir?"

Noah laughs chestily. "Something like it happened to me once. Long ago. You and I are two peas in a pod; more than you know."

———————————◦◦⊂⊘⊃◦◦⊂———————————

SUPPER AT THE LORD ADMIRAL'S HOUSE is a more sedate affair than expected, though the right mix of people is in attendance: a Church of England theologian, two philosophers from the Continent, and a smattering of near-royals, some lesser nobles such as Lord and Lady Saint Ives, as well as a few amiable commoners having temporary business with the Lord Admiral, such as the Ameses.

Still, despite all the footman's talk of the Lord Admiral's great desire to meet Lord Jonathan and Lady Jessica (and the Lord Admiral's undeniably courtly reception of them), Noah can't help but harbor the feeling that he himself was the reason for the family's invitation. Or perhaps these thoughts are merely the product of Echo whispering in the ear of Narcissus. Time will tell.

At the end of the meal, before the men retire to the parlor and leave the ladies to their spirits, the Lord Admiral says (to all in attendance, as it strikes Noah), "I wonder whether anyone has seen or heard from Leveson since the standoff at Ludgate. I've been trying to get hold of him, but he seems rather to have disappeared."

The assembled are extraordinarily quiet, awaiting the outcome of the Lord Admiral's inquiry.

Jonathan, after waiting a decent interval for others of higher station to speak, breaks the awkward silence. "Leveson testified at the trial of Lords Essex and Southampton, Lord Admiral, as I expect you are aware. I personally searched for him immediately afterwards, but was unable to find him."

"Where did you search, Lord Jonathan?" asks the Lord Admiral.

"I searched the carriage area immediately outside Westminster Hall," replies Jonathan. "As I grew increasingly alarmed, I confess I took the rather extreme measure of opening the doors of departing carriages to see if he was there."

From the opposite end of the dining room, a tipsy older gentleman rises with mock indignity and says, "So that was *you*!"

His wife, a stern-faced older woman seated beside him, says with some irritation, "Oh, sit down, Philip! You're embarrassing yourself." This is greeted with general merriment and calls for more wine.

Lord Jonathan rises with his cup in his hand, bows apologetically to the fellow (who bows in return), and says: "I sincerely apologize to you, sir, and to any whom I offended that day. Although my actions were unforgivable, I can plead that it was all in a good cause." His apology is greeted with general applause.

Before sitting down, Jonathan takes a good look at the fellow and his wife. They're roughly the same age. He does indeed remember the fellow from the day of the trial, but the woman in his carriage that day was younger than his wife by a good thirty years.

The Lord Admiral, never wont to indulge general gaiety, turns to Noah. "And you, Serjeant Ames, have you any idea where Leveson might be?" he asks, then hastens to add, "Or do you know anyone *else* who might have cause to know?"

Noah's practiced law long enough to know that when someone asks a second question before any attempt has been made to answer the first, it means the first was mere pretext.

He's heard that Lady Leicester has consulted with me, and suspects she's had Leveson abducted, he thinks. Regardless that Noah's representation is being conducted under the pretext of helping Lady *Essex*, his "secret" consultation with Lady Leicester is probably well known in the upper echelons of the court—and *no one* is more highly placed than the Lord Admiral, nor closer to the Queen.

But what of the Lord Admiral's suspicion that Lady Leicester's had Leveson abducted? While the Lord Admiral *might* have heard that Noah has conducted more than one interview with Drury, there's no obvious way for him to draw a connection between Drury and the interested party, namely, young Robert Dudley. And, it's even more unlikely that the Lord Admiral could guess that her object is to suppress the publication of letters in the custody of his current "guest," namely, Sir Henry Neville.

All of which means that, by whatever back channels, the Lord Admiral has heard that Leveson was abducted at Lady Leicester's behest, and he probably couldn't care less what personal reasons she might have had for doing so.

Noah smiles apologetically at the Lord Admiral. "Alas," he says, "I have no idea where Master Leveson is, Lord Admiral."

The Lord Admiral is visibly disappointed.

"But I *do* have," adds Noah, "a strong suspicion who might be responsible and, although I cannot divulge who that might be, I assure the Lord Admiral that I shall handle the necessary interview expeditiously."

The Lord Admiral smiles furtively and nods to Noah that he's confident his unspoken message has been received.

Noah rises and raises his cup. "To the Lord Admiral, England's savior!"

WHILE THE AMES LADIES and their escorts mill about in the Lord Admiral's vestibule all bundled up and ready to depart, the Lord Admiral's footman approaches Noah with a letter in his hand and politely takes him aside.

"Yes, Matthew," says Noah with surprise. "Did a letter come for me here?"

"Yes, Serjeant, one did," says the footman. "I hasten to add that the staff is under strict instructions not to interrupt the meal for any reason, and I sincerely hope the brief delay will not cause you any inconvenience."

Noah steps aside and opens the letter. It's brief and to the point. *Kindly attend me at Lady Essex's rooms tomorrow morning at 10 sharp. I have received a note from our mutual friend falsely accusing me of having him thrashed.* It's signed *Lady Leicester.*

Noah smiles. So Lady Leicester's taking the fall for little Timothy's interference. *Good.*

He turns to the footman. "No inconvenience," he says, palming him a coin. "None whatever," he says patting him on the back.

CHAPTER 17

BEFORE HEADING OFF to Lady Leicester's the next morning, Noah sits before the fire in his study reviewing the statement given by Sir Henry Neville to the Privy Council the day after being escorted home from Dover.

As he recalls, when Sir Henry handed Noah the transcript, he'd warned him that he wouldn't like it.

And he most assuredly doesn't.

Before the council, Sir Henry admitted seeing Sir Henry Cuffe, who invited him to meet with Southampton and Essex's man Sir Charles Danvers at Drury House. Sir Henry testified that, at four o'clock on Candlemas Day, he was leaving Serjeants' Inn when he saw a passing carriage carrying Essex, Southampton, Blount, and Danvers. The testimony that follows sorely tries Noah's temper.

There, after some ordinary salutations, Sir Henry testified, *because I had never spoken with my Lord of Southampton since he was a child in my old Lord Treasurer's house, my lord began to break to me their plans.*

Noah shakes his head in dismay, as Sir Henry's statement that he hadn't seen Southampton since childhood was a bald-faced lie—readily disproven—that will doubtless be used by prosecutors to cast doubt upon every word of Sir Henry's testimony. The *one thing* he'd implored Sir Henry not to lie about was the closeness of his acquaintance with Southampton, which turns out to be the only thing he *did* lie about.

Almost as bad is the phrase *my lord began to break to me their plans,* which is comprised of five poetic feet, each consisting of two syllables with the accent always on the second. In other words, the line is framed in *iambic pentameter,* as all the works of Shakespeare are widely known to be. The line could be inserted undetectably after the first two lines of *Romeo and Juliet*: Two 'households, 'both a'like in 'digni'ty/ In 'fair Ver'ona, 'where we 'lay our 'scene/ *My 'lord be'gan to 'break to 'me their 'plans.*

His blood boils. Why would someone denying he's Shakespeare choose to frame his testimony precisely as Shakespeare would have done for the public stage? There's evidently some confusion in Sir Henry's mind between his fantasy world and brutal reality. He needs to be reminded that the executioner's axe head is not woven of gossamer, but hammered out of cold, hard steel.

At quarter past nine, Tom brings Bucklebury around. As Noah begins his short trip to Essex House, he mentally prepares himself for a likely confrontation with Lady Leicester, the outcome of which may depend upon how artfully he frames his demand and how desperately she feigns outrage at it.

⸻ ◦◦ ⸻

ESSEX HOUSE APPEARS peaceful enough, reminding Noah of an ancient battlefield. The compacted snow of the rebellion has thawed, and the particles of soil formerly suspended within it have settled back into the earth of the garden. The blood has likewise seeped into the ground leaving no trace of color—no doubt to nourish some trivial shrub in the coming spring.

So be it. Dust to dust.

Noah hands off Bucklebury to the stableman and knocks on the front door. The footman answers, and Noah shows him Lady Leicester's note inviting him to appear at ten.

"Please come in, sir," says the footman. "M'lady is expecting you."

But before the footman can lead the way, young Lady Essex appears, kneading her hands, although whether with cold or worry Noah cannot tell.

Noah bows deeply and meets her gaze. He cannot but think how fortunate Essex has been to have this soft creature to share his life with. He wonders if soon she will become like her mother-in-law, striking out at a world that seems intent on stealing everything from her. *Is that what widowhood does to a woman?*

"Please come in, Serjeant Ames," says Lady Essex. "Lady Leicester awaits." She leads Noah into the parlor and disappears like a will o' the wisp, leaving him alone with Lady Leicester, who glowers at him from her upholstered chair like an ancient matriarch.

"Madam," he says, bowing low, "your ladyship's note reached me last evening."

Lady Leicester regards him skeptically. "Yes, I heard you were invited to the Lord Admiral's for supper. *My,* but we're moving in lofty circles now, are we not, Serjeant?" She flashes him her most insincere smile and gestures for him to take a seat near her.

He sits on the edge of the chair. "On certain occasions when the Lord Admiral has found some earthly use for your humble servant," he says, "my family has been invited to share a meal at his lordship's home. Although the Lord Admiral's generosity is much appreciated, I would hardly call that 'traveling in lofty circles.'"

"Of *course* you wouldn't," says Lady Leicester. "You, who appear before the *Queen* at will." She waves her hand dismissively. "Who is the *Lord Admiral* to one of your lofty stature?"

"Madam," says Noah, "I assure your ladyship that I appear before Her Majesty at *her* will, not mine own."

"And yet, here I sit banned for life from Her Majesty's court. To what do you attribute your advantage?" she demands.

Noah finds this quibbling tiresome and, worse, it's off the point. "Perhaps it's that I never married the man she loved," he says. It's out before he can stop it, and he's sorry he said it. Not only is it insulting, but it's even *further* off the point.

At first, she looks as though she's been slapped in the face. But instead of responding with fury, her face falls in resignation, and every line upon it seems more deeply etched than before.

"You don't mince words, do you?" she says, deflated.

Noah sits at attention and makes sure he looks sincerely downcast. "That was unforgivably insolent on my part, madam, and I beg your ladyship's forgiveness."

She sighs. "Well, you'd got as bad as you gave, hadn't you? Let's get down to business, shall we?" She removes a paper from her pocket and hands it over.

Noah opens it. He recognizes Drury's handwriting immediately, although it's a bit off kilter, giving rise to the conjecture that it was written while his wounds were being bound up. It reads, *Dear Lady Essex, You may add to your concerns the possibility of an action of civil battery to be commenced by my solicitor. For the time being, however, I have agreed with your ladyship's lackey to let matters between us rest for two years, so long as no further beatings are delivered at your gentle ladyship's kind behest.*

"It's unsigned," remarks Noah.

He takes from his pocket Drury's original note to Lady Leicester and compares the handwritings. As expected, Drury has once again written with his disfavored hand, having no doubt forgotten which hand he used to write the original note. "The hand in the present note is a bit shaky, but it appears to be the same as in the first." He hands her both notes and invites her to examine them herself.

"Very like," she says. "But you *do* realize that I arranged no beating for my … anonymous correspondent? I don't even know who he is. Do *you*?"

"I hesitate to say, madam," he replies, "in light of the liberties one of your station may be tempted to take against someone deemed adversarial."

She scowls at him. "But I just told you I'd nothing to do with the beating."

He nods. "And, though *my* credence counts for nought, madam, I do believe you. My concern does not arise out of the beating."

"What else gives you cause for concern?" she asks.

He delays his answer for later. "The man's name is Thomas Drury, madam. When I left Whitehall to meet your ladyship here on the first occasion, I realized that I was being followed. So, I turned the tables on my pursuer and had *him* followed."

She smiles in grudging admiration. "Clever."

"Thus," says Noah, "we discovered his identity. Almost immediately thereafter, I happened to come across him in a legal matter. His landlord had sworn out a warrant for his arrest, accusing him of firing a musket to frighten him away." He shakes his head. "And his landlord took offense, if you can imagine."

"I can't imagine," says Lady Leicester with a note of humor.

"In executing the warrant, a settlement was reached, and in the settlement agreement, I had Drury write out certain words in his own hand. Comparing them to the original note which your ladyship now holds, I saw that the handwritings were the same. Later, I privately confronted him about his note to your ladyship."

"Ah," she says, "now I begin to see."

"Master Drury is a man of good family," he says, giving the devil his due, "but poor personal reputation. Nevertheless, as you can see from his latest note, I managed to extract from him a solemn promise not to disturb your ladyship with this nonsense for at least two years." He bows apologetically in his chair. "I'm sorry that I could do no better for your ladyship, but there's a fair chance he'll keep his word and, if he does, at the remove of an additional two years the matter may no longer seem so interesting to him, nor to young Master Dudley, who apparently had no knowledge of Drury's interference."

"Well," she says equivocally, "it's *something*—but it hardly gives me the peace I crave."

Noah shrugs. "I have considered how to obtain such peace, madam, but anything you do now is as likely to inflame matters as to put them to rest. I ask only that your ladyship not take ... *extreme* measures to terminate the threat."

"Extreme measures?" she says dubiously. "Such as?"

"Such as having Drury abducted," he says, readily imagining the chill running up her spine.

"Having him *abducted?*" she says defensively. "Why, I would *never* do such a thing."

He looks at her coolly. "Wouldn't you, though?"

To his great relief, she blushes—as sure a confession as he could ever hope to attain. Now he has her. "As you've done with Master Leveson," he says.

Her face is still red, and she's near tears. "You *insolent* man," she says. "You've no idea what it's like to have your first husband die, your second husband die with the cloud of an earlier betrothal hanging over your head, and then have your third husband and your son taken from you and cast into the Tower, where they will very likely be put to ... death."

She weeps.

For the first time today, Noah has some sympathy for her, as he realizes that his ploy would not have worked if she hadn't retained some shred of decency. "No, madam, I have no such experiences and only wish that I could do something to help you in those regards, but alas I cannot. While your travails have been many and deep, I must also feel for poor Master Leveson's wife, however, bereft at Gray's Inn wondering if she'll ever again see her husband alive."

Lady Leicester wipes her eyes with a handkerchief.

"Abduction is a felony, of course," he says, "but hardly comparable to a charge of *murder*."

"*Murder?*" she echoes incredulously. "It was never the plan to have Leveson killed."

"I speak not of Sir John's murder, madam. For that, I'll take your word. No, I was referring to the grisly death of Sir Henry Neville that will inevitably take place if Sir John is not released in time to testify in Sir Henry's behalf. For Sir Henry is, as you know, under arrest on suspicion of high treason."

She sits agape at having her machinations so blatantly exposed.

It occurs to him that he's never discovered how she learned that Sir Henry might possess letters from Leicester acknowledging an earlier marriage. But without such knowledge, she'd have had no reason to have Leveson abducted.

"Well," he says, "that was the plan, wasn't it? Sir John withheld from testifying, Sir Henry put to death, and then Sir John released. Wasn't that it?"

She says nothing, but cowers.

Noah continues with *sang-froid*. "Neither Sir John nor Sir Henry knows aught of your involvement in any of this, nor does anyone else. And, if Leveson appears in the next few days in good condition, they need *never* know. Nor need anyone know that *I* found out any of this, a prospect which appeals to me even more. Sir John will simply appear to his wife, as Athena from the head of Zeus. And justice will follow its natural course."

Lady Leicester becalms herself. "The next few days?" she asks dubiously.

Noah nods. "As soon as possible." He rises. "Now, if m'lady has no further use for your humble servant, I would take my leave."

She absentmindedly waves him away.

He bows, and takes a last look at her before going. She'll release Leveson all right. She's frightened to death.

And damned well *ought* to be.

CHAPTER 18

AT THE TOWER OF LONDON, in the early morning hours of Ash Wednesday of 1601, an executioner's block at the center of the scaffold awaits the neck of the Earl of Essex. Her Majesty has granted Essex clemency to the extent of sparing him a "traitor's death," which would have been a public four-and-quartering at Tyburn, in favor of a simple beheading in the comparative privacy of the Tower.

To one side of the block stands a hooded executioner, his hands resting on the handle of the biggest, shiniest axe Noah has ever seen. The other side of the scaffold is sparsely populated by a few solemn-faced statesmen, most familiar of whom are Robert Cecil and Lord Chief Justice Popham. Off to one side stand a few weeping family members, including Lady Essex and Lady Leicester.

The courtyard before the scaffold is crowded with politicians, lawyers, and a few gawkers. Office-holders such as Noah, generally referred to as the "Queen's men," sit a-horseback, so that their recognizable faces can be seen by one and all, thus assuring the rabble that the slaughter about to take place is by no means the product of caprice, but rather undertaken with the full sanction of law.

Noah pats Bucklebury's withers to keep him calm. On foot beside the horse stand together Jonathan Lord Saint Ives and Sir Walter Raleigh.

Jonathan's face is pale and full of dread. Noah can hear his voice from nearly ten years ago at Gray's Inn. *It may take me ten years,* he said, *but I will see that man taken to the knacker's.* And now, at the knacker's, there's neither joy nor relief in Jonathan's eyes. How experience changes us!

By comparison, Sir Walter's face is ruddy and tense, his expression a combination of barely suppressed anger and determination. His attitude is readily understandable, as he was a chief target of Essex's groundless accusations of insubordination and disloyalty. Always a determined fellow, Sir Walter no doubt wishes to deny *on the spot* any slander that

Essex might choose to speak from the scaffold.

The Lord Chief Justice waves, catching Noah's eye. Noah looks at him questioningly. The Lord Chief Justice, his face stern, points toward Sir Walter and makes a subtle but unmistakable wave of dismissal.

Noah nods and leans down from the saddle. "Sir Walter?" he says softly, vainly hoping for Sir Walter's attention alone. While both Sir Walter and Lord Jonathan look up at him, fortunately no one else does.

Noah beckons them closer with two fingers. Sir Walter looks up at him skeptically. Noah leans down even further.

"Sir Walter," murmurs Noah preparing for a possible outburst, "evidently, your conspicuous attendance on this occasion is upsetting to the family. The Lord Chief Justice asks you to watch from the armory."

Sir Walter simmers with suppressed anger. Just as Noah is about to despair of keeping the peace, Lord Jonathan places a hand gently on Sir Walter's shoulder.

"Come, Sir Walter," says Lord Jonathan. "Won't you escort me to the armory? I'll be pleased to have you there. I don't know that I can bear to watch this barbarity so close up."

Sir Walter looks at Jonathan and his face softens, but he's still not letting it go. He says to Noah, "What if Essex begins spewing his venom at me from the scaffold? Have I no right to defend myself?"

Noah shakes his head. "This is not a court of law, Sir Walter, and you are not on trial for any crime. To the contrary, Essex's execution for treason would rather strongly support your side of the story, wouldn't you say?" He sighs. "And, for what it's worth, for two days Essex pointed at everyone he could shift blame to—with nary a mention of your name. And, for the past *three* days, he's been doing nothing but praying. He's in another world now, Sir Walter, where you and I are not. Moreover, Her Majesty has given instructions that Essex's mere mention of anything political is to be cut off as surely as his head. Please escort Lord Jonathan to the armory, if you would be so kind. You'll have a clear enough view there. I shall remain here—as all other officers are forbidden to leave—and ensure that no imprecation against you goes unrebutted."

Sir Walter equivocates for a moment, but then turns to Lord Jonathan with resignation. "Come to the armory with me, m'lord. There's no reason m'lord should stand so close as to be sprayed with traitor's blood." He marches off with Lord Jonathan close behind, passing a small train of men going the opposite way.

At the center of the approaching group is the tall Earl of Essex, dressed in a somber black suit of velvet and satin, wearing a black felt hat and a small ruff. Upon seeing the ruff, it occurs to Noah that, if Essex wears it when he's struck by the executioner's axe, the resultant horrific image will be that of a white lily spraying blood from its central style.

Essex climbs the scaffold with a demeanor nearly beatific. He raises his eyes up to heaven and addresses the lords, ladies, and others, freely confessing the sins of his past life. Though he admits the "bloody, crying and infectious sin" of the rebellion which will forever bear his name, at no point does he confess any intention to harm the Queen. Alas for him, thinks Noah, the trial judges held no such intention to be necessary in the proof of high treason.

Essex begs the forgiveness of the Queen and her ministers, praying for her long life and prosperity, thanking God that he had never been an atheist or a papist, but had placed all his hope and confidence in the merits of Christ.

"May God protect me from the terrors of death," he said, "and now I ask all those here today to join me in a short prayer."

Upon completion of the prayer, the executioner begs him for forgiveness. Essex turns to him, fully composed of emotions and faculties, and says, "Thou art the minister of justice. Spare not, nor be not afraid." He recites the Creed and the Lord's Prayer. He deftly removes his outer gown, ruff, and doublet, exposing a scarlet undervest. "In humility and obedience I prostrate myself to my deserved punishment. Thou, O God: Have mercy on Thy prostrate servant. Into Thy hands, O Lord, do I commend my spirit." He lies down on the scaffold with his neck on the block.

In a split second, the executioner's axe falls hard on the earl's neck. Although the earl seems to be rendered insensate by the resounding blow, yet is it insufficient to sever the head from the body. It takes two more mighty blows to drop the earl's head to the scaffold with a bloody thud.

To Noah, every blow after the first only strengthens his sense that beheading is needlessly cruel. Perhaps in the future someone will come up with a kinder method of death-dealing.

The executioner picks up the earl's head by the hair and exhibits it to the assembled. "God save the Queen!" he shouts, and the assembled echo in monotone without applause or celebration, "God save the Queen."

TENSION IS THICK in the armory, where Lord Jonathan and Sir Walter stand alone at a window looking out onto the scaffold.

As soon as the first blow falls upon Essex's neck, Jonathan's gorge rises. By the striking of the third blow, he's searching for a slop bucket. Fortunately, one is at hand. He kneels before it and ejects what little he ate upon rising this morning.

A young Yeoman Warder appears with a fresh pitcher of water. Jonathan grunts his thanks, pours some water into a wooden cup, and takes a sip, sloshing it about in his mouth before spitting it out into the soiled bucket.

Sir Walter, never taking his eyes off the unfolding scene on the scaffold, mutters an order to the Yeoman Warder. "Out to the pit."

The Yeoman Warder takes Jonathan by the arm as though to escort him out. Sir Walter turns, gives the young fellow an impatient stare, and points to Jonathan. "Not him," says Sir Walter. He points to the bucket. "*That!*"

The Yeoman Warder bows in smart military fashion and removes the bucket from the armory.

Jonathan turns to Sir Walter. "I regret doing that, Sir Walter."

Sir Walter turns with a skeptical look. "What, the bucket? No bother, my lord. It held far worse as recently as this morning." He sighs. "Tell me, m'lord. I know you've killed adversaries in combat before now. Have you ever been rendered sick to your stomach by it?"

Lord Jonathan gives it some thought, and shakes his head. "Never."

"Why do you suppose that was your reaction to this execution?" asks Sir Walter.

Jonathan shrugs. "It doesn't seem like a fair fight."

Sir Walter nods. "An astute observation, m'lord. It's *not* a fair fight. It's not a fight at all. It's the slaughter of a trapped animal. Puking is the only sentient response." He looks back out on the courtyard, where the spectators have begun to disperse. "The only reason I don't vomit ... any longer ... is that I've seen it so bloody often."

IN AN ANTEROOM off the Throne Room at Whitehall, Noah awaits a scheduled audience with the Queen, when he spies a pretty blonde he's quite certain he's seen before. Before he can recall precisely where it was, she walks up to him with a pleasing smile.

"Her Majesty is prepared to see you now, Captain," she says, and her error reminds him of who she is. She's the blonde lady-in-waiting who very nearly addressed the Queen as *King Richard*. "I'm afraid it will be a bit of a walk, as Her Majesty is receiving in her living quarters only." She leads him down the passageway to the living quarters.

"Is she unwell?" he asks with concern.

"Her Majesty is not … at the very *peak* of her health," says the girl, "yet, she has no illness with a name."

"Ah," says Noah, "*world-weariness*, perhaps?"

The girl turns to him, a bit confused. "Her physicians gave it no name, Captain. But, if you say so."

"Serjeant," he says.

"I beg your pardon, Captain?" she says as they walk along. She shoots him a winsome smile, and he begins to see how a witless beauty manages to ingratiate herself. "If you're addressing me, I possess no military rank."

"Nor do I," says Noah.

"No?" she asks.

"Well, I am *called* Serjeant," he says.

"I'm so sorry to hear," she says ingenuously. "Have you been demoted from your captaincy?"

"I have never been—" he begins, but thinks better of it. "Perhaps you might tell me more of Her Majesty's condition."

As they reach a closed salon door, she says, "I'm not the right person to ask." She knocks at the door.

"Come," says the Queen's wan voice.

The lady-in-waiting opens the door and enters first. "Captain Ames, Your Majesty." She curtseys, but the Queen takes no notice.

Noah enters. As the Queen stares contemplatively through a window overlooking the overcast winter afternoon, he waits silently to be recognized.

The blonde leaves, closing the door behind her.

The Queen's face, lit by the harsh daylight, seems agèd.

He stands and awaits her attention for a considerable time, which becomes so long that he begins to wonder whether she's forgotten he's there.

A harsh gust rattles the window, startling her.

Ah, he says to himself, this will surely bring her to her senses.

But it doesn't. She simply stares at the same fixed point, which he guesses to be perhaps a thousand yards away.

He's begun to wonder if she's entered into a daze of some kind when at last she speaks, albeit with little energy.

"They have begun to turn on me, Noah," she says intimately.

"Of whom does Your Majesty speak?" he asks.

There's another long wait before she replies. "Everyone," she says, and then adds, "people."

"I know of no such general feeling, Your Majesty," says Noah. "I've been sent to inform you that the sentence has been carried out upon Lord Essex."

She shivers, and tears begin to run down her otherwise impassive face. "I loved his stepfather, the Earl of Leicester," she says so quietly he can barely hear, "but Lettice stole him away." She speaks of none other than Lady Leicester, of course, who she's unaware has had Leveson abducted.

"That was long ago, Majesty," he offers, "and his lordship *left* us many years ago."

She nods almost imperceptibly. "And what have I done with those years, Noah? Hmm?"

"Your Majesty has maintained England's independence from the papist powers," he says. "Under Your Majesty's reign, the wealth and wisdom of England have been greatly enhanced."

"To be a king and wear a crown," she says, "is a thing more glorious to them that see it, than it is pleasant to them that bear it." She shakes her head slowly, as though in a dream. "England, England, England. *Bother* England," she says. "I *might* have married. Leicester was not my only suitor."

"Madam," says Noah, "every nobleman in the realm has pursued Your Majesty at one time or another."

"But *I* had to have a Frenchman, or so they told me. All of them. Even Burghley. Even his dwarf son Robert." It's rare for her to speak disparagingly of Lord Robert, though her pejorative mention of his small stature is not unusual for her.

"I expect they were concerned to assure England's peace with France into the future," Noah offers in their defense.

"England's future peace, assured through my woman's belly," she says with disgust. "Has an Englishwoman no right to *choose* whose child she'll bear?"

"Most do, madam."

"Our *basest beggars* have the right to choose a husband," she says, "while their Queen has none." Her tears, having stopped for a moment, begin afresh. "Now Essex is dead: the stepson of the man I would have married. Between Leicester and myself, though we might never have assured England of lasting peace with France, we would at least have assured that England would be ruled by an Englishman, not some errant Scot. England would have had a natural-born king. My father would have had a grandchild, and I"—there's a catch in her voice—"I would have had a *child*."

Noah is reminded of his first meeting with the Queen, when she was still quite young. Even so long ago she was preoccupied with motherhood. He runs his fingers anxiously through his hair, having been caught at unawares by the depth of her despair, and feels his own tears of sympathy coming on. But he's not a liberty to let them out, for 'tis violation of law to pity the Sovereign.

At last, she turns to him. "Noah, you are now the nearest thing I have to a child." She returns her gaze to the same spot through the window. "But you came to me whole, the child of another woman."

He swallows hard, and forbidden tears run down his face. "I am sorry to have failed Your Majesty," he says.

She shakes her head slowly. "You have *not* failed me," she says. "*I* have failed me—and England in the bargain. Never have I allowed myself the free rein of a woman, confined though it might be in comparison to a man's." She sighs. "I *unsexed* myself," she says with audible disgust, "and let my womb be made a commodity. And now am I left with nothing but regret, having sacrificed all … for *England*."

She's silent for so long that he wonders whether she's fallen into a trance. At last, she speaks. "Things will never be the same again. Leicester is dead. Essex is dead. My womanliness—" she says, rubbing her woman's belly, and her voice trails off. "Off with you now," she says as though dismissing a child. "I shall call upon you anon."

He bows low.

"And, please find William Shakespeare. Robert Cecil seems content to let the matter languish."

He bows again, and lets himself out.

As he mournfully retraces his steps out of the living quarters, a settled hate rises in his stomach for Essex—Essex, that stupid, selfish man. By destroying himself, he has destroyed the Queen of England and the nearest thing Noah has to a mother. *What now?* he wonders.

And blast Lord Robert, as well, as the burden of finding Shakespeare has now fallen upon me!

CHAPTER 19

IN THE SILENCE of an early morning with the sun not fully risen, Sir Henry enters his solitary study at the Lord Admiral's house. He draws out a new quill pen and clean sheet of paper, courtesy of his host.

Sir Henry's assignment has been made quite clear by the Privy Council. He's to amplify his initial statement, explaining discrepancies between his testimony and those of other witnesses, especially that of the Earl of Southampton, who testified that he'd spoken with Sir Henry many times since their boyhood days in the school at Lord Burghley's house.

Oh, why did I not listen to Noah? thinks Sir Henry, shaking his head. If he had, there would have been precious little discrepancy to speak of. As it is, he'll need to distract from, and elide over, the discrepancy. And in the most persuasive language possible, of course.

As he's about to set pen to paper, the Lord Admiral's footman Matthew enters with a bow.

"Sir Henry," he says, "please pardon the interruption, but the Lord Admiral asked me whether you were expecting a visit from Serjeant Ames today, and I found that I was unable to give a definite answer."

Sir Henry wonders if perhaps he should take this opportunity to postpone Noah's visit to a more propitious time, but he decides against it. It would be most helpful to have Noah's advice before writing, and there will be ample time to prepare the statement after he's left.

"Serjeant Ames told me that I should expect him at noon," says Sir Henry.

Matthew smiles. "The good Serjeant will be staying for dinner, I take it."

"That's my expectation," says Sir Henry. "Besides, his visit will be a welcome intermission from the daunting task of writing this statement."

"An *intermission*, sir?" says Matthew, seeming confused. "I'm sorry if no one told you, Sir Henry, but I'm under orders of the Privy Council to collect your … statement … and bring it to the council personally by eleven this morning."

Sir Henry opens his eyes wide. "Eleven?" he says in astonishment. "*Eleven?* How the devil am I supposed to finish something so weighty in—what—four hours?"

"Well, sir," says Matthew, "I expect I can get it to Westminster in a half hour—Westminster's not so far away, after all—but I will need at least that much time. So, that leaves you something like three and one-half hours."

Sir Henry tilts his head skeptically. "Tell me something, Matthew. If I'd told you that the Serjeant would be arriving at two in the afternoon, would the Privy Council's 'instructions' have allowed me till *one*?"

Matthew smiles, which means that Sir Henry has guessed rightly. Matthew's orders were given not by the Privy Council, but rather the Lord Admiral, who wishes Sir Henry's statement to reflect his immediate recollection, rather than hours of forethought and the advice of an experienced barrister.

"Well," says Sir Henry with a sigh, "we must respect our host's wishes, mustn't we? Now, please don't interrupt me until half past ten."

<hr/>

AT NOON SHARP MATTHEW, having returned from his errand to the Privy Council, escorts Noah up to the solitary study, where Sir Henry is seated in a comfortable chair, though without his accustomed glass of spirits.

"Would either of you gentlemen care for a spot of sherris?" asks Matthew.

Sir Henry shakes his head morosely, which Noah regards as signifying reluctant acquiescence to his request that Sir Henry not drink himself to death.

"None for me," says Noah. "Thank you, Matthew."

Matthew bows and departs.

"I've submitted my *amplified* statement as demanded by the Privy Council," says Sir Henry. "You will be pleased to learn that it was entirely truthful"—he sighs wearily—"but I question whether it will be enough to save me from an adverse verdict." He shrugs. "Perhaps if I'd had more time …"

"It may make no difference," says Noah.

"No difference?" asks Sir Henry. "What are you thinking?"

"I'm thinking," says Noah, "that if I'm Sir Henry Neville, the last thing I want is a trial."

"Should I then willingly offer up my belly for a traitor's death?" asks Sir Henry skeptically.

"Not in the least," says Noah. "But let me tell you what I expect will happen if you *do* stand trial—even privately, as in Star Chamber."

"I'm all ears," says Sir Henry.

"Assuming Sir John Leveson returns in good condition from his current predicament—and there is some reason to expect he will, given sufficient time—he could testify at trial that you renounced your support of Essex by arranging for Leveson to bar Essex's advance on Westminster."

"Do you think it would turn the trick in avoiding a guilty verdict?" asks Sir Henry.

Noah shakes his head. "No—notwithstanding that I expect Sir John's testimony to be credited by *any* group of men. You see, essentially your defense would be one of *renunciation*. Unfortunately, the adequacy of such a defense is often left to the judge for determination, and I doubt any judge would take it upon himself to dismiss these charges."

"Why such reluctance?"

"Because," Noah replies, "the Crown will probably not so much as *attempt* the difficult proof that you were an active participant in the rebellion. For one thing, you were already on your way to France by the time the rebellion commenced—or at least it might appear so. For another, I expect you would be able to muster witnesses to testify that you advised Southampton that the rebellion would be a suicidal folly." He pauses. "It would be much simpler for the Crown simply to charge you with foreknowledge of the plan and failure to reveal it to the authorities, which is known as 'misprision'. Such a charge is quite sufficient to support a guilty verdict in a case of high treason, and I expect the Crown can readily bear its burden of proof on that score. And, if you think about it, one cannot 'renounce' his misprision without spilling his guts before the event."

Sir Henry frowns. "Then, what hope?" he mutters.

Now that Noah's lowered Henry's defenses, he begins to reveal what's truly on his mind. "I will share with you some advice that I gave the late Earl of Essex, may he rest in peace, though he was too bull-headed to listen. A guilty verdict is virtually assured against you, so the case you *need* to make will be in support of your petition to *Her Majesty* seeking clemency in your case. If you make a full confession (which the law greatly encourages), thus effectively pleading guilty (which the law greatly *dis*courages), you can spring Leveson's testimony on the Crown for the first time at the *clemency* hearing. The Crown, having had no opportunity to prepare, will be without evidence to rebut it." He shrugs. "Leveson's testimony would be difficult to rebut in any event, as it would be the truth. Besides, who would refuse to believe the royally commended hero of Ludgate?" He turns to Sir Henry. "It's not a sure thing, but it's the best you've got, and I expect that it *will* be sufficient to keep you alive long enough to survive Her Majesty's initial wrath. She has a long, long memory, but in time her womanly kindness often prevails."

The gleam has returned to Sir Henry's eyes. "Do you truly think so?"

Noah nods. "I am given hope," he says, "by something you and I have not discussed."

Sir Henry regards him inquiringly.

"The Earl of Southampton liveth still," says Noah.

"What hope for me in that?" asks Sir Henry.

"Such things certainly are not written in stone," says Noah, "but the Crown tends to execute its death warrants against those convicted together within hours of each other. Yet, no move has been made to put Southampton to death. That usually means one thing only." He looks expectantly to Sir Henry.

"It means the Queen doesn't wish him dead," says Sir Henry.

Noah nods.

"But how can we avoid a trial?" Sir Henry asks.

"You can't avoid it completely, but thanks to your position as Ambassador to France, you may be tried privately in Star Chamber. As I said, you could offer your confession to a charge of treason by misprision, thus relieving the Crown of the need to present the most damning evidence against you. And if we could arrange for the trial to be held at a later date, say sometime in early July, that would give you additional time to petition for clemency before Her Majesty, and it should also give us plenty of time to assure Leveson's testimony at a clemency hearing. At least that's *one* way events might play out. There's an additional grounds for clemency that could be offered on your behalf, but—to quote a great man—you're not going to like it."

Sir Henry cocks his head uncertainly.

"It might be possible," Noah whispers, "to inform Her Majesty ... privately ... that her favorite playwright in all England is none other than ... you."

Sir Henry's eyes are agog. "*How did you ...?* Favorite playwright?

You mean …" He stops short. "Oh, I couldn't, for then *everyone* should know."

Noah scoffs. "You afford Her Majesty insufficient credit for discretion, sir."

"But, as she's so angry with me, she'll be tempted to disclose it to the public." Sir Henry shakes his head. "You don't understand, Noah. My inheritance—and my wife's and children's—depends upon my maintaining a low profile. The circumstances of my birth have always been questionable. Some might contend I was conceived out of wedlock, as my father was dallying with his second wife rather prematurely. My father had other children of the same marriage who might well seek to upset my ownership of Billingbear, and of much more."

"And if you're put to death," says Noah skeptically, "do you expect that your relatives will *not* contest the circumstances of your birth?"

Sir Henry considers. "Damned either way," he says.

"That seems to leave you with two alternatives," says Noah. "One is to trust in Her Majesty's discretion, pay a hefty fine … and live. The other would be to take your theatrical secret to the grave"—he raises an eyebrow archly—"and that *presently*."

While Sir Henry seems to wander in thought, Noah continues the argument. "Besides, there are at least two *selfish* reasons for Her Majesty to honor your secret. First, your writing is, I assume, a source of considerable revenue, which could be applied to payment of the inevitable fine. Second, without the true Shakespeare, there would be no more Shakespeare *plays*, and Her Majesty seems to enjoy little else in her advancing years. I saw her recently. She was as miserable as I've ever seen her."

"Do you think she might simply impose a fine?" asks Sir Henry.

"Hard to say," Noah replies. "Her Majesty *has* deemed it satisfactory to impose steep fines upon certain others who were far more involved in the rebellion than *you* were. So long as they pay, I expect they shall be absolved. But I doubt not that it shall go harder for you, Sir Henry. If the fine assessed against you were too high for you to pay, you might be detained *during Her Majesty's pleasure*."

"You think it will go harder for me?" he says. "Why *harder*? I never lifted a finger to assist in that madness!"

"Nor did you lift a finger to frustrate it," Noah reminds him, "until it was already underway. Such concealment might be regarded as a lesser offense if done by an accused lacking the Queen's trust. In this, however, your strength is likewise your weakness. She has known you since birth and has relied upon your counsel since you reached majority. In short, she has ever thought of you as a *friend*," he says. "But a *true* friend would have warned her of the danger—perhaps in secret—but surely he would have turned 'pickthank' and spilled all well ahead of the event. That makes your silence well nigh unforgivable. At best, I expect you will be spending significant time in the Tower, Sir Henry, although how much I cannot tell. Have I your permission to discuss these matters with Her Majesty in private? And perhaps come to terms?"

"Damn! Where is Matthew?" says Sir Henry, rubbing his forehead. "I could use a spot of sherris just now."

"We can share a sherris at dinner in a few minutes," says Noah, "but I'd sooner have you decide such an important matter *uninfluenced* by spirits."

Sir Henry is silent for a long time, and ultimately says, "Do whatever you *can* for me, Noah, but please prevail upon the Queen to keep my secret. I would hate to save mine own erring life by squandering my children's inheritance. And I'd surely prefer not to risk their inheritance if it *won't* save my life."

———————⊰∘⊱———————

"I MUST INTERVIEW Augustine Phillips," says Noah.

Lord Robert frowns, puts down his quill, and walks to his office window. Fortunately, in Noah's experience, Lord Robert's frown betokens contemplation, rather than disapprobation.

"Why must you?" asks Lord Robert.

"Her Majesty has asked me to find William Shakespeare," says Noah. "Evidently, she's concerned that he's an unindicted co-conspirator, and suspects he's dangerous."

"*Dangerous?*" he asks skeptically, and chuckles. "You mean, to *others*?"

Noah declines to join in the mirth. "Regardless whether he's a threat to the Crown, Lord Robert, Her Majesty *thinks* he might be, and she'll expect him to be interviewed."

"No doubt," says Lord Robert, "but what if we can't find him?"

"Why, then, we can't find him," says Noah. "But you've already told Her Majesty that Master Phillips has remained in London. She'll expect we *can* find him."

"Hmm," says Lord Robert, stroking his beard, "I see your predicament. I know you've *met* Phillips," he says, "but are you aware of what a subtle fellow he is?"

"I have that *impression*, but I'm not sure of the full extent of it."

"Have you ever conducted an interview before where you don't *wish* to know the answers?" asks Lord Robert.

"No," says Noah, "but I expect you conducted a few in my interests after my ... unfortunate experience at the Saracen's Head."

Lord Robert smiles wryly. "Now you've got the idea. I shall first tell *you* how it's done, and then send someone to Phillips. Besides, he has no idea how to find Shakespeare."

No, thinks Noah. *Perhaps I do, but let's hope it never comes up.*

———————⊸∘⟨⊘⟩∘⊶———————

SOME DAYS AFTER Essex's death, his bereaved mother Lady Leicester haunts the nocturnal halls of Essex House clad in a heavy robe worn over a simple nightgown.

All the mourners are gone for the day. The new widow, Lady Essex, has retired for the night, seeking relief in one or another type of spirits, evidently her only means of passing into an uneasy sleep.

Never has Lady Leicester felt so alone.

The servants (as good servants will do in a time of mourning) have taken to giving her wide passage. Though always within summoning distance, they're ever beyond sight. Like efficient ghosts in the night, their presence consists of little more than occasional footsteps shuffling from one room to another. And they seem always to know where she's going, as they vacate each room just before she appears, leaving a taper alight for her.

She compares her own predicament to Lady Essex's and cannot help but feel that she herself has the worse of it, with her son already dead and the trial and likely execution of her husband looming on the horizon. She wonders idly what she might have done to anger the bloodthirsty gods.

She enters the library overlooking the dreary Thames. The opaque curtains have been drawn shut—but for a small gap left by the servants so she can see whether it's night or day, though it's a distinction that makes little difference to her now. A low, dull roar comes in off the river, such as one might hear when clouds race across the sky, portending a change of weather. She feels a sudden chill, draws her collar close to her throat, and collapses into an upholstered chair.

A sudden series of furtive taps on the window frightens her nearly out of her wits. Her heart pounds in her chest and she shoots to her feet in alarm. She fingers the dagger in her dressing gown and draws her collar even closer, listening vigilantly.

Perhaps it's a bird who lost its way in the frigid turbulence over the Thames. *Yes, that must be it.* But just as she's about to settle back into her accustomed chair, the tapping comes again. Though it's no louder, the source of the repeating pattern can only be human.

She steps out of the candlelight and sidles up to the gap between the curtains. Peering outside, she spies a man in the moonlight and recognizes his face.

It's Mullin, who abducted Leveson at her instruction. While she's been meaning to contact him to obtain his prisoner's release, she's been dragging her feet. There's something about this man she finds deeply unnerving. For one thing, his social class is entirely unclear. He speaks more or less like an educated gentleman, but his clothing is gaudy and distasteful.

She allows herself to be seen, and points him toward the door he may use to enter the library. He tips his cap and disappears from the window moving in the direction of the door.

She catches his attention through the little window by the door and places her finger to her lips. With a nod, he acknowledges the need for quiet, and she lets him in. He enters with a bounce in his step and twirls his cap in his hand.

"Good e'en, m'lady," he whispers with an airy bow.

"Master Mullin," she whispers, "I had intended to summon you in the morning."

His eyes open wide with surprise. "'Think of the devil and he shall appear,'" he says mildly, with no evident appreciation of the irony in his chosen saying. "Why did you wish to speak with me, madam?"

"There's been a change of plans," she says cautiously. "I'm afraid it has become necessary to return our ... quarry ... to his lodgings. I trust he has come to no harm, and that he has never seen you or learned the reason for his abduction."

Mullin nods, as though to say, *of course.*

She says, "I know that you and I spoke of a fee of one hundred pounds, but as he's been with you only a matter of weeks, and as it appears I shall be unable to accomplish my goal, I was hoping there might be ... a reduction."

He looks down at his shoes for a moment with some consternation. "The fee, you say?" he says. "There's another strange coincidence, madam. It's why *I* came to see *you.*"

"Oh?" she says, hoping for some flexibility.

"I'm going to need a *thousand* pound," he says as though he'd like to help her but his hands are tied.

"*A thousand pounds?*" she asks with some confusion. "But the agreed fee was a *hundred*. You haven't the temerity to ask of me a *thousand pounds!*"

He gives her his most patronizing smile. "I could it make it *two* thousand," he proposes.

Her stomach leaps into her chest. "A thousand pounds?" she whispers. "But why would you ask so much? He's been in your charge for nary a few weeks."

"Do you think me a common *tradesman*, m'lady?" he says, obviously relishing her distress. "Your ... friend is a bit feisty," he says, dusting off his clothing as though in demonstration. "He's delivered more blows while manacled than others would have while entirely free of restraint. Besides," he says, "I've acquired ... a partner."

"A partner?" she says incredulously.

"Oh, yes," he replies matter-of-factly, "quite an affable, educated fellow."

She places her hands on her hips but maintains a subdued voice. "I don't see what your 'partner' has to do with it. Joining with him was *your* choice, not mine. And I would have protested if you'd suggested it. You'll recall there was to be only a *single* captor."

He shrugs. "Well, I needed some extra muscle to handle your friend."

"But how can you justify such an enormous increase in your ... fee?"

"Mum," he says insubordinately, "I'm risking my neck for you. That justifies the increase all on its own."

She shakes her head in protest. "But you *knew* the risks when we struck our bargain."

"How about *you*, madam?" he says with a leer. "Do *you* know the risks?"

"A thousand pounds is a king's ransom, and I *shan't* pay it," she says with quiet finality.

"What *choice* have you, madam? Will you call the constable?" he asks derisively. "Because, your neck would be in the noose as quick as mine."

Her mind is racing. "I—I *can't* pay that amount," she says breathlessly. "I don't have that much. My income arrives slowly, from those who farm our land. We don't have so much in *lucre*."

"That's unfortunate," he says with a shrug, "for, if you don't pay it—and promptly—one of these mornings your friend shall certainly wake up dead."

She feels faint.

"Look," he says with feigned concern, "I know this all comes as a shock, but I'll give you a few days—"

"A few *days*?" she says. "You might as well demand it all now!"

"I'll be back in a week," he says, as though his willingness to forbear for such a lengthy time is proof positive of his reasonableness. "I'll return at this same hour to your lovely garden on the Thames," he says sardonically. "If you have a reasonable amount for me then, I shall grant you a brief extension. But, please understand, there are rather severe demands upon me to bring this matter to a rapid conclusion." He bows perfunctorily, but before turning to go out of the door, he says, "And don't even consider bringing anyone else into this matter or having me met here by someone else. As you know, I have a confederate now and, if you do any such thing, he'll be under strict instructions to kill your friend and report to the Crown your whole involvement in this tawdry business."

He opens the door and struts out before closing it quietly behind him.

So distraught is she that it never occurs to her to sit down before beginning to weep. In a short while, she becalms herself and wipes her eyes. She draws herself a cup of wine and goes to the desk, where she takes a leaf of paper and a pen and spends a moment collecting her thoughts.

She dips the pen in the ink and begins to write,

Dear Sjt. Ames ....

CHAPTER 20

NOAH PREPARES TO CONDUCT the interview of Augustine Phillips in the room adjacent to Sir Walter's office that was cleared out for his recent interview with Thomas Drury. Instead of sending a compulsory writ, Noah sends Phillips a cordial note two days before he's to appear.

The late-February morning of the interview is dreary and cold, as many are in London. Fortunately, the fireplace is well stocked.

Looking out over the Tower courtyard toward the tradesman's entrance, Noah readily spies the unmistakable Augustine Phillips approaching in theatrical stride, robes billowing behind him in the breeze. On his head sits a black hat with an outlandishly wide brim, and in his hand is a cane being put to no present use.

Phillips catches sight of Noah watching through the window. He smiles, stops in his tracks, bows dramatically with a sweep of the arm, and resumes his approach. Though Noah's door is open, before entering Phillips doffs his hat, which would otherwise be too large to fit through the doorway.

"Welcome, Master Phillips," says Noah pleasantly. "I'm pleased that you have arrived early." He gestures an invitation for Phillips to take a seat, which the old man gratefully accepts.

"A life in the theater has taught me much, Serjeant Ames," says Phillips. "There are two things one must *never* be late for; the first is a meal, the second ... the opening lines of a play."

Noah takes Phillips' remark as a veiled acknowledgment that what's about to take place will be rather more play than reality. He's confident that Phillips has been adequately prepared for the interview, as Lord Robert promised.

"If you have time, Serjeant Ames, before we begin," says Phillips, "how is your lovely, patriotic, and strong-willed daughter Lady Jessica? I've heard that she now has a strapping young baby boy—*your grandson*, if I'm correct." He smiles broadly.

Noah cannot help but smile in return. "Lady Jessica is quite well,

Master Phillips, as is young Arthur. Thank you for asking."

"Ah. *Arthur*," echoes Phillips, mulling over the baby's name. "So you acknowledge that your family's unfortunate absence from this realm for many years never deprived you of your essential Englishness."

"That's part of it," says Noah, "but choosing the baby's name was, I think, a bit simpler. Arthur was born on the very day of the late rebellion, when a young barrister friend of mine was killed in action; his name was Arthur." Noah fights off his many fond memories of Arthur, lest he be inundated with grief once again.

Phillips looks down and scowls, his thick grey eyebrows threatening to hide his eyes completely. "That is most unfortunate," he says. "I understand there were *several* good men killed that day. And for what? So Essex could be King? *Pshaw*." He sits back in his chair. "The strapping Lord Saint Ives is Arthur's father, if I'm not mistaken."

"He is," confirms Noah. "And his lordship is also well. Tell me, Master Phillips. How fare your relations in Cornwall?"

Once again, Phillips' expression turns quite serious, though he speaks wistfully. "I have many happy relatives in Cornwall, Serjeant … which is all to the good. I see all my young cousins playing on the beach, boating, doing all the things I did there many years ago … but I truly *know* nary a one of them. You see, by the time one has attained my years, one is accustomed to seeing fewer and fewer of those he grew up with. When I look at any one of my young cousins, I need to be reminded which of my former companions he or she sprang from. But, in nearly every case, their progenitors are … long past." His eyes smile through the pain of loss. "You'll experience this soon, *grandpapa*." He says this last with a peculiar combination of fondness and foreboding.

"By God's will," says Noah. "Now, as we have touched upon the late rebellion, let us speak of the singular theatrical performance staged at the Globe on the previous day."

"Let us do so," Phillips concurs. "How shall we proceed?"

"Well, that depends," says Noah. "Have you any knowledge of the performance?" He begins taking notes of each question and answer.

Phillips nods. "A fair amount, although I didn't watch it."

"I take it the play that was mounted that day was not in the company's scheduled rotation, is that right?" asks Noah.

"Correct. In fact, it had been little staged in the past few years, and the players had little confidence in its ability to attract much traffic. Though the play contains some of the most beautiful lines ever written for the English theater, the English public, despite its love for its native tongue, would prefer to see characters being poisoned, slashed to death, and so on. So that's what they're given."

Noah shakes his head at the foibles of the public. "I'd like you to begin, if you would, by telling me who first broached the possibility of commissioning such a performance."

Phillips looks at the ceiling, evidently to refresh his memory. "It was those two Percy boys, both knights. Charles was the elder, and the younger was, I want to say ... *Joseph*?"

"Joscelyn?" suggests Noah.

"Yes, that was it," says Phillips with certitude. "I suppose I couldn't remember, as his name always strikes me as a Christian name for a *girl*. Anyway, one evening last autumn—I couldn't say precisely which day or week it was—they accosted me at a little tavern at Bankside."

"Had the tavern a name?" asks Noah.

"I expect it did. I suppose a deliveryman would need some way to distinguish one tavern from all the others. Perhaps, the *Falcon*?" He shakes his head. "But that's mere conjecture. In fact, I believe it was a bit further south of the Thames."

"No need to guess, sir," says Noah breezily. "And what did the Percy brothers say to you?"

"I was a bit annoyed by their accosting me so late in the evening, rather than coming to see me at the Globe during the daytime, but they said they didn't wish to be seen with me." He laughs quietly.

"And what was the play they wished to have performed?" asks Noah.

"*Richard the Second*, a historical tragedy," says Phillips. "Anyway, I told them such a performance would cost them dearly, but they seemed unimpressed."

"Did they say *why* they wanted to have the play performed?" asks Noah.

Phillips shakes his head. "That's no concern of the players, Serjeant Ames. So long as they're paid, they couldn't care less."

"Did the Percys tell you where they were staying in London?" asks Noah.

For the first time, Phillips seems to be calculating the effect of alternative answers. Choosing his words carefully, he says, "Just before leaving the tavern, they said they could be contacted at Essex House or Drury House."

"I see," says Noah. "And when were the arrangements for the play actually made?"

"A few weeks later," says Phillips.

"Is there a standard fee for mounting a play such as this on short notice?"

"There is," replies Phillips.

"Is the standard fee what was charged?" asks Noah.

Phillips seems reluctant to go into the question, but he does so regardless. "Sir Gelly Meyrick came to fix the date with me and to agree on a price. He and I dickered a while, and we came to terms on a fee which was a bit higher than the standard."

"How much higher?"

Phillips makes it evident that he'd hoped not to be asked such a question. "It was ... one pound more than the standard."

"Twenty shillings more?" asks Noah.

"Correct."

"How large was the audience for the performance?" asks Noah.

"I was told the receipts were modest," says Phillips, "but that at least a dozen or so known associates of the Earls of Essex and Southampton attended."

"The Percy brothers?" asks Noah.

Phillips glares blankly at Noah, tacitly communicating that he's been assured that this line of questioning would be avoided. "The Percys were in attendance," he replies.

"Did they remain till the end?" asks Noah.

"They did," replies Phillips, "but I know little else about those who attended."

Noah smiles. "Actually, I had no further questions along that line."

Phillips smiles knowingly.

The next question would naturally have been whether the performance was attended by Sir Gelly, but the response would have led immediately to the question whether Sir Gelly stayed for the whole performance. As Noah and Phillips are both aware that Sir Gelly left the theater early—in the company of none other than their mutual friend Sir Henry Neville—the question has gone unasked.

"Master Phillips, I must ask you quite a grave question now," says Noah.

Phillips smirks. "It's not every day an officer of the Crown deigns to ask me *any* questions, sir. I've assumed that every one of your questions is quite grave."

"William Shakespeare appears to have disappeared," says Noah. "Do you know where he may be found?"

Phillips makes a show of taking a long time to answer, scratching his beard, rubbing his brow, shifting in his seat this way and that. At last he shakes his head. "No, sir. For the life of me I could not tell you where he might be found. The gentleman is a valued shareholder of the player's company, and I can only hope that no harm has come to him."

"*When* did he disappear?" asks Noah.

Phillips shrugs. "I could not say, sir. I was not wont to see the gentleman often, unless he was appearing in a current production. It's not as though he announced his departure. From what I've heard from others, one day he was there, the next he was gone, although his absence went unnoticed for a few days. I'm afraid I can't tell you when that occurred. My last clear recollection of seeing Master Shakespeare was well prior to the day of the rebellion, and I have no reason to suspect he had any hand in it."

"He was not a player in the performance we've been discussing?"

"Most certainly not," replies Phillips. "The expense catalog for that performance makes no mention of Master Shakespeare."

"Does the catalog list the name of *every* player appearing in the current play?"

Phillips chuckles quietly. "Oh, every player makes *sure* of it," he says.

"And why is that?" asks Noah.

"Because if a player's not listed, he's not *paid!*" Phillips says in good humor. "That's a rule that dates back to Henslowe's management, before he left us for the Admiral's Men ... nearly a *decade* ago now."

"Very well, Master Phillips," says Noah. "That concludes my inquiry for the moment, but will you remain available for further questioning, should that become advisable?"

"Why, certainly, sir." He looks at Noah's notes of the interview, still lying open on the desk. "Are we off the record now?"

Seeing Phillips's concern, Noah puts down his pen, and blots and folds up his notes. "Certainly, Master Phillips. Was there something else you'd care to discuss?"

"This is a small matter and may seem irrelevant now, but ... do you recall upbraiding Master Shakespeare after seeing the play about the Jewish merchant in Venice?" asks Phillips.

"I do," says Noah. "As I recall, I was rather harsh with him, as he'd taken the given names of my daughter and her husband for two of his characters."

"Precisely," says Phillips. "Have you forgiven him for this *faux pas*?"

Noah smiles knowingly. "I no longer blame Master Shakespeare. It was a slight indiscretion that might have been made by ... *anyone.*"

Phillips cocks his head, as though not quite sure whether Noah has signaled his knowledge that Shakespeare didn't write the play.

Noah rises and extends his hand. Phillips rises and shakes it, still looking for confirmation. Noah draws him closer by the hand, winks, and says softly: "Yes, I know who wrote the play."

AS THE SUN RECEDES below the horizon, Noah returns home. To his surprise, some small work appears to have resumed on Jonathan and Jessica's new house. Though not much has changed, a few lines of twine have been stretched between corner stakes to guide the placement of new bricks.

He hands off Bucklebury to Tom the stableman and opens the front door.

Marie awaits him inside, wearing an expression he's come to recognize as indicating that she has some new gossip to share. On his way in the door, he picks up a pair of letters that were slipped under it. One is a bill from the dressmaker, the other is sealed in a finely made envelope bearing Lady Leicester's initials. His name as addressee is raggedly penned, as though inscribed in a rush.

Marie waits patiently for him to greet her.

"Good e'en, darling," he says, kissing her cheek. "You seem to have something you'd care to share with me."

Her eyebrows rise. "I would have thought myself not nearly so transparent as all that," she says.

He smiles. "It's one of those endearing things about you that I've learned to love with all my heart." *Take that, David Killigrew!* he thinks. *You're not the only one who knows how to talk to a woman.*

She kisses him on the cheek and says, "Did you know that the Earl of Leicester was once married to one of our neighbors' cousins?"

Noah is taken aback, and he wonders if he's talked in his sleep. Why else would Marie have the least interest in a prior marriage of an earl who's been dead for more than a decade?

"Wh- what?" he says. "Please explain, my love."

"Lord Sheffield's cousin was once betrothed to the Earl of Leicester!" she says with glee, while trying to hold her voice down.

"Marie," he says wearily, "what has that to do with anything in today's world?"

"Evidently," says Marie, "*someone's* been stirring up trouble for Lady Leicester. Lady Sheffield says if it's proven that the earl married Sheffield's cousin before marrying Lady Leicester, then his marriage to Lady Leicester would be deemed unlawful on ground that it was ... *um* ... oh, what's the *word?*"

"*Bigamous?*" suggests Noah.

"Yes, precisely," says Marie. "And, if that were found to be so, Lord Sheffield's cousin or her son would sweep up all of Lady Leicester's land and titles!"

He regards her as though she's a bit mad. "How did such a thing even come up?" he asks with exasperation.

"Oh, you know the ladies. We talk."

"Yes, that much I know," he replies, "but is there no rhyme or structure in ladies' choice of topics?"

"Not really," she says, "that's the joy of idle conversation."

"*Gossip*, you mean. Marie, who raised the topic of Leicester's first marriage?"

"Why, Lady Sheffield, of course!" says Marie.

"Of course," he says indulgently, "but why did she think to raise it now?"

"Evidently, someone is trying to stir the pot," says Marie, "and Lady Sheffield thought it ... interesting."

"Well," sighs Noah, "if that's so, is not Lady Leicester to be pitied greatly, with her son having been executed a few days ago and her husband to go on trial for his life a couple of days hence?"

Marie evidently rethinks her bemused reaction to the news. "I suppose that's so. But to look on the bright side, Lord Leicester's cousin may have much to gain."

"Marie," says Noah, "I hope that you will keep your views on such matters to yourself, and that you will avoid further discussion of them with anyone but me. As you may know, Lady Leicester was once a good friend of Her Majesty. If ever there were a time for Her Majesty to ... *assist* her old friend, it would be presently."

Marie regards him suspiciously. "You already knew all this, didn't you?"

"Perhaps," he says, showing her the envelope. "This letter has just come to me from Lady Leicester."

Marie's eyes open wide. "So, you are *assisting* her?"

He holds her close. "I can only say, dear, that you should speak nothing of this any further, whether to Lady Sheffield or anyone else, for you and I are involved in it more than anyone should know."

"I?" she asks, amazed.

He snickers. "Yes," he says, "by marriage." He sniffs some interesting, spicy scents emanating from the kitchen. "Do you suppose there'll be supper soon? I'm famished."

"Of course, let's go in together."

He shakes his head wearily. "I'm afraid I must read this letter in the quiet of my study first," he says. "Might I ask who else will be here for supper?"

"Lord Jonathan, Lady Jessica, Esther—"

"Cheerful?" he asks.

"Perhaps, but I think he's supposed to be at Oxford," says Marie.

He laughs. "He's *always* supposed to be at Oxford, yet somehow he never seems more than a few feet away from Esther. Will Jacob be at supper?" he asks. "Or Timothy?"

She looks down morosely. "Sadly, they cannot both leave Leah alone for so long. I've had Cook prepare food for the three of them, and the boy will come to fetch it in a few minutes."

He beams at her. "Marie, you are the very picture of charity. I love you."

They kiss, and Noah wanders off to his study.

Lady Leicester's note, while intriguing, imparts little information: *I apologize for the intrusion, but could you please attend me alone this evening just after dark? I have sent the servants away. Come to the Thameside library, where I alone shall await you.*

<hr />

THANKFUL FOR THE full moon, Noah takes the short walk to Essex House alone, leaving both horse and torch at home. When he reaches the house, he sees it's just as well he didn't bring Bucklebury, for the stableman is evidently one of those who's been given the night off.

Essex House looms silently before him in the moonlight. As he lets himself in through the wicket, he shakes his head at the irony of fortune. If anyone had suggested, when he was held prisoner here a few weeks ago, that he would be invited back urgently several times in the weeks following Essex's execution, he would have dubbed them mad. But, of course, it's long been established in his mind that the world *is* quite mad. Such things are to be expected.

He shuts the wicket quietly behind him and walks around to the library. Taking extra care to avoid slipping on the wet stones, he steps up to the library door and lightly taps his finger on it.

Lady Leicester appears at once, carrying a candlestick. She opens the door and furtively ushers him in. She's wearing a heavy robe, as though she wishes the rest of the household to think she's preparing to retire.

"Won't you sit down, Serjeant Ames?" she says, and leads him to a chair. She takes a seat very near his, so they can keep their voices down.

"Would you mind, m'lady," he whispers, "if I were to ask who else is in the house at the moment?"

"Only Lady Essex," she replies then adds as a cynical afterthought, "and the one the Scots call 'John Barleycorn.'"

It takes a moment for Noah to catch on to the reference. "I take it her ladyship currently seeks surcease from sorrow at the bottom of a bottle," he speculates. Lady Leicester nods sadly. "It's to be expected, I suppose. I must observe, m'lady, that *your* presence of mind under these circumstances is a marvel to me. And most admirable."

She nods, near tears. "It takes its toll, Serjeant. It takes its toll."

"How may I assist your ladyship?" he asks.

"As you are no doubt aware," she says, "Master Leveson has not been released."

An image flits through Noah's mind, of Leveson lying at the base of a ditch with his head bashed in. "I have noticed that, madam. I hope no harm has come to him." He steels himself for bad news.

"None that I know of," she says, "though no villainy seems beneath the brigand who's holding him. He has demanded a *thousand* pounds, instead of the hundred agreed upon. Can you believe it?"

In the dim light, he observes her stricken face. Though ordinarily he'd be tempted to deride her credulity in expecting fair treatment from an abductor-for-hire, instead he pities her and takes refuge in a commonplace saying.

"No honor among thieves," he says. He considers the abductor's proposition. "A *thousand* pound?" he marvels, "*Have* you that much at present?"

"Of course not," she says. "I tried to explain to him that I receive my money only gradually over time, but he … didn't believe me … or didn't care. I suppose there are many landless merchants nowadays who require a great deal of money to conduct their affairs. Alas, 'tis not so with the landed gentry."

"When is he demanding the money be delivered?" asks Noah.

"He came here last night unexpectedly, through the same door you used just now. He said he'd come the same way in a week's time to collect it, but that so long as I make a substantial payment at that time, he would consider extending the terms." She frets openly. "Oh, what am I to do?" she asks, and weeps.

"He's coming back here next week?" asks Noah.

"Yes, but, *oh,* he said that if anyone else were to meet him here, he would instruct his confederate to kill Leveson. *Oh, that poor man!*" she cries in quiet anguish, chafing her hands anxiously.

Again a flush of anger rises in Noah's gut. She has the temerity to lament the peril of a man *she's* had abducted for the purpose of assuring the death of yet an *additional* innocent man.

"Do you know the man's name?" he asks.

"The confederate?" says Lady Leicester. "No, he didn't say. He referred to him only as his new *partner*, and implied that his partner was the reason for increasing his … fee."

"I meant the name of the man who came here last night, madam. Do you know *his* name?"

"*Mullin,*" she says. "I'm sorry. In my confusion, I thought I'd mentioned his name earlier."

"Mullin," he echoes. "What does he look like?"

"He's an average-looking man. Considerably shorter than you are, Serjeant, and facially not much to look at. He does have a few things in his favor, I suppose. One is that he speaks as though he's educated, and dresses as he probably *believes* educated men dress. But they don't, of course. His taste tends rather to the … gaudy. He fancies himself stylish, I'd imagine."

"Do you know where he might be found?" asks Noah.

"I know nothing else about him," she says. "He was recommended by a servant who left me years ago, a footman … whom I later discharged for stealing."

My God! thinks Noah. *What will such a credulous woman do without a husband to protect her from such rabble?* Well, as that's beyond his control, it's likewise beyond his care. "How much can you scrape together to give him upon his return?" asks Noah.

"Aren't you going to *arrest* him?" she asks.

"Madam, the first thing he'll do is to accuse *you!* No, we can't have him arrested." Noah sighs. "I'm afraid his use of a confederate alone renders that impracticable, m'lady, unless you want the blood of both Leveson *and* Neville on your hands."

"Of course I don't," she says with a shiver.

He shakes his head. She was more than prepared to have *Sir Henry's* blood on her hands, but apparently adding a *caitiff's* blood would be simply too much for her immortal soul to bear.

"Besides," says Noah, "if instead we have him followed, there's a chance that whatever you give him could be recovered."

She becalms herself and seems to be assaying her resources. "I suppose that, without troubling friends, I could assemble a hundred fifty pounds or so."

"That *might* do the trick," he says. "At least, I hope it's enough, or we'll have our hands full right quick."

"What do you mean?" she asks with a worried look.

"Well," he says, "what if he feels you're withholding from him? He could murder Leveson or make his confinement far more miserable. Or he could try to take more from you before he even leaves this house."

Her eyes flash with terror.

"Of course," Noah assures her, "we'll have someone nearby to ensure that he doesn't get carried away with m'lady, should that happen."

She nods. "Then, what's your plan?"

"First I must see whom I can get to carry it out before I can form it fully, madam. Though at need, in other cases, I could muster the full might of the Crown, it's extremely important to keep this particular matter as quiet as possible for your sake."

She regards him inquiringly as he begins to form a plan in his mind.

"There may be violence," he says after a few minutes, and bows before going.

CHAPTER 21

THE NEXT MORNING, Noah is summoned by the Queen to the living quarters at Whitehall. On this visit, he's escorted from the entrance by the brunette lady-in-waiting who was upbraided by the Queen some weeks ago for answering a question on behalf of her hopelessly ignorant blonde friend.

"Are you leading me," asks Noah with a note of worry in his voice, "to the same small parlor where Her Majesty received me on my most recent visit?"

"I expect so," says the lady, turning to him. "You sound disappointed, Serjeant."

"Not in the least," says Noah, "but Her Majesty seemed … *preoccupied* on that occasion with the passing of the Earl of Essex. It seemed to put her out quite. It has not been her custom to receive her counselors in such small quarters."

"Truth be told," she says, "Her Majesty does seem a bit reluctant to receive visitors in the larger rooms lately. Perhaps she's just simplifying her life."

"Perhaps," says Noah, but he doesn't believe it. Something's wrong with the Queen, even if everyone around her is too anxious to notice or mention it.

The lady knocks on the parlor door.

"Come," says the Queen.

The lady opens the door and announces Noah, curtsies, and leaves.

The Queen turns to look at Noah, who bows and rises again. There's something odd in her countenance. She's looking *toward* him, but her eyes are focused upon a point far behind him. As there's a wall there, the point she's focused on is outside the room. It gets no better when she speaks.

"Noah," she says, "thank you for coming on such short notice." Once again the gray light from the window deepens the wrinkles about her eyes.

He bows again. "Yours ever to command, Majesty."

Again, there's a long silence in which she seems to be having a conversation within the confines of her own mind, complete with changes of expression. All that's missing is the words.

To end the awkward pause, Noah says: "Is Your Majesty expecting Lord Robert to join us?"

She shakes her head. "No, 'tis just you and I. I was very ... open and honest with you the other day, Noah." She blushes. "I hope that my trust was not misplaced, and that you have not repeated anything I said then."

"Not misplaced," he says, shaking his head. "I was privileged to hear Your Majesty's innermost thoughts, and would not violate that privilege for all the world."

"I sounded ... bitter, did I not?" she asks with a slight cringe.

Noah shakes his head. "Yours was the voice of long experience, Majesty, the voice of inner reflection. I hope that you will always feel free to speak your mind with me. Always."

She is sufficiently satisfied with his reply to abandon her fugue state and focus on him once again. He finds it reassuring that she seems capable of rejoining the world at will.

"And you, Noah," she says, "will you be equally open and honest with your prince?"

"I shall, Majesty," he says. *What is she getting at? Or is she still in a trance despite appearances to the contrary?*

There's a knock at the door and the lady-in-waiting enters with a small tray of elaborate biscuits. The lady places the tray down on a small table and bows out. The Queen shows not the slightest interest.

"Please help yourself, Noah," she says.

"Madam," he says gingerly, "have you no interest in such delicacies?"

She shakes her head. "None of late," she says, as though it's a matter of no importance. "I have not invited Lord Robert this morning, as he seems remiss in failing to do something I've asked him to do. I thought it wise to summon my Hebrew baron to discuss it."

Noah smiles at her pet name for him, which she generally reserves for only the most intimate occasions. "Anything, madam," he says. "May I ask what remissness you have found in Lord Robert?"

"I've asked him to interview William Shakespeare, which he has repeatedly told me he cannot do, as Master Shakespeare appears to have been detained on serious business at some location outside London."

Detained on serious business outside London? Those are likely the very words Lord Robert used. True, but evasive. To avoid being questioned is, he supposes, *business* of a sort. As for Shakespeare's location? Even Noah's house on Holborn is technically *outside* London, as is the Globe Theater, so that says nothing about how far away Shakespeare might be.

She continues. "A few days ago, I asked *you* to find Master Shakespeare, Noah. Have you made any progress?"

"Since Your Majesty so commanded, I have interviewed Augustine Phillips, the business manager for the Lord Chamberlain's Men," says Noah, "but Master Phillips responded to my direct question with his assurance that he knows nothing of Master Shakespeare's location."

"What else did he tell you?" she asks.

"He told me how the performance was originally arranged. That he was asked by the Percy brothers, Sir Charles and Sir Joscelyn, whether the player's company would be prepared to stage *Richard the Second* at the Globe, and that Phillips replied that they would be prepared to do so for the right price. Some weeks later, Sir Gelly Meyrick dickered on the price with Master Phillips, paid the fee, and the play was later staged. There were a dozen or so followers of Lord Essex in attendance at the play, but receipts from the public were modest."

"What was the fee negotiated by Phillips?" asks the Queen.

Noah searches his memory. "It was the players' usual fee for such a showing, Majesty, plus a premium of twenty shillings."

She sneers. "*Twenty* pieces of silver?" she says. "They sold their souls cheap! Wouldn't *thirty* have been more in keeping with the long-established rate for betrayal?"

Even to a Jew, the Queen's allusion is unmistakable. She's likening the premium received by the player's company to the bribe paid to Judas Iscariot to betray Jesus at Gethsemane.

Noah can feel his face fall and a sweat break out. "Madam, I don't know what to say. I did not get the impression from Master Phillips that he regarded the premium as a price for betrayal. As he pointed out, the play had been staged many times before without ill effect."

"*Not* without ill effect, Noah," says the Queen, "but with an *incremental* corrosive effect."

"I see," replies Noah.

She regards him sternly. "Neither Lord Robert nor you seems especially concerned that Master Shakespeare has authored a play obliquely challenging my right to the Crown." She seems genuinely irritated, even alarmed. "Why am I alone in perceiving Shakespeare as a possible threat?"

"Madam," says Noah, "Master Shakespeare is no threat to either Your Majesty or the Crown."

She bangs the table with her open palm in time to her next question. *"Why isn't the author of that play in Crown custody?"* she demands. With evident interest, she watches the equivocation in his face.

Sir Henry has authorized me to proceed with the Queen in hopes of gaining clemency, and the time has come. He cannot hold out any longer.

His mouth dry as the deserts of Arabia, at last he speaks. "In this unique instance, madam, may I rely upon the same confidentiality that Your Majesty expects from your humble servant?"

At first she regards him skeptically, then nods her assent. "You may, in this singular instance."

He inhales deeply. "I have reason to believe that the author of the play poses no threat to the Crown, and is indeed already in Crown custody."

Anger flashes over her face. "But you just told me you don't know where Shakespeare is."

He's in a cold sweat now. "My assurances to you have *all* been true, madam. I so swear."

He stands mute and waits for her to draw what, to him, seems an obvious conclusion. Of course, this information is all brand new to *her*, as she must first overcome some firmly held (but mistaken) beliefs.

Slowly, her face changes from surprise to horror, then to barely suppressed fury.

"And where was this 'author' arrested?" she demands.

"At Dover, Majesty, by Lord Saint Ives and your humble servant."

She seethes a moment, breathing heavily. "Thank you for your loyalty, Noah. It's all the loyalty I seem to have got lately, and I must be grateful for it. I must think on this privately. Meanwhile, you may rest assured that I will maintain your confidence in this matter." Barely containing a strong swirl of emotions under the serene mask of her face, she says as gently as possible, "You may go."

But Noah wishes to mention the mitigating circumstance of Sir Henry's renunciation of the rebellion, even though he'd much prefer having Leveson at hand for proof. *"If I may,* madam—"

But she slams her open hand on the table, cutting off all conversation.

"Get out!" she shouts, trembling with anger, her eyes focused once again on a point well past the wall behind him.

Noah bows and turns, all the while wondering whether he's just saved Sir Henry's life … or killed him.

———————⟳⟳⟳———————

JUST AS NOAH EXPECTED, Cheerful has not yet returned to Oxford since last term's examinations. On one hand, that's unfortunate, as it's delaying the award of his degree; on the other, it assures that he'll be available to assist in the hugger-mugger that's become an unavoidable part of Noah's position.

Noah is not seriously concerned about how quickly Cheerful attains his degree, as there's considerable wealth in the Killigrew family, and Cheerful (being everyone's favorite) will quickly find employment in some lucrative part of his family's enterprises.

After supper, Noah invites Cheerful into his study to discuss the dangerous matter of Lady Leicester's extortionate abductor.

Timothy follows Cheerful into the study like an uninvited puppy and insinuates himself as near the fire as he can without scorching his clothing.

"For purposes of this conversation," says Noah eyeing Timothy cautiously, "I'll refer to the lady in my story as simply 'the lady.'"

"Approximately where does she live in relation to your home?" asks Cheerful.

"Fairly close," says Noah, "close enough that getting there will play little part in our planning. The problem is that the lady has caused a certain … man to be abducted." He turns ever so subtly in Timothy's direction. "*Not* Shakespeare, thank you."

Cheerful says, "But, sir, as you'll recall, Timothy and I are already aware of the identity of the missing gentleman. That is, if it's the same man."

"Of course you do," says Noah, turning to Timothy. "I take it, Timothy, that you have no new leads on where he might be stowed."

"None, suh," says Timothy. "I thought, since things didn't turn out so well last time, I'd stay out of the rescuin' business till I'm asked to return to it."

"A sound practice," remarks Noah, "although I'm not quite sure I'll ever be prepared to ask you to return to such a rough business. Anyway, I persuaded the lady to instruct her abductor to release the gentleman, but when she did so, he defied her, instead multiplying his unlawful fee tenfold. He's returning to the lady's house for an initial payment under cover of darkness this coming Tuesday evening."

Cheerful takes a moment to respond. "So far, a rescue is sounding feasible. What's the pitfall?"

"The abductor apparently has acquired a confederate," says Noah, "whom he calls a partner. He says that if anyone 'greets' him at the lady's house or attempts to interfere, his confederate will kill the prisoner."

Cheerful folds his arms and, after some thought, says, "This could get quite sticky, sir. Have you considered calling in the Warders?"

Noah sighs and shakes his head. "The abduction was done at the lady's instructions. As I've been instructed to *assist* her (up to a point), we can't expose her to arrest."

"What do we know about the abductor?" asks Cheerful.

"Not very much, I'm afraid."

From the corner, Timothy pipes up. "Do you know his name, suh?"

At first Noah's undecided whether to tell Timothy the abductor's name, but he already knows who's been abducted. *In for a penny, in for a pound.*

"Mullin," Noah replies.

A faint smile melts away from Timothy's face, and he becomes in turn angry and sad. Even in the firelight, the reddening of his face is evident.

Cheerful casts a knowing look toward Noah, and the two wait for Timothy to regain his composure.

When it becomes clear the boy will not speak until spoken to, Noah asks, "Do you *know* the man, Timothy?"

Timothy shrugs. "I suppose there must be more'n one man goin' by that name in London. Does this Mullin talk a like gentleman and dress like a ... stage player?"

Noah's eyebrows pop up. "That's more or less as he was described to me."

Silence.

"Well," says Timothy at last, "I can tell you he's no gentleman."

"How can you be sure?" asks Cheerful.

"Because no gentleman would ask a young boy to do what he asked *me* to do," says Timothy. "In fact, I can't think of *anybuddy* you could ask to do that without gettin' slapped for it. But that's not the worst of it."

Silence again, then Timothy resumes his tale.

"About a year ago, I met this one boy. He'd been livin' hand to mouth on the street like me for a couple o' years. We stole food together and found places we could sleep in the same room. Our friendship lasted but a few weeks. He called himself 'Choth.'" He pronounces the name to rhyme with *doth*.

"Choth?" says Cheerful. "What sort of name is that?"

Timothy continues. "He had a harelip, y'see, and he couldn't write anything (and who on the street could *read* it if he could?), so we called him what he called himself. Choth. It wasn't until some weeks later that I learned what he was tryin' to say all that time. With his *talkin'* problem, he had a hard time of it on the street, although (truth be told) I think he would have had a hard time of it *anywhere*."

"Surely," says Noah, "there are places for young people with that affliction. Are there not?"

Timothy nods sardonically. "Oh, yes, suh. If he wanted to, he could freeze and eat the swill they'd feed 'im in a foundlings' home. He lived in one till he was old enough to escape. I asked him why he left—'cause even though they *talk* about it bein' freezin' in those places, it never *truly* gets cold enough to freeze—and he told me he was always afraid they'd think 'im mad and toss 'im in the Bedlam." Timothy's eyes well up. "Because he couldn't talk right, y'see. He was clever enough, once you got to know 'im, but he couldn't make himself ... understood, unless ye gave him a *lot* o' time.

"Anyways. Early one day at the Saracen's Head, I was buildin' a fire, which was one of the small jobs I'd do every mornin' so the tapster wouldn't toss us out in the cold. (When ye live hand to mouth, ye learn how to make yourself useful.) Choth was still sleepin' in the back room, up against the stone of the fireplace. Stone keeps givin' warmth even when a fire's been out a long time. Anyway, in walks Master Mullin. The tavern wasn't even open for business yet, and he walks in like he owns the place. So, I ask him if there's somethin' I can do for 'im, and—real soft-like—he makes his ... indecent proposition. At first, I thought he was jokin', but then he pulls out tuppence and waves it in front of my nose. And that's when I realized he's *not* jokin'. So I told him he'd better get out of there right quick—before Master Tapster come—if he knows what's good for 'im.

"To my surprise, he takes my hand and puts the tuppence in it, and tells me there's another comin' my way if I find another young boy who'd do what he asked. I almost threw the coin at 'im. But when yer livin' hand to mouth, you don't throw away money for nothin', least of all fer yer pride. So I told 'im I'd ask the others, but he better be leavin' anyway."

Cheerful gets up and rakes the coals in the fireplace. They wait for him to resume in his own time.

"So later, when Choth wakes up and sees me kind of angry, he asks me what 'appened, and I told 'im. Not for one second did I think he'd actually go lookin' for Mullin, but that's just what he did. I didn't see him that day, nor that night, nor for a few days after. Then, one fine day, I see 'im in a *carriage* of all things, sittin' next to Mullin. Since Mullin's lookin' the other way, Choth waves to me, and I wave back. I couldn't see too much of 'im, but I could see a flower pinned to his raggedy jacket, just like a 'real' gentleman."

"Was that the last you saw of him?" asks Noah.

Timothy shakes his head and sighs sadly. "No, suh. I saw him one more time. A couple o' weeks later, some other children—like me— come runnin' and tell me they found his body in a ditch not far from the Saracen's Head. So I went to see. It was him all right. He still had that stupid flower pinned to his jacket, 'cept it was all muddy by then. Some men picked his body up, and I followed 'em all the way back to the foundlings' home. How they recognized 'im, I don't know. They took his body to a graveyard in the back—no coffin or nothin'—and the priest come out and mumbles all the things they say over dead bodies. As there was nobody else there, I stepped up to the grave to hear better. When the priest sees me, he stops mumblin' and says out loud what a shame it is that this young man has been cut down in the prime of his life, and how sorely he'll be missed." Timothy scoffs. "And then the priest looks straight at me and asks me if I 'ad any fond memories of *Charles* that I'd like to tell." He gulps as though holding his supper down. "I didn't say nothin'. I just run away."

"Did you ever see Mullin again?" asks Noah.

"Nah," says Timothy. "He never dared come back to the Saracen's Head. If he did—and I caught him before he come in the door"—he glances at the refined gentlemen rapt with his story—"well ... he'd be sorry."

Noah shakes his head darkly. "We'll reconvene tomorrow night, after supper. Timothy, how are Jacob and Leah faring?"

Timothy shrugs. "Mistress Leah is quite feeble, suh. Very ... 'fragile' is what Jacob calls 'er."

Noah sighs, smacks his hands on his thighs, and rises. "And now to bed."

CHAPTER 22

ON THE SECOND DAY of March, Noah accompanies Jonathan and the historian Camden to Westminster Hall to witness another trial on charges of high treason. The defendants—knights all—have long known each other well: Sir Henry Cuffe, Sir Gelly Meyrick, Sir Christopher Blount (who is the late Essex's father-in-law and husband to Lady Leicester), Sir Charles Danvers, and Sir John Davies.

As they're marched into the courtroom, only Sir Gelly has the presence of mind to nod to Noah and bow deeply to Jonathan before turning to face the Court.

During the arraignment, Blount, Danvers, and Davies ask whether they may plead guilty to the portion of the indictment accusing them of participation in the rebellion, but not to the specification that they intended harm to Her Majesty. Before addressing their request, the Court has Cuffe and Meyrick physically separated from those making the request.

As at the trial of Essex and Southampton, the Court informs the three defendants that they will not be permitted to split their plea in the manner requested, as even the least participation in a conspiracy to rebel is conclusively presumed at law to envisage the murder of the Sovereign.

The Court then urges upon Blount, as evidence of his guilt, both his own confession and that of the deceased Earl of Essex. When the latter confession is read aloud to him, he writhes as though it could not be more false. Looking heavenward, he cries aloud, "Thou, O God, knowest from what manner of designs I *dissuaded* the earl!"

The Court then urges upon Blount the confession of the deceased Thomas Lea, the sailor whom Noah helped to capture. At the mention of Lea, Noah feels his face redden, and he casts his eyes down in regret. Seeing his reaction, Lord Jonathan pats him comfortingly on the shoulder.

The Queen's Solicitor then turns to Danvers, who listens patiently to the charges and responds with nothing but a simple statement that his participation in the rebellion arose solely out of his blind devotion to the Earl of Southampton, who once saved him from a charge of murder by transporting him out of the realm to France until he could obtain Her Majesty's pardon.

Davies then confesses to the peripheral accusation that he's been instructed in the popish religion and that he continues to profess that faith, having been encouraged in it by Blount. When Blount immediately objects, Davies reframes his statement to the effect that he would have continued his popish worship regardless of any encouragement from Blount.

Cuffe and Meyrick are then brought forward.

Cuffe is confronted with the confessions of Danvers, of the late Earl of Essex, and of Sir Henry Neville.

Essex's confession assigns full blame to Cuffe as the prime instigator of the whole plot.

Sir Henry's confession accuses Cuffe of having cautioned him, upon his return from France the previous August, that Sir Henry would surely be blamed for the failure to reach agreement on the Treaty of Boulogne. Sir Henry's confession goes on to say that Cuffe often attempted to enlist him in the rebellion, persuading him to visit with the late earl, and then persuading him to come to Drury House to hear of the preparations being made for the rebellion, which Sir Henry immediately condemned as wicked and impractical.

Upon hearing this, Cuffe makes no objection, although, ever the academician, he dwells on the inadequacies of the indictment in accusing him of engaging in rebellion on grounds that he merely occupied Essex House on the day it occurred. Hearing this, Crown counsel leaps to his feet to deny Cuffe's criticism, as the indictment specifically outlines each participant's assignment in the conduct of the rebellion, and that so long as a man knew the general object of the conspiracy, he thereby rendered himself liable for high treason.

When it comes to Sir Gelly's turn, the prosecutors seem to drone on in a needlessly long peroration, essentially accusing Sir Gelly of having prepared Essex House for defense.

Always a man of action rather than words, Sir Gelly merely shrugs and says, "Essex first raised me up, and Essex has now thrown me down."

The jury of twelve returns a verdict of guilty against every one of them.

Sentence of death is pronounced first upon Blount and Danvers, each of whom requests the death of a nobleman, that is, by beheading. Davies, upon hearing his death sentence pronounced, requests the same death; as he's not of noble blood, he asks that at least he not be quartered, so that he might be given Christian burial.

Meyrick and Cuffe are each condemned to die at Tyburn. As neither of them was accused of acts of violence, however, they're spared the horrors of being four-and-quartered, and are sentenced rather to hanging.

Before leaving the courtroom, Noah bows to Camden. "Sir," he says, "it has been more than a pleasure to have your company these past days. Though I expect it may be some time before we meet again, I very much look forward to the hour."

Before Camden can reply, Lord Jonathan asks Noah, "Aren't you going to attend the executions?"

Noah shakes his head sadly. "I've had my fill of such sights, m'lord. I would go only if I were ordered to do so. I hope you will understand."

"But will you not come to see Sir Gelly dispatched?" Lord Jonathan urges.

Noah sighs. "If your lordship would have me there, I shall attend—but that one alone."

Camden bows. "I expect I shall see you both there."

<hr>

IT'S FULL DARK at Thameside, but there's too much moonlight for Noah to be confident he's fully hidden from view, even behind the trunk of a thick old oak. Listening for Mullin's arrival from his perch on the southeast corner of Essex House, Noah's ears become ever more attuned to the gentle sounds of the night, the lazy slapping of wavelets against the Essex House dock and the clopping of a few sets of hooves along the Strand.

Though he's confident he can't be seen by anyone approaching Essex House from the street (one would have to be on the river to see him), there can be no certainty that Mullin will come the obvious way. After all, he's a scoundrel, and surely has more than one trick up his sleeve.

A brief rustling in the bushes on the opposite side of the dock breaks the rhythm of the night. It's followed by a brief glint of moonlight off a metal blade, which is Cheerful's prearranged signal that someone has entered the grounds through the wicket on the Strand and is now coming 'round the house along its western face.

Noah's eyes dart toward the river to confirm that no one's watching.

There's no one there, at least no one he can see. Remembering the dagger given him long ago by Uncle Avram, he locates it in his pocket next to the mask he's brought along for the occasion. He firmly grips the dagger.

A few moments later, a man saunters past the place where Cheerful and Timothy are hiding, showing no fear of apprehension. His obvious confidence only makes Noah that much more nervous.

The man walks up to the library door and knocks gently three times. Even with the aid of moonlight, Noah can't see precisely what the man's wearing, but he does seem to be dressed for a jaunty night out.

The library door is opened from inside, and candlelight briefly illuminates both Mullin's face and Lady Leicester's. There's a murmur of furtive conversation between the two. She sounds nervous, but not terrified, as she admits Mullin to the library and closes the door, cutting off the light.

Noah imagines young Lady Essex asleep upstairs, and prays she hasn't suddenly deviated from her newly acquired habit of drinking herself to sleep.

While awaiting Mullin's exit, Noah's teeth are set on edge by the sound of a horse clopping in place. That would be Cheerful's mount, which has been tied off on a tree by the Strand in case Cheerful sees a possibility of following Mullin undetected.

The clopping quickly dies down. Perhaps it means nothing. Surely a horse must perform that little dance-in-place at least a dozen times on an average evening, but no one notices it until silence becomes the order of the day.

After waiting a few minutes, Noah begins to worry that something has gone amiss. All that was supposed to happen was for Lady Leicester to hand him some money and explain that she'll have more in another two weeks, which should have taken only a minute or two.

Noah finds his attention fixed on the dim candlelight escaping through the single opening between the curtains. Momentarily, it seems to flicker. Well, that's to be expected, he tells himself. But then the candlelight begins to gutter, fading until he wonders if it's been extinguished. Should he go inside to see what's happening? No, the moment Mullin hears him, Lady Leicester will be in peril and Leveson a dead man.

Then a dim light upstairs draws his eye. It's bouncing a bit. It's probably the same candle. Whoever's holding it is walking. Did Mullin insist upon receiving additional monies immediately? Has Mullin sent her to fetch additional monies? In which case, he could have remained in the unlit library. Could he be looking out this window for Noah right now?

Or did Mullin accompany Lady Leicester upstairs? Is she in immediate danger? What of the sleeping, vulnerable Lady Essex? Noah breaks into a cold sweat. He detests waiting, especially when it's impractical for him to intercede. The candlelight upstairs begins to fade, and he shifts his attention back down to the library. And waits. And waits. Once he's waited for a longer time than it took for the candle to move upstairs, he realizes what's happened. Mullin has asked her to let him out through a different door, probably the door onto the Strand.

Noah would like to move along the eastern side of the house shadowing the candle's movement, but there are too many windows through which he might be seen. And if Mullin were to leave from one of the side doors, he'd be sure to see Noah, which would end in disaster. On the edge of hearing, Cheerful and Timothy appear to be having a disagreement, no doubt mirroring his own concerns.

Suddenly, a horse and rider burst out of the trees and gallop eastward on the Strand into the night. But Noah can't be sure it was Mullin until Lady Leicester emerges from the house, looking for him.

At last she emerges through the library doorway, appearing exercised, but unharmed—except for her loss of the money that Mullin just escaped with.

Timothy races across the yard to Noah.

"I can still catch him, sir," he whispers breathlessly. "May I take the horse?"

"Now, young man," replies Noah, "you know that was not the plan."

Timothy's face falls in exasperation. "But the plan has failed, suh!"

Cheerful comes up behind Timothy and places his hands on his shoulders. "There'll be another chance, Tim," he whispers and the boy's shoulders slump with disappointment. "Now you return to Jacob's side. I expect he needs you right away."

Timothy stamps off full of disappointment, and Noah and Cheerful watch him until he disappears from view.

"Come," says Noah to Cheerful, "let's go inside." As they enter through the library door, Noah takes a long look at the river, and shivers to think how readily they could be seen from any vantage point out there.

Once the door is closed, Lady Leicester quietly upbraids Noah for letting Mullin get away.

"But, your ladyship," says Noah, "our plan required you to let your visitor in and out through the same door."

"But he wouldn't be satisfied with the amount I offered him," she says defensively. "He insisted that I give him more, and then insisted upon following me to the place where I keep my money."

"How much did you offer him at first, madam?" asks Noah.

"I handed him fifty pounds," she says, as though anyone should have been satisfied with that.

Noah notices that Cheerful is quietly amused.

"But, madam," says Noah, "that's *half* the amount upon which you mutually agreed! Why would you expect him to accept that? Besides," he says, thinking back to an earlier conversation, "didn't m'lady say you could muster one hundred and fifty pounds? Why did you not proffer him at least that much?"

She regards him indignantly. "No doubt you'd like me to pay him the thousand pounds he's demanded, Serjeant!"

"Not at all, madam," he protests. "How much more did you give him when he forced you to take him upstairs?"

"I gave him an additional fifty pounds," she says, "so now he *should* regard himself as paid in full. Yet, I still haven't secured the prisoner's release, so he's been overpaid and failed to complete his task." She puts her chin up. "Why, I should take him to court!"

Noah's mouth literally hangs agape, as he's amazed at her disconnected logic. "Where you would be arrested upon filing your complaint," he says. Becalming himself, he adds, "M'lady will of course move her cache of money to some other location."

"Of course," she says. "Well, what do we do now that your attempt has failed?"

"Can m'lady tell me what else was said during this somewhat prolonged visit?"

"He wanted more money," she sniffs.

"So I've gathered, madam," he says, "but did he tell you anything that might be helpful to our cause? Did he say anything about his confederate?"

"Nothing."

"Did he say when he would return and how much he would demand?"

"He said he'd return in another two weeks as I'd suggested, and that he'd expect the remainder of his thousand pound." She regards Noah darkly as if she knows what he's thinking. "No, Serjeant, I cannot raise such a sum presently."

"I wasn't thinking that, madam," he says, distracted by dark thoughts, "for I'm beginning to suspect we may never see Leveson alive—no matter how much you pay."

CHAPTER 23

TWO DAYS LATER, the wind roars high above the gallows known as Tyburn Tree. Nearer the ground, the region's split-tailed hawks known as "kites" circle eagerly in their hunger for the bloody entrails occasionally burnt and discarded here.

Seated on horseback beside a substantial crowd, Noah, Jonathan, and Camden ruefully await the proceedings.

Two carts complete their passage from Newgate and clatter up to the scaffold. The first carries Sir Henry Cuffe. In the second stands Sir Gelly Meyrick. Each prisoner has his hands already tied in front of him, and a single-knotted noose about his neck.

The crowd seems disappointed as word circulates that the condemned men will be hanged without quartering. Noah glances above; evidently, the kites haven't heard, for they circle still.

Cuffe's cart is the first to be rolled to the scaffold. The free end of the halter rope is tossed up to a man on the scaffold, who takes up the slack and fastens his end to the "tree." Notwithstanding that there's no one by who can help him, Cuffe addresses the crowd in his usual meandering way, justifying his conduct and repeating the same legally irrelevant distinction he emphasized at trial, namely, that he intended no personal harm to the Queen.

"Enough," cries the sheriff. "Do not wrong the truth by distinctions, nor sew fig-leaves together to cover your fault, but rather get on with it!"

Cuffe sends the sheriff a dirty look for cutting short the little time afforded a man who shall never have any *further* time, to whom "later" no longer has meaning. He turns back to the crowd and says: "For my part, I never excited any man to take up arms against the Queen. But whereas I have brought that noble knight Sir Henry Neville into danger, I am heartily sorry for it, and I earnestly entreat him to forgive me."

He falls to fervent prayer, protests his faith in God, and craves pardon of God and Queen.

When he's finished speaking, the gate at the rear of the cart is opened. The horses are urged forward, pulling the cart out from under his feet. After a short drop, he dangles there, jerking for a few minutes, then hanging inert for some time.

The cart carrying a stoical Gelly Meyrick then draws up to the scaffold, and the process begins anew, except that Meyrick, saying nothing in his own interest, rather urges the granting of clemency to any he might have led astray. As he finishes, he nods respectfully to Lord Jonathan and curtly toward the sheriff, who urges the horses forward.

For a long time, Jonathan stares at Meyrick's corpse dangling next to Cuffe's, and makes no sign of leaving.

Noah turns to him. "Come, my lord," he says sympathetically with Camden nodding in agreement, "there's nothing for us here. All that could be done *has* been done." The three of them clop mournfully away.

The disappointed kites who've circled all the while rise now, climbing into a gale that lifts them up and carries them away.

———————⟶∘⟨⟩∘⟵———————

TWO DAYS LATER on Tower Hill, Danvers and (Lady Leicester's third husband) Blount are beheaded, and the Essex Rebellion is well and truly done.

But remaining to be decided are the fates of the Earl of Southampton and Sir Henry Neville.

———————⟶∘⟨⟩∘⟵———————

NOAH FINDS HIMSELF in the same salon, alone with the Queen. He cannot imagine how she escapes the company of Lord Robert for so long without piquing his curiosity. But then he realizes that, although Lord Robert knows everything that happens in the palace and everything Her Majesty does, she can escape his company on her slightest whim—because she's the Queen, and Lord Robert answers to her. The Queen answers to God alone.

"Tell me what the Nevilles think of me, Noah," she says equably.

"Majesty?" he says, searching his memory for an answer and a careful way to frame it.

"Oh, come, Noah," she says. "Everyone has an opinion of the Sovereign."

"As you can imagine, Majesty," he says, "I know little of the Nevilles' views on their Queen, except perhaps for Sir Henry's."

"Did you know his father, *old* Sir Henry?" she asks.

"I met him only once, Your Majesty. At Billingbear."

She taps her head with her forefinger, as though faulting herself for forgetting. "Oh, that's right. You visited with him at Billingbear during that awful plague year. What was it?"

"1592, madam," he replies. "It was during the Lopez matter."

She nods. "A matter that I expect the late Lord Essex is lamenting as we speak."

He says nothing, but remembers his fury at Essex at that time, and wonders whether it's possible Christians have it right in their understanding of heaven, hell, and the afterlife. For his own part, he doubts it. In fact, of late he seems to doubt everything.

"Did Old Sir Henry speak of me?" she asks.

"Yes, madam," he says. "I recall him expressing the opinion that, in his experience, Your Majesty was the Sovereign *most* deserving of praise."

She regards him doubtfully. "Truly, Noah?"

"As God is my witness," he replies. "He remembered Your Majesty fondly and had nothing critical to say of you."

She paces by the fire. "As I was his favored Sovereign and he lived through the reign of King Henry the Eighth, then he must have held a lesser opinion of my father."

Although she hasn't posed a question, she obviously expects an answer.

"Old Sir Henry let on," he says, "that he felt his father, Sir Edward Neville, had received unfair treatment at King Henry's hands."

"Indeed," she says, evidently unsurprised, "Sir Edward was beheaded at Tower Hill on my father's warrant. Though the charge was advancing the interests of de la Pole at the King's expense, in fact the execution was conducted to advance Thomas Cromwell's claim to certain real property sought by Sir Edward."

While this is news to Noah, he admires the Queen's objectivity about her father's flaws. "Old Sir Henry made no mention of the grounds for his father's execution, madam, whether true or false."

"And what of your younger Sir Henry?" she says. "Has he ever told you his opinion of me?"

He nods. "He also held Your Majesty in high esteem, telling me that your inner kindness once forbade you to kill a deer in Windsor Forest."

She regards him sternly. "Perhaps if I'd acted more like my father and killed the blasted deer, Sir Henry would have feared me more.

Perhaps then he would have *told* me that a rebellion was brewing ... for fear of losing his own head."

Noah can only shrug and say, "Perhaps. But your regard for young Sir Henry has not been entirely unrequited, madam. Judging by the gallows confessions of the conspirators, Sir Henry was adamant in his insistence that their cause was wicked and idiotic."

She nods dubiously. "But as a loyal subject, he should have told *me* of it." She peers into his eyes. "Do you doubt it?"

"I doubt it not a whit, madam," he confesses softly. "To say his conduct is a disappointment to me would be to grossly understate my view of his ... lapse."

"Did you know of his ... lapse ... prior to the rebellion?" she asks.

"I did not, madam," he replies, feeling very much as though he's on the witness stand himself. "Sir Henry well knew that if I'd caught a whiff of it, I'd go straight to Lord Robert."

"But not to your Queen?" she asks.

"I would have had no doubt that Lord Robert would handle it with as great a dispatch as Lord Burghley before him. By the time Your Majesty learned of such a plot, there would have been several heads pricked down for pikes at London Bridge, and Essex would have lain in the Tower awaiting Your Majesty's pleasure."

"And what of Southampton?" asks the Queen. "Would Lord Robert have had him, too, in the Tower?"

"I expect so, Majesty," says Noah. "Lord Robert is well aware that it would have been solely *Your Majesty's* prerogative to reduce the punishment to be meted out to the Earl of Southampton."

"And to which jail would *Sir Henry* have been sent?" she asks pointedly.

Noah squirms uncomfortably and rubs his beard. "I would have told Lord Robert of Sir Henry's knowledge of the rebellion. But at that point, Your Majesty would have been well clear of danger, and the rebellion would have been quashed on information I'd received from Sir Henry, whose lapse in informing the authorities would have been cured by *my* actions."

"Ever the lawyer," says the Queen with subdued admiration. She shakes her head. "It's not possible to cure someone *else's* moral failings, Noah. All you can do is to cover for them, a path that's often ill-advised. You would have protected me, but Sir Henry would have escaped punishment—*yea*, even so much as *detection*."

Noah shrugs. "A will o' the wisp, madam. We must be speaking of an alternative world where such things come to pass, for in the present one they never did."

"And Lady Anne," says Her Majesty. "Had she an opinion of her prince?"

"None that I know of, madam," Noah replies. "And of late her hearing has been so poor that conversation has been quite limited."

"You go back quite a long way with Sir Henry, do you not?" she says conversationally. "I understand you went on European tour with him as a young man."

"I *do* go back a long way with him, Majesty," he replies, "even further back than the tour. We go back to our days at Oxford together."

"I understand," she says coyly, "that he was quite the ladies' man on that tour."

Noah cannot help but smile. "Indeed, madam. One of my most important functions was to defend him from punishment for indiscretions of that kind."

She arches an eyebrow. "No less a personage than King Henri of Navarre told me that Sir Henry wound up in jail for carousing more than once, and that you fished him out of such situations with a minimum of embarrassment."

Noah smiles and jovially adds, "And a minimum of *expense*, madam."

"Even then he was mindful of his money, I see."

"He's ever been so, in my experience," says Noah. "But, truth be told, if it hadn't been for the benevolent intercession of King Henri, Sir Henry would have ended up in the jakes despite my efforts." His feeble attempt at levity is lost on the Queen, as her mind has already moved on.

"I have noticed," she says, "that Sir Henry has ever been mindful of his money. Of course, as his branch of the family is untitled (though not entirely unlanded), I suppose Sir Henry is part of the 'money' economy that has come into fashion since my father's coronation." She looks directly at Noah. "Do you suppose that's why he writes for the public stage?"

"Madam?" asks Noah, unsure what she's getting at.

"Do you suppose Sir Henry writes for the *money*?" she asks.

"As to whether that's his primary motive, madam, I cannot say, but it's my belief that he is paid for his playwriting."

"And he was furious with me for taking him to task for selling cannon indiscriminately to foreign powers," she observes. "I expect that such dealings had brought him a good deal of money."

Noah's quiet, as he's not sure where she's going with this.

The Queen removes further doubt without ado. "And Sir Henry was constantly bemoaning the Exchequer's arrears in paying him the money for his embassage." She smiles as though she's decided something that was bothering her greatly. "Money is what he cares about most. Very well. If money is what he loves, then I shall have his. I shall fine him until he *weeps*." She sits back smugly and says, "Thank you, Noah, you may go."

Noah kicks himself, alarmed that he was lulled into thinking he could speak freely to the Queen without consequence. And he's unwittingly led her by the hand to a form of punishment that Sir Henry is sure to find quite painful.

"Madam," he blurts out, "I shall be able to produce evidence that Sir Henry attempted to frustrate the rebellion—and in fact succeeded in doing so."

She cocks her head with interest. "Oh? When can you produce this evidence?"

He kicks himself again. He can't tell the Queen that he expects to rescue Sir John, as that would imply that he knows where Sir John is being held. And that would raise the question *how* Noah came upon such knowledge, which would in turn require him to disclose that Sir John was abducted on orders of the Queen's old friend Lady Leicester, to whom Noah now owes a professional obligation to keep her confidence. *What a tangled web!*

"It may take a few weeks," he says feebly.

"I shall look forward to seeing it," she replies. "You may go now."

NOAH IS INVITED once more for dinner at the Lord Admiral's house, and once again the Lord Admiral is not at home. After dinner, Noah and Sir Henry move into the upstairs parlor.

"Matthew," says Sir Henry to the Lord Admiral's footman, "please leave us alone for a few minutes. Serjeant Ames and I have important affairs to discuss."

Matthew bows out.

Sir Henry swishes the sherris around in his glass. "You were saying?"

Noah shifts uneasily, and completes the thought that he started over dinner. "Evidently, Her Majesty intends to impose a hefty fine upon you."

"And from whom did you learn this?" asks Sir Henry.

Noah flashes Sir Henry an unmistakable expression saying *you know quite well whom.*

"Was *hefty* the word that was used?" asks Sir Henry.

"Not exactly.

Sir Henry takes another sip. "How hefty is hefty?"

"I don't know, to be honest. I know that fines are under consideration for several participants in the rebellion, such as the Earl of Rutland, Bedford, Sands, Monteagle. The Percys will likely get off the lightest, and even that fine would likely be five hundred pound ... perhaps more."

Sir Henry frowns. "She can't possibly place me in a category with Rutland or some of those others you mention. They were active participants right through the day of the rebellion." He shakes his head. "Besides, those men are quite wealthy. Is she *limiting* their punishment to payment of the fine?"

"I don't know," says Noah. "That is, no one knows. I doubt Her Majesty herself knows as yet. In the past, many men fined for high treason have paid their fines and avoided execution, but there's something the Crown has done in the past that would make your life even more miserable."

"What's that?"

Noah sighs. "The Crown could keep you imprisoned at the Tower until the fine has been fully paid."

Sir Henry's face fills with dread. "Do you suppose she might do that in my case?"

"I don't know," replies Noah, "but I can tell you that she's more furious at you than at any of the others I just mentioned."

"But why?" he asks, full of consternation. "*Why?*"

Noah takes a sip of his own sherris and gives the question some thought. "Other than your betrayal of her trust in you, as we've already established, the only two possibilities I can come up with—and mind you she has said nothing about either—I suspect she blames you for allowing Southampton to get involved in the rebellion."

"How could she blame me for that?" asks Sir Henry incredulously. "How could she *possibly*? Everyone knows he and Essex were thick as thieves. They were bed mates, for heaven's sake."

"Well, now that she's aware of your writing, she's probably realized that your two long poems were publicly dedicated to Southampton, meaning that there was a long-standing relationship between the two of you. And your attempt to deny that relationship in your first statement to the Privy Council has no doubt reinforced her notion that you were close enough to Southampton to extricate him from any thought of rebellion. She loves Southampton. *Why?* I don't know." He shrugs. "He's thought to be a comely and courtly young fellow. She has a soft spot for such people, you know."

"Not soft enough to save Essex from the block," says Sir Henry. "What's your other possibility?"

"You just put your finger on it. She may even blame you for Essex's rebellion."

"Why, that's madness!" says Sir Henry. "I never had *any* control over his lordship, and precious little influence."

Noah nods at the unfairness of it all. "The rebellion forced her hand to sign Essex's death warrant. Once it took place, she had no choice but to see him put down for good and all. And there was one thing you could have done that would have frustrated the rebellion entirely."

Sir Henry lets out a long sigh. "I could have told her it was coming. God, that's so unfair. Was I the *only* adult in the room?"

There's a short blast of cold air, as though someone has come in through the front door downstairs. In a moment, Matthew trots up the stairs and enters the parlor. "The Lord Admiral has arrived and wishes to join you gentlemen for a nightcap."

Noah and Sir Henry rise just in time to greet the Lord Admiral.

"Please sit, gentlemen," says the Lord Admiral. He turns to Matthew. "Bring us some of that old brandy, Matthew. I assume these two gentlemen will be joining me."

"Thank you, Lord Admiral," say Noah and Sir Henry.

The Lord Admiral looks askance at Noah. "Serjeant, why is Leveson still not at liberty?"

Noah can feel his face redden. "If I may be so cryptic, Lord Admiral, one attempt has been made to recover the gentleman. Though it failed, the abductor is none the wiser for the attempt."

"When will the next attempt be made?" asks the Lord Admiral.

"In three days' time, Lord Admiral," replies Noah.

"See that *this* attempt does not fail, Serjeant."

Just then, Matthew walks in with a tray holding three glasses and an ancient-looking bottle.

"Ah, here we are," says the Lord Admiral.

Noah and Sir Henry take their glasses.

The Lord Admiral leads them in a familiar toast: "God save the Queen."

CHAPTER 24

AS COLD NIGHT FALLS on Holborn and supper is cleared away, Noah and Cheerful prepare once more to keep watch over Lady Leicester's house in hope of following Mullin from Essex House to the place where he and his confederate are holding Sir John Leveson. Noah labors under no illusion; he's well aware it will be perilous indeed.

Noah regards Cheerful blankly. "Where's Timothy?" he asks. "Considering how he clamored to be included in our plans, it's remarkable that he's nowhere to be seen."

Cheerful shrugs. "I believe he's chatting with Esther upstairs. She asked me to send him to her."

"For what purpose?" asks Noah. Barely has he got the words out but Timothy stamps down the stairs.

"'Evening, gentlemen," says Timothy. "Sorry to keep you waiting."

"I hope you're timelier if things get out of hand," says Noah.

"I'll be at the ready, suh," says Timothy with a smile.

"Have you your mask?" asks Noah.

"It's in my pocket, suh," replies Timothy. "Wouldn't want to strut it about, would I?"

The three of them don their heavy coats and head out to the stables. Tonight, Bucklebury will come along in addition to Cheerful's horse. This way, in case one of them loses sight of his quarry, the other can continue the chase. An additional advantage of having two horses is that they can be tied off at different locations.

There are only three ways for Mullin to travel when he leaves Essex House: west on the Strand, east on Fleet Street, or north on Chancery Lane (where he's sure to pass Marie's house). If he goes west on the Strand or north on Chancery, Cheerful's horse is to follow first. If he goes east, Bucklebury will be at the ready for Noah himself to lead the tail. Whichever way Mullin chooses to go, once the pursuit is underway, Timothy will return to Marie's house to await the outcome. At least, that's the plan.

Noah looks up at the sky. The light seems dimmer than it was during their first attempt to follow Mullin, the moon now lending half the light it lent last time. Still, while it will be more difficult to see Mullin at a distance, Mullin will have a harder time seeing his pursuers.

As the three begin their short move to Essex House, Noah has a sinking feeling in his belly. *What's to ensure Mullin won't escape the same way he did last time?* With so much at stake, he suddenly feels foolish for relying on a mere two men, plus what little an eleven-year-old boy can bring to bear, despite his having experience well beyond his tender years.

But, what choice has there been, really? His mind fleetingly conjures up images of other possible participants, such as Jonathan, Andres, Arthur, and Chester. But it's about time Jonathan were treated as the baron he's become and ... more importantly from Noah's viewpoint ... a husband and a father. Andres is up in Cambridge. Arthur is dead, and much lamented. And Chester works for the Queen.

It doesn't escape Noah's sense of irony that *he* also works for the Queen, but that's no advantage in this instance. Noah simply cannot do anything to compromise Lady Leicester's position—which he was appointed to buttress, after all. To enlist more men would surely have exacerbated her jeopardy.

As they reach the Strand, Cheerful turns west to conceal his horse and himself in the brush.

This time, Timothy is to remain with Noah. Together, they turn east, and Noah ties off Bucklebury in the woods off the Strand. The two take up their position behind the oak tree where Noah hid on their first try. Timothy sits on a nearby stump. While Noah can't help but admire how cool the boy seems in this most perilous situation, there's no sharing in his equanimity. All Noah can see in his mind's eye is the Lord Admiral's face, glowering at him for failing in his assigned task yet a second time.

They need wait only a few minutes for Mullin to appear. As he did the other night, he enters the grounds through the wicket, but this time he chooses a route 'round the eastern face of Essex House to the door leading from the dock to the library, which takes him past a point no further than ten feet from Noah and Timothy. As Mullin passes, Noah looks inquiringly to Timothy. Timothy nods sullenly; it's the same Mullin.

Mullin knocks jauntily and, once again, the door opens from the inside. This time, there's no conversation before Lady Leicester admits him to the library and shuts the door behind him.

Barely a moment has passed when a horse begins clopping excitedly on the other side of the house. Noah rolls his eyes. *What is wrong with Cheerful's horse that he cannot stand quiet for a half-hour on end?* But, instead of quieting down, the horse begins to shiver and whimper. Noah can hear Cheerful trying to comfort the beast with his voice, but it does no good; the horse continues to fuss. There's something ineffably sad in its whimpering. If a horse could weep aloud, thinks Noah, this horse would be doing so.

The equine noise rises to the point where it simply *must* be audible inside the library. Noah prays that Mullin doesn't come out to investigate.

Noah's heart begins pumping hard. *What the devil is happening to that horse? Is there nothing to be done to quiet it down?*

Then, as if by magic, the horse quiets down.

Mullin soon emerges by the library door and whistles past Noah on his way back to the wicket. The man is both shameless and heedless of his own jeopardy.

Noah and Timothy follow Mullin a short way behind.

Mullin lets himself out through the wicket, mounts, and canters calmly west toward Westminster.

Is Cheerful following Mullin? Has his mount recovered?

Noah counts to thirty, then exits through the wicket and turns west. Mullin is gone from sight. Perhaps Cheerful's horse has recovered, thinks Noah, and horse and rider are now following Mullin according to plan.

But as soon as Noah comes close enough to see Cheerful, he realizes that disaster has struck once again. Cheerful's horse is *lying down* as though mortally wounded, breathing heavily, his eyes nearly closed; Cheerful is stroking his withers and speaking to him in low, comforting tones.

Horrified that they have failed in their mission a second time, Noah places both his hands on his head and runs to Cheerful with Timothy hard behind.

"What happened?" asks Noah in an excited whisper.

Cheerful rubs his worried face with his hand. "I can't be sure in the dark, but I think he was ... bitten! It must have been the same thing that was worrying him a few days ago in this same spot. A small animal ... I don't know. Perhaps a fox."

"But why would it bite him?" asks Noah.

Cheerful glances over his shoulder in the moonlight, and speaks as if in a dream. "He must have got a bit too close to the fox's burrow. The den probably had pups in it. Mother Fox must have come out and bitten him on the ankle. Surely, that's what startled him. He tramped in place the way a worried horse will do, but then … he got his foot caught in a gully, and the ankle snapped in two." He winces to recall. "I could *hear* it."

"You're sure?" asks Noah.

Cheerful nods glumly.

Noah regards the horse skeptically. "What calmed him down?"

Cheerful sighs. "An elixir that Lord Jonathan gave me some months ago. Said it would calm a worried horse for several hours." He removes the empty vial from his pocket. "Oh, but I'm sure I gave him too much."

"How much did you give him?"

Cheerful shrugs. "The whole thing."

"What were you *supposed* to give him?"

Cheerful is crestfallen at the results of his own panic. "Jonathan said not more than two drops."

Noah places his hand comfortingly on Cheerful's shoulder. "It's just as well. He's sedated now. There's nothing *for* a snapped ankle is there?"

Cheerful shakes his head glumly.

"You'll have to put him down, then," says Noah gingerly.

Cheerful nods. "I couldn't very well do it while that … that *bastard* was talking with the lady, could I?"

"No," says Noah. "Of course you couldn't. You did exactly the right thing." He pats the horse on the muzzle. "Wait ten minutes, by which time Mullin will be a long way off. Then you must shoot this poor brute." He looks back at the house. "I must go now to speak with Lady Leicester." He throws his hands up. "Oh, what a *filthy* night!"

With Timothy by his side, Noah races around the house to the library door.

The door's wide open. Lady Leicester stands before it, her arms folded imperiously in the moonlight. "And now I have lost *three hundred pound!*" she scolds him in a hoarse whisper. "What ever were you doing? Did you follow Mullin?"

Noah shakes his head apologetically. "I'm afraid there was a mishap with one of the horses, madam, and my man … was unable to follow. The horse will need to be put down."

"You *foolish* man!" she says contemptuously. "What do I care if a horse needs to be put down? You should have followed him yourself."

"I could not, madam," says Noah. "By the time I realized what was happening, Mullin had already ridden off. Even if I'd got to mine own horse immediately, I wouldn't have known which way to go."

She glowers at him. "A fine mess you've made of things!"

"I, madam? *I*?" He struggles to control his anger. "Was it *I* who had Leveson abducted in order to disable Neville from defending himself on trial for his life? Was it *I* who proffered so little to the extortionist on his previous visit that he insisted on following m'lady about the house to gather more, so that we were unable to guess which door he'd exit from? To add to that, now m'lady scolds me for my failures, rather than telling me what Mullin said this evening. What guidance have you for me, madam? What *guidance*? Or shall we give up?"

Chastened, Lady Leicester frowns and chafes her shoulders in the cold river air. "I don't know what guidance I can provide," she says. "He asked me for the money, and I gave it to him. He was in a jaunty mood, very happy with his crony. He begged me not to send a children's crusade to beat him, as well." She fumes. "Oh, if only I knew the children who'd do it."

"What?" demands Noah. "*What* did you say?"

Noah looks toward Timothy, but finds the boy has suddenly vanished into the night, presumably toward home, as planned.

Lady Leicester looks confused. "I—I was telling you what happened—"

"No," says Noah, interrupting without apology. "What was it he said to you? Something about a *children's crusade*?"

"Yes," she says, remembering. "That I should not send a children's crusade to beat him." Seeing that Noah imputes some significance to this turn of phrase, she becomes apologetic. "I assumed he'd heard what happened to the other extortionist—Master Drury."

Noah scowls and shakes his head. "No one at Westminster has heard a thing about that incident with the children. It's not the kind of thing Drury could very well complain about at law. Nor would he allow it to become general knowledge, as it does him little credit as a schemer. To the contrary, it would make him seem very much … the loser."

He suddenly realizes where Timothy darted off to in such an all-fired rush, and counts himself the dunce for taking an extra minute to draw the obvious conclusion. Without so much as a bow, he races toward Bucklebury.

"Where are you going?" the lady demands after him.

"To get your money," he replies with thinly disguised contempt, then adds under his breath, "and Leveson."

ON THE SOUTH LANE of the Strand, Cheerful continues his lonely vigil, stroking the fallen horse, wondering when the elixir will wear off and the devastating pain will return in full force.

Dimly aware of a few heated shouts between a man and woman behind Essex House, Cheerful peers east to the place where Bucklebury is tied off, roughly where the Strand becomes Fleet Street. In a moment, there's some hurried movement there, which he assumes is Noah preparing to mount. Evidently, he's correct in that assumption, for a robed rider quickly mounts Bucklebury and gallops east into the night.

Though Cheerful might be heard by the rider if he were to shout, the painful truth is that he has nothing to say. Until this horse is put out of its misery, his sole business is right here.

"Good boy," he coos, stroking the horse's throat another few minutes, reluctant to do the necessary. "You've been a fine steed, m'lad. I shall remember you until I have no memory left, and perhaps we'll meet again hereafter." The horse gazes up at him mournfully. Cheerful comforts himself with the thought that there's a hint of love in those sad, sad eyes. It's as though the horse is saying, *I love you, but I can bear this no longer, so get on with it.*

Cheerful removes a kerchief from his pocket and places it over the horse's eyes. The horse does nothing to shake it off or resist.

Cheerful looks up again to make sure that Noah has disappeared into the dark, then mournfully removes the pistol from his pocket and assures that the charge is still in place.

In a cold sweat, he steps backward and takes aim above the eyes.

QUIETLY PASSING SAINT PAUL'S CATHEDRAL, Mullin hears a pistol shot in the distance behind him—at least, he *thinks* it's behind him. It's difficult to tell sometimes, with the report bouncing off the many tall buildings in this part of town.

If he had to guess, the shot came from the southwest, in the general vicinity of Essex House, which he left shortly before. For a fleeting moment, he wonders whether the shot might have had something to do with him—a general alarum, perhaps, summoning men of law enforcement to gather in aid of Lady Leicester.

But he nearly laughs aloud at himself. Lady Leicester wouldn't dare call the constable on him. As she well knows, the first thing he'd do if he were tracked down (an unlikely scenario) would be to point the finger back at her, and say he was loyally doing her ladyship's bidding having not the *least* idea what private griefs m'lady bore poor Sir John Leveson, who seems such a fine fellow.

In fact, until he met Drury, Mullin had been treating Sir John rather cavalierly. Surely, he'd been kept warm and fed, and been allowed to relieve himself a few times a day, but he'd remained chained to a support beam the rest of the time, and the blindfold had stayed on without exception.

It was Drury who'd established, shortly after joining his scheme, that if no firm plan were to be made to kill Leveson, he ought to be treated humanely. After all, if he were ultimately released, he could come looking for them and, having once identified them, put an end to them both.

Mullin had conceded to his newfound friend that, on an academic level, the argument contained a great deal of merit—at least in the event of Leveson's escape—but it only reinforced Mullin's prior notion that every effort ought to be made to prevent Leveson from ever finding out their true identities. They'd jointly decided that, whatever accommodations were to be made for the prisoner's comfort, a (slightly more comfortable) blindfold would need to remain in place the whole time. Drury had kindly acceded to Mullin's superior reasoning, as any man of breeding needs must.

Mullin has never revealed to Drury that he fully intends to murder Leveson once no further payment can be withheld on condition they provide proof of life. After all, one can't be "done away with" by a dead man. And Leveson's death certainly wouldn't be the first mark of Cain earned by Mullin, just in case anyone is keeping score, which he roundly doubts. Far from it, he's had numerous young "lovers," as he describes them to himself, who'd been treated well during a term only he decided, and ended up face-down in a ditch.

Mullin earnestly hopes that Drury never finds out about his "habits," as experience has shown that such knowledge makes some men queasy, despite their superior breeding.

He disregards the pistol report, draws up his collar, and continues in his plodding pace.

NOAH'S BEEN CARRIED by Bucklebury all the way to Candlewick Street by the time Cheerful's pistol report reaches him. He begins to worry that he's traveling too quickly and thinking too slowly. He tugs the reins, and Bucklebury slows to a walk.

Mullin's remark to Lady Leicester about a children's crusade has made it almost certain that Mullin's co-conspirator is none other than Thomas Drury, who's recently been set upon by children. Still, that's no assurance that Drury has remained at the same cottage he occupied a few weeks ago. After all, Drury had inadvertently caused a great deal of damage to the cottage, so that, even if he paid for the repairs, the landlord Groatsworth might have ejected him nonetheless.

Noah decides he has no choice but to proceed on the assumption that he and Mullin are heading for the same destination, for if Drury has moved his temporary residence, then Noah has no *idea* where Leveson is being held, and this is but a mirthless chase and a waste of time.

Noah shakes the doubt from his mind, relying mostly on Drury's temporary penury. Hadn't he said he couldn't afford the three pounds needed for the repair? Then, as the three pounds Noah lent him for that purpose had been delivered by the constable directly to the landlord, Drury would still be without funds. And yet he's managed to stay in London for another week or two, probably on credit. (He really must place a note in the file to the effect that Groatsworth is an idiot.)

Where would Drury have got the money to move his residence? A new landlord would no doubt have demanded the first month's rent plus a security deposit, which would amount to a few pounds, at least—a few pounds that Drury didn't have. No, he's still there in the damaged cottage, Noah feels sure.

But that still leaves an immediate problem. If Noah and Mullin are traveling at the same time from the same point of origin to the same destination, then it stands to reason that their paths would cross at least once, leaving open the substantial possibility that he will be seen. (He shudders to consider the catastrophic consequences of their arriving at the same time; for the moment, he excludes that possibility from consideration.)

How might he conceal himself? He could put on his mask, but that would make him rather *more* conspicuous, especially in such light traffic. This evening is not a holiday calling for masquerade. Although, if he were seen, the mask would initially conceal his identity, it would also mark him as someone *needing* to conceal his identity, which would draw suspicion. So, there's little to be gained by donning a mask so early. He draws his cowl up far enough to conceal his face from the moonlight. That will have to do.

As far as his route, what are his alternatives? It would be best to avoid crossing Mullin's path entirely, and that would require him to deliberately overshoot Bishopsgate and double back to conceal himself somewhere he's likely to see Mullin pass through Bishopsgate without himself being seen.

And he knows just the place. Just east of the point where Camomile Street meets Bishopsgate. He shakes the reins and Bucklebury begins to canter.

—————————⋄∘C∕∕∕∕⊃∘⊂—————————

TO REMOVE THE hazard to traffic, David struggles alone, tugging the horse's carcass a few feet further off the Strand. Having completed that Herculean task, he drags himself up Chancery Lane to High Holborn.

What seems an eternity later (but could not have been more than a few minutes), Tom appears at the Ames's stable door to greet him. When Cheerful comes close enough for his wretched expression to be seen in the moonlight, Tom's smile drops away.

"Problem, suh?" asks Tom. Glancing about, he says, "Where's your horse?"

David shakes his head morosely. "Shattered an ankle, I'm afraid."

Tom's eyes open wide. "Was that *your* pistol shot, suh?"

David nods. "'Twas. After the poor thing received a fright from his injury, he suffered little. I put him at ease as best I could, before … putting him down."

"Oh, I'm so sorry, suh," says Tom. "I know how fond you were of him, and I'm sure he knew, too. Ye done the right thing, suh."

David shrugs, accepting no comfort. "I did the *only* thing."

"I'll call the knackers at first light, suh," says Tom. "Is there anything else I can do?"

Cheerful shakes his head. "Not really, Tom. Just make sure the knackers return the bridle, the saddle, and the saddlebags—which were empty, so you need not concern yourself with the contents."

"Sure thing, suh," says Tom. "Never you worry. Now you best be off to the house, as Miss Esther seems quite worked up about you."

David bounds up toward the Ames's house. *Never you worry,* the stableman said, but all he can *do* is worry. Especially about Noah.

He knocks on the front door, which is instantly swung open by Esther, whose beautiful face is marred by worry.

"Oh, David," she says. "Are you all right?"

He nods. "As you can see," he says impatiently, looking over her shoulder into the house. "Where's Timothy? He was supposed to remain here."

"He was here but a moment," she says, "and he wanted me to tell you that he'd gone off to assist Serjeant Ames."

"Did he take a horse?" asks David.

"No," she replies, wringing her hands. "He left on foot."

"On *foot*?" he says with astonishment. "Then Serjeant Ames must be nearby indeed. Did he tell you where Serjeant Ames was?"

"All he said was"—she searches her memory—"'Muggins is in cahoots with Jewry.'"

Mullin's in cahoots with Drury! David kisses Esther's cheek and sprints back to the stables.

"Hoy, Tom!" he shouts.

Chapter 25

NOAH ARRIVES AT Camomile Street overlooking Bishopsgate. As far as he can tell, he's successfully avoided crossing paths with Mullin on the way here. While he can't preclude the possibility that Mullin spied him while himself escaping detection, that seems unlikely. There were few travelers on the road on such a dark night, and Noah was careful to avoid making himself conspicuous.

While Noah has passed Camomile Street many times in the past (as one necessarily does when passing through Bishopsgate), he's always been too preoccupied to look past the wild daisies that thrive here through much of the year. Now, at the end of winter, there are no flowers, and the little surviving vegetation remains blanketed under a thin layer of snow. Little did he know that beyond the daisies that catch the traveler's eye were … more daisies. The nearest structure is a good hundred yards from the gate.

Fortunately, there's a tall oak much closer than that, broad enough to shield horse and rider from the revelatory rays of moonlight. He ties off Bucklebury behind the trunk, removes Uncle Avram's dagger from its scabbard and holds it in his right hand, placing both dagger and hand in his pocket. He regrets appointing Cheerful to be the sole pistolier for this occasion, as one can never be sure when a pistol will come in handy.

Noah prays he can avoid a fight. He's well aware that he'll be out-armed and outnumbered. Both Mullin and Drury (presumably, both armed) will be arrayed against him, and Leveson, his natural ally, will be bound and out of the fray.

Having woefully assayed his many weaknesses, Noah assays his strengths. He has civil authority on his side, and he's in the right. With enough bluster, he should be able to persuade his adversaries that the Queen's men are on their way here, and that their only chance of escape is to go at once, leaving both Lady Leicester's money and Leveson behind.

He waits by the oak, hoping to see Mullin appear from the west then disappear north through Bishopsgate.

And he waits.

And he waits, long enough that he begins to wonder if perhaps he's got Mullin's plan all wrong. Perhaps Drury and Leveson have *not* situated themselves at Groatsworth's cottage at all, and Mullin is *not* coming tonight. Or perhaps Mullin passed through Bishopsgate some time ago, and he and Drury are long gone with both money and prisoner.

From the west, Mullin slowly appears on his mount at last, ambling along with no notion of haste, taking so long to reach the gate that Noah imagines himself shouting, *Oh, get on with it!*

Finally, the tail of Mullin's horse swishes through the gate and disappears behind London Wall.

Now it's just a matter of choosing the most propitious moment.

Noah soothes Bucklebury before leaving him, steps up to the wall at the eastern end of the gate, and peers around the corner toward Groatsworth's cottages, earnestly wishing there were more light to help him see.

Mullin pulls up to the cottage formerly (or presently) occupied by Drury, where a taper burns in the window, a sure sign that someone has been there all the while. So, the division of labor was as Noah first imagined: Mullin goes to collect the money while Drury guards the prisoner.

Mullin ties his horse to a post on the far side of what was once the porch. In place of the porch there stands a temporary structure of rough wood cleverly designed to render the cottage habitable until a new porch can be installed come spring, at which time Groatsworth no doubt plans to rent it out at the earliest possible moment. Until then, at least the roof has been sealed from the elements and the front door rendered functional.

Before stepping inside, Mullin removes his gloves in a manner so genteel as to parody, rather than emulate, a gentleman. He lets himself in and shuts the door quietly behind.

Noah approaches the windowless side of the cottage and presses his ear to the wall. He hears two men engaged in subdued conversation. The next thing he hears is the spilling of heavy coins onto a wooden tabletop.

Remembering that Timothy spoke of a small window in the rear of the cottage, Noah searches for, and quickly locates it. He looks through it, moving as little as possible to avoid detection, and sees Mullin and Drury sitting at the counting table in the front room. Closer to Noah sits a man wearing a hood covering his head, Sir John Leveson no doubt, momentarily unattended. The hood renders it pointless for Noah to try for Sir John's attention, as he couldn't see anyway.

Noah takes a deep breath, steps up to the front door, and pounds on it three times in rapid succession, loud enough to alarm those in the cottage but, he hopes, not the neighbors.

From inside comes the sound of men hastily bustling about. He just hopes neither of his adversaries has grabbed a firearm in the process. Just to be sure he's not hit in such eventuality, he takes a sidestep from the door.

The door swings open and Mullin steps out angrily, deftly pulling the door shut behind him so Noah can't see in. He looks menacingly at Noah.

"Who are *you*?" he demands in a whisper.

"Who am I, Master *Mullin*?" he whispers indignantly. "I am Serjeant Noah Ames, Queen's counselor."

Mullin's eyes dart about in near-panic, and he puts his finger to his lips. Seeing no one to lend this intruder aid, he beckons to Noah to follow him behind the cottage. With some hesitation, Noah follows.

Mullin glares at him suspiciously and speaks quietly. "You're the Queen's Jew, aren't ye? I've heard o' you. How'd ye know *my* name?"

"It makes no difference how I learned your name, Master Mullin," says Noah, "nor that of your fellow conspirator Thomas Drury who sits inside this very cottage as we speak, nor even that of Sir John Leveson, whom you've feloniously abducted and now detain here. For if you fail to comply at once with my demands in the Queen's name, soon *everyone* shall know your name and they'll all come out to see you hanged on Tower Hill. From your viewpoint, I should think it far more important to know that I've summoned the Queen's Guard, and they shall be here within this five minute."

Mullin draws a dagger and points it at Noah's belly. "What if I was to kill you right now, and then run? Then nobody'd know *who* was here to greet you." He smiles cruelly. "Would they?"

Noah shakes his head. "The Tower Guard knows I've come here to fetch Sir John Leveson from the clutches of two nameless scoundrels," says Noah with false bravado. "And a *single* well-placed member of the Guard knows that those scoundrels go by the names of Mullin and Drury. If you so much as lay a hand on me, my man's been instructed to identify you to the rest of the Guard, and you will be fugitives for the brief remainder of your brutish lives." He shrugs. "On the other hand, if you go now, leaving Sir John unharmed and abandoning Lady Leicester's ransom money, I assure you no one will learn it was you two who committed these capital offenses."

Mullin seems to equivocate and, just as Noah planned, begins to sweat for having to decide so quickly; he continually glances at Bishopsgate as though expecting to see a contingent of burly armed men tramp through at any moment. He regards Noah suspiciously. "Mebbe I should just hold you hostage, so they'll let us get away."

Noah shakes his head. "You'd just add another corpse to the butcher's bill, for I'd *probably* be killed." He casts Mullin a smug expression. "But you and your confederate would *surely* be killed, if not tonight, then a few weeks hence, for all the good such a postponement would do you."

Mullins holds the dagger up to Noah's chest and urges the point through his coat into his robes. "Y'know what I think? I think you're full o' *shit*, Jew. I think *nobody's* comin' through that gate. I think you're gonna take the money fer *yerself*, like your kind'll always do."

Noah conspicuously glances toward Bishopsgate. "You and I are not cut from the same cloth, Master Mullin. I don't betray those for whom I work."

Whether out of pique or in furtherance of some larger plan, Mullin pushes the dagger point the remainder of the way through Noah's robes until it's touching his unprotected skin, and drags it across his chest, slicing as it goes.

Noah suddenly sees a white light, and the cut stings him like a thousand bees, recalling that moment at Oxford when the late Sir Gelly dragged his short sword across Noah's chest. Noah loses his grip on Avram's dagger and hasn't time to find it in his oversized pocket.

"Fine, Master Mullin," says Noah, glancing back toward the gate. "Let's you and I await the Queen's men together."

"I *could* just kill ye now," says Mullin, looking as though he'd very much like to do so, if just to get even.

Noah has no choice but to ignore the blood oozing down his belly from the painful cut, for he has almost nothing to fight with but convincing bluster. "Master Mullin," he says through gritted teeth, "you disappoint me. For you, this is an opportunity to choose freedom ... or certain death. It's your choice." He shrugs and forces a contemptuous smile to his lips.

"You Jew bastard, stickin' yer hook nose where it don't belong!" says Mullin. He takes a step toward Noah and raises the dagger over his head, preparing to bring it down hard.

Noah steps back heedlessly, tripping on a rock and falling backward to the ground, his hand grasping furiously to find Avram's dagger.

Although he's taken his eye off Mullin for only a moment, as he fixes upon him again Mullin's dagger-hand drops to his side.

Noah, unable to take his eyes off the knife, watches in amazement as Mullin's fingers spread wide and the dagger drops to the frozen ground. He squints through the darkness to see the details of Mullin's face.

Mullin's eyes are wide open, and he appears to be searching for something in the distance. Though his expression betrays horror, it's dominated by *shock*. His splayed fingers move urgently toward his neck, but never touch it. Instead, they tremble spastically a few inches away, while from his throat bubbles up a hideous gurgling, followed by a desperate gasping for breath.

Noah leaps to his feet to reap advantage from his adversary's distraction, and takes a bold step forward, brandishing Avram's dagger, which he's found at last. But Mullin takes no notice, and it's not until Noah takes another step forward that he detects Mullin's grievous injury.

Protruding from Mullin's throat is the hilt of a dagger. And it's *only* the hilt jutting out, the full length of the blade having evidently penetrated all the way through his neck to his spine, cutting his windpipe in two and slicing at least one major artery, for blood pulses from the wound onto Mullin's doublet and gushes onto the snowy ground before him.

Mullin's eyes roll up into his head, and he collapses in a heap into the warm puddle that's already collected at his feet. Even in the near darkness its red hue is visible.

As Noah returns to his senses, it occurs to him that there might be a madman in these woods who regards his mission as having been accomplished only halfway. That Mullin was the first to be attacked doesn't mean he'll be the last.

Noah frantically scans the woods for a madman. In a moment his eyes light on … Timothy, skulking guiltily in Noah's gaze.

The boy appears unhurt—in fact, unsullied. There's no sign of injury upon him … and no sign of blood. Yet, it's obviously Timothy who stabbed Mullin through the throat.

Noah regards the boy in utter disbelief. "Timothy," he whispers and, after a momentary loss for words, he grunts, "Thank you."

"That was for Choth," Timothy whispers sullenly. "Does this mean I can't stay with Lord Jonathan any longer?"

Noah takes the boy in his arms and hugs him tightly. Though Timothy tenses up at first, evidently unsure whether Noah's hug is one of pure affection, at last he relaxes.

"Of course not, son," says Noah. "You are welcome to stay with us ... always."

"Sir, you're bleedin'," says Timothy pointing to Noah's chest. "Don't it hurt?"

Noah nods. "Like the fires of hell, I'm afraid. But don't you worry, I've been hurt in the same way before, and I'll be returning to the same surgeon who patched me up then. I'll be fine."

The boy weeps quietly on Noah's shoulder, a relief to them both. It occurs to Noah that this is the first time he's seen this street urchin react like a child who's been cared for.

In light of their perilous predicament, Noah draws away from the boy and looks him in the eye. "But there's something you must do now. I'd ask you to return to my house at once, but I know you wouldn't do it." He points to Bishopsgate. "Bucklebury is on the other side of the gate. Tend to him quietly, while I attend to my remaining business here."

"But, sir," says the teary-eyed lad, "I need to be able to see you, so that ... I may come to your aid again, if need arises."

Noah sighs, but relents. "Very well, then," he says, "stand on the other side of the wall, but *don't* allow yourself to be seen. Can you do this?"

"Yes, sir," says Timothy. Wiping his eyes on his sleeve, he jogs off to the gate and instantly disappears from view.

Just then, Noah hears the makeshift door to the cottage creak warily open behind him.

OUTSIDE BISHOPSGATE, Cheerful Killigrew dismounts, and ties his borrowed horse to a tree. Slowly, he inches along London Wall, peers through the gate and quickly identifies the cottage that Lord Jonathan identified some days ago as having been occupied by Drury.

Though the light is dim, he can see that Noah was correct in his surmise that Mullin and Drury are working in league. And Noah's evidently already made his presence known, as Mullin is leading him toward the rear of the cottage and Noah appears to be following willingly.

The cottage door is closed and a candle burns within, barely silhouetting the shape of a man seated at a table inside, probably Drury, which makes it likely that Sir John Leveson is also inside, though he can't be seen from this angle. At the far end of the makeshift porch, a horse is tied off, looking asleep.

Cheerful decides he'd better move closer to the place where any action is likely to take place. Relying on the darkness to shield him from view, he ambles up the opposite side of the road a little way, then crosses the road and ambles back toward the cottage. He stops and listens only a few feet from the door.

Sounds emanating from the opposite side of the cottage give him cause for concern. Noah's voice sounds anything but friendly, and Mullin's downright hostile. The voices die down, although there's a stamping about that might indicate a tussle. He hears an indistinct gurgling as though someone's clearing his throat, then the voices stop.

Though Cheerful earnestly wishes he knew what was going on between Noah and Mullin, he daren't cross the porch, for he'll alarm the horse and the noises outside will surely draw Drury out.

But when the door remains closed for a few seconds, Cheerful decides to avoid the door and go the other way 'round. He creeps to the back end of the wall and peers toward the woods behind the other side of the cottage, where he sees a little blond boy being comforted in Noah's embrace.

As there's no sign of Mullin, Cheerful assumes that the tussle ended successfully for Noah. He wonders in passing whether Timothy played any part, but he has no time for contemplation. He returns to the porch without delay, as Drury will no doubt be making his play soon.

The moment he reaches the porch, the door opens and a man emerges, facing the opposite way, clumsily dragging out another man, presumably Leveson, whose arms and ankles are bound, and whose head is covered by a hood.

Recognizing this as his cue for immediate action, Cheerful draws the pistol from his pocket by the barrel and, with the butt, clubs Drury twice in the back of the head with all his considerable strength. Drury collapses to the porch's wooden floor like a sack of grain.

Mullin's horse awakens and shuffles about. Cheerful pats him comfortingly and he calms down without a fuss.

Cheerful turns his bludgeoning victim over to make sure he's truly insensate. Satisfied that he is, Cheerful approaches the hooded prisoner, who instinctively jerks away.

"Master Leveson?" whispers Cheerful.

The figure nods his head vigorously.

"We're here to rescue you," whispers Cheerful. "First off, can you confirm that there only two captors?"

The figure nods again.

Though Cheerful needs to ensure that Mullin has been put out of the way, he first needs to ensure that Drury is securely bound, in case he returns to his senses before the fight is finished. He also wishes to unbind Leveson at the first possible instant, as the poor fellow's evidently been held in this miserable way for weeks on end.

"If I undo your restraints," Cheerful whispers, "do you promise to quietly tie up this fellow I just bludgeoned, and put the gag and hood on him?"

The figure nods slowly, and Cheerful can sense the urge for revenge in that simple motion.

Cheerful unties the rope around Leveson's hands and removes the hood and gag. Leveson sighs with relief, and grabs Cheerful's right hand, shaking it gratefully.

Cheerful can't help but smile. "Introductions later, sir," he whispers, and steps off the porch. He draws the pistol from his pocket, checks the charge, and points the business end away from both Leveson and himself.

Prepared to shoot at anything looking remotely hostile, Cheerful quickly turns the corner and finds Noah alone, leaning against the side of the cottage, holding his hand to his chest, writhing in pain. At Noah's feet lies Mullin in a pool of blood, presumably his own.

"Good evening, Serjeant Ames," Cheerful says quietly. "'Tis I. David."

Noah looks up at him with a start. "Have you subdued Drury?"

"Yes, sir," replies Cheerful, "Sir John is presently tying him up and blindfolding him. Are you hurt badly, sir?"

To Cheerful's amazement, Noah shakes his head. "Hurt … but not badly." He looks down at Mullin. "At least, not as badly as *he* is." He turns to David. "Did Drury see you?"

Cheerful shakes his head. "He couldn't have. I struck him in the back of the head before he had a chance to turn about."

"Good," says Noah, apparently hatching a plan.

"Sir John is on the porch with Drury," says David.

Noah uses his elbow to shove himself away from the side of the cottage. He stops momentarily, overcome with pain. Cheerful assists him by the arm and they go to the porch together, where Sir John is finishing the job of putting Drury in all the restraints he's just shed himself.

Upon seeing Noah, Sir John's eyes open wide with recognition.

Noah immediately puts his finger to his lips and beckons Sir John to join them on the side of the cottage, where they can't be heard.

"Before you speak, Sir John," whispers Noah, "Please understand that I'm not here." He points his chin toward Cheerful, bringing a nasty reminder from his wound. "Nor is this young fellow."

"Neither of you is *here*?" asks Sir John, his voice hoarse from disuse.

"No," replies Noah. Thinking that he and Cheerful (and the concealed Timothy) need to make quick work of their disappearance, he says to Cheerful, "Go and fetch the coins on the table inside. Put them in the bag that Mullin used to bring them here."

Cheerful nods and goes.

"No, Sir John," confirms Noah. "We were never here. What happened was that you managed to untie your restraints and awaited your moment. When Mullin went to the jakes, you clubbed Drury in the back of the head—twice—and tied him up. Then you came outside and lay in wait for Mullin. When you confronted Mullin, he drew out his dagger and fought, and you were forced to kill him where he now lies. Y—You stabbed him through the throat." He looks uncertainly at Mullin's corpse. "You'll need to come up with an explanation for the second dagger—the one through Mullin's throat—but I expect you can just say you found it in the cottage."

Sir John sneers with contempt at the thought of his chief captor. "That's fine," he says, "though I myself might have made his suffering last a bit longer." He smiles at Noah admiringly. "A most unfortunate incident all 'round," says Sir John, tongue in cheek. "I see you're wounded," he says with concern.

Noah shakes his head. "A mere flesh wound, I assure you. I'll be fine tomorrow. When you speak with the constable, don't mention anything about me or this young man. Don't mention anything about *money*. A great deal depends upon your supporting this story. Several innocent young people, as well as your humble servant, have risked a great deal to rescue you. We must never be questioned about this."

Sir John nods earnestly. "You need say no more."

"Well, there are three things remaining," says Noah. "First, I shall hold you to your promise to tell Her Majesty of Sir Henry's enlisting you to frustrate Essex's movement toward Westminster."

Sir John nods. "And the second thing?"

"I'm afraid I must ask you to let Drury go," says Noah. "He knows too much about your abduction and, if pressed hard enough, could point his finger at some very ... important people for whom I'm bound to secrecy."

"I thought, according to our story, he was tied up," says Sir John doubtfully.

"Yes, that's what you *thought*, but evidently you hadn't tied him quite tightly enough. He must have untied himself and escaped when you weren't looking. When he regains his senses (after *we're* well away), tell him the story I just told you, and tell him that if he contradicts it, or returns to London sooner than in two years, you have friends who'll see him hanged." Noah darts a glance about. "I don't see Drury's horse here. I expect it's tied off somewhere nearby. If it's not, and he's short a horse, let him take Mullin's."

"And if he doesn't need Mullin's horse," says Sir John, having trouble warming to the idea of letting one of his captors go, "what should I do with it?"

"Keep it," says Noah with a shrug, then thinks better of his answer. "Better yet, I know someone who had no choice but to put his horse down recently and could use a good horse. Send the horse over to me if you wish, and I'll find him a good home."

Sir John nods. "And your *third* item of unfinished business?"

"Well," says Noah with a wry smile, "your lovely wife *did* offer me a hot meal."

Sir John seems about to slap Noah heartily on the back until he remembers the chest wound. Instead, he bows. "At your pleasure, sir. You shall always be welcome at our table."

Cheerful returns with a bag of coins and bows to Noah. "It's all here, sir, every farthing."

Noah feels he owes Sir John at least a comment about the money. "I shall return this bounty to the ... person who gave it to Mullin under duress. Please, Sir John, never investigate this matter further."

Sir John concedes with a shrug. "If that's the price of getting my life back, consider it done. But whom shall I summon after letting Drury go?"

"See that cottage over there?" asks Noah, pointing to Groatsworth's. "Knock on the door. The fellow who lives there owns this place." He smirks. "I only wish I could wait here to see his face when he once again finds his precious cottage in an uproar—and a bloody corpse in the bargain."

NOAH AND CHEERFUL fetch Timothy and Bucklebury.

Timothy shares a saddle with Cheerful, clinging to him from behind.

Noah regards them both affectionately. "Now, I'm going to tell you both never to discuss the events of this evening again. Not with me. Not even with each other."

Cheerful says, "Not even with Esther?"

Noah shakes his head. "She knows most of what you're going to say before you say it, anyway, so why bother mentioning it aloud? We're leaving both horses at our stables. Timothy, we're leaving you at Jacob's. David and I then have a small errand to complete."

AT THAMESIDE OF ESSEX HOUSE, Noah is relieved to see a taper still burning in the window. Leaving Cheerful outside, he approaches the door, which is anxiously opened by Lady Leicester herself.

Noah bows deeply. "Madam, may I come in briefly?"

"Certainly," she says, though quite uncertainly.

Noah steps indoors and hands her the bagful of coins.

"Madam," says Noah, "here is *all* your money: both the amount you paid to have Leveson abducted *and* the amount you paid to save him from certain death at the hands of his abductors." It seems … polite … to allow her that fig leaf, even though she probably never gave a second thought to the man whose life she imperiled.

She accepts the heavy bag, and her burden seems to have lifted by an equivalent amount. "And Mullin?" she asks.

"He shall never trouble m'lady again," says Noah.

Lady Leicester seems disquieted by the incompleteness of his answer.

Noah sighs, as—despite his best effort—his heart wells up with pity for this woman, who's so recently lost both husband and son to the executioner. "Mullin was killed in the fray, I'm afraid. No great loss there."

Lady Leicester nods thoughtfully. "And his 'partner'?"

"A matter of no consequence," he replies. "Although he escaped, he can't very well go to the authorities."

"Couldn't you have—?" She stops herself.

"Couldn't I have *what*, madam?" If she's asking him what he expects, she's damned well going to have to ask him aloud.

She hesitates demurely, unable to bring herself to pose the question.

He shakes his head dourly and answers her unspoken query nonetheless. "I have a professional scruple, madam, never to execute someone without a trial."

She regards him with feigned horror. "Oh, I would never ask you to do that," she says.

"Of *course* you wouldn't," he replies sardonically.

She looks at his person and notices the stains on his silks though, to be fair, the reddish brown color is difficult to make out in the dim light of the taper. "I fear you are hurt, Serjeant," she says.

"It looks worse than it is, madam," he says. "I'll be fine by morning."

"Will there be an ... honorarium?"

"Madam?"

"A *fee* ... for your services?"

He shakes his head. "All covered by the Crown, madam. All in a day's work."

"Well, Serjeant," she says, "you have my eternal thanks for what you have done. I regret having been petulant at any time. Is there nothing I can give you for your troubles?"

He nods. "Two things. The first I shall insist upon. I expect your ladyship shall do nothing further to hinder Sir Henry's success either at trial or in applying for clemency."

She nods in agreement.

"Second, I would ask that your ladyship never seek my help again."

She's quite a sight, standing there holding a bag of coins he just handed to her, looking as though she's been slapped.

"Good evening, madam," he says. He bows and walks away.

———————⇀∘〰∘↼———————

NOAH AND CHEERFUL begin their walk to Marie's house.

"Don't you wish to see a surgeon?" asks Cheerful, full of concern.

Noah smiles. "Tonight, I shall be seeing the surgeon who assisted me with a similar wound these ten years ago."

"Do you even know where to find him?" asks Cheerful.

Noah laughs quietly, and says, "I'm married to her."

CHAPTER 26

A FEW WEEKS LATER, as the New Year begins on the twenty-fifth of March, Noah gazes out over the Thames through the upstairs window of the Lord Admiral's house in Chelsea.

"Quite a year that's just closed," says Sir Henry, seated in the comfortable chair he's appropriated as his favorite during his extended stay.

Without turning, Noah says, "I was just thinking the same thing. It occurred to me that the gift Marie made for Her Majesty this past yuletide is only now being presented." He shakes his head. "It seems so long ago. So much has happened. So much … death." He discreetly rubs the wound on his chest. Though Marie was quick to clean and bind it, it hasn't healed as quickly as that given him by Sir Gelly ten years ago. Of course, that's mostly a commentary on his being ten years older and slower to heal.

"Let's hope the new year doesn't bring any further death," says Sir Henry, no doubt contemplating his own peril. "I hope that Southampton—pardon me, *Wriothesley*—is well?" As Her Majesty has ordered Southampton stripped of his titles, all loyal subjects are forbidden to address (or refer to) him as *Southampton*, or even *lord*, or to bow to him in a manner befitting his former estate. He has been reduced to *Master Wriothesley*.

Noah nods. "I visited with him the other day at the Tower," he says. "That's one of the perquisites of working there. I'm allowed to visit all but the very few prisoners on the 'forbidden' list and, honestly, I have little interest in them in any event."

Matthew enters with a bow. "A message to you, Sir Henry, from the Lord Admiral at the Tower," he says, handing Sir Henry a folded note and patiently awaiting Sir Henry's instructions.

As Sir Henry reads, his equanimity is quickly replaced by anxiety. He looks up first at Noah, then turns to Matthew. "It appears, Matthew, that I shall not much longer enjoy the pleasure of your service and companionship."

Matthew's face falls into a sadness. *Well executed,* thinks Noah, *one could swear he didn't read the message before bringing it.*

"Sir?" says Matthew.

"The Lord Admiral informs me," replies Sir Henry morosely, "that a place is being *set* for me at the Tower, beginning one month from today." After a moment lost in thought, he turns to Matthew. "Thank you, Matthew," he says. "There shall be no reply."

Matthew turns to go, but then turns back, his face red. "If I may, Sir Henry," he says with evident sincerity, "it is indeed rare to have someone staying with the Lord Admiral who is such a pleasure to serve." He bows and quickly disappears.

"The dream came again last night," says Sir Henry. "There I stand on the cart at Tyburn, bound hand and foot as the executioner cuts off my privates, slices my belly open and pulls out my entrails—"

Noah interrupts. "It will do you no good to frighten yourself to death, Sir Henry," he says. "No one in this ... affair has suffered that penalty. Nor shall you."

"Has Her Majesty assured you of that?" he asks.

Noah shakes his head. "She assures me of nothing, except that she will hear Sir John's testimony in considering your punishment. She appears to want only one thing from you, and that's for you to suffer. Whether she exacts a fine or imposes a lengthy term of imprisonment or some other penalty, her object is the same."

"To make me suffer," mutters Sir Henry. His face brightens a little. "When will she hear from Sir John?"

"That's all quite secret, Sir Henry," he replies. "No one knows."

Sir Henry offers him a supplicating smile.

Noah shakes his head, but ultimately gives in.

"Next week," he whispers. "but we shan't learn a result until the Star Chamber rules."

SIR JOHN APPEARS a bit nervous as he's escorted to Whitehall Palace on horseback by Noah, Lord Jonathan, and Cheerful.

"I don't know much," says Sir John, "about the protocols for appearing in the Presence of Her Majesty."

Lord Jonathan chimes in. "Well, I suppose it's not too different from appearing before an earl, and all London knows you've appeared before one of those ... at Ludgate."

Noah says, "Lord Saint Ives is being facetious, of course, but it's not so very different. Of course, you may not *touch* Her Majesty. Some years ago, I situated myself so as to catch her, as she appeared about to fall; to hear it spoken of later, you'd have thought I rushed her with a broadsword. Don't approach her unless she bids you to do so. Don't speak unless she speaks to you. Don't sit while she stands, nor eat until she does, unless she commands you to do so in each instance. And don't turn to go until she expressly dismisses you—and even then you must bow out of the room, never turning your back to Her Majesty until you've taken three steps backward."

Cheerful adds, "And if she tells you to jump, jump. If she tells you to fall on your sword—"

"David!" says Noah sternly.

"How long do you suppose she'll want me to be there?" asks Sir John.

Noah shrugs. "There's no telling how long. You're there until she's good and through with you. But, remember, Sir John, you've been commended for coming to her aid in the face of armed opposition, and you won the day, keeping at bay those who might have done her violence. She'll be inclined to credit what you say. She'll also likely be prepared to show you some forbearance, should the need arise—though I wouldn't bet on it."

"And what should I say of Sir Henry?" asks Sir John.

Noah smirks. "That I may *not* say, except to advise you to tell the full truth of what happened on the day of the rebellion."

"Why can't you advise me what to say?" asks Sir John.

Noah smiles. "If I were to advise you of that, then, if asked, you'd have to tell her that I did so, and that would give her cause to doubt your veracity, on the theory that a truthful witness needs no coaching. On the other hand, if I *don't* advise you, your truthfulness shall ne'er be in doubt."

"What a world you lawyers inhabit!" says Sir John.

Noah and Lord Jonathan shrug at each other.

Cheerful and Lord Jonathan remain on their mounts outside the palace while Noah and Sir John climb the palace steps and proceed to the Throne Room together.

WHEN THE LORD STEWARD admits Noah and Sir John to the

Throne Room, the Throne is vacant.

"Her Majesty shall be here anon," says the Lord Steward. He exits.

Sir John chafes his hands fretfully. "What if she doesn't like me?" he asks.

Noah smiles indulgently but has insufficient time to reply, as Her Majesty and Lord Robert Cecil enter together from behind the Throne.

Noah and Sir John kneel and bow their heads.

The Queen takes her seat on the Throne, and Lord Robert beams beside her.

"Rise!" says the Queen cheerfully.

They rise together. Noah steps away, ceding the floor to Sir John, who respectfully waits to be addressed.

"Sir John," says the Queen, "Serjeant Ames informs us that he has expressed to you our commendation for resisting Essex's armed attempt to advance on this palace through Ludgate."

"Yes, Your Majesty," replies Sir John, "and I thank Your Gracious Majesty for noticing my small contribution to the cause."

"Small?" says the Queen skeptically. "*Decisive,* we should say."

Sir John bows modestly.

The Queen arches an eyebrow. "You appear before us today on behalf of your cousin Henry Neville, is that right?"

Noah is privately jarred by her omission of Henry's title as a knight.

"That is correct, Your Majesty," says Sir John, evidently a man of few words.

"What is it you wish to impart to us on his behalf, Sir John?" asks the Queen, as she rests her chin on her hands.

"I wish to confirm to Your Majesty that, although Sir Henry—"

"*Just* Henry," says the Queen, interrupting.

Sir John glances at Noah. "Please pardon if I offend, Majesty. I've come to confirm that *Henry*—although he clearly knew of an impending rebellion and had evidently failed to come forward with such information until that day—renounced any intent to permit or further the rebellion—"

"It would have been a simple matter for him to come forward," says the Queen, "would it not?"

Sir John is perspiring about the face. "I imagine," he says hesitantly, "that he could readily have come forward to either Lord Robert or Serjeant Ames here, both of whom were well known to him."

"Was there anyone else he could have told?" asks the Queen.

"I suppose he *might* have told Your Majesty directly," admits Sir John.

The Queen nods indulgently. "Pray, continue, Sir John. In what way did Henry Neville manifest his renunciation of Essex's rebellion?"

"Your Majesty," says Sir John, "Master Neville asked me to muster such men as I could, to stand athwart Ludgate and deny Lord Essex and his men westward passage toward this palace or elsewhere in Westminster."

"We see," says the Queen indulgently, as though it's the first she's learning of this, which is ridiculous but polite. "When you refused passage to the earl and his men, in which direction did they retreat?"

"South toward the Thames, madam," he replies.

"Tell us, Sir John," she says, "what would you have done if Essex had led his men north to Newgate, where, if he'd crossed through the gate, he might have entered Westminster from the north? Had you anticipated that contingency?"

Sir John nods morosely. "I considered what to do under those circumstances, Your Majesty, but only briefly, given what little time I had to prepare. As I knew of no one guarding Newgate, I couldn't take the chance of Essex's going north. If he had, I would have ordered my men to catch up with his lordship's band before they could reach the gate and"—he casts down his eyes—"slay them in the streets, if need be."

The Queen feigns surprise. "The earl, too?"

Sir John briefly equivocates, but only in his facial expression. "If possible, Majesty, I would have reserved to myself the duty of arresting the earl. If he'd resisted, however, I *would* have slain him, as would have been my duty as a loyal subject."

The Queen sits back with a satisfied sigh. "Then we commend you again, Sir John, for that would have been *precisely* your duty."

Sir John bows respectfully.

Up to this point, Noah is more than satisfied with the day's proceedings. But the Queen continues, as she often will.

"Serjeant Ames informs us," she says, "that you were abducted from Westminster Hall immediately upon testifying in the earl's trial for high treason, and that you were held captive for some days."

"That is so, Your Majesty," Sir John confirms.

"How ever did you escape?" she asks.

"I managed to free myself from the rope that bound me, madam. When one of the two captors went to … relieve himself, I subdued the other and bound him up—not tightly enough, as it turned out. Then I surprised the one who'd left. When he resisted, I slew him. But when I returned, I found that the other varlet had escaped on horseback."

"Did you get a good look at either of them?" she asks.

"I'd been blindfolded the whole time, Your Majesty, so I hadn't seen either of their faces. It was quite dark in the room where I subdued the one who later escaped; I never caught sight of him again. The one whom I slew was still on the ground in the morning, of course. Although I expect his face had been somewhat altered by death (as most are), I took a good look at him and felt certain I'd never seen him before."

The Queen regards Sir John sympathetically. "Have you any idea *why* they would have abducted you in the first place?"

"No, madam," replies Sir John. "I can only conjecture that it was the intention of—whomever they were working for—to ensure that the information I am today supplying to Your Majesty would never have come forth, so that Master Neville might be put to death for lack of proof in support of his petition for clemency. I earnestly hope, madam, that his life will be spared."

"We expect it will," says the Queen with a shrug, as though such weighty questions are never truly left to her—when in fact they *always* are.

Noah breathes a dizzying sigh of relief.

The Queen shoots him a reserved glance. "Of course," she adds, "whether Master Neville will be *pleased* with the quality of his future life, that we cannot warrant." She turns back to Sir John. "However, we have instructed the Exchequer to compensate Sir John and his wife out of the Treasury for any damage either of you has suffered arising out of your faithful execution of duties to the Crown, and to add to that sum our gift of one hundred pounds."

"*One hundred pounds?*" exclaims Sir John, shaking his head at the great size of the gift. "Surely, there is no need for that, Majesty."

"Sir John," the Queen asks with a pert smile, "need we inform your dutiful wife that you have declined this small favor from the Crown? After she has suffered *so* ... and dutifully awaited your return?" She purses her lips in an appealing pout.

Sir John beams in good humor. "Nay, Your Majesty. I shall gratefully accept your bounty. And I hope that my concession will obviate any need to inform my wife."

The Queen titters. "Thank you for coming, Sir John. You may go."

Sir John bows out, withdrawing three counted steps before turning from the Queen.

When Noah simply stands there, the Queen dismisses him with a friendly gesture of the hand.

CHAPTER 27

A FEW MONTHS LATER, on July 9, 1601, Noah wanders about Henry's quarters at the Tower awaiting his friend's return. How many other prisoners, he wonders, would have been quartered so comfortably? In fact, the accommodations seem only slightly less sumptuous than those housing the erstwhile Earl of Southampton, presently residing down the hall.

On the main table lies a large sheet of parchment with a great deal of writing. Though Noah wishes not to pry, he can't help but notice that the handwriting changes somewhere in the middle of the sheet. At the top is an elaborate, formal style of writing known as *court*, while the lower half becomes a more utilitarian writing known as *secretary*. There are numerals sprinkled throughout.

The main door to the quarters opens and Noah steps away from the paper.

Henry enters and sees Noah awaiting him. "Ah, yes, they told me you'd be here. How are you, Noah?"

"How am *I*?" he replies. "I am well, thank you, but I expect the question should rather be turned about, as *I* was not tried at Star Chamber yesterday."

"Star Chamber? Is that what it was?" asks Sir Henry with a shrug. "It wasn't located at that room in the palace where Star Chamber customarily sits, but rather at York House."

Noah nods. "I believe that the room known as 'Star Chamber' is being refurbished. Who was in attendance?"

"Sundry members of the Privy Council," says Henry, "a few judges."

"That will pass as Star Chamber, regardless of the room," says Noah. "Did you bring your own counsel?"

Henry wags his head. "They encouraged me to do so, but I'd already spoken with you and knew what to expect. Besides, as you couldn't represent me, I'd no desire to consult with a lesser barrister."

"You flatter me, sir," Noah replies. "What was the outcome?"

"Well," says Henry with a sigh, "I'm here at the Tower awaiting Her Majesty's pleasure. In the meantime, the Court—in addition to looking down its nose at my 'unforgivable' remissness in failing to come forward with news of the rebellion—imposed a heavy fine."

Noah gulps with dread and waits for Henry to tell him.

"Ten thousand pound," says Henry wearily. "I don't know where I'm going to come up with it, but that's what it is." He points to the document Noah was viewing when Henry came in. "That's my first attempt at some sort of statement of all my sources of income." He shakes his head. "See how *fair* I began to write it. It was too much of a labor to take it all down in court, so I switched." He shakes his head with disapproval. "In an age where so few can write, is it not ridiculous that those having the skill must learn to write in numerous *hands*?"

"Can you *pay* ten thousand?" asks Noah skeptically.

"Not remotely," replies Henry. "I've tallied it all up, straining to think of every reliable source of funds (and there are few such nowadays). I might—by impoverishing myself and my family—pay three thousand or, if she gives me enough time, possibly as much as five."

Noah remains skeptical. "Can you truly pay *five thousand pound?*"

"I probably could," says Henry, "but how the devil am I to earn it while I'm trapped in *here*? Earlier, I was lamenting having sold the ironworks but, truth be told, I couldn't operate it from inside the Tower anyway." He looks at the walls and shakes with frustration. "And I know her. She's going to keep me here until it's fully paid."

"Can you do *anything* to earn money while you're in here?" asks Noah.

Henry becalms himself and slowly nods. "I can write," he replies.

"And none of these mincing masques for the parsimonious peerage, neither. Scripts for the *public* stage. For *everyone*—from the lowest rabble to the Sovereign himself—as long as they *pay*."

"That's the spirit!" says Noah, amazed at his friend's unexpected determination. But it hasn't escaped his notice that Henry's referred to a *male* Sovereign, thus betraying his hope that the present *female* Sovereign will soon be quitting this world. On that, he and Henry will never see eye-to-eye.

"Well, what do you expect?" says Henry. "I'm responding to the warning words of an old friend. *I'm too poor to give up.*"

Noah can't imagine why *he* would ever have said that to Henry, as Henry always seemed to have money for anything that suited his fancy. "I don't think I've ever said anything quite *like* that," says Noah.

"What makes you think it was you?" asks Henry. "I have *other* friends, you know." He laughs. "Of course it was you! And if you didn't say it quite that way, you *should* have."

Noah's delighted by his friend's unexpectedly grand perspective.

"Besides," says Henry, "we're going to negotiate this fine to a fine point. Forgive the pun."

"*We?*" asks Noah suspiciously.

"Well … *you*," concedes Henry.

Noah nods with chagrin. "I might have known." Something else occurs to him. "Henry, there's something I haven't asked you that's been preying on my mind of late."

Henry sits down heavily on an upholstered chair and leans back. "Out with it," he says.

"Did Old Sir Henry leave behind … papers?"

Henry's expression turns skeptical. "You've been losing sleep over my father's papers? The man's been gone ten years."

"Humor me, Henry. You can start by answering my question."

Henry strokes his beard. "Well, he left behind all his *legal* papers, of course—indentures and such—mostly with his solicitors, I should think. Is that the kind of papers you're talking about?"

Noah shakes his head. "No. More like … private correspondence."

Henry thinks back. "My father corresponded extensively with two classes of people: first, his dearest friends; second, those he expected might do him some good. But, alas, on his deathbed, he burned it all."

"He left no items of correspondence between him … and *anyone*?" asks Noah.

"No," replies Henry gravely. "I went through his things when he passed. In fact, I went so far as to search the library for, as you may know, men have ever been wont to conceal their papers in—or behind—books. I suppose the reasoning is that, with enough forest about, one's enemies might overlook a tree here and there."

Noah sits silently for a moment, his mind spinning. So … Lady Leicester was mistaken in her assumption that Old Sir Henry left his correspondence behind, her fear being that it might contain a letter or two in which her husband acknowledged the validity of his prior marriage. As it turns out, she needed never fear, as any such letters had been burned ten years earlier. Noah wonders whether, if he'd discovered that before matters got out of hand, Mullin might not have extorted money from Lady Leicester—and been killed for his pains. But if Noah *had* told her, would she have believed him? And when would the occasion have presented itself for him to so inform her? It all seems so speculative. He puts it aside for another day.

"Care to tell me why you want to know?" asks Henry.

"Not important," replies Noah blithely.

CHAPTER 28

UNTIL THE QUEEN can be persuaded to address the sentences of Neville and Wriothesley, both their fates remain uncertain and both men fraught with anxiety. In this posture, Henry's burden is actually lighter than Wriothesley's, for Henry feels assured he'll be released once his fine is paid (having been committed to the Tower *at the Queen's pleasure)*, where Wriothesley remains under the same sentence of death as was *executed* against Essex.

Countervailing the notion that Wriothesley's execution is a foregone conclusion is the Queen's well-known fondness for the handsome, well-spoken, and penitent Wriothesley, a fondness which, it is widely believed, might well overcome his fatal sentence.

And eventually, Lord Robert meets with success in persuading Her Majesty to commute Wriothesley's sentence to life in prison.

As yet, the Queen has made no move toward releasing either Wriothesley or Henry Neville from the Tower, and time crawls at the snail's pace best known to those serving time in prison.

―――――――――⟶◦⟨✦⟩◦⟵―――――――――

EIGHTEEN MONTHS HAVE now passed since the day Henry asked Noah to renegotiate the ten-thousand-pound fine. Since then, there have been some remarkable and unexpected successes: The fine has been halved to five thousand pounds, and Henry has been granted leave to pay it in installments (with which, thus far, he's miraculously remained current).

In point of fact, however, it's been Lord Robert who's borne the heavy lifting. A practicing barrister such as Noah cannot represent Henry's interests against his employer, the Crown. It's been Lord Robert who's brought the matter up to Her Majesty countless times—far more than anyone else would have been suffered to do. Time and again, Noah and Henry together have anxiously awaited word of Lord Robert's further progress in bringing Henry one step further from insolvency and closer to freedom.

Noah now occupies Henry's favored chair, chosen not to displace Henry, but rather because every other seat in Henry's quarters is occupied by books, scrolls, and loose papers. Henry himself stands at the window, reading by daylight in an old book.

In Noah's lap is the notebook that formerly occupied the chair in which he now sits. In it, Henry seems to have made (and seems still to be making) sundry notes taken from various records of the Tower.

On the desk before Noah are books containing dramatic works by Aeschylus, Sophocles, and Euripides.

"The Greeks?" remarks Noah. "These sources are a bit erudite for the public stage, aren't they?" He leafs through the table of contents. "Are you adapting the Greek *Orestes* for the English theater?"

Henry finishes reading a short passage before looking up. "A Greek *Orestes*?" he says. "Seems superfluous, as I've already adapted the *Danish* one."

"*Hamlet?*" asks Noah with surprise. "That was yours?"

"Certainly," replies Henry absentmindedly. "Well … my *Hamlet* was closely based on Belleforest's French version, but I had to translate it myself and adapt it for the stage in my own verse. I'm rewriting it with a view toward the Greeks' penchant for drama; hence, the books."

Noah nods. "Yes, I forgot your French was quite as good as your Latin."

Henry scowls. "That's not all you've forgotten, Noah. Nevilles *are* French, or partly so. So are *Tudors*." He pauses, gazing out the window. "So are *Stuarts*. As you know, Mary Queen of Scots was French-speaking; so is her son King James, at least insofar as he *can* be, surrounded as he is by Scots. Here, have a look," says Henry drawing a gold coin from his pocket and tossing it to Noah. "It's a Scottish eighty-shilling piece bearing a portrait of King James the Sixth. That's just so you'll know what he looks like before you see him in the flesh."

Studying the golden image of King James, Noah sighs and lapses into melancholy. King James the Sixth of Scotland is commonly understood to be Queen Elizabeth's choice of successor. Unless he changes the name by which he rules, he'll be King James the First of England. And that will happen when the Queen dies, which seems more imminent with every passing month, especially now, with tales of the Queen's trances and girlish conduct escaping the inner sanctum of her advisors.

"No one lives forever, Noah," says Henry sympathetically, as though reading his thoughts. "Our beloved Queen has reigned for forty-three years, and she was already a grown woman by the time of her corona- tion." When Noah does not reply immediately, Henry asks, "What have you heard of Her Majesty's health of late?"

It's a sore topic between them. While Noah wishes the Queen would occupy the Throne for the remainder of his life, Henry's best chance of leaving the Tower before growing old is for the Queen to ... meet her ghostly forbears.

Noah shrugs. "I've been summoned to appear before Her Majesty only sparsely of late," he says. "When I do appear, I perceive *some* recognition of me in her eyes, but I doubt she recalls precisely when or where—or how—she and I met. Robert Cecil says her presence of mind has been intermittent, that she seems to be ... slipping away."

"That's how the aged tend to go," says Henry. "They fall into a sad- ness, then into a fast, thence to a watch, thence into a weakness, thence to a lightness ..." His voice trails off.

"Then into a madness?" says Noah. "That's how it goes, is it not?"

"Well, let's hope it never goes so far," says Henry. "I couldn't bear to see her suffer so."

Noah nods in agreement. "Lord Robert says that, when the Queen sees someone look upon her with sympathy, she acts the young girl and dances for them a little, as though to say, 'not a whit of it.'"

"I think we all do that sort of thing in advancing years," says Henry. "Not only to demonstrate to others that we are not overwhelmed by infirmity, but to tell ourselves the same lie."

Noah looks up at Henry. "Do you know that, in all the years I've served Her Majesty, I've never actually *requested* an audience? I think I shall do so."

"Why?" asks Henry with concern. "So you can torture yourself fur- ther?"

Noah shakes his head. "I must *know*."

"Know *what*, Noah?" asks Henry. "That she's beginning to depart this earth? You already know that."

"I must know ... if I am remembered."

"What does it matter that you're remembered," says Henry, "when she who remembers you will soon be no more?"

Noah finds himself considering the truth of Henry's point, but rejects it when he realizes that, as we will *all* vanish someday, it implies that nothing we know or do means a blessed thing. And that thought is simply too painful to consider.

NOAH FOLLOWS THE brunette lady-in-waiting toward the same room where the Queen summoned him two years ago, a few weeks after the rebellion.

As he enters, the Queen is staring out of the window. But there's no wonderment in her aspect this time—only sadness. The lines about her eyes and mouth are deep, as though etched into a pale marble bust fashioned to serve as a *memento mori*.

The lady-in-waiting curtseys and vanishes without a word.

The Queen turns with a forbearing smile and looks upon Noah's face. "You wished to speak with me privately?" she says.

Noah swallows hard. Why is he troubling this agèd woman who already bears the weight of the world on her shoulders? "I came not to ask anything of you, Your Majesty. Rather came I to offer my services in any way that might be useful to you. You have found so little use for me of late, and I wished some assurance—selfishly, I suppose—that I have done nought to lose Your Majesty's … affection."

She looks at him with puzzlement. "Have I said or done anything to express my disapproval?" she asks. Her question seems sincere rather than Socratic. She's not teaching him, but asking whether he recalls something she does not.

"No, madam," he says, a bit chagrined. "It is rather that you have said nothing to me at all." He steels himself to say directly what he's had on his mind for months. "Do you … remember me, Majesty?"

At first she seems vaguely offended at this insult to her power of recall, but her expression softens immediately. She takes a step toward him and gazes at his face, searching no doubt for some clue to his identity. For a few moments, she seems to despair, but then looks into his eyes again with a glint of recognition.

"Once … I believe, you brought me a potato," she says with a mixture of sentiment and pride.

Despite his best effort, tears well up in his eyes and run lightly down his cheeks. He clears his throat. "And was proud to do so, madam."

She scowls at her own failing memory and looks more closely at the details of his face. "But you are grown older now," she says, "and I confess I cannot recall your doing so." She brushes some lint off her sleeve. "Oh, I suppose I've grown older, too."

"In that you are mistaken, Majesty," he replies. "In mine humble eyes, you are … forever young."

She purses her lips skeptically. "Now you merely flatter, sir," she says demurely, as though he were a suitor caught at being naughty.

But as her face softens again, he realizes that what remains of him in her heart, while not all of their long history together, is her gentle feelings for him, her kind regard.

And in that moment he's surprised to realize that that's all that matters, and that he's somehow been granted the ineffable gift which he sought in coming, but which he never expected to receive.

"Not a whit, madam," he assures her. "Thank you for sharing this time with me."

"Must you go so soon?" she asks.

"Nay, madam," he says. "'Tis not I, but Your Majesty for whom the affairs of England cannot wait. Lord Robert admonished me not to be heedless of Your Majesty's time." He bows.

She smiles wistfully at him and keeps him in her view for a long moment. "You may go, of course," she says a bit reluctantly.

WRESTLING WITH ANGELS is what the Bible calls it, and Noah's done it since closing his eyes. In the middle of the night, his nocturnal struggles end, and he awakens. Instead of a gnawing feeling in his stomach, he feels a wave of … peace, and lies in the dark enjoying it for a few minutes.

For some reason, he rises early. He washes his face in the basin of water left by his bed each night. As it's only late March, the water is quite chilly and brings him 'round quickly to full awareness. He puts on his silks. and has descended to the midpoint of the front stairs when he spies a lit torch through the window. By its location, it seems to be affixed to the cottage that Jacob shares with his wife and young Timothy. He quickly dons his coat and opens the front door, where he's greeted with the most heart-rending scene imaginable.

Timothy stands outside in his shirtsleeves, shivering and weeping. Noah glances up and sees a somber Jacob, torch in hand, making his way to Noah's porch from the cottage.

"Come in at once, Timothy," says Noah in a hoarse whisper, so as not to raise the rest of the house.

Timothy rushes into Noah's embrace, placing his strong arms about

Noah's chest and squeezing as for dear life. Noah can't help but notice how strong the boy's embrace is. No longer an eleven-year-old, Timothy's nearly fourteen and has begun to attain the height and strength of a young man.

The boy begins blubbering into Noah's shoulder. "She just passed so quickly, suh. There was nothing I could do for her. She just labored to breathe for a minute. Next thing I knew, she just ... stopped breathing." He looks up at Noah's face. "And she was dead. Dead, suh." Another year or two, and it will be Noah looking up into Timothy's face.

By this time, Jacob has reached the door. He enters the house and closes the door on the cold wind. "I'm sorry, Serjeant Ames. The boy has no recollection of losing his mum and dad. I shoulda known he would take it this hard. I should never 'ave let 'im tend to the old girl."

"You speak only of the boy, Jacob?" says Noah skeptically. "Have you nothing to say of your own feelings? Shan't *you* miss Leah?"

Jacob looks Noah in the face with truly one of the most pathetic expressions Noah has ever seen. Jacob struggles to speak. "I—I loved her as my own life, suh. No one shall miss her as much as me. She was my world, and now my world has come to an end." He sighs, but he's adopted a somehow ... defiant attitude. "It ain't right how a man can live so long that he outlives his beloved." He looks toward the heavens with contempt. "There's nothin' left for me now."

Noah recognizes that look. Jacob intends to take his own life, he's sure of it.

As though realizing that Noah has read his thoughts, Jacob turns to go. "If you need me, suh, I'll be back in the cottage. I hate to leave her alone."

"Are you sure Leah has passed?" asks Noah.

Jacob nods sadly.

"Did you close the cottage door before coming here?" asks Noah.

"Aye, suh."

"Then, please go to my study," says Noah in what sounds remarkably like an order. "Please. I'll be there in a few minutes, after I attend to Timothy."

Jacob equivocates a moment, but accedes. "Yes, suh," says Jacob and lumbers off.

As Noah leads Timothy toward the kitchen, he passes a window, through which he can see that daybreak is upon London. Unless he's mistaken, in the distance he can make out the distant clamor of alarum bells at the Tower of London.

Noah leads Timothy to a seat at the kitchen table. "Are you hungry or thirsty, Timothy?" he asks.

Timothy wipes his tears on his sleeve and shakes his head. "Nothin' like that, suh. But thank you."

Noah takes a seat next to him, strokes his blond hair, and waits for him to calm down.

Timothy looks up at Noah. "I'm sorry for carryin' on like this, suh, only—only you don't know what it's like to lose a mother. And now I've gone and lost a *second*."

Noah's heart sinks as a new set of bells—much closer—joins in the general clamor outdoors. From their low and heavy sound, Noah recognizes them as the bells of Saint Paul's.

As he's about to answer Timothy, it dawns upon him what the bells are clamoring to tell him and all the world, why he wrestled with angels last night and awoke with a sense of peace.

She's gone.

Noah looks at Timothy. "The Queen is dead," he whispers in a state of wonder, then shakes his head in dismay. "Long live the King."

Timothy regards him as though he's mad. "Suh?"

Joining Timothy in his grief, Noah hugs the boy to his chest. "Timothy, you and I—we orphans must hang together."

Timothy looks at him with shock. "You, suh?" he says. "You're an *orphan*?"

Noah nods. "I was brought to this country from the Continent many years ago after losing both my mother and my father to religious bigotry. And now, those bells—do you hear them?—they ring to tell me that, like you, *I* have lost my second mother."

ON THE WAY to the study, Noah must pass the front door. As he does so, there's a knock, and a note slips under the door. Dreading written confirmation of what he knows in his bones, he unfolds it nevertheless.

I regret to relate to you, old friend, that Her Majesty, whom we both have loved so well, is no more. She died during devoted prayer, so we need have no fear of her soul's destination. I'll write as soon as I may to tell you whether I have persuaded our new Sovereign to retain you in the same capacity as Her Majesty did whilst she lived. I write also to ask that you not come to see me at any of the royal palaces until I write you, which may be some time after the coronation of King James, long may he reign. You may, of course, visit Wriothesley and Neville at the Tower. I am at Richmond Palace now (where Her Majesty passed), which has been reclaimed in every sense by a veritable flood of the Peerage. I fear it's just a matter of time before they throw me out. If you wish to attend any of the public commemorations, of course that is entirely up to you, but I wish that, like you, I might have the privilege of grieving privately, for this is so great a loss for both of us that the prospect of conducting public obsequies sickens me. I commit you to God's Protection.—RO CECIL.

He tucks the note in his pocket and proceeds to his study, where Jacob pokes the fire with an iron. "I didn't mean to presume, Serjeant," says Jacob pointing at the fire, "but I thought ye'd wish to heat this room up a bit, knowin' how much time ye spend in here."

"Not at all, Jacob. Please permit me first to express my condolences for your loss. Leah was a wonderful woman who gave you many wonderful years and memories. Her death is a great loss to us all, not least to Master Timothy." He points to the note in his pocket. "I am only just informed that Her Majesty passed last night, as well." Jacob's face registers shock. "That's what all the bells are about. I hope that Leah and Queen Elizabeth travel together wherever they go."

"Oh, Serjeant Ames," says Jacob, "that only makes me feel the worse, as I know how much affection ye had for Her Majesty, and could see how much ye risked and sacrificed for her sake."

"Thank you, Jacob," says Noah. "And thank you for allowing yourself to be detained here a moment in this your hour of great grief." He takes a step forward and lowers his voice. "I wished to speak with you alone because earlier I saw in your eyes a despair that I didn't know you had in you. It quite frightened me."

"How do you mean, suh?" says Jacob evasively.

"I mean, sir," says Noah, "that I saw in your eyes the intention to do yourself harm."

Jacob casts his eyes down. "I—I thought that your *niece* was the one with the second sight."

Noah looks at him askance. "I *need* no second sight, who am only a few years younger than yourself and have recently felt the dint of a loved one's death. Do you count your heart unique, Jacob?"

Jacob shifts uneasily. "I'm common as dirt, suh," he says.

"Then so am I, Jacob, as there's not a thought in your head that hasn't haunted me for months on end. Things will be hard for you without Leah. I have no doubt of it. You will spend months, perhaps years, haunted by her memory and the loss of the life the two of you shared."

"That's certain, suh."

"But the gods have given you more life, Jacob, and it would be insolent of you to refuse it."

"What life is that, suh?" asks Jacob.

"That boy who awaits you in the kitchen—who loved Leah so *much* he could not contain himself and so—in the middle of the night—bolted coatless from the cottage in grief over his unbearable loss. That boy's to be reared in the house of Lord Saint Ives and my beloved daughter, to be kept on as a helpmate and advisor to my grandson. Timothy needs you to be a father, Jacob."

Jacob shakes his head. "I'm old enough to be his *grandfather*. What use has he for a broken-down old Jew like me?"

"Perhaps you would not ask that question if you gave a moment's thought to *his* predicament. He has no one *of his own*. Sure, he'll have my daughter's family, but he brings no one to it but himself alone. He needs you—another outsider—to sit up awaiting his return from school, to cheer him on in competition, to commiserate in his failures and exult in his victories, of which I expect there will be many. I know it may not seem like much to you at this moment, Jacob. But you have many joyous years left to your life and (heaven knows) nowhere to rush to. Leah would not want you to give up—or worse, to destroy yourself. Remember that in our tradition, no less than the Christians', to take one's own life is to spit in the face of the Lord. And remember that the trial of the offense takes place but a moment after death, so you'll have no time to prepare which, for a barrister such as I, is most frightening of all."

Jacob smiles at Noah's remark on his profession and ponders his main point deeply. "Lord Jonathan told me, Serjeant," says Jacob, "that you came to England as an orphan and rose to the position o' Queen's advisor with neither a mother *nor* a father."

Noah scowls. "I had the *Queen of England* on my side, Jacob. She became a second mother to me. *Why?*"—he shrugs—"I do not know. If it was the Lord's trick, I can only wish for more. But how many an orphan boy begins life with a *queen* in his corner, Jacob? Timothy has no queen. He needs a father. He needs *you*."

Noah regards the old man askance and takes the devil's goading posture. "Or is the path forward simply too *treacherous* for you, Jacob? You, who were among the few to survive the first English voyage around the globe? You, who fought at sea too many times to count? Who faced down every terror the sea could hurl your way and risked a watery death a *thousand* times? Will it be too frightening for you to kiss a boy on the pate when he does well? Too taxing to scold him when he acts selfishly? Too difficult to remind him daily—by your continued unwillingness to give up on him—that he is *cherished*, that he *counts* for something in this cold world ... that he is not *alone*?"

Jacob bends at the shoulders and faces the fire, pretending to poke at it as he weeps silently, each tear sizzling as it strikes the hearthstone.

Noah pats him on the back. "And remember, Jacob. Despite the way things may seem at this moment, neither are *you* alone." He sighs heavily. "In fact, the way I feel right now, you're not even the only broken-down old Jew in this house."

To Noah's amazement, Jacob's shoulders quake with silent laughter.

"Wipe your eyes, Jacob, and come fetch Timothy in the kitchen. Bring him with you to make the ... necessary arrangements. Let him know you must be there for each other."

Jacob nods and sighs.

"Do you recall the end of the English mother's blessing?" asks Noah.

Jacob shakes his head. "I've heard it recounted many ways, suh."

"It concludes, *And may you die a good old man.* And so you shall, Jacob, but many years hence."

Jacob nods, manfully holding back his tears, and follows Noah from the study.

CHAPTER 29

BY EARLY APRIL 1603, King James, though not yet crowned, is universally accepted as successor to Queen Elizabeth.

Noah comes to the Tower to see Wriothesley and Henry Neville released and restored to their rights and titles by the new King's written order. Making his way through the families of the two men, Noah bows first to the restored Earl of Southampton.

"M'lord," says Noah, "please allow me to extend my best wishes to your lordship for a long and fruitful life."

Southampton, in his modest way, nods respectfully and says, "I have two things to say to you, Serjeant Noah Ames."

Noah's eyebrows rise. "M'lord?"

"The first," says Southampton, "is to express my deepest thanks for all you have done for me and Sir Henry Neville during these trying months. Without your many intercessions on our behalf and the news you faithfully brought to us, our stay here would have been infinitely worse."

Again Noah bows. "You're most welcome, m'lord."

When Southampton makes no sign of continuing, Noah says, "M'lord? Was there something else you wished to say?"

Southampton nods and draws him aside by the elbow. "Please accept my apologies, and also pass them along to your lovely wife, Marie. Tell her how much I regret having failed to come to her aid at once when her husband was murdered. Although I cannot seek her pardon on such grounds, I was under the questionable influence of Lord Essex at that time. And please add my apology for asking her for compromising information about *you*. Though both these things happened more than a decade ago, my actions, which were seriously misguided, still sit heavy on my conscience, and I regret that I've made no effort before now to make amends with either of you. Can you forgive me, Serjeant?"

Noah smiles broadly. "I am most grateful," says Noah, "for your lordship's affections, and do heartily forgive any breach. And I shall pass your sentiments along to Marie as soon as I return home. I expect you'll be hearing from her."

Southampton pats him heartily on the back and returns to his family.

Noah leaves Southampton's lodgings and goes to Sir Henry's.

As soon as he enters, a smiling Sir Henry hugs him so hard that he nearly loses his breath.

"It's good to find you in such high spirits, Sir Henry," says Noah.

"If it weren't for your efforts, my old friend," says Sir Henry, "I would have no spirits at all. They would long ago have fled this earth."

"Surely, Sir Henry, you exaggerate."

"I surely do *no such thing*," says Sir Henry. "Incidentally, did you attend the public funeral for Her Majesty?"

Noah looks down sadly. "I did not," he says. "I was about to do so when I heard about ..." His voice trails off.

"The effigy?" asks Sir Henry sympathetically.

Noah nods. "I could not abide the prospect of seeing Her Majesty's coffin straddled by a dressmaker's effigy bedecked with her clothing and jewelry."

Sir Henry regards him sympathetically. "A violation, perhaps, of the Old Testament's proscription against graven images?"

Noah shrugs. "Well, hers was not an image of God, but ... something like that, I suppose."

Sir Henry pats him on the back. "Those who knew Her Majesty in life have no call for an effigy. To us, such an image is a poor, lifeless mockery of one we loved dearly. Your reaction is shared by more than you know. Lord Robert went, of course. So did Camden. But neither had a choice." Sir Henry gazes through the window of the quarters he'll shortly abandon. "Such displays are put on to remind the groundlings that they're still ruled by the monarchy; they're useless to eyewitnesses to history who have, all along, trodden the stage."

⸺◦c✦◦c⸺

WHEN NOAH RETURNS HOME, Marie awaits him at the door. She kisses him and hands him a letter that was slipped under the door. He pockets it without so much as a glance.

"Lord and Lady Sheffield," she says excitedly, "have invited us to dine with them out of doors the day following the Coronation. It's to be a very large reception."

"Have Jonathan and Jessica been invited?" he asks.

She laughs. "*All of us* have been invited."

"*All?*" he asks dubiously.

"Both households. Lady and Lord Saint Ives and young Arthur and his entourage of Aunt Beth, Jacob, and Timothy. Also, Esther and David, Stephen, and my younger two. Lady Sheffield even asked me to write to Andres and Barbara in Cambridge!"

He arches a reserved eyebrow. "And Bucklebury?"

Marie rolls her eyes. "I've little doubt your horse will be the *guest of honor*, Noah," she says sardonically.

Noah shrugs. "Very well, then. I'll go, too. Why the sudden expansiveness on the part of Lord Sheffield?"

"Evidently," says Marie, "he's in a good mood, now that life has been breathed anew into his cousin's effort to prove her prior marriage to the Earl of Leicester."

"Marie, I told you—"

"I'm ever mindful of what you told me, Noah," says Marie, "but I had nothing to do with this, nor have I commented upon it. Oh!" she exclaims, digging into her pocket. "The letter I just handed you came with these. The messenger said he was afraid to insert them in the letter for fear they'd fall out."

She extends her hand toward him with her palm down, and drops three shiny one-pound coins into his hand.

"Thank you, dear," he says. "I shall look forward to Lord and Lady Sheffield's reception with great anticipation." He shuffles for a moment, thinking how best to proceed with the next topic. "Meanwhile, I promised Lord Southampton that I would convey to you his deepest apologies for two instances of misconduct that took place about ten years ago: first, his failing to come to your aid that day when the elder Stephen Rodriguez was killed; second, for asking you for 'dirt' about me."

She stiffens noticeably. "He surely took his time about it," she grumbles. "Besides, on the latter point, 'tis *you* whose forgiveness he should be seeking."

Noah nods. "He apologized and begged my forgiveness today, which I freely gave him. And I suggest that you do the same. Life is too short to hold grudges against those who've been near and dear to us."

"But—" she begins to protest.

He interrupts her, as he rarely does. "Marie, the man's spent the past two years in confinement at the Tower. Part of that time, his sentence has been one of death, and the remainder perpetual imprisonment. He's been reprieved by chance alone: the confluence of Her Majesty's death and

King James's decision to let him start over. Do you truly wish to be the only one *not* wishing him well?"

She sulks, but says nothing.

He kisses her on the cheek. "Of course," he says, "you're free to do as you wish, but if you write him a heartfelt note, you'll place yourself in good stead with an earl newly returned to his life and fortune. Life is long, Marie, and there's no disadvantage to having such a man on your side." He brushes a stray hair off her face.

"I shall write to him in a few days," she says, and marches up to her study.

Noah goes to his own study, where he fishes the note from his pocket and slits it open. As he expected, it's from Drury.

I deeply regret having taken so long to repay my financial debt to you, sir, but it truly slipped my mind until I once again contemplated coming to London. The messenger carrying this note should have handed you three one-pound coins. If he failed to do so, please let me know; I'll send you three more such coins by return messenger, and have the thief roundly whipped.

Years ago, I was advised that my debt to you was in fact far greater than money can repay. (Someone who felt I'd wronged him said he would have slain me were it not for your strict instructions to the contrary.) I belatedly thank you now for your courtesy on that occasion.

Now that my agreed-upon absence from London has lapsed, I expect that Lady Leicester may soon have her hands full again in matters arising out of her husband's prior marriage. I am gratified, however, that your honorable self and I have treated each other as honest gentlemen all the while. And perhaps her ladyship will take some comfort from the assurance that she shall never again be bothered by that colorful fellow who, the last time I saw him, seemed quite done in.— Thos. Drury

Noah shakes his head. If a stranger were to read this note, he'd no doubt deem it a tepid exchange of pleasantries between gentlemen, while in fact it's an expression of barely repressed hostility from quite a dangerous man.

And yet, the writer has no thought of misleading his reader. To the contrary, the writer's so devoid of moral compass that *in fact* he believes a modicum of conversational skill suffices to overcome any depth of moral depravity. Evidently, the late Mullin believed so, as well. A well-matched pair of scoundrels, indeed.

Chapter 30

THOUGH CORONATION DAY was quite warm, the evening cooled off nicely for the various receptions taking place throughout London, or so Noah has heard tell, as Lord Robert has not written to summon him to court.

The following day, which is the day of the Sheffields' reception, dawns with a cool mist over the grass, and the sky promising a bit more in the way of clouds, though they're the high, wispy type portending drier weather.

Shortly after dawn, Noah peeks out of his bedroom window upstairs and takes in the view of Jonathan and Jessica's stately new house across the way. The central living quarters and two wings of the structure are complete and beautifully finished, as are the front gardens. An additional wing, to extend toward the rear yard, remains under construction, but it promises to be a tasteful and detailed addition to the existing house. While things seem quiet over there for the moment, Noah's fairly certain that little Arthur will have them hopping shortly.

Before Noah turns away, his eye cannot help but light on the small garden that's been planted near Jacob's cottage in memory of his dear departed Leah. Jacob and Timothy are getting on better than Noah could have imagined in his wildest dreams; they're not related as father and son, but they might as well be.

<hr/>

MARIE AND NOAH'S HOUSE has somehow become the place for the whole family to dress and gossip. After a small late breakfast, everyone dresses in his or her very best clothing. As neither Jacob nor Timothy had any finery to speak of, Marie summoned the tailor to fashion a good suit of clothes for each of them. Even though they're traveling no more than a quarter mile, the stableman has thoroughly cleaned both Marie's and Jessica's carriages to a bright shine.

When Tom brings both carriages up to the front, the house empties its occupants onto the drive. And a lovely family they are, thinks Noah, the women resplendent in all their finery and the men tugging at their jackets and shirts that seem both too bulky and too tight-fitting at the same time.

"Gafatha!" exclaims little Arthur as he toddles toward his grandfather. On his head sits a makeshift paper crown.

"What sort of cap is that, young fellow?" asks Noah.

"*Cown!*" replies the boy excitedly.

"Ah!" exclaims Noah, as though he would never have guessed. "Well, it's quite becoming, Arthur. Were you crowned yesterday with the new King?"

The boy looks up at him in confusion, as his vocabulary is not quite up to conversation. Jessica comes up behind Arthur, placing a hand on each of his shoulders.

"Grandfather," says Jessica, "Arthur is merely *playing* at wearing a crown. This is not the Crown of England, is it Arthur?"

The boy turns to Noah. "Not *Cown England,*" he explains, and Noah cannot contain his laughter. Stooping to address the boy on his level, he leans in and whispers so that only Jessica and her son can hear. "I have *seen* the Crown of England!"

Arthur's eyes open wide with amazement. "You see Cown of England?"

Noah smiles. "Yes, m'lad. Many times. You see, I knew the Queen of England who wore the Crown of England."

Arthur looks up at his mother, who replies for him. "Grandfather, we are not quite old enough to understand all those words, but we'd love to discuss this with you at length once we've learned more!"

Noah nods earnestly, and replies to the boy as though his mother had merely passed along his thoughts. "And I look forward to having that discussion with you, my grandson." He kisses the boy on the pate and stands up to full height.

Now approaching Arthur comes Timothy, with the slightest bit of blond fur on his philtrum and clean blond hair wafting in the breeze.

"*Timmofee!*" the child exclaims with delight, as though the mere mention of the name were a full pronouncement, and rushes into Timothy's arms.

"My best friend in the world. Arthur!" replies Timothy in slightly more subdued tones.

"I have *cown,*" Arthur says to Timothy, pointing to his cap with childish delight.

"Well," says Noah, "now that that's been firmly established, perhaps it would be appropriate for us all to step up into the carriages to go and see our neighbors."

Tom the stableman takes the driver's seat at the front of Jessica's carriage, Jacob does the same for Noah's, and both await Noah's instruction to proceed.

"Noah!" calls Marie from the doorway, "a letter's arrived for you!"

"Please leave it there, my sweet, and come along!" says Noah with exasperation.

Marie folds her arms and regards Noah skeptically. "Serjeant Ames, do you not forget yourself?"

Noah stands there a moment, undecided what to do.

"Serjeant Ames," comes Esther's voice, her head jutting out of the carriage window, "it's getting very warm in this carriage."

"Papa, Esther's right!" confirms Jessica from the other carriage.

"*Gafatha, Etta ripe!*" pleads young Arthur ingenuously, echoing his mother as best he can.

Arthur's mangling of his mother's words results in general merriment.

Noah goes to his wife, who stands at the house's open front door with the letter in her hand. Once he's close enough not to be overheard, he says, "Marie, this is unlike you. We receive so many letters at this house, and—"

"It's from Lord Robert," she says, quietly glowering at him.

"No matter," he assures her. "I don't need to read it immediately. Look about you. We're surrounded by all that matters. Just for this one day, let us enjoy this wonderful life that you and I have worked so hard to build together."

"But," she says, "what if the letter contains news of a place for you at the new court?"

Noah sighs. "This blessed kingdom has remained afloat without my participation for all these months since the passing of Queen Elizabeth. May it never founder (God forbid), but I'm humble enough to know that, if it were to do so, it wouldn't be because I personally failed to navigate it overnight—at least not *this* night. Hand me the letter, dear." He accepts it from her and places it in his pocket. "I promise you I'll read it first thing in the morning. But—please, Marie—just be present with me this e'en, with no distractions, no politics, no court intrigues of lords and ladies"—he glances at Jessica's carriage—"except those we bring with us, of course."

Marie kisses him on the cheek and accompanies him to the carriage holding Esther and Cheerful, and Stephen and his younger siblings.

Though Noah breathes a partial sigh of relief, he's conscious that—somehow—that blasted letter has found a way to accompany him. He feels it in his pocket, like a piece of gravel in his shoe.

———————

LORD AND LADY SHEFFIELD'S REAR LAWN is set up in a series of long tables, at which members of each family can spend some time enjoying a bit of intimacy and occasionally circulate among the tables of other families.

Marie converses with Lady Sheffield near the rear door, as they jointly survey the bustle of guests.

"M'lady," says Marie, "you have outdone yourself, and your seating arrangement is a revelation. I have never seen anything like it, and I expect tongues will be wagging about this reception for years to come." She adds darkly, "I expect you'll also have your share of imitators."

"Thank you, Mistress Ames," says Lady Sheffield. "I justified this bit of extravagance to Lord Sheffield by pointing out to him that he'd squandered our welcome at Queen Elizabeth's court by hanging about at Essex House for so many months. I told him that we need to make a great impression on our peers in order to establish ourselves as a force to be reckoned with at the court of King James."

Marie smiles at her cagily. "A wise move, m'lady, and well timed. I expect this is just the thing to do it!"

———————

NOAH STANDS AT a table with a cup of wine in his hand, conversing with Lord Jonathan, David, and Stephen Rodriguez.

"No matter how much a man dedicates himself to public life," says Noah, "sometimes all you can do is tend your own garden. You know, protect and grow your own family. I've learned over the past few months that there can be great satisfaction in that." He glances about. "I wonder where Sir Henry is. He said he would come here with a guest."

"Which guest might that be?" asks David, who seems to have become more earnest since his betrothal to Esther.

Noah shrugs. "I'd conjecture it's the Earl of Southampton, whose fortunes have taken a giant step up in the past few weeks."

Little Arthur, still wearing his paper crown, toddles up to Noah and seizes one of Noah's legs. "I *love* you, *gafather*."

Noah, his heart pierced, bends down to kiss the boy's cheek. "What can grandfather do for his favorite grandson, Arthur?"

The boy seems stuck for words, but once again his mother comes to the rescue.

"I expect Arthur seeks your blessing of his crown," says Lady Jessica.

Noah sits, and takes the boy up onto his knee. The others gather 'round to hear what he has to say.

"I bless you in every way, m'lad," says Noah. "May you have a long and happy life. May you serve the Crown of England with pride and distinction for all your days." Noah looks up to see Lady Jessica welling up with pride.

"As for this imitation of a crown," says Noah, growing more serious as he gently removes it and hands it reverently to the boy, "enjoy it until you outgrow it, for it is my utmost hope as your grandfather that you neither wear a real crown nor covet one, for I've seen what a real crown can to do to the life of whoever wears one, what sacrifices are exacted, what punishments await." He kisses Arthur's cheek and somehow feels as though, notwithstanding the boy's limited vocabulary, he got the gist of Noah's blessing. Noah looks up to see some serious faces which, mere moments ago, were full of joy.

As Lady Jessica draws Arthur away, she turns back to Noah. "Why did you have to add that last, Father?" She shakes her head impatiently. "He's just a child."

"Children grow up," Noah mutters under his breath. "I want only what's best for him."

Seeing Noah's serious frame of mind, Lord Jonathan says, "Father, won't you share with us a memory of our late departed Queen?"

Though Noah knows he's already a bit in his cups, he takes up the gauntlet, pouring himself yet another cup of wine and rising with his back to the house, addressing the family members at his immediate table.

"Ladies and gentlemen," he begins, "it was my privilege to serve our dear departed Queen Elizabeth for many years, as her barrister, as her unofficial advisor, and as her most dedicated subject." He hears a slight commotion behind him, but ignores it. His listeners grow silent and serious, as befits his speech on this occasion. "Queen Elizabeth's name will ring true in the hearts of Englishmen as long as this island is inhabited by men of true hearts and devotion to decency and justice. She will be remembered for assembling the right men at the right time to save our precious shores forever from the Spanish Armada."

His listeners fall to their knees as though expecting a benediction of some sort. Though the demonstration is touching, it seems out of place, so he resolves to bring them all back to the present. "And now we have a new King," he says, "who deserves our support, our respect, and our love as much as did our dear departed Queen Elizabeth. So, won't you join me in drinking his health?" He raises his cup before him. "To King James the First of England!"

To his dismay everyone's eyes remain downcast. Only one person looks up at him. It's Timothy, who points over Noah's right shoulder, concealing his index finger as well as he can from everyone else.

Noah looks to his right, where he sees the face of a man who looks vaguely familiar, though he's seen it only once before. On the coin that Sir Henry showed him at the Tower. It's King James in the flesh.

Noah's eyes open wide and he drops to his knees in embarrassment. "I'm so sorry, my liege. I didn't know—"

The King places his hand reassuringly on Noah's shoulder and holds forth in a thick Scots brogue, no doubt exaggerated for the occasion. "Your family seems to know an old homily which has escaped you, Serjeant Ames. That is: Speak of the devil and he shall appear."

All the assembled laugh at the jest, but keep their eyes downcast.

Evidently pleased with his reception so far, the King adds, "You may all rise. By the way, in Edinburgh, that homily has another line that appears to be unknown outside Scotland. The two lines together go thusly: "Speak of the devil and he shall appear; drink to his health, and *he'll ne'er go home!*"

Noah rises with his cup before him. "By your leave, Your Majesty," he says. Turning to the assembled, he pronounces, "God save the King!"

"God save the King!" they respond and drink as one.

"And now," says Noah with a bow, "by the words of the Scottish homily, Your Majesty shall ne'er go home."

The King pats Noah on the back and begins to circulate among the other tables.

Feeling rather full of himself, Noah watches the King's progress with warmth.

"You always did have a knack for saving your bottom," says the impatient voice of Lord Robert.

Noah looks down to the man himself. "Lord Robert," says Noah, "I didn't hear you arrive."

Lord Robert shakes his head in admonition. "The next time I send you a note, I'll instruct the messenger to read it aloud to you, and then hit you over the head with it!"

THE END

HISTORICAL NOTE

The series *In the Den of the English Lion* is a work of historical fiction, a sort of "what if" winter's tale, written for the reader's amusement. A great deal of research went into it, but it should not be relied upon for scholarly purposes, other than to excite further inquiry. Book 1, entitled *A Second Daniel*, Book 3, *A Dragon in the Ashes*, and Book 4, *All the Men as Mad as He* contain historical notes which, among them, cover the story through the end of Book 4. This note is intended to cover events in Book 5, *Shakespeare's Treason*.

Many characters introduced in Book 5 are fictitious, such as Mullin, his nemesis young Timothy, and various servants. However, others appearing in the series for the first time were real people, such as the historian William Camden (author of the *Brittania* and the *Annals* of Queen Elizabeth's reign), as well as several principal characters featured in the abduction subplot, such as Lady Leicester, Lady Essex, young Robert Dudley, and Thomas Drury. More on this subplot appears below.

Many lines spoken in the story, especially those spoken aloud during the trial of Lord Essex and Lord Southampton, were lifted nearly verbatim (with minimal modernization and editing) from primary sources, or secondary sources relying directly upon primary sources.

The Essex/Southampton trial is one of the earliest at British common law for which we have, in the case of nearly all witnesses, something resembling the kind of verbatim transcript one would find in a trial today in Britain or the United States. For some unexplained reason, the only (or nearly only) witness whose live testimony was summarized instead of being reported verbatim was Sir John Leveson. (The author has converted the summary of his testimony into dialog, with little embellishment). Another source that has come down to us is the invaluable report of the trial by William Camden who, by his own account, personally attended it. Essex's execution is faithfully reported in the story, as is Raleigh's watching it from the armory.

The trial of the other principal conspirators, although there is no verbatim report, is recounted accurately in the story. The story is also accurate in stating that Peers of the Crown were not subject to disqualification from participating at trial on any of the grounds mentioned.

The reader was already familiar with the events of the Essex Rebellion from Books 1 through 4. Nonetheless, as the Essex/Southampton trial occupied only one day, the writer thought it best to bring the reader along as a spectator, albeit with benefit of Serjeant Ames's commentary. Although the author made some redactions from the trial transcript and a few emendations to it, the conduct of the trial is as accurately portrayed as the author could make it without dwelling on matters extraneous to the story.

Where records survive, the content of the final speeches of various conspirators is reported and contextualized as accurately as possible.

The incident resulting in the arrest and execution of Thomas Lea a few days after the collapse of Essex's rebellion (reported by Camden) is modified in the story only slightly to make a place for Serjeant Ames.

Queen Elizabeth was indeed interested to learn the circumstances under which Essex's men hired the Lord Chamberlain's Men to stage *Richard the Second*. Those circumstances were accurately described in Book 4. In Book 5, the specific fee that was negotiated has been accurately provided, as has the amount of the premium charged by the players' company for performing the play at the Globe out of turn.

As depicted in the story, there is no record indicating that William Shakspere of Stratford (referred to in Nevillean studies using the original spelling "Shakspere") was ever so much as questioned in connection with the rebellion or the play's performance. The story's attribution of that omission to Robert Cecil's having had Shakspere detained and kept out of sight is fictitious, although if it were true it would not be entirely surprising. Augustine Phillips, business manager of the Lord Chamberlain's Men, was in fact questioned by the Crown in connection with the exhibition of the play but, as in the story, nothing came of his testimony.

The Queen's line, spoken to a lady-in-waiting: "*I* am Richard the Second! Know ye not that, foolish girl?" is attributed to Queen Elizabeth in several historical sources, although the setting in the story was supplied by the author's imagination. Queen Elizabeth is also reputed to have said: "To be a king and wear a crown is a thing more glorious to them that see it, than it is pleasant to them that bear it."

Which of Sir Henry Neville's contemporaries knew that he had penned the plays and poems now attributed to "William Shakespeare"? That's unknown. The common speculation that Robert Cecil and Lady Anne knew it is not farfetched, if only because of their day-to-day familiarity with Sir Henry. From the author's readings about Queen Elizabeth's intelligence and learning, it seems entirely possible that she came to suspect as much, at least after the rebellion's collapse. The author has posited that Shakspere knew of Neville's authorship, as it seems implausible that Shakspere, a shareholder of the players' company that mounted Neville's plays, had no arrangement with the author of plays eventually attributed to William Shakespeare.

Noah Ames's recitation of the marriages of Lettice Knollys (Lady Leicester) is accurate, as is Lady Leicester's recital of both her relationship with young Robert Dudley and the terms of his father's will. Noah's analysis of the legal effect of Lady Leicester's predicament (as spoken to Lady Essex) is as accurate as the author could make it.

The conflicting interests of Lady Leicester and young Robert Dudley concerning the estate of the late Earl of Leicester came into being upon the earl's death in 1588. However, young Robert evidently found the earl's testamentary gifts to him so agreeable—and the will's references to him as "my base son" so daunting—that the dispute remained nascent for many years. Drury did in fact instigate young Robert's prosecution of a lawsuit in 1603 against Lady Leicester. However, Book 5's report of Drury's instigation in 1601 is fictitious foreshadowing, included to suit narrative purposes. It was not until 1603 that the actual dispute erupted into an abortive trial, a travesty of justice resulting in judgment in favor of Lady Leicester and punishment of possibly perjurious witnesses for Robert Dudley.

Sir John Leveson, the hero of Ludgate, was in fact a distant relation of Sir Henry Neville and attended Queen's College at Oxford University, as Sir John recites in the story. As the author did not come upon any generally available sources indicating precisely how Sir John came to be at Ludgate with a contingent of armed men on the day of the rebellion, it seemed a good opportunity to posit Sir Henry's intercession, as that provided an opportunity to unite the main plot with the subplot of Leicester's prior marriage. In fact, however, there is no reason to believe that Sir Henry urged Sir John to defend Ludgate; that's fictional. Moreover, there's no reason to believe that Sir John was ever abducted, whether to prevent him from testifying in support of Sir Henry's application for clemency or for any other purpose. Although Essex's hat was shot off at Ludgate, we have no reason to suspect Sir John of that.

Robert Dudley, the Earl of Leicester who died in 1588, was in fact well known to old Sir Henry Neville (our Sir Henry's father, who died in 1593). We know nothing of any correspondence between them.

Readers who'd like to cartographically visualize Andres's pursuit of Drury through the streets of London (and the turnabout pursuit) are strongly urged to examine the invaluable interactive copy of the Agas Map operated online under the designation *Map of Early Modern London*. It will give the reader some idea of not only the locations, but also the distances between various places.

Camden's observations concerning the invention of the hammer beam and its use in the construction of Westminster Hall is accurate.

John Daniel did in fact steal Lady Essex's important jewelry, resulting in a Star Chamber inquiry. Although in the story Camden remarks that Thomas Drury was known to spend time in Daniel's company, there is no basis in fact for that remark.

Though a couple of riders were sent to retrieve Sir Henry Neville from Dover, they were (obviously) not Noah and Lord Jonathan.

Sir Henry Killigrew (father to Lady Anne Neville) in fact refused to admit the Nevilles to the Lothbury house until being ordered to do so by the Crown.

In reality, as in the story, Sir Henry Neville was placed under house arrest at the Lord Admiral's in Chelsea. Sir Henry's recitation of other notables who'd occupied that dwelling is accurate.

Although Sir Henry's two statements to the Privy Council are accurately touched upon in the story, both statements are widely available for verbatim review.

As depicted in the novel, the Lord Admiral rushed Sir Henry to write his statement in one morning so that he would not have time to adjust it.

In England in 1601, the New Year was indeed celebrated on March 25.

There's no reason to believe that Sir John Leveson received any amount from the Crown in thanks for his heroics at Ludgate.

The parchment sheet on which Henry Neville recorded his various sources of income in multiple handwritings is real, and exists today. It is depicted in one of the photographs appearing in Brenda James's seminal *The Truth Will Out*. There's also (the author believes) an oblique reference to it in the second quarto of *Hamlet* (V, ii, 33-39), apparently written by Neville while imprisoned at the Tower. In the play, Hamlet recounts to Horatio his scheme to trick the King of England out of putting him to death: "I sat me down/ Devised a new commission, wrote it fair:/ I once did hold it, as our statists do/ A baseness to write fair and labour'd much/ How to forget that learning, but, sir, now/ It did me yeoman's service."

King James in fact ordered the nearly immediate release and restoration of Southampton and Sir Henry upon the death of Queen Elizabeth.

To the extent that there is disagreement among the sources on a few trivial questions, it is hoped that the reader will defer to the author's need to decide such questions for narrative purposes.

ABOUT THE AUTHOR

Neal Roberts and his wife live on Long Island, New York, where they have two grown children. Neal is a practicing attorney and adjunct law professor, and spends as much time as possible researching his next novel while enhancing his lawyer's pallor. When he's not writing Elizabethan politico-legal novels, practicing law, or teaching, he's an editor of an international peer-reviewed publication in the field of intellectual property law. Neal is also an avid student of Elizabethan literature and politics, which subjects form the basis of his first novel, A Second Daniel. His analysis of Shakespeare's Sonnet 121 has been extensively cited by some of the most important authorities seeking to identify the true author of the poems and plays attributed to William Shakespeare. Connect with Neal at his website (authornealroberts.com) or on Facebook (Facebook.com/authornealroberts) and join his mailing list (bitly.com/FreeHistorical) to know when upcoming books release and to grab your free short.

ALSO BY NEAL ROBERTS

A Second Daniel, In the Den of the English Lion, Book 1 (Historical Mystery): London 1558. An orphan from a far-off land is renamed "Noah Ames," and given every advantage the English Crown can bestow.

London 1592. Now an experienced barrister, Noah witnesses what appears to be a botched robbery outside the Rose Theater, a crime he soon suspects to be part of a plot against Queen Elizabeth herself. Steadfast in his loyalty to the Queen, Noah must use every bit of his knowledge and skill to lure her most disloyal subject onto the only battlefield where Noah has the advantage ... a court of law – though in doing so he risks public exposure of his darkest secret, a secret so shocking that its revelation could cost him everything: the love of the only woman who can offer him happiness, his livelihood ... even his life.

The Impress of Heaven, In the Den of the English Lion, Book 2 (Historical Mystery): LONDON 1600. When the Earl of Essex is removed from command and placed under arrest for reaching a forbidden truce with the Irish rebels, Serjeant Noah Ames reluctantly accepts a commission to investigate the earl's fitness for command, and the two are pitted against each other once again. Meanwhile, Noah's beautiful daughter, Lady Jessica, has sought to remarry into the nobility, but events have thus far frustrated her plans. One day, Noah attends a briefing where the Queen's new commander displays maps of English military positions in Ireland. Noah's suspicions are aroused when he sees that one map is missing a watermark appearing on all the others. When he informs his young barrister friend Jonathan of his concern, he inadvertently sets in motion events that throw Jonathan and Lady Jessica together on a journey across England into ever greater peril.

A Dragon in the Ashes, In the Den of the English Lion, Book 3 (Historical Mystery): LONDON 1600. When an attempt is made on Queen Elizabeth's life, Serjeant Noah Ames races to her rescue, then sets out to identify the culprit among a band of foreigners who've newly arrived from the Continent to join with the seditious Lord Essex. In the course of his investigation, Noah uncloaks an unmitigated rein of evil that has resulted in the murders of kings, queens, and religious minorities ... and which now threatens Noah's life for reasons no one would ever suspect. Will Noah pay the ultimate price for forgetting that the past is never past?

All the Men as Mad as He, In the Den of the English Lion, Book 4 (Historical Mystery): LONDON 1600. Though Queen Elizabeth has ordered the Earl of Essex's release from confinement, she's thwarted his return to social and military grace by barring him from court for an indefinite term. Unsatisfied with this humiliation, the Queen considers whether to cut off his sole remaining income, as well. Noah Ames strongly advises against it on grounds that the Queen will thereby lose any remaining influence over Essex's conduct and also place him in desperate financial straits. When several seemingly unrelated men are found murdered, Noah begins to suspect that such murders reveal Essex's treasonous intention to return to court in bloody defiance of the Queen's order.

www.ingramcontent.com/pod-product-compliance
Lightning Source LLC
Chambersburg PA
CBHW031940260626
47157CB00016B/843